BOX OF BONES

Also by Peter Morfoot and available from Titan Books

Impure Blood
Fatal Music

PETER MORFOOT

A CAPTAIN DARAC MYSTERY

BOX OF BONES

TITAN BOOKS

Box of Bones
Print edition ISBN: 9781783296682
E-book edition ISBN: 9781783296699

Published by Titan Books
A division of Titan Publishing Group Ltd
144 Southwark Street, London SE1 0UP

First edition: April 2018
10 9 8 7 6 5 4 3 2 1

Did you enjoy this book? We love to hear from our readers.
Please email us at readerfeedback@titanemail.com or write to us at
Reader Feedback at the above address.

To receive advance information, news, competitions, and exclusive offers
online, please sign up for the Titan newsletter on our website:

www.titanbooks.com

For Clare and Bryan

1

A world of sound and light awaited them in Place Masséna.

'We've got here far too late,' Darac shouted over the spit and thump of a high-energy dance track. 'Maybe we should forget it.'

Erica Lamarthe gave a sad little nod. 'Yes, who wants to have fun, anyway? Let's just give up and go.'

A largely traffic-free space flanked by gardens, fountains and statuary, Nice's Place Masséna had a pleasant, relaxed vibe for most of the year. For three weeks in early spring, it was the epicentre of one of the most spectacular carnivals in France. Starting and finishing in the Place, the nightly Parade of Lights was a living lava flow of giant figures, fantastical creatures, dancers, jugglers and musicians.

Darac swept an arm across the scene. 'Well, look at this. There must be twenty thousand people here.'

'Twenty thousand... *and two*. So what we do...' Erica threaded a slender hand through the crook of his arm and held tightly on to it '...is think *rugby*. Come on! We can do this!' Taking a deep breath, she put her head down and shoved into the scrum.

'Rugby?'

'Move!'

He moved.

'I love… the theme this year.' Playing prop forward was straining Erica's voice. 'Don't you?'

'Dunno. What is it?'

'*King of Harmony.*'

From a gantry high above the Place, a searchlight gyrating around the night sky suddenly raked the crowd. Darac scrunched his eyes as it found him. 'Sure it's not *Escape from Colditz?*'

Erica's smile was tart. 'Quite sure.'

Over the PA, a voice like a machine gun announced that the parade had formed up 'off-stage' and would be entering the Place in less than ten minutes.

'Plenty of time.' Erica redoubled her effort. 'Come on.'

The circular bulk of a colonne Morris stood away to their left. In the swell of bodies, an unhelpful current was dragging them toward it.

'Do something, Darac. We don't want to get stuck against that.'

A hit with the silly stringers, the colonne was hung in webs of psychedelic snot.

'Don't worry. It wipes off, according to Bonbon.'

'Stuck, as in not being able to move, I mean. Pull to the left.'

'I *am* pulling to the left.'

'Pull harder!'

Moments later, they made landfall against the colonne.

'Clockwise?' Erica said, her nose pressed against its circular display.

Still bound together, they began waddling their way around the obstacle.

'I feel like a wind-up penguin.'

'I told you it would be fun. Now, we're not going to get anywhere unless we work harder. What we need is a big five minutes. Big five! Come on! What do we want?'

Where had all this come from? 'Erica…'

'I can't hear you.'

'A *big five*.' Darac shook his head. 'Jesus.'

'That's it. Ready? Hup!'

Five minutes of determined scrummaging followed. At the end of it, they were further from the action than they had been originally.

'Look,' Darac shouted over his shoulder, 'I'm meeting my father for a drink later and you've got a date, right? So why don't we cut our losses and—'

Erica tugged sharply on his arm. A meaningful silence followed. With some difficulty in the press of bodies, he turned to face her.

'Darac, do you actually like Carnival?'

'No.'

'Not even the Parade of Lights?'

'No.'

'No. Alright. But you do want to see Marco's samba band? And the boy – the one you lent your guitar to?'

'Freddy. Well, ye-es.'

'So stop playing the moaning Minnie and start using your shoulders.'

'I have been using them.'

'You have. Uh-huh.' Erica pursed her lips. 'Okay: new tactic.' Gripping his arm once more, she took a deep breath. 'Police! Make way, everyone! Brigade Criminelle!'

The warning went unheard, buried under an avalanche of PA announcements. Among them was the promise that the head of the parade was now only two minutes away. Around the Place, sound and light crews eased down the blare and bump. Disco hour was over.

'Thank God for that.' Darac cocked his ear. 'Listen.'

In the distance, he heard whistles, drums and trumpets. And dancing above it all, an electric guitar.

'Is that Marco's band?'

'He said they were near the front.' The pair were still completely hemmed in. 'Seriously, we may just have to miss them.'

But then, by some obscure principle of the motion of bodies en masse, pockets of space suddenly opened up in front of them. Trimming the angle of their shoulders, the pair took off into the first, side-slipped smartly through the next, and then following a series of zigzagging passes, came in to land right on the parade route.

'See? We did it!'

'Yes.' Darac released her arm. 'We did.'

Erica's eyes were everywhere. 'I *so* love this!'

Darac's attention was on the roadway. 'Still no barriers.'

'Still? What do you mean?'

'Haven't been to this thing since… for years. Suppose I expected changes.'

A Police Municipale sergeant was drawing laughs as he walked the line. 'This is a street party, so no enjoying yourselves now, people. No smiling, laughing or dancing. But if you have to go nuts, do it safely. Safety first, guys. And watch your wallets. Wallets, cameras and phones.' Recognising familiar faces, the sergeant gave his shtick a rest. 'Evening, Captain. Mademoiselle. No need to tell officers of your calibre to be careful when it all starts coming through, is there?'

Erica gave him a *sympa* smile. 'I like your patter, Sergeant…?'

'Magne. Thank you. It's better to keep it light for things like this.'

Amid cries of protest, a couple of young men stumbled on to the road behind him.

'No pushing!' Rolling his eyes, Magne sidled off toward them. 'Did you two hear what I just said?'

Glancing at her watch, Erica stood on tiptoe and peered into the distance. Marco's samba band wasn't getting any louder. 'Still can't see them. They must be holding them further down the avenue.'

'Wouldn't you rather have been sitting up there?' Darac gave a nod to the temporary stands erected on the opposite side of the parade route. 'Better view. And you'd be the first to see anything.'

'No, no. You're not part of it up there. You've got to be down on the street.'

Taking a shove in the back, Darac found himself all too literally on the street.

'Sorry, monsieur.' Many hands helped him up. 'There was a surge.'

Like a mother fussing over a child, Erica started brushing him down, then thought better of it. 'You alright?'

'Yeah. Nobody's fault.' He scanned the scene behind and realised the culprit was a stocky, red-faced man wearing a denim jacket. Pushing a bow wave of irritation, he was thrashing his way through the crowd as if his life depended on it. 'I take that remark back.'

Erica shook her head. 'Poor man. Claustrophobic, probably.' She looked more closely. 'Or stinking drunk.'

For a moment, Darac considered giving chase but abandoning Position A wasn't an option. Besides, another victim appeared to have grasped the nettle. Issuing apologies to the crowd, a man wearing a red scarf and a blue jacket was in determined pursuit of the drunk.

Erica turned away and stared hard into the mouth of Avenue des Phocéens. 'Come on, people!'

Across the street, ushers were showing invited guests into a fenced-off area at the foot of the stands, a temporary gated community for bigwigs. Darac ran an eye over the Great and the Good: some footballer who was the guest of honour; the five-strong carnival committee and their guests; and finally, front and centre, the mayor and his entourage.

'I have a feeling things will move any second now, Erica.'

'About time.'

'Check out Jacques Telonne.' Suave and smiling, Telonne was the chair of the carnival committee, one of the fattest of Nice's fat cats and the potential next mayor of the city. The man's smile faded as he cast an eye over the mayoral party. 'Look at him sizing up the even bigger wigs. You can practically see what he's thinking from here.'

'Really?' Erica murmured, not looking.

His eyes still on Telonne, Darac leaned in to her. 'He's wondering which of them will back him for the top job if we the suckers vote him on to the council.' He gave a dry little chuckle. 'You're worrying about the wrong people, Jacquie boy. You've got enough mates in high places. It's winning over us plebs first that's your problem.' He gave Erica a look but she wasn't listening.

'This is starting to get a little...' Her eyes widened. 'Wait.' A frisson crackled around the Place. 'Aha!' She went up on to her tiptoes as the drums, whistles and guitar grew louder. 'Here we go.'

The head of the procession came into view. Erica took it upon herself to give a running commentary. 'First is… a float. What's that say? Oh boring. It's just some corporate thing. Look at the number of people milling around it, though! Can't see the road at all.' A stronger charge jolted the crowd. 'Now *this* is more like it! A dragon, is it? Yes. It's huge! And further back, the king, look. *Storeys* high!' Erica's fine blond hair swished like a pennant as she jetted Darac a glance. Her face was so aglow with excitement, it touched him.

'You're not sitting on my shoulders, if that's what you're after.'

She gave him a more considered look, smiled and returned her attention to the parade.

As the dragon in all its scaly, smoke-belching vileness bore down on them, Darac was contemplating something altogether more serene. Jaume Plensa's *Conversation à Nice* was a grouping of seven sculpted figures that lived permanently in the Place. Each sat atop a pole-mounted plinth, the figures changing colour over time, acting and reacting in a complex interplay with its neighbours. They were mainly blue at the moment.

'It's about communication, you know,' Erica said.

'What?'

'The sculptures. The value of people talking. To each other.'

'Absolutely right.' He smiled, coming back to the here and now. 'Sorry.'

The dragon was quite something, he had to admit.

Using combinations of rods and wires, the beast's black-clad animators looked like Lilliputians on a night-fishing expedition. Somehow, their presence didn't spoil the illusion. On both sides of the route, the crowd gasped as the beast shook itself like a wet dog, then reared up and puked a plume of pink smoke in the direction of the bigwigs on the dais. They seemed to take it in good part. To sustained cheers, the dragon gathered itself and clattered away to begin the sequence all over again.

'Wasn't that fantastic?' Erica was already turning to the next thing. 'Is this him? Marco?'

Darac grinned. 'Oh yes.'

Riding a float tricked out as a tropical paradise, Marco's band was chanking out a slow and slinky samba. Ahead of them, lines of women wearing little but crested headdresses were moving like waves breaking on a white sand beach.

'*Oye como va, mi ritmo, Bueno pa gozar – mulata…*'

Her eyes on Marco, Erica leaned back into Darac's shoulder.

'The white suit really sets off his beer belly. And that beret-ponytail combination? Class.'

'He's turned out in worse for the quintet, believe me.'

'He's positioned himself right at the front of the float, I notice.'

'Playing timbales behind these girls for two hours? He'll think he's died and gone to heaven.'

Unable to resist the beat, Erica began to move to it.

'This is jazz, you know,' Darac said. 'Of a sort. The stuff you're supposed to hate.'

'No-ooo. It's Latin.' Raising Darac's hand, she circled sinuously under it. '*Oye como va, Da-da-dah…*'

Marco spotted them, celebrating the moment with a fusillade of rim shots. 'Darac!' Indicating the dancers, the drummer mimed going at the knees as he returned to the number's elusive clave beat.

'Is he always like that?'

'Always.' Darac finally caught sight of the guitarist. A star of JAMCA, one of the local youth orchestras run by Marco, the young man was leaning against a palm tree at the back of the float. 'Hey, Freddy!'

The boy's open face lit up and he stepped forward, hanging a lissom little riff around the head of the tune as the dancers swayed this way, then that. After a couple of variations, he brought the sequence to a close with a rapid upward arpeggio.

'He's wonderful,' Erica said, trying to clap in time with the number. 'How old is he?'

'Fifteen, I think.' Darac gave him a thumbs-up.

'How sweet of you to lend him one of your guitars.'

'It's special, that one, actually. It was the first really good instrument I bought.'

'*Really* sweet.'

'I've got four nicer guitars. I *could* have lent him one of those.'

'Well, you tight bastard.' Flicking up a shoulder, she turned back to the parade. '*Oye como va…*'

Sergeant Magne came shimmying alongside.

'Nice moves!' Erica called.

Magne responded with an extravagant flourish but then, gazing past them, his party face fell. Darac followed his gaze.

A squeal of tyres. Airbrake hiss. Shouts. Dragon handlers

down. The dragon itself, half a tonne of wire, sheet metal and fibreglass lolling unfettered over a scattering crowd. Screams. Samba float stopped dead. Dancers: some down; some scrambling away; some looking to help. People in the stands on their feet, watching, helpless. Marco's six-strong band all down, some still on the float; others, including him, pitched on to the road. Timbales rolling like stray hubcaps in all directions. Magne running up the road to the head of the parade. Behind him, the fallen samba girls hobbling around. None of their injuries looked serious.

'Marco!' Darac dodged between the walking wounded toward his friend, who was lying on his back, eyes closed. He looked the worst off of anyone they could see.

'Ambulances!' Erica shouted into her mobile, following him. 'Plural. Place Masséna. Now.'

'Medics? Any medics here?'

No takers.

'How's your first aid, Erica?'

'Hope yours is better.'

A couple of the dancers were fluttering ineffectually over Marco. Others were shouting at the samba float driver. 'You ran into us! Arsehole!'

'Police! Gangway!' Darac tried to remember the routine as he knelt at Marco's side. 'You girls alright?'

'Yeah but no thanks to the driver. He bumped right into us.'

'Uh… Okay, he's breathing. And his airway is… clear.' Darac began taking Marco's pulse. 'One, two…'

Deep cuts to Marco's cheek and forehead were starting to bleed profusely. Taking tissues from her handbag, Erica set about staunching his wounds.

'Mustn't press too hard. Look at the swelling. Cheekbone may be broken.'

'Marco? Can you hear me?'

The samba float driver joined them. He was shaking. 'Something happened at the front and then the dragon went—'

The girls weren't having it. 'You were watching that instead of us, you arsehole!'

'Hey, if I hadn't jumped on the anchors when I did, I would've gone right over you, not just bumped you on to your backsides.'

A shuttering crash to their left. The dragon had finally collapsed, cartoon-like puffs of pink smoke enveloping the wreckage. Darac was still staring at his watch.

'Seventeen. Eighteen… Anybody under that? Twenty…'

'No, don't think so,' one of the dancers said, craning her neck.

Voices washed around them.

'What's happened?'

'Some guy went under the float. The one at the front.'

'One driver brakes, then they all brake, don't they? Domino effect.'

'Front wheel went right over the guy's head.'

'Burst like a melon.'

'Pissed, he was.'

'Look at what he's caused. Arsehole.'

'I bet it was that drunk,' Erica said, maintaining an even pressure on Marco's cuts. 'The guy who was pushing everyone.'

'Thirty-one… Sounds like it. Any sign of the ambulances? Thirty-three…'

The dancer acted as Darac's eyes once more. 'Can't see them.'

Lapel radios buzzing, a wedge of officers spearheaded by Magne was sweeping along the road toward them.

'Keep the road clear for emergency vehicles!' he shouted. 'Keep it clear now!'

Darac relinquished Marco's wrist. 'Doubled that makes… ninety-six. Not too fast, considering.'

The patient's eyes opened.

'Marco? Can you hear me? Marco? Do you know where you are?' The drummer's gaze was fixed, unfocussed. 'Look at his eyes.'

Erica nodded. 'Glassy.'

Feet trampled around them.

'Move back, everyone!' Darac said.

'I couldn't help it,' the float driver repeated, walking away. 'I had to jump on the anchors. Got a line of girls right in front…'

Erica bent low over Marco. 'Can you hear me, sweetie?'

He made an affirmative sound in his throat.

'That's good. Help's coming, okay? But for now, can you see my finger?'

'Ye-es.' The word was no more than an exhalation.

'Try to follow it.' She moved it slowly in front of his eyes. There was some response. Slow, but it was there. 'Hey, not bad.' She gave Darac a little nod of encouragement. 'Okay, let's try again. Tell you what, Marco, forget it's a finger. Think thongs and feathers. Swaying. *Oye como va…*'

Darac smiled at Erica's strategy. And it worked: Marco's eyes held the finger first one way, then the other.

'*That's* better. Just concussion, I think.'

'Concussion?' Marco's voice was a little stronger. He tried to sit up. 'Jesus.'

Darac laid a hand on his chest. 'Stay still a second, mate. Just in case.'

Young Freddy came limping up. 'Marco... is he alright?' The boy's face was a mask of concern. 'I saw him fall.'

'He's doing fine.' Erica applied fresh tissues to Marco's cuts. 'Did he land directly on his back?'

'He fell forwards, mademoiselle. On to his head. Then he tried to get up and sort of collapsed. I saw it.'

Magne's phalanx was almost alongside.

'Where are the medics?' Darac shouted across to him.

'On their way!'

Nearby, he could see the TV reporter Annie Provin already doing a piece to camera. 'Carnival Committee Chair, Jacques Telonne, must come up with a lot of answers,' she said. 'And there are decisions to make. Monsieur Telonne, will tonight's parade be aborted? What steps will you take to make sure citizens are safe?'

Stern-faced, Telonne stepped forward to respond, but Darac didn't hear any more. Sergeant Magne's lapel radio blurted out a message. 'Say again?' He looked across at Darac. 'I'll tell him. Over.'

'I'm alright,' Marco said, trying to blow a trailing end of tissue paper away from his lips.

Erica removed it. 'Good. The bleeding is stopping.' She applied two fresh tissues. 'These are the last.'

'Marco? Keep lying there, but can you move everything? Start with your toes.'

Everything moved as it should.

'I think we can sit him up.'

Darac and Freddy helped him. Once upright, Marco gave the boy a wink. 'A tip: never headbutt a road.' His hand went to his face. 'Mademoiselle? Thanks, but I can hold these tissues on now.'

'How's your cheek feel?'

'Bashed.'

'Looks it. There… Got them?'

Darac felt Sergeant Magne's hand on his shoulder. 'You're needed up at the front there, sir. The guy who went under the float? Some are saying he didn't fall, he was pushed. Since you are right here, sir… And we don't have full powers of arrest. Although that's a bit academic as it turns out.'

'The suspect *is* held, isn't he?'

'He got away in the crowd.'

Darac ran a hand through his thick, wavy hair. 'Alright. Witnesses?'

'Some. And more coming forward. We've started taking statements.'

'We may have got a glimpse of him ourselves. Back view, anyway.'

A couple of the other samba players joined them. 'Freddy? How's Marco?'

The boy filled them in as Darac took a final look at the fallen.

'You go,' Marco essayed another wink. 'I'm alright.' He indicated his torn jacket sleeve. 'Better off than my suit, anyway.'

Darac gave Marco's arm a pat. 'Anything's better than that suit.' He took out his mobile, telling Magne, 'Just need to make a quick call.' Away to his left, the dragon's handlers were starting to pick over the carcass. 'Any injuries there?'

'Couple of the guys have ricked themselves pretty badly. Another's broken his leg, I'm hearing. But they kept the thing airborne long enough so it didn't land on anybody. That's the main thing.'

'Indeed.' His father answered at the first ring. 'Papa? I've got caught up in something.'

'But it's important I see you, Paul. Can't you turn whatever it is over to Granot or Bonbon?'

'Listen, I'll be there. I may be a little late, that's all.'

'Oh, okay. Good, I'll see you as and when.'

'Bye.'

Sirens whooped dissonantly in the far corner of the Place.

'And now, the Parade of Ambulances,' Darac said. He gave Marco a look. 'Only be a minute, mate.'

Erica touched Darac's forearm. 'I can't imagine there'll be a tech aspect to it, but do you want me to come anyway?' She glanced at her watch. The minute hand was just reaching Captain Haddock's beard. 'I've still got an hour or so before I'm meeting Serge.'

'It won't be pretty up there.'

'I know that. Will you stop treating me as if…' She was suddenly aware of Freddy and the others. 'I'll be fine.'

'Okay, then.'

A second Police Municipale officer joined them. 'Captain? They're all waiting for you.'

'One second. Magne, could you liaise with the medics? Apart from the cuts and the swelling on his cheek, Marco here might be concussed. His pulse is a little fast, but he can move everything.'

'Sure.'

'I'll stay with him, as well,' Freddy said.

'Okay, we're off. See you later, guys.'

'I'll go and round up the drums, Marco,' Darac heard one of the samba players saying. 'Don't trust this crowd.'

'Just a second, Erica. Freddy?'

'Yes, monsieur?'

'You do still have the guitar?'

2

There was a carnival of its own going on in the squad room at the Caserne Auvare: Darac's boss, Commissaire Agnès Dantier, was playing host to a delegation from Europol. In a lower key, Lieutenants Roland Granot and Alejo 'Bonbon' Busquet were awaiting an instruction from the public prosecutor's office; and young detectives Yvonne Flaco and Max Perand were catching up on paperwork. Or they had been until Darac had turned up unexpectedly.

'It's the old classic this, isn't it?' Bonbon grinned, his tawny eyes twinkling. '*Did he fall or was he pushed?*'

Darac handed Granot the witness statements. 'The consensus is he fell.'

'Fell? I thought pushed was the call.' Bonbon took a white paper bag from his pocket. 'Sheep's eye, anyone?'

No takers.

'Granot?'

Shifting his bulk, Lieutenant Granot peered into the bag like a polar bear contemplating a hole in the ice. 'What are they, really?'

'Liquorice and nougat.'

'I'm on a diet, suddenly. What about this push call, chief?'

'The couple who read it that way were some way off. Those nearer reckoned the chaser was trying to pull the victim out of the way of the float, not push him under it.'

'If he didn't push the guy, why did he run off?'

'No one saw him do that. He just wasn't there when they turned around.' Darac gave the report a nod. 'It's all in there.'

Granot gave a little grunt as he skimmed through the witness statements. 'I see you haven't added a description yourself?'

'I'll give you one now.' Darac drew up a chair. '1972 Gibson SG Standard. Cherry finish. All original hardware and pickups. Serial number—'

'Not of your guitar.' Granot shook his jowly chops. 'Of the chaser.'

'Alright, it's not a Brigade case, strictly speaking. Or at all. But that guitar *is* worth a couple of thousand euros, you know.'

'I know. We all know, especially Flak and Perand, who are co-ordinating the search. But possible homicide trumps theft, doesn't it? Even of your 1972… whatever it was.'

'Gibson. SG. All original.' Leaning back in his chair, Darac craned his neck around Granot. 'Anything yet, Flak?'

'Foch have got several uniforms working on it, Captain. No eyewitnesses as yet. And so far, nothing on a personal camera. Looks as if people only had eyes for the dragon. But there'll be TV and CCTV to check later. The thief could well have been picked up there.'

Perand gave the stubble-blackened side of his face a slow scratch. 'For the time being, Lartou and his telly addicts are only looking at the murder/accident/suicide moment.'

'Fair enough.'

'Speaking of that?' Granot picked up his pen. 'You saw him, didn't you?'

'Only from the back. Navy blue jacket; red scarf; balding. But the witness statements from the business end of the thing aren't much better.'

Bonbon peered over the mountain range that was Granot's shoulder.

'"Tall"; "medium height"; "stocky"; "slim".' He nodded. 'Useful.'

'Well, they all agree he had a goatee beard. That's something. And a couple of the later ones said they'd be able to pick him out of an ID parade. I asked Astrid to take her sketch pad down there. Or tablet or whatever she's using now.'

'"*Balding*."' Granot completed Darac's description with a conclusive stab on the full stop. 'Yes, it seems no one paid much attention to the chaser. It was the victim, the loud and drunken Monsieur Michel…' he checked the surname, 'Fouste, that drew all eyes.' He turned the page. 'I'll just continue with these. Talk amongst yourselves.'

Bonbon wrapped himself back into his chair. 'Why all the mayhem? Floats stop and start all the time in parades, don't they?'

'People seeing a man's head explode is why. One of the dragon handlers fainted dead away at the sight; another fell over him, breaking his leg. That made the beast slew to one side. For a second, it looked as if it might collapse on to the crowd.'

'What about the float your mate was on?'

'All the driver's fault. Transfixed by what was going

on at the head of things, he bumped into the samba girls in front of him and then jumped too hard on his brakes. The thing submarined and the band toppled off it like skittles.'

'And it was while everyone was picking themselves up and so on that—'

'Someone saw my guitar lying unattended, grabbed it and made off into the night.'

Making a trenchant point to the Europol delegation, Commissaire Agnès Dantier arrived on the scene at that moment. The visitors concurring vigorously, they began forming an orderly group behind Granot's desk.

'But that's enough on the European Court. May I introduce my second-in-command, Captain Paul Darac?'

Agnès's eyes met his. A discreetly raised brow was answered by an almost imperceptible nod. Assured that everything was fine, Agnès introduced the others, made a couple of observations, and led the delegation away.

'Now, back to our top story,' Bonbon said, clocking that Granot had finished reading the statements.

The big man tossed the pages on to the desk. 'Here's a summary: those nearest to the incident believe that Fouste fell under the float under his own steam, that the chaser was trying to prevent him from so doing, and that he then must have left the scene while everyone was gazing at the stricken Fouste.'

Granot's desk phone rang. 'It's Lartou. How's the CCTV looking?' He listened for some moments, and then, eyeballing Darac and Bonbon, gave an encouraging nod. 'And that was on the CCTV? What about the chaser? Sure? Okay.'

Darac performed some modest air guitar. And then repeated it more extravagantly.

'Oh yes, on to the theft of the century, Lartou… Indeed it *was* the captain's guitar. In all the mayhem, the kid left it on the float… Well, just do your best. That's it.' He hung up.

'It's clear on the CCTV that in trying to avoid the chaser, Fouste lost his balance, failed to grab an offered hand, and stumbled right under the float.'

Bonbon shook his tawny head. 'Splattered all over the road… He should've just taken a bollocking from the guy.'

'And the chaser?' Darac said. 'Although it's academic now.'

'No shot of him – well, not of his face – on either CCTV or broadcast TV. There's material from one further camera to check out, though. Should be available tomorrow. Some sort of technical problem at the moment.'

'Okay.' Darac swiped his mobile. 'Astrid? You hook up with those eyewitnesses yet?'

'Yeah, a couple of them. Still a few to see.'

'You can give your pencils or your stylus a rest. The chaser's in the clear.'

'You won't be needing my sketches?'

'Doesn't look like it. Sorry I wasted your time.'

'Hey, my rate's the same whether you use what I do or not. And I'm keeping my pencils out – there's a whole new portfolio in this for me: *After the Carnival, a Post-Apocalyptic Vision of… Something.* They've got the dragon up, by the way. Be good as new by tomorrow, they think.'

'I'll tell Erica.' He looked at his watch. 'Got to go.' He

ended the call. 'Okay, this all seems to be heading in a
conclusive direction. If there's anything on the guitar, leave
me a message.'

Once outside the squad room, his mobile rang almost
immediately. The number wasn't familiar.

'Monsieur Darac?'

'Yes?'

'It's Freddy. I'm sorry to ring, monsieur, but Marco gave
me the number. I hope you don't mind.'

'No, no. How's he doing?'

'Good. Well, concussed like the mademoiselle said, but
they've let him go home.'

'Excellent. Thanks for calling.'

'I also want to say, monsieur, that I'm done in about
losing your—'

'You didn't lose it.' Darac gave duty officer Béatrice
Lacquet a wave as she buzzed him out of the building.
'Some arsehole stole it. We'll get it back. Don't worry.'

Bzzzzzzzut!

In a freshening wind, the hand rail was cold to the touch
as Darac took the steps down into the compound.

'If you don't, monsieur, I'll pay you what it's worth. If
you don't mind waiting.'

Darac smiled; Freddy was a sweet kid. 'Mate, don't worry
about it; it's insured. In any case, we'll get it back. Whoever
took it doesn't know what they're up against, do they?'

'No, I guess not. Uh… If you put flyers in all the music
shops and that, you know – flyers with a picture and details
of the guitar and "stolen" on it, that would help.'

Those flyers were already being printed, Darac knew.
'Nice idea. We'll do that. And a lot more, Freddy.'

'Yeah? Cool. But I shouldn't have just left it there like that.'

'Hey, shit happens.' Should he have said that? 'It could have happened to anyone. Right?'

'Thank you, monsieur. Thank you very much.'

Darac ended the call and headed for his car. When he got there, Vice Squad Head Captain Francine Lejeune was pulling into the adjoining space. They exchanged greeting kisses.

'Heard about the fun and games, Frankie?'

'Just now on *France Info*,' she said, sweeping a cloud of kohl-black hair from her forehead. 'Gruesome.' Her voice, a perfectly enunciated yet soft contralto, made a concept like 'gruesome' seem all the more horrible, somehow. 'And then confusion reigned, by the sound of it.'

'For a minute or two, it did. I was there.'

Her brows lowered. 'Were you?'

'Our drummer was playing.' There seemed little point in mentioning the guitar. 'And Erica had a spare ticket. Next thing, a drunk falls under a float and we're putting in a spot of unpaid overtime.'

'Just an accident, then?'

'Yes. And get this: CCTV confirms it.'

Frankie drew down the corners of her mouth. 'You mean it actually came in useful?'

'Well, it had to come up trumps some time.'

'*France Info* just reported that the remaining parades might not go ahead.' She gave him a knowing look. 'Refund all that ticket money? It could happen, I suppose. Telonne's giving a press conference about it tomorrow.'

'They'll just put crash barriers up, won't they?'

'If they go *that* far. But obviously, press conferences will be the last thing on your mind tomorrow.' Frankie reached for his hand. 'I hope it all goes well, Paul.'

Darac's signature expression, a sort of amused empathy, lost all its levity for the moment. 'I'm off to meet Papa now, actually.'

'Oh?'

'I think he has something he wants to tell me.'

3

Most of the second-class hotel bars of Nice's palm-studded Promenade des Anglais charged first-class prices for drinks, most offered evenings of faux jazz, and most were unsuitable places in which to hold discreet conversations. Apart from the presence of a white baby grand, mercifully *sans* pianist, Hotel Brunswick's Le Phare Blanc seemed an exception to the rule.

'Welcome, Captain. Monsieur Darac is seated in the corner banquette.'

To even the most casual of observers, Darac's resemblance to his father, Martin, was remarkable. From him, he'd inherited the light-heavyweight build, the black wavy hair, and the strong, broad-boned face. The humour that gave his expression its relieving lift was a blessing from both parents.

The embrace was warm and prolonged.

'So Frankie is still wearing *Marucca*,' Martin said, sitting. 'Or someone is.'

'It's Frankie.' Darac smiled at the familiarity of it. A perfume industry 'nose' for almost thirty years, his father could never resist the challenge of naming a scent, however faint its traces.

They ordered Courvoisiers and, as if sticking to a mutually agreed script, chatted light-heartedly while they sipped them. It was during a second round that the elephant in the room finally got to its feet and joined them.

'Paul…' Martin stopped swirling the cognac around in his glass. Its shimmering surface came to a rest before he continued. 'With tomorrow in mind, this may seem to you exactly the wrong moment to say what I'm about to but…' He stalled.

'I can't judge until you say it.'

Trepidation vying with earnestness, Martin looked his son squarely in the eye. 'I'm very, very serious about the woman I've been seeing. So serious, that… I'm thinking of asking her to marry me.'

Darac gave a slight shrug. 'Congratulations.'

Martin exhaled deeply. 'Doesn't the identity of the accused at least interest you?'

A small man wearing a tuxedo and a disappointed expression sat down at the piano and lifted the lid. After a moment, 'Night and Day' came limping lame and leaden across the floor.

'It's Martine, I imagine.'

Martin's eyes hardened. 'That was over some time ago. You know that.'

'Oh yes. Well, it was for the best. Martin and Martine?' He made a moue. 'Not ideal.'

Martin took a deep breath. 'She's called Julie Issert. She's forty-one, she lives here in Nice and she runs a travel agency. Well, a personalised travel service.'

After just a few bars, 'Night and Day' was already segueing into 'They Can't Take That Away from Me'.

'And you've known her for…?'

Martin downed his cognac. 'Another?'

'No thanks.'

Martin caught the waiter's eye and held up one finger. 'Look, Paul… I don't have to account for anything in this. I don't need your permission—'

'How long have you known her?'

'Four months. I don't need—'

'Why her? Why not Lorena? Mariette? Adriana?'

'Why? Because I didn't love them.'

'Right.'

'And four months doesn't mean anything. I knew within four *hours* of meeting Mama that I wanted to be with her for the rest of my life.'

'That was Mama, though, wasn't it.'

'She was special, yes. She was fabulous. But so is Julie, Paul. She's full of life and energy. And she has that same…' As if the quality he sought could be extracted from air, he made a sifting movement with his hand. 'Well, you'll see when you meet her.'

'You realise that this is exactly what you said about—'

Martin shook his head. 'This is ridiculous! I'm fifty-six, for God's sake. And you—'

The waiter arrived. He seemed to take an age to remove the new glass from the tray and put it on the table and put the empty back on the tray and wipe the table and step by halting step, slope slowly out of earshot.

'And you, Paul—'

'I'm still twelve. Is that what you think? Is that why you've chosen this day of all days to let me in on your plans? To test my mettle?' Their eyes met in a slipping of gears that was almost audible. 'Well get this: I went to the carnival tonight. How's that? Do I pass?'

The fight went out of Martin suddenly. He reached out and squeezed his son's knee. 'Paul, that night had no bearing on what happened. None.'

'Yes, so they said.'

'You know…' Martin hesitated. 'Mama would have hated this. Hated it.' Another squeeze. 'You have to let her go. For everyone's sake.'

It was Darac's turn to stare at his drink. 'You're not driving home, are you?' he said, at length. 'Three cognacs is one too many, you know.'

'Uh… no. I'm staying here in Nice. I'll get a cab.'

Darac nodded. 'With Julie?'

'Yes.'

'She feels the same about you, I take it?'

'I hope so.'

'Uh-huh.' A sip of cognac. 'So she runs a travel service? Handy.'

'Yes. Air miles, freebies. All that.'

At the piano, Monsieur Disappointed's mood showed no signs of lifting as he gate-crashed 'Puttin' On the Ritz'.

'I'm heading off to the Blue Devil. Anders Bergcrantz. Trumpet. Great player.'

'Well… enjoy it.'

'I could drop you off en route. Save you the cab fare.'

'Julie lives up in Saint-Sylvestre. It's ridiculously out of your way.'

'Alright.' He got to his feet and for the moment, just stood there. 'You know Mama's death and all the things that surrounded it? I *have* let it go.'

If an actor were ever called upon to convey paternal love, exasperation and incomprehension in just one facial expression, they could not have bettered Darac *père* at that moment. 'Then why…?' He gathered himself. 'Then why have you always been so disapproving of my women friends? All of them, practically. Why have I been petrified at the thought of even mentioning Julie to you?'

Unsure of how to frame his response, Darac *fils* said nothing at all. It didn't thrill him that conversations on this topic tended to bring out an unsuspected judgemental, even passive-aggressive, streak in him. Whoever his father chose to spend his life with was nobody's business but his own. Yet, when it seemed so obvious that Martin's love of love never brought him any real happiness, Darac had to say *something*, didn't he? His eyes slid to the piano. 'I just don't want you to end up like him.'

'I won't. But I reserve the right to run that risk.'

They embraced.

'See you tomorrow, Papa.'

4

The kitchen was faced with oak, granite and terracotta. Sleek, flush-fitted and devoid of protruding buttons, an ensemble of top-of-the-range appliances maintained the hard, clean lines. From microwave to flat-screen TV, everything in the room worked without any obvious means of control.

Slipping on to a perch at the breakfast bar, a top-of-the-range woman wearing a white towelling dressing gown reached for a remote and waved it lazily in the air. In a frisson of static, larger than life-size heads appeared on the wall opposite. The woman kept her eyes absently upon them as she raised a teaspoon of yoghurt-moistened berries to her mouth. A press conference with the carnival committee was in full swing, and the floor had just been opened to questions.

'So, Monsieur Telonne,' Annie Provin began, 'you have decided to go ahead—'

'*I* have not decided, Annie,' Jacques Telonne replied smoothly. 'The *committee* has decided.'

'Very well – the *committee* of which you are chair has decided that the remaining five parades, and the climax of the season, the burning of the king, will go ahead. But last night, monsieur, a man was killed in Place Masséna. Surely—'

'Annie – a man was killed last night in Toulon. Another in Grenoble. Last week, a family of three was killed on the N98 near Saint-Raphaël. Such accidents are regrettable. They are tragic. But unless we are all to stay at home wrapped up in cotton wool, accidents will always happen.'

Setting down her spoon for a moment, the woman retied the belt of her dressing gown.

On the television, a second journalist had piped up. 'Monsieur Telonne, that is a very partial answer. I know it would change the street-party atmosphere to an extent but simply by erecting barriers around the Place, this particular tragedy could have been averted.'

'Had there been barriers, Jean,' replied Telonne, 'there could have been more loss of life than there was. If you were a football fan as I am, you would know what disasters can happen when a body of spectators is penned in to an enclosure from which there is no ready egress.'

'But Promenade des Anglais has barriers for the Parade of Flowers,' Provin said.

'That is because there are far more lorry-style floats in the Parade of Flowers than there are in the Parade of Lights…'

Wearing a thigh-length Aphex Twin T-shirt, a girl in her mid-teens padded bare-legged into the kitchen and crossed behind the breakfast bar. 'Any pizza left?'

'Good morning, Laure,' the woman said, without turning around.

'Yeah, ye-eeah.' In mid-yawn, Laure ran her fingers through her hair, a dark-brown mat that sat on its undershaved sides like a cheap toupee. 'Pizza?'

'There isn't any. Besides, you don't want pizza for breakfast.'

Laure dabbed a panel on the fridge door. It opened in a controlled glide. 'No? I thought I did.'

'I'll rephrase that. You shouldn't *have* pizza for breakfast. Or at any time. Apart from anything else, it's bad for the skin.'

'Bad for the skin? It isn't me who has a tattoo on her left, no, right arse cheek.'

The woman stiffened but said nothing

'Even if it is a pretty little butterfly.' Laure smiled with exaggerated sweetness. The smile disappeared. 'Coffee?'

'No, thank you.'

The fridge door set off on its return journey. 'I meant is there any?'

Still absently watching the screen, the woman gave a sideways nod. A chrome cafetière was sitting on a worktop.

'Where's the glass one?'

'Dropped. Shattered.'

'Tut, tut.'

The woman turned up the television. Annie Provin's voice rose above the sound of coffee being poured. 'And in the ensuing mayhem, three wallets, a handbag, two cameras and more significantly, a valuable musical instrument were snatched by thieves. As a potential mayoral candidate, you cannot be happy—'

Laure glanced at the screen as she set the cafetière back on the table.

'As a potential mayoral candidate, you cannot be happy—'

'What are you suggesting now? That opportunists taking advantage of an extraordinary circumstance constitutes a crime wave? Let me tell you something, Annie. Thanks to our policy of zero tolerance, the city of Nice has never in its entire history been as safe and as free of crime at all levels as it is now.'

Capping the pronouncement with a belch, the girl grabbed a couple of croissants and headed back to her room.

'Laure?' The woman finally turned. 'Remember what we said. Keep it down.'

'Keep what down – my breakfast? Bulimia's your thing, Mama dear. Not mine.'

Of the fifteen rooms in the house, Laure's bedroom was the smallest. She had chosen it deliberately. A note for visitors scrawled on the door read: YOU WILL CRASH AND BURN. Back-heeling it shut, she picked her way to her bed and, hitting the play button on her laptop, slipped on a pair of headphones. It wasn't a concession to her stepmother. The track was her latest composition and she wanted to listen to it critically.

As chaotic and colourful as the kitchen was sterile, the place was part bedroom, part DIY recording studio. Following circuit diagrams and wielding soldering irons held few fears for Laure – she'd put in most of the electronics herself. Keyboards were her thing. But as she listened to the track, she realised it needed something else. A different sound. Coffee soaking into the croissant began to scald her fingers as her eyes slid to the corner of the room. There, propped against the wall, was the solution. She smiled, a bubble of transgressive pleasure rising in her stomach. She knew that the guitar was an old Gibson SG Standard. She knew that it was sought-after and valuable. Best of all, she knew that it was hers now.

5

Darac had never been a good time-keeper. Late for school. Late for band practice. Late for this, late for that. But on 27 February every year, he was always the first to arrive at the old cemetery in Vence. Set on a terraced hillside just outside the town walls, it was a classic burial ground in the local style; no sylvan idyll but a conurbation of stone tombs and statuary laid out in a strict grid. A tiny city of the dead.

Usually dormant, Darac's sense of his mother's loss, deepened by convictions that allowed not the slightest hope of eventual reunion, awakened with some force as he waited at the gates for the others. He was never quite sure how to deal with the emotion. Give himself up to it? Snap out of it? He turned away for a moment and looked back toward the living city.

It was an overcast but warm morning for early spring, as was often the case for the anniversary. All around, there was a feeling of life freeing up, breaking out, burgeoning. Small birds flitted from branch to branch of a nearby shrub, flashing particoloured patterns against the pale green leaves.

'Goldfinches. A charm.'

Darac turned. The woman was elderly, rail thin and, with her spry demeanour, somewhat birdlike herself.

'That's what they call a group of goldfinches.' She smiled. 'A charm. Lovely, isn't it?'

'Yes.'

'We used to get them in our hibiscus when we lived in Antibes. Almost sixty years, we were there. Of course, I'm over in the apartments now. La Belle Vue. Do you know it?'

There wasn't a centimetre of Vence that Darac didn't know. 'Yes, I do.'

'It's very nice. But it's not the same.'

Darac was carrying a spray of perfect white roses. The woman's eyes alighted on it, darting with unconcealed pleasure from bloom to bloom.

'How beautiful.'

'She would have loved them,' Darac found himself saying. And then wondered why he had. 'Mama, that is.'

The woman smiled with a sort of knowing gravity. Leaning into him, her eyebrows rose as she touched his arm. 'She *does* love them, my dear. By God's good grace, she loves them at this very moment.'

However well-meaning, Darac didn't need it. 'Yes, well I must be going.'

'Of course, monsieur.' As if listening for a faraway voice, she canted her head slightly toward the avenues of tombs laid out beyond the gates. 'Yes, she is *so* happy you're here.' She nodded. 'I know, you see.' Her face was riven with concern, suddenly. 'I hope you are not the only one for her?'

But before Darac could answer, she spotted something behind Darac and her face lightened. 'Ah good, I see you have company. Your friend obviously didn't notice you.'

Darac looked over his shoulder. A man in a black coat, carrying a huge bouquet of lilies, was walking briskly through the cemetery gates. After a moment's hesitation, he began slow marching along the nearest rank of graves, reading each inscription in turn.

'As I say, I really must be—'

'Yes, you go and join him. What was your mother's name, by the way?'

Some medium you are, Darac thought. But at least the woman had asked the question directly, not recited a roll-call of initials until the connection with the 'other side' was made by nothing more supernatural than a process of elimination.

'It was Sandrine.'

The woman was only partially satisfied. 'Sandrine…?'

Enough was enough. 'Sandrine.'

'Yes.' The woman gave him a slightly straitened look. 'Forgive me. But remember what I said, monsieur. She *does* know. Goodbye.'

'Goodbye, madame.'

It was a further ten minutes before the first of the party, his mother's older brother Clément, joined him at the gates. And then in short order, his aunts Sophie and Antoinette, assorted cousins and old friends of the family, and even a few former students from the school at which Madame Sandrine Darac had been head of mathematics. As the appointed hour arrived, only one person was absent.

'He'll be here shortly, Paul.' Aunt Antoinette gave him a reassuring smile. 'Got a bit held up, that's all.'

Trying to hide his irritation, Darac said nothing. Other well-meaning people uttered well-meaning excuses for Martin as the minutes ticked by. Just as someone suggested that mobiles be switched on after all, a red Citroën swung into the street, stopped and reversed sharply into a parking space. The passenger door opened and Martin jumped out. Behind the wheel, a striking-looking woman with a head of auburn hair watched Martin hurry toward the party. The woman, it was clear, was Julie Issert.

'Clément, I can't tell you how sorry I am to be late.' Checking the pink carnations he was carrying had survived the dash, Martin greeted everyone in turn. He left his son until last. 'Paul, I'm—'

'Let's go in.'

A live CCTV camera was set up in the street that skirted the right-hand wall of the cemetery. Had staff at A1 Security been paying attention to the live shot it was relaying, they would have seen the Darac party walking in an informal group toward the graves clustered in the far corner of the site. They would have seen, on a parallel path, a large bouquet of lilies laid at the feet of a stone angel, and leaning against it, a man wearing a black coat, head down, weeping. And then, they would have seen the image turn to grey as the camera tilted suddenly skywards.

A whole family of Daracs resided in the neighbourhood of his mother's grave, a plain stone tomb mounted on a stepped plinth. A headstone carved in the form of an open book was its only sculptural flourish. On it was inscribed: OUR BELOVED SANDRINE THÉRÈSE DARAC, 18 AUGUST 1954–27 FEBRUARY 1988. Beneath it, the tomb itself was carpeted in flowers.

Clément said a prayer; Darac and Martin remained mute. Martin said some words at which Darac, and Martin himself, shed tears. And then all shared in a moment of silence.

Shots rang out. Bullets whining and ricocheting all around them. Darac was the first to react. 'Take cover!' he shouted, shepherding the others.

Bullets pitted the stonework as they huddled behind the tomb. Flowers exploded in a fragrant shower of petals. Caught in the line of fire, the man in the black coat ran for cover, falling twice in the process. Using the wall as a shield, the shooter was firing from the street that ran around the far side of the cemetery.

The shooting stopped.

'Anyone hit?'

No one.

Darac stood. The *stèle* had been ravaged, his mother's forename obliterated. He started to run as hard as he could toward the wall. A chorus of voices went up.

'Stop, Paul!'

'Come back!'

'For God's sake!'

He kept running. At any second, the shooter might reappear, firing at him point blank. He kept running. A car door slammed in the street beyond. An engine started and powered away. Darac vaulted the wall. The car, a grey Renault Mégane, was already making the turn into the street that led past the cemetery's main entrance. He ran on – his own car was parked next to the gates. He could be away and after the Renault in seconds. He ran hard around the corner. His quarry was still in sight. And then, another car burned away from the kerb, a red Citroën with a red-headed woman at the wheel.

'What is she doing?'

As the shooter went to overtake, the Citröen jagged hard

into his path, trying to ram the near-side flank, but the momentum was with the Renault. The Citroën cannoned off into a line of parked cars and stopped dead. The stricken Renault lurched and snaked but, missing everything else, continued along the street. Darac arrived at the Citröen as Julie Issert, thrown on to the passenger seat by the impact, grabbed the steering wheel and pulled herself up.

'Are you alright?' Darac said, breathing hard as he yanked open her door.

'I heard shots and then he came screaming around the corner.' Her words flew out in a single rapid burst. 'I had to do something…'

Staring intently at her, he reached in and turned off the engine.

'*Are* you alright?'

'Yes, yes. Was anyone—?'

'No one was hit, madame, okay? No one.' He jetted a glance toward the end of the street. The Renault was braking for the turn. 'Let's get you out.' She didn't show any sign of injury, moving freely. The Renault was nearly out of sight. 'I have to go now.'

Leaving her at the kerb, he jumped into his own car and tore away. In the rear-view mirror, he saw Martin jog through the cemetery gates. Arms outstretched, Julie went to meet him. As they were about to embrace, Darac made the turn and they disappeared.

He put out an APB call, then leaned on the horn and hammered the throttle. No feel for the racing line, he drove on pure adrenaline, missing walls, parked cars and street furniture by centimetres. Darac lost sight of the Renault. *Slow down to go faster,* he remembered. *And think, think,*

think. Initially, the road layout offered two escape routes for the shooter. The decisive junction was less than four hundred metres away. A roundabout. Which exit would the shooter take? A right would allow the Renault to double back to town; left led on to the open road to Cagnes. Hoping he would have caught the shooter before he needed to make the call, Darac pressed on. And there was another possibility, he realised. The shooter might abandon the car altogether. Perhaps it had already been ditched.

Brake lights flared ahead of him. Darac's heart beat a little faster. Was it? Yes, it was the Renault. Darac pressed harder, the car dipping and snaking along the twists in the road. Two hundred metres to the junction. Another glimpse of the brake lights. He was gaining. Who the hell was the shooter? He couldn't think of anyone with a grudge that strong against him. A hundred metres to the roundabout. The road straightened. Darac could see the Renault clearly now. He could read the number plate. With fifty metres to go, he was almost on top of it. Left or right?

The Renault attempted both, feinting right before jinking left. Too fast to make the turn, it took off, flipping and somersaulting into the grassed area in the centre of the roundabout. Darac skidded to a stop and got out. Was the shooter still alive? Still holding the gun? Darac ran in a zigzagging crouch to the driver's door.

Concerns about stopping a bullet evaporated with one glance.

6

Darac called various crews to the crash scene. By the time he left them to it, the investigation into the shooting incident itself was well underway in his absence.

There were three routes back to the cemetery: scenic, more scenic, stupendous. Today of all days, it had to be the last. With John Coltrane's 'All or Nothing at All' along for the ride, Darac hadn't gone more than a few metres before his mobile rang. Concerned colleagues had been phoning ever since news of the shooting broke, but this time he saw the caller was Didier Musso, leader of the quintet in which Darac played guitar. There was little point in enlightening him.

'Hey, Didi.'

'Some gig last night, eh? Bergcrantz – what a trumpet tone! He could charm the birds out of the trees with a sound like that.'

Darac pictured goldfinches. 'Absolutely.'

'Listen, I've been talking to Marco and he says he'll be fine for Thursday's gig. He also says you and that pretty blond girl, you know, the tech queen?'

'Erica.'

'Erica, yes. The two of you saved his life, he says.'

'That's just Marco being Marco. Simple first aid is all we did.'

'He also mentioned your old Gibbo got nicked. Young Freddy's beside himself, he says. Poor kid.'

'Everything's cool and I've told him that. Didier, I'm in the middle of something so…'

'Yeah, you get back to it. See you tomorrow night.'

'I won't be able to make it, but sign me on for the gig anyway?'

'Okay. See you Thursday.'

As the road shelved around the spur above Les Baumes, Darac slowed and pulled over. The cloud cover was all gone now. Under a sky of deepening azure, he stood for a moment, the vast panorama of the Alpes Maritimes laid out before him. It was a view dominated by the Baous, four up-thrust knuckles of rock that seemed to pull taut the high, thyme-scented ridge that stretched between them. It was a landscape he'd known all his life. A landscape his mother loved above all others.

Darac hadn't noticed the mud-splattered 4x4 that had fallen in behind him as he left the crash site. Still turning things over in his mind, he didn't notice it as it rolled to a stop alongside his Peugeot, screening it from the road. In the vehicle were three tough-looking individuals. Each was heavily armed. A rear window slid silently down. An assault rifle pointed at Darac's spine.

'DutDutDutDutDut!'

Darac flinched.

'Now you really are dead, Captain,' the officer said.

Deploying the Armed Protection Unit proved to have been Commissaire Agnès Dantier's idea. Darac called her.

'How many of these guys are there altogether, Agnès?'

'Six. The other three are dotted around outside the cemetery.'

'I don't need them now.'

'Our dear Prosecutor Frènes had to dig deep into the budget for them, so be grateful.'

'Dug willingly?'

'His little arms were going like pistons once I suggested he might be the next target.'

'It has to be something like that, something political. But the shooter's dead, Agnès.'

'And suppose he's part of a group?'

'If he was the best they had, they're not much of a group. He was a real amateur, believe me. Crap driver, too.'

There was no gainsaying her. At least Darac knew the guys wouldn't get in the way. You saw the APU only if they wanted it that way.

Lieutenant Christian Malraux peered at what was left of the headstone and grinned. 'Aw, that's sad, isn't it? Mummy died when he was only a kid.' He straightened. 'Can turn you into a complete arsehole, that.'

The crime-scene photographer lowered his camera. 'Shift,' he said. 'And mind where you put your feet.'

The immediate area was still littered with flower debris.

'Yeah, wouldn't want to spoil them.' Malraux trod with exaggerated care between the chewed-up blooms. 'I don't know, Marcel, I call in as a courtesy and this is all the thanks I get? I'm over in Cannes now, you know. Full lieutenant.'

'We miss you terribly.'

The camera's motor drive whirred away.

'Our paths will still cross, my friend.' Malraux winced, screwing up his eyes. 'Ah, shit.' He reached under his overalls and took out two small plastic vials. Tilting his head back, he emptied one of them into his pink, lashless left eye. '*And* he had his guitar nicked didn't he? Talk about a bad week.'

The camera went silent once more. 'You're still in the way.'

Blinking like a faulty light bulb, Malraux repeated the procedure with the other eye. 'Captain Fantastic having his arse nearly shot off… I tell you, if I was still around, it wouldn't have happened. I've saved his life once already.' His head still tilted back, Malraux shuddered, freezing cold, suddenly. Trying to force his eyes open, ghastly images started crowding into his head. He pictured the entombed body beneath him rising through the stone slab and coming for him. The skeletal hands of a woman reaching out and closing around his throat. Blinking blindly, Malraux staggered backwards, dropping the vials.

More camera whirrs. 'Sting, do they?' Marcel said. 'The drops?'

Gulping in air, Malraux put his hands to his neck and felt all around it. His eyes clearing, he kept them on the grave as he retreated another couple of paces. 'Just cold,' he said at length. 'The stuff does that.'

'I never realised you were such a sensitive soul.'

Malraux's vision settled. He began to calm down. Not that he would ever admit to anyone that he'd just suffered a panic attack. 'Because that's definitely what it was,' he said aloud, still staring warily at the grave.

'What was definitely what?'

Slowly, Malraux gathered himself. He looked at his watch. 'Got to go. Hate hanging around these places anyway. Give me the fucking creeps.'

The whirring stopped. 'Oy! Don't leave your shit behind.'

'You chuck them,' Malraux said, not looking back.

Darac was standing by the cemetery wall, glowering at a mark on the ground when he heard a car draw up beside him.

'I gather we missed Malraux,' Bonbon said, getting out of his car. 'Came to pay his respects, he made out. Flak called me. She reckons he was just snooping.'

'I don't care either way.'

Bonbon gave his boss a long, appraising look. 'So?'

'I'm fine.'

'Uh-huh?'

Darac grinned. 'Alright, I'm still a bit shaken. So the sooner we—'

'...get down to business, the better?'

'Something like that.'

'Okay, but have you had a chance to talk with your papa and everyone?'

'Yes, he's gone off to sort something out. For the family.'

'Right.' Bonbon stared at the red circle sprayed on the pavement that Darac had been inspecting. In the centre of it was a card marked with the letter A. 'The shooter fired from there?'

'Be my guest.'

Conveying just how weird he found it, Bonbon put

himself in the position of the gunman and squinted over the wall. 'Where exactly—'

'See that baroque monstrosity with the angel? The one sporting the equally baroque bouquet of lilies? Follow that line for about twenty-five metres.'

Bonbon's face crumpled. 'Mate,' he said, 'I don't know what to say.'

'Yeah, well…' Darac thought back to the old woman at the cemetery gates. 'She is *so* happy you're here,' she'd said. 'It's just a box, you know, Bonbon. A box of bones.'

Bonbon didn't speak straight away. 'And he parked right here, the shooter?'

'Not to start with. According to the one statement we've got so far, he parked first under that oh-so-useful CCTV camera further down the street.'

'The one pointing at the sky?'

'It is now. Although the witness didn't see it because he'd gone by then, the shooter must have tipped up the camera, decamped to here and opened fire.'

'Tipped up? You usually have to undo bolts.'

Behind them, Chief Forensic Officer Raul Ormans was stowing equipment in his van. Dark, barrel-chested and imperious, Ormans had the look of a thespian who had played kings in his time. 'You don't have to undo bolts,' he said, in his deep, resonant tones. 'Not if the thing's a lightweight piece of crap mounted on a simple swivel. These high-tech devices were all it took.' He pulled out a couple of lengths of plastic downpipe, push-fitted them together and mimed the action. '*Voilà.*'

'Great.'

'Notice this drain, gents?' Ormans nudged a pebble

through the grating with his foot. 'Wait for it.' Some seconds elapsed before the splash. 'Not the worst spot to lose a gun, is it? Yet he took it with him.'

Darac shook his head. 'It's deep, alright, but it's a place we'd more than likely look. I don't think he even thought about it, though. Have you had a chance to examine the thing yet?'

'The gun went straight to the lab from the crash site. Did you get a good look at it yourself? Other than when you were running straight toward it, I mean.'

'Jesus,' Bonbon said, exhaling deeply and conveying by a shake of the head that Darac's hot-headedness was, once again, a source of concern to him.

'At the crash site? No. Just the end of the barrel, R.O. What was left of the guy was covering the rest of it.'

'We'll have something later.'

A woman's voice called out from down the street. 'Captain!' Patricia Lebrun was the technician responsible for signing personnel in and out of the crime scene. Martin Darac was standing next to her. 'May he?'

'Suit him up, Patricia. Bullets, R.O.?'

'Recovered six so far. Forty-five calibre. Can't tell you any more at the moment.'

Bonbon's mobile rang. 'Go for it, Perand.' He opened his notebook. 'Spell that?'

While he waited for Bonbon, Darac looked back over the wall toward his mother's grave. He could still scarcely credit what had happened. Despite his sympathy for anyone subjected to an attack, he'd often felt frustrated at the paucity of detail that victims, or merely witnesses, were capable of recalling after a traumatic event. Now here *he* was, feeling a huge range of things himself and one of them was simple confusion. How many shots had been fired? He'd asked that at scenes a thousand times. It was less than two hours after the shooting and he had no idea. Ormans had found six bullets so far. Maybe that's all there would be. Maybe nearer sixteen had been fired, though. Twenty-six, thirty-six; he just didn't know. He was sure of only one thing. Without the shield of his mother's grave, he and several other members of his family would soon have been moving in alongside her.

'Okay,' Bonbon said. 'The shooter was one Carl Auguste Halevy. Fifty-three years of age. Accounts manager. Cagnes-sur-Mer address. Married. The wife is already en route to the morgue for the ID.' His tawny eyebrows lowered. 'But here's the interesting part. He had a completely clean record. And as far as Perand has been able to check so far, his close associates have no more than traffic offences or other trifles to own up to.'

'No potential grudge-bearers there. Did Perand check on a gun licence?'

'Yes, and Halevy held one. For a forty-five-calibre Browning. An antique.'

'It fires well enough,' Darac said, staring off. 'But why the hell was he firing it at me?'

'Perand has informed the wife we'll need to talk to her later.'

'Right.'

Martin Darac joined them. 'It's a cliché, I suppose, but I feel like an astronaut wearing these overalls.' He gave Bonbon a look. 'Would you give us a moment?'

'Of course. I'll be over with Patricia. Give me a shout when you're ready.'

Father and son waited until he was out of earshot.

'The mason says he can do something by next week,' Martin said. 'Does that work for you?'

'Yes. I'll have released the site in a day or two.'

'Good. It will have to be a whole new construction, obviously.' He gave Darac a loaded look. 'When it's done, the priest will have to re-consecrate the grave. A lot of piety in Latin, that means.'

'Whatever we may think, all that matters is that Mama would have wanted it.'

Martin smiled. 'She would. Although it wasn't so much that she was a believer, you know; more that she believed in not completely *dis*believing. What your Aunt Sophie calls "believing in her own way".'

He looked across at the bullet-pocked masonry of her grave. 'Very much in her own way,' he said with a smile.

One occasion in particular came back to him, a spin around Monoprix when he was about eight. Having brilliantly finessed sneaking an extra jar of Nutella into her basket, he'd then suffered a miniature crisis of conscience. 'Mama,' he'd asked. 'Is God really real?' 'Well, Paul,' she'd said, putting the jar back on the shelf – she had of course spotted his legerdemain – 'some people think of it like this. You may as well believe He is real because if you don't, you would miss out on an awful lot of things if it turns out He *is*.' Pascal's Wager for the under-tens. At the time, it had made a sort of sense to young Paul Darac. It was only some years down the line that he realised it didn't work and that his mother, a maths teacher after all, was holding back more precise propositions on the subject until he was older. Darac looked past Martin and gave Bonbon a beckoning nod. 'So… you've all made statements, Papa?'

'That young Officer Flaco took them. Impressive girl.'

'She's that and more.'

'Chloë.'

'Yvonne.'

'Not her name; her scent.'

'Ah.'

'Too floral for her but I didn't say anything.'

'Just as well.'

'Aniseed twist, monsieur?' Bonbon said, rejoining them. 'Useful in cases of shock.'

'No, I'm fine, thanks. We all are, in fact. Even Sophie, my sister. I tell you, a soufflé collapses and she has to be practically sedated but turn the family plot into a shooting gallery and she sails right on through.'

'Remarkable, monsieur.'

'And speaking of remarkable, Paul, what about Julie? Wasn't what she did fantastic?'

'It was. It was also fantastically reckless.'

Martin gave a brisk nod. 'Ah, yes, of course. Reckless. She could have killed herself trying to help but let's just forget that.' He exhaled deeply. 'So what now?'

'We know who the shooter was, Papa, but as yet, we've no idea why he wanted to…' The point ran off into a siding as a new thought rolled in. 'I've been guilty of making a bit of an assumption here, haven't I?'

Bonbon nodded. 'Just a bit, chief.'

'What assumption?' Martin said.

'That as a homicide detective, I was the likely target. I've arrived here at ten o'clock in the morning every 27

February for over twenty years. The shooter, I reasoned, must have known that. He therefore also knew that for some minutes, his target would be standing still, absorbed, unprepared, and almost certainly unarmed. A perfect time for a hit. That was my thinking, anyway.'

Martin's face creased in a sort of perplexed admiration. 'What a job you do.' He waved the thought away. 'What's the problem with that conclusion?'

'There isn't one. But there are other possible scenarios, are there not?'

'Such as?'

Seeing the difficulty of the situation, Bonbon intervened. 'Monsieur Darac – please don't infer anything critical in this but do you know of anyone who might want *you* dead, for instance?'

'Certainly not!'

'Think.'

'Who, for example?'

'I don't know, monsieur. A business rival?'

'No, no. The perfume industry can be a cut-throat business but I've never made any real enemies.'

Bonbon gave his boss a questioning look. And got the nod. 'Well then, perhaps a spurned lover?'

'What is this? No! Emphatically not.'

'Or perhaps the target was another member of your party?'

'You'll be saying that Paul's Aunt Sophie has a contract out on her next.'

'Papa.' The look was as neutral as his son could manage. 'Carl Auguste Halevy. Does that name mean anything to you? Think before you answer.'

Martin thought about it. 'No. I have never heard that name. He was the man, I take it? The would-be assassin.'

'He was.'

'No. Never heard of him. Look, might not the shooting have been just a random act? Perhaps this Halevy was a lunatic.'

'It can't be ruled out,' Bonbon said. 'But it's the least likely scenario.'

Officer Yvonne Flaco joined them. Plump as a pony and with a scowling mien, Flaco radiated strength, diligence and toughness. And apparently, Chloë.

'Witness statements, Captain,' she said, handing them over. 'This is what you gave me on the phone, these are by various members of your party, and finally, these are from people who were in the vicinity at the time.'

'Quick work, Flak.'

'That's because there are so few of them. There are two significant things, though.' She tapped the topmost statement with the tip of an unvarnished nail. 'Madame Lécame, who walks her dog past the cemetery a couple of times a day, says that the shooter appeared to be parked here most of yesterday. And he was here this morning when the cemetery opened at eight o'clock.'

'*Was* he?' Darac put his hands on his hips and stared at the ground. 'You didn't happen to get anything on the other mourner, did you? The man in the black coat who ran off?'

'That's the second thing.' Flaco handed him a poly bag containing a folded sheet of printed paper. 'A uniform picked this up just over there. It must have dropped out of a pocket when he fell.'

'Look at this, Bonbon.'

The paper was a current account statement for the Crédit Bal-Med bank dated 23 September 2003. The account holder's name was one Sylvie Galvin, and it showed a deposit made mid-month of €400,000 as a cheque from the same bank.

Bonbon's eyebrows rose. 'Four hundred grand? Lovely.'

'Why would a man be carrying around someone else's eight-year-old bank statement?'

He intended the question for Bonbon but Martin spoke up. 'Perhaps he didn't realise it *was* in his pocket. I only wear this suit once in a blue moon. For funerals and so on.'

'You could have something there.'

'Anyway, I must be getting back. Will you be joining us, Paul? We'll all be at the house.'

'I'm not sure. There's a lot to do, still. I've detailed a couple of the armed protection unit to keep an eye on you, by the way.'

'That's not necessary, surely?'

'Almost certainly not.'

Martin didn't hide his exasperation. 'How long will they be around, for heaven's sake?'

'Only for a few days. But you won't notice them much.'

'Well… if you insist.'

Business finally over, Darac *fils* looked his father in the eye and nodded. 'Right.'

'So.'

Further nods. Glances at feet.

Bonbon caught Flaco's eye, inclining his head toward the cemetery. The pair took their leave.

Darac shook his head, admitting defeat. 'Ah, there's just too much to say.'

'Yes there is. Absolutely. But look... come to dinner soon. So you can meet Julie properly.'

'Alright.'

'When?'

'I don't know. Soon.'

'What about tomorrow?'

'Tomorrow?' Darac wasn't used to being pressured like this by his father.

'Or the weekend. I'll give you a call.'

'Yes... alright.'

'Good.'

Their crime-scene overalls making a forlorn rustling sound, the two men embraced for some moments and then went their separate ways.

Darac joined Bonbon and Flaco at the baroque angel grave. The occupant's name was almost lost among verses of scripture but he found it and read it out. 'SYLVIE MARIE GALVIN. BORN 1 SEPTEMBER 1984; DIED 19 APRIL 2008.' Twenty-three at her death, he reflected. His mother had been ten years older. And that had been no age to die. 'Any thoughts?'

'No reference to her family, notice,' Bonbon said. A photo roundel showed a sad-looking, fleshy-faced young woman with small, deep-set eyes. 'Doesn't look like a girl who has four hundred grand in the bank, does she? Maybe the photo was taken before.'

Flaco took another look at the bank statement. 'She was nineteen when she received the sum. An inheritance? She may have needed it, by the look of things. The account was only a few hundred euros in credit at the start of the month. Not much to live on.'

'She could have had other accounts as well.' Bonbon checked out the address on the statement. Appartements Solferino, Les Moulins, was not one of Nice's more exclusive residences. 'Scratch that.'

Darac pursed his lips. 'So what's the story? What do you think, Flak?'

'Just on the age of the statement, like your papa said, people often do leave things in clothes they don't usually wear. But what was the man doing with it in the first place?'

'Quite. And look at how elaborate and expensive this grave is. Yet Sylvie seems to be the sole occupant.'

'A mausoleum for one.' Bonbon's police armband slipped down his skinny sleeve. 'It *is* unusual.'

'And another thing. Why was he here, the man in the coat?'

'Well, to visit the departed.' Bonbon absently pulled his armband back up.

'Why now? It's neither the birthday nor the anniversary of the death of this Sylvie Galvin.'

Flaco evidently didn't understand the objection. 'Does it need to be a special occasion to visit a grave here? Back in Guadeloupe, we often do it.'

Darac indicated the bouquet. 'That's quite something for a casual visit.'

'It's quite some grave,' Bonbon said.

'Yet the man had no idea where it was. I saw him walk through the cemetery gates, stop at the very first grave, check out the inscription, then turn to the next. Two hundred or however many graves it is later, he finally found the one he was looking for.'

Bonbon pulled his rubber-band mouth into an upside-down U. 'So he's a visitor. From afar, possibly. Literally a distant relative?'

'Maybe. Think of the significance of the shooter turning up here not at five minutes to ten this morning – the time, as I say, my party has been gathering for the last twenty plus years – but two whole hours earlier. And he was here most of yesterday. What does that suggest?'

Raul Ormans' large, patrician head appeared under the angel's wing. 'It suggests a degree of corroboration with my own findings.' He set down an evidence case. 'When you look at the nature of the weapon used, the ammunition, the trajectories and everything else, it's difficult to arrive at any conclusion but this: the man standing here wasn't caught in your line of fire; you were caught in *his*. Or rather, you were the backstop to it. He was the target, happily. Happily for the Daracs of this world, that is.'

Darac made an affirming sound in his throat. 'Agreed. It was the man in the coat the shooter was waiting for. He knew he was coming, he just didn't know when, exactly.'

Flaco nodded her tightly corn-rowed head. 'And it explains why he fired from where he did. If you'd been his target, Captain, he would have secreted himself somewhere he could get a much closer shot.'

'Succinctly put,' Ormans said, heading back to his van. 'Later.'

Bonbon's foxy eyes were following trails. 'He wasn't winged as he got away, was he? The man in the coat, I mean. If he was, he'll be seeking medical help.'

Flaco pointed toward a pedestrian gate set in the rear wall. 'He went out that way. Dr Mpensa's team examined his route all the way and a bit beyond. They didn't find a single drop of blood.'

'Pity.'

Hands on hips, Darac stared at the ground. 'So let's reframe our original question. Why was the apparently clean Monsieur Carl Auguste Halevy shooting at the man in the black coat? And who is that individual? It may still be a matter of life and death that we find him even though it was Halevy who wound up being killed.'

Flaco's scowl deepened. '*He* might contact *us*, surely? To report that someone just tried to kill him.'

Once again, Bonbon's armband decided it had had enough of the high life. 'Depends, Flak, doesn't it?' he said, unconsciously pushing it back up. 'On just *why* Halevy was shooting at him.'

'If the man reports in – great,' Darac said. 'But we're not relying on it.'

'It's a pity no one got a good look at him, Captain.'

'I know someone who may have – an old lady I was talking to before this all started.'

He gave Flaco a description and told her the quickest way to get to La Belle Vue, where the old lady had said she was living.

'I'll go over there now. How many apartments in the building?'

'About thirty or so. If you find her and she can describe him, ask Astrid to follow it up with a sketch.'

'Right, Captain.'

Darac's mobile rang. 'It's Perand. Hang on, Flak, I'll put it on speaker.'

The three of them attuned their ears to a voice that was

the aural equivalent of scrawled handwriting.

'Yeah, Lieutenant Granot's asked me to tell you Madame Halevy's up to being interviewed and he's gone off to do it.'

'I'll call him in a second. We've got developments here.' Darac outlined them. 'Anything else?'

'Yeah, I've had Foch on the line about your guitar.'

'And?'

'No leads – excuse the pun. So unless the outstanding CCTV footage shows something, it's not looking good on that score. Every instrument shop and pawnbroker in the area has flyers, though. And they're emailing the details nationwide.'

'Good. Thanks for that, Perand.'

Darac ended the call wondering if he'd seen the last of his first really good guitar. But he had more pressing matters to attend to. Selecting camera mode, he aimed his mobile at Sylvie's roundel photograph. No one had the heart to say 'smile'.

7

Madame Yvette Halevy was a slender, bitter-faced blonde with a style of grieving all her own.

'Carl was a waste of space.' She took a deep drag on her Gauloise. 'Oh, I don't mean he was incompetent. He did well enough in his job. But it's typical of him that he would wind up... like this.' She gave the air an offhanded slap. 'Typical.'

The apartment was a well-appointed duplex in Cagnes-sur-Mer with an uninterrupted view of the château at Haut-de-Cagnes. A simple crenelated box surmounted by a flag-festooned tower, the château had the look of a toy fort.

'Madame,' Granot said, scarcely able to conceal his incredulity, 'I don't think you understand the situation. Your husband tried to murder someone. In the coldest of cold blood. And then in fleeing the scene, he was killed in a car crash. He's dead, madame.'

'Haven't I just identified his body? Idiot.'

Whether Madame was referring to her husband or to him, Granot wasn't sure. 'Alright, let's start with the shooting.'

'Pah.'

'The shooting, madame.'

'I can't imagine why he did it.'

'Did your husband have any enemies? Can you think of anyone he might have wanted out of the way?'

'What part of "I can't imagine why he did it" didn't you understand?'

'This attitude isn't helping, madame.'

Another deep drag. 'Carl had no enemies. He wouldn't say boo to a goose.'

'Does the name Sylvie Galvin mean anything to you?'

'No.'

He handed Madame Halevy his mobile.

'There's a face to stuff food into. Who's this – your daughter?'

Granot's jowly chops reddened. 'It's Mademoiselle Galvin. Do you recognise her?'

She handed it back. 'Never seen her.'

Granot continued with a description of the man in the black coat.

'It could be anyone.'

'This man, the man your husband shot at...' The possibility he was entertaining seemed remote to him but he had to pursue it. 'Is he your lover? Your husband found out and decided to act?'

A deeper drag. 'I don't do lovers, monsieur.' She stubbed out her cigarette emphatically, as if the prospect of it rekindling was a clear and present danger. 'And they don't do me.'

'About the gun he used...'

The interview dragged on for ten further fruitless minutes.

'Right, that's that,' she said at the end of it. 'Are you driving back into Nice, now, Lieutenant?'

'Yes.'

'Then you can give me a lift. I need to make the funeral arrangements.'

8

Laure loved her new guitar. It was ballsy and loud and it played like a dream. She banged out a few low-end riffs, then started exploring its upper register in a series of keening screeches.

Despite the warning to visitors, her door opened.

'Laure!' Her stepmother's screams were no match for the Gibson. 'Turn! That! Down!'

Laure eyeballed her, cranking up the volume a notch before sliding a huge chord down the neck of the instrument. Buried in the stacks of equipment, an idling amplifier hummed a tense undertone to the silence that followed. It was the stepmother who finally spoke, placing her words across the chasm between them with the contained precision of a tightrope walker.

'When you are making your… music, would you please wear your headphones.'

'Take your plastic tits and get out of my room.'

'I said when you are making your—'

'Listen, I was living in this house before my father even met you. Fuck off!'

The woman flew at her, slapping and kicking. But she was no match for Laure. In less time than it took to say 'top of the range', she was bundled out into the hall and dumped on to her backside. Picking herself up, she did two things she'd vowed she never would. She called out: 'Wait until your father gets home!' And then she burst into tears.

9

The extraordinary events of the past twenty-four hours had persuaded Commissaire Agnès Dantier to bring the monthly case review meeting forward by a day. Darac arrived back at the Caserne just as it was about to get underway. He could hear the lively mix of banter, argument and jokes in the squad room from well down the corridor – the 'storm before the lull', Agnès had once dubbed it. The buzz dropped to a murmur as he walked in.

'Something I said?'

Scanning faces, he exchanged a look with Frankie of such meaningfulness that the rest of the room seemed to disappear momentarily. But it was Erica who got up to embrace him.

'I leave you alone for five minutes.' Her eyes misting, she removed a flower petal fragment from the collar of his jacket. 'Thank God you're alright.'

As the simmer gradually went back up to a boil, Max Perand turned to Flaco.

'This is supposed to be a police station, no? Not a fucking…' A suitable comparison evaded him. 'He's already had the boss practically weeping down the phone, they say.' He thought it politic not to mention that 'they' was Adèle Rousade, resident rumour-monger at the Caserne. 'And Frankie Lejeune was the same, apparently.'

Flaco stared at him, saying nothing.

'Sickening,' Perand persisted. 'Don't you think?'

Flaco decided to play, after all. 'He's got a lot of faults, hasn't he, the captain? A hot temper being just one of them.'

'Tell me about it.'

She continued as if explaining something to a child. 'But because he's warm-hearted, supportive—'

Two positives were enough for Perand. 'Yes, yes, yes.'

'Because he's those things *and* more, some people actually like him. And they're relieved he wasn't shot dead today.'

'Flak – he was shot at by accident.'

'Shot at while standing at his mother's graveside.'

'He wasn't the target, alright?'

Flaco's withering stare was a potent corrective. But Perand wasn't finished. 'Anybody could have been hit. *I* could have if I'd been there.'

The stare was Flaco's last word on the matter.

Perand threw up his hands. 'Alright, I'll burst out crying and give him a kiss. How's that?'

Drawing up a chair behind him, Drug Squad Head Captain Jean-Pierre 'Armani' Tardelli flicked the saggy neck of Perand's *Down by Law* T-shirt. 'If you want to go gay, Maxie, you'll have to dress better than this.'

'Funny, Captain. Very funny.'

Granot and Bonbon were the last to arrive, taking seats next to Frankie. Agnès was sitting at the head of the room, a stack of folders on the desk in front of her. Slipping out of her shoes, she unclamped her reading specs from her ash-blond bob and called the meeting to order.

'Alright, everyone, we'll start with…' She made a moue.

'Your stolen guitar, Paul. Perand – where are we with this?'

'The good people over at Foch have pushed the boat out for us but as yet they haven't come up with anything.' He detailed the measures being taken. 'Lartou, you've got something, right?'

Crime scene co-ordinator Jean-Jacques 'Lartou' Lartigue nodded his shaved head. 'We should be receiving a DVD from the Mairie. There was a software issue with one of the security cameras in Place Masséna but they're almost there, they say.'

'Let's hope something comes of it. So on to the death at the carnival that kicked off this drama.' Agnès opened the file. 'The deceased is one Michel Fouste, fifty-five, who lived alone. Worked in construction. When he did work, that is. A conviction for assault in December 2009 seems to relate to a history of alcohol abuse that goes back many years. He was drunk again at the Parade of Lights. Initial concerns that the death may not have been accidental proved unfounded under further examination.' She looked up from the sheet. 'The verdict is going to be accidental death, isn't it?'

There were no gainsayers. Agnès set the file aside and opened the next one, initiating a discussion about the man who had pursued Fouste though the crowd. It was agreed that he should be interviewed, were he to come forward. Under the circumstances, there seemed no necessity to mount a search.

'Just a quick note on the future of Carnival itself.' Agnès skimmed a release from the committee office. 'Tomorrow afternoon's Parade of Flowers is going ahead... as are the remaining two Parades of Light next week. The final night firework display and the Burning of the King are also going ahead as planned.' She grinned knowingly, a look that suited her feline features. 'Surprise, surprise.'

Half an hour or so later, Agnès's stack of case files was down to just one. The mood in the room changed as she drew it toward her. 'I think we all know what happened earlier today. Would you take us through it, Paul?'

Supported by witness statements and other evidence, he recounted the incident and outlined progress in the investigation.

'So where do we go from here?' Agnès said.

'I've requested details on Sylvie Galvin, the occupant of the grave in question. The man in the black coat who was being shot at obviously knew her – he had an old bank statement of hers in his pocket. So he's possibly a relative; perhaps a close one and therefore findable. We've got one eyewitness description. Were you able to get hold of Astrid, Flak?'

'Yes – she should have interviewed the old lady by now.'

'So with any luck we'll have an image of the man shortly.' Darac ran a hand through his hair. 'The bank statement aspect is intriguing, isn't it?' He gave Agnès a look. 'I'd like us to look into that. On the shooter side of things, I interviewed some of Halevy's work colleagues on the way in. They're dumbfounded.'

'Friends are always dumbfounded.' Armani clasped his large, tanned hands together behind his head and leaned back in his chair. 'Wives are dumbfounded, husbands – everybody.'

'Sure, but from their accounts, Halevy does come across as an unremarkable sort of guy. Nervous, almost timid.'

'He did own a pistol,' Frankie said, her silk-soft contralto making gun ownership sound an appealing hobby. 'And he did fire it. Repeatedly.'

Agnès nodded. 'When timid characters crack, they often do so spectacularly.'

Granot gave a phlegm-rattling chortle. 'Maybe he mistook the man in the coat for his wife.'

A ripple of laughter ran around the room.

'Okay – anything else on this at the moment?'

A couple of other initiatives were proposed and approved and the briefing drew to a close. Darac exchanged a few words with Frankie and then turned to the usual suspects.

'Coffee, Granot? I certainly need one.'

'You're on.'

'Bonbon?'

'I don't know. They say it gives you funny ideas.'

Once in his office, Darac made straight for his beloved Gaggia espresso machine and set to work.

'Madame Yvette Halevy…' Granot's expression was a sort of awestruck bemusement as he flopped onto his usual seat by the door. 'I've been at this for thirty years and I've never come across anyone like her. I told you I dropped her off at that funeral directors' on Avenue du Ray, Contes Frères, after our little chat?'

'You made it live, mate,' Bonbon said, turning a chair around.

'You'll never guess the last thing she said to me before she got out of the car.'

Bonbon's elastic band of a mouth stretched into an even wider grin.

'What are you doing next weekend, big boy?'

'Better than that. She said, "Do you think Messieurs Contes would dress Carl's body in an Olympique de Marseille football strip for the burial?" I said, "I'm sure they would." She said, "Good. He was a Monaco fan."'

Granot's laugh rumbled under Bonbon's breathless squeak.

'Ker-tishhhh!' Darac managed not to spill any of the freshly ground Delta Diamante he was measuring into the filter holders. 'Ai, ai, ai.'

It was only after he'd recovered that Bonbon noticed a cardboard-backed envelope sitting on the desk. Darac's name was written on it in a distinctive hand.

'Chief? Astrid has already left her handiwork, look.'

'Shit. I should have looked in here before the meeting.' Enveloped in a cloud of savoury sweetness, Darac cast only the quickest glance over his shoulder – nothing interrupted the sacrament of the bean. 'Why didn't she email me a photo? Check it out, will you, Bonbon?'

Bonbon got to his feet and opened the envelope. 'Okay, there are two sketches... and a note.' He laid the drawings side by side on the desk. 'Look at these, Granot.'

Words of protest accompanying a medley of effortful sounds, the big man hauled himself off his chair.

'Read out the note,' Darac said.

'She writes: *Hi Darac, just got back from Vence. As you're always saying, it's probably nothing, but check out these masterpieces.*'

Granot gave an approving little grunt. 'Love her confidence.'

'The note continues: *Sorry I couldn't email them but my server was down. They look a million times better in the flesh, anyway. The one marked "A" I did with an eyewitness at the Parade of Lights the other night. It's of the guy you called the chaser – the one with the goatee who made off into the night. Now look at "B", which I've just drawn with the help of the old lady you met at the cemetery. A charming old soul, isn't she? Bird fancier. She and her husband used to attract goldfinches to their hibiscus, she told me. Ah, sweet. Except they trapped them and ate the poor little things.'*

'Astrid a vegetarian?' Granot said, bemused.

'Go on, Bonbon.'

'Anyway, look carefully at that second sketch. The man is clean-shaven but apart from that, he looks the same as the first guy, no? Note the basic topography of the faces and especially the eyes. The only real difference is the goatee. Anyway, I'm late for my dance class so – later. By the way, I'm glad you didn't get shot, Darac.' Bonbon couldn't resist chuckling. 'And then she signs off: *Kisses, Astrid.'*

'*Kisses*, is it?' Granot ran an eye over the two drawings. 'I never get that.'

'I'm more of a "with cordial regards" man, myself.' Bonbon's words emerged in a distracted monotone as he compared the two images. 'Hm… Both have the same puddingy face, don't they? Puddingy with little currants for eyes.'

'You're making me hungry.'

Still looking, Bonbon stepped back a couple of paces. 'I'm with Astrid. These likenesses… are alike.'

Darac took in the sketches as he handed out the coffees. 'Yes, they are alike. Very.'

Another thought struck him. 'Take a look at this.' He brought up Sylvie Galvin's grave photo on his mobile.

'What do you think? Father and daughter? Could be, couldn't they?'

'They could. Easily.'

Darac parked his backside on the desk. 'First, I had no idea how many shots had been fired at the scene. Then, it turns out I saw this guy both at the parade and in the cemetery. I just didn't register what he looked like.' He shook his head. 'I don't think much of my skills as a witness.'

'You didn't see him head on, either time,' Bonbon said. 'And people don't actually look at everything they see, anyway.'

Granot nodded. 'People see what they expect to see. Like I see what's coming next.'

'If what you're seeing is someone going to have another chat with Madame Halevy, you've got it in one.'

'Sweet Mary... So you're thinking what? Carl Halevy might have been a mate of the guy that went under the float...' Fingers clicking flabbily together, Granot searched for the name.

'Michel Fouste,' Bonbon said.

'Fouste, yes. And perhaps Halevy didn't share the view that the man with the deep-set eyes' – he indicated the sketches – 'was innocent of his death. He reckons he *did* push the man. So he digs out his old pistol and kills him out of revenge. Or tries to.'

'No, I'm not thinking that.' Darac took a sip of espresso. 'The timing doesn't work, does it? Halevy took up station at the cemetery hours *before* Fouste did his swan dive under the float.'

'Ah yes.' Granot gave his temple a reproving tap. 'He did.'

'So it's not Carl Halevy's connection with Fouste we need

to establish; it's his connection with Astrid's guy. That's why we need to talk to good old Madame H. again. We need to show her these drawings.'

'And there's the last of the CCTV footage from the parade, the camera they were having trouble with,' Granot said. 'There might be a usable shot of the man in that. A nice frontal view.'

'Don't count on it. This guy seems to have a sixth sense for security cameras.'

'Bit of a coincidence, isn't it?' Bonbon looked unconvinced. 'Astrid's man being in the cemetery as well as at the parade?'

'Half of Nice was at the parade,' Darac said.

His black desk phone rang – an internal call. He leaned back and picked it up.

'Adèle Rousade here, Captain. I've got the first bit of info you wanted. Shall I give it to you now or do you want to wait for the rest?'

'Let's have it now. Just a second.' He smothered the mouthpiece for a moment. 'Sylvie info.' He picked up a pen. 'Go ahead, Adèle.'

'Okay. Sylvie Marie Galvin born 1 September 1984 to Karen Marie Galvin.'

Darac sensed trouble. 'Got the father's name there?'

'Not known.'

'Not known,' he repeated to the others.

'The mother's occupation is listed as "various". She gave up the baby immediately. Sylvie was brought up at the Convent of the Sisters of Mercy, Vallauris. Mother died in May '87. Road accident. Sylvie left the convent in September 2002. That's it. I'll let you know the rest when I have it.'

'Thanks, Adèle.'

Granot's forehead furrowed like a beach on a retreating tide. 'Bad break, that – father not known.'

'*He* knew who he was though, didn't he?' Darac drained his espresso. 'He found her grave. Eventually.'

Bonbon gave a little nod. '"Not known" often means not declared, doesn't it? So we'll just go through her mother to find him.'

'Not possible. She's dead.' The floor was a rich source of inspiration for Darac. He stared at a worn patch next to his chair. 'So where are we? An estranged – let's say he *is* the father – an estranged father sets out to find his long unacknowledged daughter Sylvie, perhaps for reasons connected with the €400,000 he'd somehow discovered she'd come into. Sporting a goatee, he goes to the Parade of Lights. A drunk, Michel Fouste, barges into him as he barged into a lot of other people. Words pass between them. He pursues Fouste to have it out with him but the crowd delays him. Just as he catches up with him, Fouste falls to his death. Our man beats a hasty retreat. We don't know at what point he discovered that Sylvie had died, but the next day, without the goatee, he buys the biggest bouquet he can carry and goes to the cemetery to pay his respects. Whereupon he's shot at by a seemingly respectable accounts manager named Carl Halevy, who was waiting for him for the purpose.' He ran a hand through his hair. 'What the hell is this about?'

Granot gave a little grunt. 'Whatever it is, that €400,000 is at the heart of it.'

'It's likely. But whether it is or not, we've got to find this guy.' Darac beamed at the others. 'Right – who wants to show the drawings to Madame Halevy?'

10

Two entry violations in one day.

'I'm trying to work here!' Laure slotted a printed circuit board into an effects box she was building. 'Jesus!'

Trampling anything in his way, the man made a beeline for her. In one action, he yanked off her cans, grabbed the arms of her chair and spun it around to face him. Still holding on to the arms, he brought his livid face down to meet hers.

'You will never, ever, talk to Elise like you did earlier. And you will never lay your hands on her again. Do you understand?'

Laure burned with rage. She was holding a screwdriver. But she knew her limitations. And she knew his.

'Let go.' Pushing hard against the floor, she tried to force the chair back. No go. 'I want to get on with my work.'

'Work?' His eyes were bulging. 'You call farting around in this pit all day work?'

Laure stared right back at him. 'Yes.'

The music for her latest composition was staved-out on her laptop. He grabbed the computer, thick fingers pressing several keys at once, scrambling the last couple of bars.

'I'll tell you what this is.' He tossed the laptop back onto her desk. 'It is *shit*! That is what it is.'

'Be careful with that. You paid good money for it. And it's not shit. Now go away. I need to finish it.'

'Need to, do you? There's a need? A necessity? People are depending on it?'

'I've got to hand it in later or I'll fail my course. You wouldn't like that, would you?'

'This is your last warning, Laure.'

In his eyes, the blade of anger was beginning to retract.

'Or you'll do what? Beat me up? That would look good in the papers. Or on TV.'

He released the arms of the chair, shoving it back.

'Get back to your... *work*.' He turned but he took no further step. Propped against the wall was an instrument he'd never seen in her room before. But he'd seen an image of it somewhere else. 'What's that?'

'That? We call it a guitar.'

'Where did you get it?'

Sliding on her headphones, she looked him steadily in the eyes. 'It fell off the back of a lorry.'

Telonne stared, incredulous. When he spoke, the words emerged in slow motion. 'You committed a crime? In front of thousands of spectators, and God knows how many more watching on TV? And with your father sitting in the place of honour not twenty metres away?'

She smiled. 'Don't you know it "comes out better on a stolen guitar"? I thought you were supposed to be down with the kids?'

He took a step nearer. 'You stupid little bitch.'

'I am not stupid. Nobody saw me. And you weren't sitting in the place of honour, *Papa*. You're not mayor yet. You're not even on the council.'

Shaking his sleek, alpha-plus head, Jacques Telonne turned slowly on his heel and, without giving it another glance, walked past the guitar and out of the room.

11

'Do I have to go?'

Agnès Dantier made a show of pinching herself. 'No, I'm not dreaming.' She gave Darac a look over her reading glasses. 'You sound five years old.'

'I want to see the material, obviously. It's just that I'd rather do it when all the brass have gone.'

'Meeting Room A,' she said, pleasantly. 'Five minutes.'

He lingered.

Sighing slightly, Agnès looked up from her file.

'Room A,' he nodded. 'Five minutes.'

Darac ran into Bonbon in the corridor. 'How did you find Madame Halevy?'

'I must say Granot's got a knack with women. He rubs them all up the wrong way.'

They walked through the open door into Darac's office.

'Whereas you—'

'Exactly – I know how to draw a woman out.' A stained and sticky crumple of paper emerged from his pocket. 'Kola Kube?'

'From the stall in Cours Saleya?'

'Of course.'

'In that case…' Darac took one. 'So what did your masterful approach elicit from Madame?'

'Nothing. She didn't recognise the man in either version of the drawing. But she didn't bite my head off or anything.'

'A triumph, Bonbon.'

'She didn't know the guy – what could I do? Anyway, I've had the drawings scanned for the late unlamented Carl's friends and associates. Maybe they'll come up trumps.'

'Indeed. Meanwhile, we've got a movie to watch.'

'The missing Masséna CCTV footage?'

'The same. Frènes is joining us.'

Bonbon's foxy grin disappeared. 'What for?'

'You'll see.'

A good crowd had assembled in Meeting Room A. Showing on a flat-screen TV the size of a billiard table, the movie ran for a full forty-five minutes before Agnès called, 'Cut'.

Sitting next to her, Public Prosecutor Jules Frènes looked put out, momentarily. A small man with a big ego, he saw it as his role to call any shots that were going. But this wasn't the moment, it seemed, for indignation. The puckered pout gave way to an expansive smile as he stood. 'Thank you, Commissaire. That, I think, completes our picture of what happened yesterday evening. There can be no doubt whatsoever that the unfortunate Michel Fouste did not meet his death at the hand of another, but rather at his own hand reaching too often for the bottle. Other images, too, are revealing…'

Sitting on the end of the back row, Darac shrugged at Frankie. All the extra footage had achieved was to underline how Fouste had met his death. Astrid's sketches remained the best likenesses they had of the chaser, the man whom Carl Halevy had tried to assassinate the following day. A secondary let-down was that there had been no sequence showing Darac's guitar being snatched.

As Frènes droned on, Darac ran an appraising eye over Jacques Telonne. Paying full attention during the screening itself, he looked relaxed now, reacting to Frènes's points with nods and little affirming noises. Now and again, a white-out smile shone through the tan. A true politician.

After more sycophantic bleatings, Frènes's speech finally reached its climax.

'And I think that we, representing as we do the twin organs of law and order in the city, can look forward with confidence to a time of unparalleled co-operation with the Mairie, should, as I fervently hope, the next municipal elections return our guest to the city council where, as the law demands, the election of mayor shall be its first task. I should like to conclude...'

'With a song,' Darac said, not quite under his breath, to Frankie.

Frènes ploughed on. 'I should like to conclude with the observation that Monsieur Telonne has always been a friend of the Palais de Justice and it's a true mark of his commitment that he has come in person to examine this footage with us this evening.'

The man raised both hands palms outwards. It was nothing.

'Would you like to say a few words, monsieur?'

'No, no.' He stood. 'However...'

Five minutes later, the man's speech ended on a crowd-pleasing note – a promise to help fight 'in any way I can' the European Court's intention to bring French police practices into line with the rest of the continent. In particular, it seemed Telonne abhorred the move to abolish the practice of questioning suspects without the presence of 'interfering lawyers' in cases initiated by public prosecutors. 'Ours, my friends,' he'd said, 'is a system not to abolish but to cherish. It is a system which prevents more wrongdoers from falling through the net of justice than any other.'

On the last point, Darac had to admit Telonne was probably right. But the system only worked as advertised if the right kind of officer was asking the questions.

'*That* was different,' Armani said, as the meeting broke up. 'Couldn't Agnès D have just emailed the footage to Telonne? What's she up to?'

'Buttering him up?' Perand said. 'Maybe it's Telonne who's going to build the new Caserne. Maybe she's angling for bigger offices or something.'

'Frènes only showed up because he knew Telonne was coming. Wankers. Both of them.'

Telonne intercepted Darac at the door. 'Captain,' he said, his eyes following Frankie's fulsome figure out of the room. 'I hear nothing but good reports of you. One of the highest clearance rates in the country, I understand.'

A mechanical grab might just have shaken Darac's hand with more firmness.

'Thank you.'

White-out. The hand still pumping.

'And I'm reliably informed that on her retirement, you are favoured to succeed Madame Dantier as the next commissaire of the Brigade.'

Darac smiled. So that was Agnès's game in inviting Telonne, was it? She was feathering her protégé's nest with the possible next mayor of the city. Darac needed friends in high places. But he would rather snuggle up to a rattlesnake than Monsieur Jacques Telonne.

'Who knows? Perhaps.'

As Telonne at last released Darac's hand, Agnès joined them.

'Paul certainly did a splendid job as acting commissaire a little while ago. Didn't he, Monsieur Frènes?'

'In a sense, he did,' Frènes said. 'Quite remarkable.'

Weasel words. Darac had zero respect for Frènes and the feeling was mutual.

'Well, if you'll forgive me, monsieur.'

'Of course, Captain. Your case load is heavy, I'm sure.'

'And part of that case load is the guitar stolen from the parade,' Agnès said. 'No help from today's CCTV, unfortunately.'

'Indeed,' Telonne said. 'I suppose you are not devoting too many resources to the theft. Particularly after what happened at the cemetery earlier.' The look was solicitous. 'I was so very sorry to hear about that.'

'Thank you. As for the guitar – we're giving it the works. It's mine, you see.'

'Yours, but…?' Suave was out. Panic, in. 'I thought it belonged to some kid… One of the youth orchestra musicians, I mean.'

'I just lent it to him for the occasion.'

'Uh… Do you… are you getting anywhere with the search?'

'Are you alright, monsieur?' Frènes asked.

'Of course! I am just concerned that the captain's own instrument should have been the one taken.' He turned back to Darac. 'Are you near a resolution?'

'Not yet but it's very early days. There's a lot we can do.'

'Such as? I'll… need to know these things. If I'm elected.'

'May we walk and talk, monsieur? I need to get back to my office.'

'Of course.'

As if pulled by a hidden force, Frènes began to move, too. Agnès came between them. 'Monsieur – if you would wait a moment, there's a matter I need to discuss with you.'

'But…' As sullen as a grounded teenager, Frènes watched his new best friend set off without him. 'Oh, very well.'

For all his outward gloss, Telonne walked with a heavy, flat-footed step, Darac noticed. A legacy, perhaps, of his early days as a labourer on the building sites from which he rose to run one of the largest property development companies in the area.

'You say there's a lot you can do, Captain?'

By the time they had reached his office, Darac had outlined several methods of recovering a stolen object. They paused at his door.

'And which of those approaches will you try first?'

'The amnesty – no questions asked if the instrument is left in some appropriate place.'

Granot and Bonbon were in conversation further down the corridor. Darac gave them a beckoning nod.

'Presumably, Captain, you would choose somewhere where there's CCTV – or have officers posted?'

'No, no. We don't even do that when we have a weapons amnesty, monsieur. Amnesty means just what it says.' With scant acknowledgement to Telonne, Granot and Bonbon passed behind Darac into the office. 'Well, now I really must—'

'Indeed. Thank you.' Telonne extended his hand. 'Gentlemen.'

One of Darac's desk phones rang, cutting the handshake short.

As Telonne walked flat-footedly away, Darac went to take the call.

'Records here, Captain. I've got the rest of that Sylvie Galvin info you wanted.'

'Go for it, Adèle.' He wrote down the details as she went through them, and then asked, 'A couple more things: her employment record?'

'Low-paid shop work. Never did anything else.'

'And Sylvie continued to work after September 2003?'

'Uh… yes she did. Full time.'

He wrote down the last couple of places she worked – both supermarkets. 'Her address at the time of her death?' She gave it. Darac hesitated. 'Appartements Solferino? Sure?'

'That's what it says here.'

'Okay.' He noted the address. 'And finally, the cause of death?'

'It just says NCL.'

'NCL – what's that?'

'Am I a doctor? Dunno.'

'I'll find out. Thank you, Adèle.'

Darac sat back in his chair, his brow lowering.

'What?' Granot said, reading the signs.

'Okay, you're a full-time shelf stacker living in modest-stroke-shithole accommodation and you come into €400,000. Would you still be doing both of those things five years later?'

Bonbon chuckled at the thought. 'Only if the cash had gone as easily as it came.'

'Following money.' Darac gave Granot a look. 'This means you.'

The big man knew his worth as a paper trail chaser. 'Naturally, but I won't be able to follow anything until the bank opens in the morning.'

'I've got Sylvie's bank statement,' Bonbon said, 'when you want it. The one found at the cemetery.'

Darac glanced at his watch and, as if by the power of suggestion, felt all in, suddenly. 'Look, I'm tired and we can't do much more on this at the moment, can we?' He opened his notebook and folded out a page. 'So how are you fixed for tomorrow – much on?'

The trio discussed their schedules and put together a rough plan.

'See you tomorrow, guys.'

Darac stayed put.

'You're not leaving,' Bonbon said. 'I'm a detective, I notice these things.'

'Just going to put up some new stuff on the guitar theft.'

'The amnesty route?'

'You never know. It might work.'

12

Laure stabbed the C# key repeatedly. Nothing in her headphones. No power light. 'Fuck.'

She tried the simple stuff first, examining the leads, sockets, switches. The problem was more complex. 'Fucking power supply… Piece of shit!'

The door banged open. The third violation of the day. But already fired up, she was ready for him this time. Whipping off her headphones, she stood. '*Now* try and trap me in my chair.'

Telonne came no closer. Darac's guitar lay on its back on the floor between them. 'I want every hair and fingerprint cleaned off that. I want you to do the same to the case. Then I want you to put one inside the other and leave it outside this door.'

Crossing her arms, she rocked her body weight on to one side. 'And why should I do that?'

'Because, Laure, we have a window of opportunity to get it back to its rightful owner.'

'*Do* we?'

'And do you know who that person is?'

'Why should I care who the previous owner was?'

Her father sneered. '*Previous owner.*'

'Listen, it was you that taught me that if I wanted anything in life, I should go out and grab it. I did.'

'*You* listen. That guitar belongs to a police officer. But not just any police officer. Oh no. Paul Darac is his name. A captain in the Brigade Criminelle. A clever fucking hotshot with all the resources in the world at his disposal! What do you think of that?'

Laure couldn't help it. She started to laugh. She, the daughter of the man tipped to become the next mayor of the city, had put him in deep shit with none other than his *cause célèbre* – the police. She had never known anything so funny. And she would probably have kept on laughing but for the look she finally saw in her father's face. It wasn't the eyeballs-out fury she was used to. He looked calm.

'I said this was your last chance, Laure, and I mean it. If you don't do as I say, you will get nothing further from me. Ever. We've had enough. *I've* had enough. You've got an hour.'

He closed the door behind him.

Laure stomped toward the guitar and grabbed it by the neck. Ideas crowded in. She could smash it and put the pieces in the case. How would this bastard *flic* like getting it back then? How would her father like it? What would *that* do to his campaign? She held the guitar above her head, shaping to dash it against the wall. But she stopped short. The plan was no good. Her father was bound to check the thing over before he took it.

'Fuck!'

And then she had a much better idea.

13

The events of the day were playing like a movie in Darac's head as he threaded his way through the thrumming tangle of the old town, the Babazouk. Home was an apartment in Place St Sépulcre, a flagstoned courtyard squeezed into its outer edge. A car-free zone closed to non-residents, the Place had a buzzy, al fresco life of its own for most of the year. On a sharp, moonlit evening when no one was around, it had the look of a Chirico cityscape – an empty space full of sinister possibilities.

But there was nothing at all sinister about the figure who emerged from the shadows toward him. Coming together by the carved stone well head in the centre of the Place, they kissed in greeting. For some moments, the woman held on to him.

'You've heard, then, Suzanne?'

'It was on the *Nice-Matin* website. With photos.' She gave a disdainful shake of the head. 'They don't call these people news hounds for nothing.'

'Absolutely.' Setting his weight back against the well head, he ran his hand along the cold curve of its rim. 'You know, I've never noticed before but this thing wouldn't look out of place in a cemetery, would it?'

'It's the day you've had, sweetie. Everything will look different tomorrow.' She zipped up her coat. 'Right, my patients will be wondering where I am. Actually, they won't, but let's think positively.'

'Just quickly – I've got a medical question. What is NCL?'

'NCL…' Suzanne searched the roofline for an answer. 'Non-something, something… No. I don't think I've ever come across it. Sorry.'

'I'm going to talk to one of our people shortly so don't worry about it.'

'*Ciao*.'

'*Ciao, bella*.'

They clasped hands in farewell, and turned to go their separate ways. But Darac paused as a stray thought wandered into his head and out of his mouth.

'Are you a believer, Suzanne?'

'In what?'

'God. Life after death – all that.'

'Good God, no.'

Darac laughed and continued on his way.

His roof terrace overlooked the Babazouk side of the apartment house. Even on a cool evening, it was his habit to sit out for a while before going to bed. Rising sounds and smells connected him to the street life below, yet underlined his separation from it. For reasons he couldn't explain, it was a feeling he loved. With a long, slow beer and a couple of long, slow tunes, the roof terrace wind-down was one of his favourite things in the world.

Tonight though, he had a couple of calls to make first.

'Papa?'

The family debating society sounded to be going strong *chez Darac Père*.

'Paul, we're all doing well here. You?'

'Fine, yes.'

'Thanks for the message you left. It was such a relief to hear those bullets weren't intended for us.'

'Absolutely. Uh… you mentioned dinner. How does Friday sound? But here – I'll cook.'

'Are you sure?'

'Papa, I would have bet a million euros on you saying that. Yes, I'm sure.'

'Becoming predictable in my old age. Thank you, it would be lovely.'

Glad to be ending the conversation on a positive note, Darac rang another number straight away.

'Professor Bianchi's office.'

'Patricia? Deanna hasn't gone home yet, has she? She was expecting me to call.'

'No, Captain, she's here.' He heard Patricia announce him. 'She's coming. Despite everything that happened, I must say I enjoyed meeting your father earlier. Just like you, isn't he?'

'How long have we got?'

'We haven't,' she said, the smile evident in her voice even on the phone. 'Here's the professor.'

'Darac. It's been quite a day for you.'

'You could say that.'

'And are you alright? Don't just say "yeah, yeah" like you usually do.'

'In that case, I don't know what to say to you. Except, what's NCL?'

'NCL?' Deanna's tobacco-rasped voice lost all its playfulness. 'There isn't anything you've been keeping from me, is there?'

'Lots of things, I should imagine. What do you mean?'

'I'm just a bit distracted here. Why do you want to know about NCL?'

'It's cited as the COD of a young woman we're interested in. I've never heard of it.'

'Ah. And you've never heard of the Internet, either?'

'The Internet doesn't talk back. Especially at your level.'

'You have recovered the situation nicely. NCL stands for neuronal ceroid lipofuscinosis. It's a condition in which excessive lipopigments form in body tissues, with inevitable and horrible consequences.'

'Excessive pigment? Doesn't sound all that drastic.'

'It's one hundred per cent fatal. So now you know, you can stop wasting my time.'

'*That's* my Deanna. Why the wobble just now? Did you think *I'd* contracted it? I'm touched.'

'Nobody contracts NCL. It's an inherited condition.'

'Inherited?' Darac stared at the floor. 'It's rare, I take it?'

'I couldn't give you the incidence percentage off the top of my head – which you probably could get on the Internet, by the way – but it's very, very low.'

'Alright, someone has NCL. Where do they go for treatment?'

'Just one place – the Hôpital de la Timone in Marseille. '

14

'Never heard of her.'

The man was seventy years of age, grey around the temples, and grey everywhere else. Officer Max Perand checked his notebook and tried again.

'But you've been living in this block since February 2002, monsieur. Right?'

A shrug.

'You have. And you've been living in this actual apartment since January 2006. Mademoiselle Sylvie Galvin lived directly opposite you' – he made a hooking motion with his thumb – 'for over two years.'

The man scratched his scrotum. Perand, who wasn't above such moves in public himself, suddenly realised how unsavoury it looked.

'So?'

'You must have known her.'

'I knew her but I didn't *know* her, if you know what I mean.'

Perand stared away down the corridor for a moment. 'I am going to arrest you, Monsieur Pilart, for obstructing an officer in the course of his duty—'

'That is shit! That is a load of—'

'*Unless!*'

The shout echoed around the peeling plasterwork. Two or three doors opened. Heads appeared.

'Unless you start co-operating.' Perand was aware of the heads suddenly. They shot back in. 'Now, tell me all you know about Mademoiselle Sylvie Galvin.'

By the time Perand left Appartements Solferino, he had learned little of real value but some things had emerged. It seemed Sylvie Galvin had occupied the polite, reserved, shy, withdrawn band of the personality spectrum. She was described variously as 'fat', 'big', 'obese', 'solid'. Yet she was sometimes 'weak', 'sickly' and even 'frail'. Sylvie had never spoken of family or friends. No one gave any credence to the idea that she could have come into money. And no one recognised Astrid's drawings of the man who visited her grave and was almost assassinated for his trouble.

Flaco fared little better at the two Megaprix supermarkets Sylvie had worked in latterly. The flustered HR manager's dossier on the young woman characterised a 'willing and honest but limited and unconfident employee'. Frequent absences for ill health also counted against her, he confided. The manager was, of course, 'devastated' to hear of her death. Fellow checkout staff remembered her as a sad, mousy woman who nobody felt they knew.

None of her erstwhile colleagues could envisage Sylvie having come into money. And although some noted the resemblance between the man in Astrid's sketches and Sylvie herself, none had ever seen him or could recall her ever mentioning such a person.

* * *

Part place of worship, part going concern, the Convent of the Sisters of Mercy in Vallauris was an impressive set-up. While he waited for the mother superior to appear for the promised interview, Bonbon's tour of the winery, apiary, and garden furniture workshop proved interesting and instructive. It also gave him an idea about Sylvie Galvin.

He was just about to be shown the kitchen garden when, in a brisk crunching of gravel, a Toyota Land Cruiser pulled up smartly behind him. At the wheel was a sharp-featured woman with a weather-beaten complexion.

'Ah, here's Mother Anne now.'

Following the introductions, the convent's senior bride of Christ dismissed Bonbon's guide and took over the role herself. He wasted little time in getting down to brass tacks.

'Reverend Mother, apart from its principle activities, this is a highly productive, well-to-do institution, is it not?'

'I am happy to say that it is. But I thought the purpose of our meeting was to discuss Sylvie?'

'Bear with me, if you please. Mademoiselle Galvin lived very humbly, yet we know a considerable sum of money was paid into her current account five years before she died in 2008.'

If it was news to the Mother Superior, she didn't show it. 'I see.'

'From talking to a couple of the sisters here, I understand Sylvie was a dear soul.'

Mother Anne's smile was a thing of lofty forbearance. 'Lieutenant Busquet, *all* souls are dear to God.'

Bonbon, entering his twenty-first year in the Brigade, reflected that God must be a particularly forgiving deity.

'I'll rephrase that. I meant that Sylvie was a very pleasant and dutiful girl when she was here.'

'She was, indeed.'

'And that makes me wonder if, having come into the fortune I mentioned earlier, Sylvie may have given that sum away. Perhaps to you, Reverend Mother. To your convent, I mean.'

Mother Anne's attention was drawn to a novice hoeing by the far wall.

'Sister Teresa, remember to nip the weeds off with the blade! You're just pushing them around! Nip them! That's better… I'm sorry, Lieutenant. What did you say?'

'I asked if Sylvie Galvin donated a considerable sum of money to the convent?'

'She did not.'

'She could have done so anonymously.'

Mother Anne graced Bonbon with another smile. 'In that case, we would have no way of knowing if she had or not, would we?'

'A sum in the region of €400,000 would carry a pretty strong identity of its own, though, wouldn't it?'

'I assure you, Lieutenant, that for the period to which you refer, our accounts will show no such donation.' She indicated a small, single-storey brick building adjoining the winery. 'Our offices. You are free to examine the books, by all means.'

'Thank you. Before I do – do you have any clue as to the identity of Sylvie's father?'

'None. Now, if you'll excuse me?'

In the office, Bonbon examined the books with a comb almost as fine-toothed as the one traditionally wielded by Granot. By the time he walked back to his car, he'd arrived at a firm conclusion. Unless someone had broken up Sylvie's windfall into subatomic-sized particles, she had not blown the sum on the Sisters of Mercy.

Although he had ultimately drawn a blank, Bonbon didn't drive away from the convent entirely empty-handed. A half-case of rosé, an assortment of honeys and two baskets of freshly pulled veg wasn't a bad return.

Leaning back in his chair, Granot, desk phone to one ear and his finger in the other, yawned extravagantly. The obsequious young man he was talking to from the Crédit Bal-Med bank had said, 'I'll just be a minute, sir,' a full five minutes before. Granot was inspecting his finger for wax when the man finally did come back.

'Lieutenant?'

'Still here.'

'I'm so sorry to have kept you waiting, sir, but I now have the information you requested.'

Granot shifted his bulk forward and picked up his pen. 'Fire away.'

'The current account statement of Mademoiselle Galvin that you faxed me?'

Granot glanced at the original in front of him. 'Yes?'

'Mademoiselle Galvin did have an account with us and the number on this statement tallies with the number of that account. But I can find no record of the certified cheque of €400,000 referred to in it. It seems that the deposit never happened.'

Granot's eyes locked on the entry as if the figures might suddenly rearrange into an explanation.

'Are you still there, Lieutenant?'

'You say the transaction *never* happened. But could the amount have been paid in just for a second or two and then disappeared? Perhaps the result of an error?'

'That is… not impossible. I will have to look further to determine it, though, sir. Might take an hour or two.'

'That's fine. Call me back when you have an answer. Wait. Does the address on the statement tally with your records for Mademoiselle Galvin?'

'Appartements Solferino, 17, Les Moulins… Yes, that too is correct.'

'Thank you, monsieur. I'll await your call.'

He hung up and hit speed dial. 'Good – you're still here,' he said when Darac answered.

'I'm not heading off to Marseille until later. What's up?'

Granot relayed the news.

'I'll be right in.'

Granot was sitting back in his chair, his hams of forearms crossed in contemplation.

'So the four hundred grand didn't exist but the account did?' Darac said.

'It didn't exist in any real way for Sylvie.' Granot unfolded his arms and sat forward. 'But it doesn't look like conventional money laundering. There, the money definitely goes into an account and definitely goes out.' He indicated the statement. 'According to this, the money went in and stayed in.'

Darac stared off for a moment. 'You haven't seen Sylvie's grave, have you, Granot?'

'No.'

'Think Versailles.'

Darac looked at his watch. There was just time.

Marvais et Fils was one of the area's longest established firms of undertakers. Darac was greeted by a tall, sober young man wearing a sober suit. 'I am pleased to have taken your call, Captain. I am Benoit Marvais – the fifth generation of the family to have had the honour of serving the community.'

'In their various hours of need.'

Marvais didn't quite know how to take the remark. 'Indeed. Please follow me.'

Marvais led Darac through a suite of showrooms and chapels into a private office at the rear of the premises.

'So – Galvin, Sylvie Marie,' he said, booting up the computer. 'And may I say on behalf of my father and our whole organisation, Captain, that we were utterly dismayed at yesterday's events. Desecration of a loved one's grave is the bitterest of pills for the family. And to have actually witnessed it. And to have been almost killed in the process – words fail me.' The young man's expression took on even graver sobriety. 'Might I enquire—?'

'No sale, Marvais. We've approached Louis Frégaux to rebuild my mother's grave.'

Lowering his eyes, the young man inclined his head. 'Of course.'

The computer came to life. The screen wallpaper, Darac noticed, was a team shot of Nice's football team, Le Gym.

Marvais' composure slipped a couple of notches. 'Oh, I'm

sorry. Please forgive this, Captain. No one sees this as a rule. Members of the public, I mean.'

'According to one of my lieutenants, the team are a deadly bunch this season anyway. So…' Darac gave a shrug in lieu of a punchline.

'That's very good.' The smile fading as soon as it formed, the young man sat down and began scrolling through screens. 'Galvin, Sylvie Marie… I'm not familiar with the name, I'm afraid – I've only just started here, actually. I've worked at our branch down in Antibes since leaving school. I'll have it for you in a moment.'

Darac gave the place the once-over as he waited. On a filing cabinet was a stack of magazines published by the Society of Crematistes. He picked one up and opened it. And put it down again immediately. A pegboard leaning against a door that gave into a yard caught his eye. Attached to it was a display of numbered coffin handles.

'Old stock on its way out,' the young man said. 'Literally. I was on my way to the yard with it when you arrived.'

'Coffin handles *date*?' he said, idiotically picking out B3 as his handle *du choix*.

'My father doesn't think so but we must look forward. Go with the times. Ah – Galvin, Sylvie. Here we are. There appear to be two interments. Which are you interested in?'

The transfer of bodily remains from final resting place to even more final resting place was a fairly common practice in the area. But it was invariably a downscaling move.

'I think you'd better give me both.'

'Certainly.' Sobriety once more. 'On the first occasion, which was 26 April 2008, our non-living client had pre-selected the—'

'Look, Monsieur Marvais – forget the patter, just use plain language, alright?'

'In that case, the first interment was a plywood and niche job. Perfectly decent but basic.'

'Do you have a list of the mourners' names, by any chance?'

'None is kept.'

'Alright – who paid for it?'

Marvais consulted the screen. 'The deceased herself. Insurance policy.'

'What sort of occupancy did she pay for?'

'The remains would have been removed…' He checked the screen. 'After four years.'

'But the second funeral obviated that necessity.'

'Apparently so.'

'What date was that?'

'It was… 11 June last year.'

'Occupancy?'

'The term… is in perpetuity.'

Marvais read on. His face tightened. His cheeks flushed slightly.

'The cost of this second interment, monsieur?'

'Uh…' Marvais attempted a matter-of-fact lightness. 'It was twenty-five thousand euros.'

Darac nodded. 'Twenty-five grand. A tidy sum. And a conveniently round one.'

'Indeed.'

'Who paid?'

An adjustment of the tie. A dry-lipped smile. 'An anonymous benefactor paid, actually. Our lives are like stones in a pond, aren't they; they send out many—'

'Let me guess. He paid in cash, didn't he? Or she?'

For effect, Marvais checked the screen. 'Do you know, he – or she – did. Very generous.'

'Who dealt with the matter?'

'There's a note here. The instruction and the money arrived in an envelope. Cécile, our secretary at the time, opened it. It was signed simply, "a friend".'

'Let me see the screen.'

'Certainly, Captain.' Marvais was all readiness to help. 'We have nothing to hide.'

'What, this is an everyday occurrence in your industry, is it? Receiving vast cash sums anonymously to pay for a "friend's" funeral?'

'It is unconventional but it's not against the law, Captain. I assure you that all the proper offices were performed, and all the regulations were observed in relation to the second interment of Mademoiselle Galvin.'

The note tallied with Marvais' recital.

'There, you see,' he said. 'It's as I indicated. Now, if you'll forgive me—'

'Are you a religious man, Marvais?'

A knife to the heart could not have wounded him more. 'Of course!'

'In that case you'd better pray that that twenty-five grand was declared. Show me the year's accounts.'

Glassy-eyed, ashen-faced, Marvais could have stood in for one of his 'non-living clients'. 'It's not that easy. We need notice of—'

'What you need notice of is the fact that I can close down this entire operation with one phone call.'

Silence.

'Oh… very well.'

Marvais got somewhat unsteadily to his feet, yanked open a drawer and extracted a folder. He set it on the desk and riffled through its various sections, slowing as he neared the relevant month. He looked as if he might indeed be sending up a prayer as he paused before turning the final page.

'There! I told you! Fully declared and completely legiti—completely observant of the rules and regulations.'

'Good. Now let's see Cécile's note.'

'The note? I'm not sure we would have that.'

'You've got…' He performed a rough count. 'Fifteen filing cabinets there labelled "Correspondence". Try "A" for "Anonymous".'

By the time Marvais found it, an MTV screensaver had kicked in on the computer.

'Here's a receipt for the note,' Darac said, taking it. 'Which is more than your company issued for the cash. Goodbye for now.'

'For now?'

'Well, you'll want to be around when we perform the exhumation.' Shifting the handle display to one side, Darac opened the door into the yard. 'I'll go out this way.'

He left the young man to last year's hardware and Lady Gaga.

15

Pairs of identical glass doors regressing into the distance gave the corridor the look of a movie dream sequence.

'Captain?' Dream over. The consultant was short, sharp and in a hurry. A shepherding arm directed Darac into a light, bright office. 'Victor Scalette.'

'I spoke to your secretary on the phone,' Darac said, turning, but Scalette was already past him.

'Sit, please.' Facing the indicated chair was a desk on which sat just two files. Scalette sat down and opened the uppermost one in a single continuous action, though not before Darac managed to read Sylvie Galvin's name on the cover label. 'So, Captain.' Scalette concluded the utterance, as he had every previous one, with a long, impatient exhalation.

'Am I keeping you from something, Doctor?'

'I am a senior consultant,' he said, as if the question were the most imbecilic ever posed.

The man's attitude irritated Darac but he took no offence. He'd been known to push the pace along himself when the occasion demanded it. 'As I mentioned briefly on the phone, we're trying to trace—' Darac's mobile rang. 'Excuse me.' Showing versatility, Scalette blew out a column of air without saying anything first. Checking the caller's ID, Darac put the phone on *silent*. 'My lieutenant. He'll leave a message.' Darac slid Astrid's sketches across the desk. 'As I was saying, we are trying to trace and identify this man. He strongly resembles Sylvie, doesn't he?'

A glance was all it took. 'Yes, he does.'

'We believe he is Sylvie's unacknowledged and indeed, unrecorded father. As I understand it, the condition from which she died—'

'Juvenile neuronal ceroid lipofuscinosis.' Scalette closed the file. 'A form of Batten disease.'

Darac made a note and continued. 'Thank you. The condition is rare and inherited, is it not?'

'Yes.'

'Since this is the national centre for the treatment of the disease, there's a strong possibility that Sylvie's father's name, et cetera, will appear on your case files. True?'

Scalette nodded brusquely. 'We know from our records that the mother was not affected, but she would, of course, have been a carrier, since the disease is carried in a recessive gene. The same could be true of the father.'

'Be that as it may.'

Scalette thought about it and then opened the flap of the second file, half revealing a long list of names. He thought about it again and closed it. 'You have a court order?'

Well aware that at this early stage, Frènes would certainly refuse it, Darac hadn't applied for one. You had to choose which battles to fight. 'Not as such.'

'Your application was refused?'

'No, no. There just hasn't been time to apply. And speaking of that, you've been very kind and your time is obviously valuable so I'd be more than happy to continue this with your records people.' In fact, Darac had been banking on it. Preferably with a temp who didn't know any better. 'So if you'd just point me—'

'I'm not pointing you anywhere. Our admin staff are just as *au fait* with the regulations regarding patient confidentiality as I am, Captain.'

'You know, you really should do something about that breathing problem of yours.'

'What?'

'Skip it. Look, we're searching for a needle in a haystack with this thing. If the needle's name is on that list, it would make finding him at least possible.'

'*Why* do you want to trace this man?'

'You're in the business of saving lives, right? Give me a copy of what you have there and you could be saving *this* man's life.' He indicated the drawings. 'Someone tried to kill him yesterday. Many times over.'

Sitting back, Scalette drew his index fingers together and tapped them against his pursed lips. 'So it could be argued,' he said at length, 'that you need to trace the patient for his own protection?'

And because the man was at the centre of an intriguing case. But that wasn't going to play with Scalette. 'Exactly so.'

'*His own protection*,' the doctor repeated, staring off.

The concept seeming to offer a way forward, Darac detected a slight relaxation in the man's facial muscles. But there was some resistance, still. 'Dr Scalette, I infer that there are people you may have to answer to about this.'

'You infer correctly.'

'I give you my personal guarantee that not one person on that list will be approached directly or indirectly until we're absolutely certain—'

'I am going to release the list,' he said, turning on his photocopier.

'You are? Thank you.'

'Do not misunderstand, Captain. I set little store by your guarantee. But I have limitless respect for Professor Bianchi. But for her, I would not have agreed to see you in the first place.'

'Deanna called?'

Scalette copied the list and handed it over. Another shepherding arm. Another dream sequence of doors and Darac stepped out on to the apron of the hospital.

It was then that he finally played Granot's message.

16

Wearing a tuxedo and the sort of expression heavyweights sport before a bout, Jacques Telonne crossed the hall and headed for Laure's room. No stranger to betrayal and broken promises, he entertained little hope of finding the guitar case sitting outside her door.

It was there.

Half expecting it to be empty, he knelt and undid the clasps. The guitar was sitting snugly in its lined recess. He could see that she had cleaned the instrument but had she bothered to remove *all* her prints? In a lidded compartment, he found plectrums, replacement strings and a pair of nail scissors. He was willing to bet she hadn't even considered cleaning those or the case itself. Darac had said there would be no questions asked but Telonne couldn't be one hundred per cent sure. And one hundred per cent was the Jacques Telonne way. He closed the clasps and picked up the case.

In the garage, he wiped every surface of every part of the package. He was laying the instrument back into its recess when a door opened behind him.

'What are you doing with that?'

The man was aged in his early forties, strong of build and cocksure of manner.

'I am not doing anything, Picot. You are. I need you to drop this off somewhere.'

He joined Telonne at the workbench. 'Delivery boy now as well, am I? It says "site foreman" on my hard hat.'

Conveying that he was only just keeping the lid on his temper, Telonne fixed Picot with a look. The man shrugged, getting the message.

'So where do you want me to take it?'

Telonne closed the lid of the case and told him what he wanted.

'Okay.'

'Got a pair of clean gloves?'

'In the car. And a parka.'

'And you're clear on what I want you to do?'

'No problemo.'

'There'd better not be a problem. This was all I needed at the moment.'

Picot tossed the day's *Nice-Matin* on to the case. 'It mightn't be the only thing.'

Telonne snatched up the paper. As he speed-read the piece, incomprehension did nothing to lighten his mood. At the end of it, he lowered his perfectly trimmed eyebrows and shook his head.

'This affects me how? And spit it out, Picot. I'm due at a reception shortly.'

Picot respected Telonne the captain of industry. He respected Telonne the would-be mayor. He respected Telonne the man. But he wasn't intimidated by him. Not for a second.

'Think about it, Jacques.'

17

'You've had a shave, Perand?' Granot lumbered into the squad room and set down his stuff. 'You look almost human.'

The young man moved to adjust his balls, but thought better of it. 'There's a shaver in my glove compartment at all times, as it happens.'

Bonbon joined them. 'You just hadn't realised what it was for until now.' He held out a paper bag. 'Lemon drop, anyone?'

'How were the Sisters of Mercy?' Granot said, helping himself.

'Sisterly. But they weren't much help on Sylvie. None of them had any idea who her father was.' He flicked the bag with his finger. 'Flak?'

'No thanks.'

Wearing a white lab coat, Erica stepped lightly into the room. Doubly glad he'd resisted the call of his balls, Perand flashed her a smile designed to suggest the world of fascinating possibilities that lay behind it.

Her eyes were elsewhere. 'Are those orange drops, Bonbon?'

'Lemon. And to what do we owe the pleasure of your company?'

'Lemon? Better still.' She slipped one into her mouth.

'Darac left a message asking me to come over.'

'I see your young man scored another couple of tries yesterday, Erica,' Granot said. 'What is it now, twenty – twenty-five for the season?'

'Serge isn't counting them.' Nonchalance gave way to glee. 'But it's twenty-seven!'

Bonbon looked awestruck. 'Serge Paulin – the Flying Flic.' He gave Perand a look. 'You seen the man play, Max?' He formed his hands around an invisible tree. 'Calves like this.'

'Like a nice big calf, do you, Lieutenant?'

'As you can see by my own.' Drawing up handfuls of cloth, Bonbon airily flapped his trouser legs. 'Call me… Spartacus.'

Flaco didn't lose it very often but the sound of her laughter – a lawn sprinkler on helium – was a joyful thing.

Granot chose to ignore the horseplay. 'Serge could play at a higher level, couldn't he? For one of the really big clubs, even.'

Erica's face fell. 'Don't say that. If he went off to Toulouse or somewhere, I'd never see him.'

'Pity,' Perand said.

Bonbon pulled up a chair. 'Enough of the gods who walk among us. For a moment, I thought I'd cracked it at the convent. About where Sylvie Galvin's four hundred grand might have gone, I mean. I thought she might have donated it to the sisters.'

'And she hadn't?'

'No, and our paper chaser *par excellence* here discovered why she couldn't have.'

Granot accepted the compliment with a grunt. 'She never

had it to give, Erica. Not for a second.' He showed her the statement. 'This is a one hundred per cent genuine fake.'

'May I?' Erica took it.

'There are no microchips or anything,' Granot said.

'I took Foch's forgery course last year, you know.' She held it up to the light. 'And came top.'

'So what do you think of this one?'

'Good.' She handed it back. 'But not *quite* good enough. That's what you're supposed to say.'

'Sylvie is a dummy in this thing, isn't she?' Bonbon drew his knees up under his chin. 'A pawn in a bigger game.'

Flaco shook her head. 'You know if we hadn't interviewed so many people this morning who knew Sylvie, I might even question whether she really existed.'

'*That* is beyond doubt,' Granot said. 'One of the few things about this business that is.'

Making a signature entrance, Darac walked in sipping an industrial-sized espresso. 'Erica, can you scan these and get them up on the projector?' He handed her Dr Scalette's list of male NCL sufferers and the anonymous donor's note from Marvais et Fils. 'Thanks.'

Narrowing her eyes, Erica rested a hand on her hip. 'This isn't why you called me in?'

'No. Well, partly.'

'None of you geniuses knows how to use a scanner and a data projector?'

Perand was a cool, smart-mouthed boy. Except when he was around Erica. 'I can,' he said.

'*I can*,' Flaco parroted, doing her best to sound like a fawning ninny. 'We all can, Erica.'

'I just thought you'd be interested in developments,'

Darac said. 'Especially as you were there when this thing started.'

'Hmm.' Unconvinced, Erica anchored a skein of her fine blond hair behind one ear, and fed the first sheet into the scanner.

Darac parked his backside on an empty desk. 'One of the things Erica has there comes from an interesting little detour I made before I went off to Marseille.'

As Darac recounted his experience at Marvais et Fils, Bonbon, whose wiry frame had all the capacity for contortion of a pipe cleaner, bent himself into an increasingly tortured position in his chair. At the end of the account, his face was a picture of incredulity.

'Twenty-five grand in *cash*?'

Perand grinned. 'Talk about dodgy.' It was his turn for a little voice work. '*Ah, Monsieur Marvais – give us an empty tomb and look the other way a minute, will you? Here's a little something extra for your trouble.*'

'They properly recorded the transaction, remember,' Granot said.

Bonbon shook his head. 'But that doesn't guarantee everything lying under that slab is above board.'

Darac nodded. 'And it seems significant that this new grave has in-perpetuity occupancy. What you would do if you didn't want it to be disturbed at some point in the future.'

Flaco turned to Darac. 'Do you believe Sylvie's remains are actually in the grave, Captain?'

'They should be. We'll soon know. Even Frènes didn't argue over the exhumation order. That's how strange this is.'

Erica had finished her task. 'Alright, I've made and logged the files. Want to throw them into the mix?'

'Go for it.'

She threw a switch on the data projector and a list of names formed on a cleared section of wall. Most bore annotations in Darac's handwriting.

'Who are these people?'

'The Hôpital de la Timone in Marseille is the national treatment centre for NCL. It's highly likely that one of its patients is Sylvie's father. There are a hundred and eighty-seven names altogether. The men I've crossed out have birth dates that rule them out as potential fathers for Sylvie. Giving plenty of latitude, that leaves forty-seven names. There are a number of approaches we can adopt…'

Silently mouthing one of the entries, Bonbon sat back in his seat, tapping his chin. For a moment, he couldn't place it. Then it came to him. 'We may only need one of them, chief.'

Next to him, Granot gave the desk a rap. He was there, too.

'Delmas. Pierre Delmas,' they said, more or less in unison.

The name only half registered with Darac. 'Delmas?' He stared off. 'It's familiar but I can't pinpoint it.'

Granot shifted his weight back in his chair. 'That's because you didn't have anything to do with the case. You were on your secondment in Paris.' His grizzled old mug took on a nostalgic look. 'Twelve glorious months without a single reference to jazz. Those were the days.'

'Yeah, yeah. And the case was?'

'The Société Provençale Robbery of 2003.' Granot smiled proprietorially. 'Ever heard of that?'

'So-Pro? Of course. The gang was unusually astute, wasn't it? It was bad luck for them that they were up against Agnès; even though, in the end, it took a tip-off to close out the case. You were on it from the start, Granot?'

'I most certainly was.'

'I wasn't on the strength until some months later,' Bonbon said, typing Delmas's name into the police database. 'I was here for the trial, though.'

'What was the most notable thing about this robbery?' Granot enjoyed playing quizmaster. 'Come on, Captain Brains.'

'Easy. It was a copycat of the Société Générale job of '76. More or less.'

'It was indeed.'

Even Perand seemed impressed. 'So-Gén? It's world famous.'

'They made a movie of it,' Erica said, attracting the young man's gaze once more. 'And there are documentaries.'

Flaco nodded. 'I saw one not long ago. The thieves left a message in the vault: *We did this without… weapons or violence or…?*'"

Granot smiled, warming to his role as *éminence grise* on the case. '*Hate*, it was. Now fast forward to May 2003 and the Société Provençale. The thieves got into the vault on a Friday evening. By dawn on the Monday, they'd chalked the exact same message on the strongroom wall and made off with over nineteen million in cash, jewellery and other valuables. A perfect crime – the "So-Pro" robbery in more senses than one. But it turned out the gang hadn't been quite as Pro as the press gave them credit for. Just a few days later, everything was recovered. Everything. The "So-Am" robbery, they called it, in the end.'

'That's who Pierre Delmas is.' Darac clicked his fingers. 'He went down for it, didn't he? In fact, he was the only one of the gang who did. He was, what – the getaway driver?'

'He was the inside man. Worked for a firm that handled security at the bank. Got ten years.'

'Question, Captain?' Flaco said. 'It's an interesting development and I can see the connection Delmas *might* have to Sylvie Galvin through this disease. But so might others. Delmas could still be in prison, even.'

Bonbon angled his screen to Granot. The big man nodded. Bonbon turned it to face the others. 'Have a look at this mug shot, guys.'

A balding man with a fleshy face and dark, deep-set eyes stared back at them.

'It's Astrid's sketch.' Perand yawned. 'All over again.'

'Now I know who he is,' Bonbon said, 'I'm not sure why I didn't think of it before.'

Granot shook his jowly chops. 'I saw a lot more of him than you did and I didn't get it. His face is a lot fatter now, to be fair.'

Bonbon scrolled the page. 'Well, look at that. You were wondering if the man is still inside, Flak? He isn't. Got out a couple of years early.' The foxiest of grins. 'Two days ago, to be exact.'

Erica gave Darac a look. 'That's the day we went to the Parade of Lights.'

'It is indeed.' He ran a hand through his hair. 'Fresh out of prison and straight to the parade. Interesting.'

Perand treated the others to one of his smugger looks. 'Delmas was the only one of the gang to go down? I bet I know where the others are. At least some of them. They're residing in a cash-sale grave in Vence.'

18

'There was no one in, Lieutenant.'

Granot's reply began with a belch. 'Sorry, Perand, my guts are rotten this morning. No one in? So get the owner or the concierge to *let* you in.'

'Delmas is the owner. And there's no one on site who *could* let me in at the moment.'

'Got a man staked out?'

Perand kept the mobile to his ear as he knocked on the apartment next door. 'Yes. Next time Delmas shows, he'll pick him up.'

'Good. Tell him to be careful.'

The door was opened by a slight, elderly woman with prominent cheekbones and sparse white down for hair. A questioning expression suggested she was a sharp-witted old soul. Still holding the mobile to his ear, Perand showed the woman his badge. She shrugged noncommittally but didn't retreat.

'Okay, the next-door neighbour is in, Lieutenant. I'll get back to you.' Perand turned off his mobile. 'Sorry about that, madame. Do you know a Monsieur Pierre Delmas?'

The woman nodded as if she'd known that someone like him would come eventually.

'I was wondering if you had any idea when he might be back?'

'In a couple of years, isn't it?'

That was one hurdle crossed.

'Uh, no, actually. He was released a couple of days ago.'

'Time off for good behaviour?' She gave an enigmatic little smile. 'Come in.'

Perand loped lankily into a surprisingly upbeat space of pastel-washed walls and light-toned wood. 'You are…?'

'Otaphu, Katja.'

She directed Perand into a bentwood armchair. At his back were bookshelves containing several works on ancient history by one K.J. Otaphu – the one place in the room a visitor wouldn't notice them.

'So you haven't seen Delmas, Madame Ota…?'

'Phu. O-ta-phu.' She sat in the chair's twin, opposite him. 'No, I haven't. But when I do, I shall ask him in for a coffee.'

She hadn't offered *him* one, Perand noticed. 'It's clear Monsieur Delmas's criminal past doesn't revolt you.'

She made a sound halfway between a disdainful snort and a laugh. 'There are things in this life far more worthy of one's revulsion than the unarmed robbery of a bank, don't you think?'

'We don't think, Madame O-ta-phu. We just find things out. Do you expect to see Delmas on his return?'

'Unless his period of incarceration has induced amnesia.'

It seemed Madame was not acquainted with the state of Delmas's health.

'Was he a friend of yours, particularly?'

'No. I scarcely said a word to him in the…' A raised eyebrow appeared to be necessary for the calculation. 'Fifteen years, it must be, that we've lived next door to one another.'

'Was he a friend of anyone else in the building?'

'I don't think so. And I don't recall any visitors. He was a man who very much kept himself to himself.'

Perand produced Sylvie Galvin's photo. 'Have you ever seen this person?'

'No. But she bears quite a resemblance, does she not, to Monsieur Delmas?'

As bright as he was, knowing which questions to ask, when to ask them, and when to stop asking them was sometimes a struggle for Perand, but the interview at last concluded with a thought-provoking observation.

'Overall, how would you describe Pierre Delmas?'

'Cool. Reserved.' She thought about it a moment. 'Proper.'

'Proper? He may have been the brains behind a nineteen-million-euro bank raid.'

Madame Otaphu gave another little snort. 'The other members of the gang, the ones who weren't caught, they were brainier still, it seems.'

A1 Security occupied part of the top floor of a glass and concrete block in Saint-Augustin. Perhaps worryingly for its clients, the building was ideally sited for its staff to make a quick getaway: Nice Côte d'Azur Airport, the busiest in France outside Paris, sprawled behind the chain-link fence on the opposite side of the boulevard.

Darac had decided to open with managing director Vincent Leroux, a handsome individual with a strong jawline and a matching handshake.

'Let's go back to 2003,' Darac said, once the preliminary

niceties had been observed. 'You were Pierre Delmas's immediate superior?'

'Briefly, yes.' Leroux had the air of a man used to being called superior. 'The company has a policy of blooding new senior staff on the shop floor, as it were.' He glanced at his watch. 'I am sorry but could we limit this to ten minutes?' Swivelling his chair, he turned to face the windows that formed the side wall of his office. 'I'm leaving for Geneva shortly.'

'Don't worry.' Darac was speaking to the man's profile. 'The world is still out there.'

'It's not the world that worries me. It's my flight. Our pilot gets very upset if we're late. So… Pierre Delmas, the most infamous employee in the company's history. That's all there is to say, really. What more can I tell you?'

Whatever it was, Darac felt like getting into Leroux's face to hear it. But he stayed put. 'He was released from prison a couple of days ago. Are you expecting to see him?'

Leroux produced a derisory laugh. 'It's hardly likely.' He swung his chair back into line. 'Don't you think?'

'Is it likely he would seek out anyone else here?'

'I've no idea.'

The next nine minutes simply flew by.

A visit to HR proved more useful. At the end of it, Darac had compiled a list of all those who had been working at A1 at the time of the robbery. Aside from absences for ill health, Delmas had been considered a steady, reliable employee. Until he had tried to bust So-Pro for nineteen million euros, that is. Darac's subsequent meetings with the Bank Protection Department and Accounts yielded little of further significance.

Darac fared better in Maintenance. It seemed that Artur Rigaud, a short, lively individual in his mid-forties, had an ear in every office in the building. And a matchstick in every terminal in the gang socket he was repairing.

'I'll just finish this off while we talk.' He glanced at a volt meter plugged into the socket. 'Still flat-lining. And this connects to the most important bit of kit in the whole place.'

'Not one of the servers, surely?'

'My espresso machine.'

Darac smiled. 'I understand perfectly.'

'So what did I make of Pierre Delmas? Quiet. Pleasant enough. A bit… dull, I suppose is the word. One thing that always struck me as funny: for a clever bloke, he could be a bit slow-witted. No, slow-witted isn't the right way of putting it.' Artur wiggled one of the matchsticks and then jammed a second in next to it. The needle on his power meter did a little dance to celebrate. 'That's got it… Yeah, you couldn't tell him a joke, for instance. That kind of thing.' The thought seemed still to perplex Artur. 'I tell you what, though, you could have knocked me down with—'

'A matchstick?'

'Something like that – when what he'd been up to came out.' Artur began filling in a job sheet. 'And then, poor sod, he was the only one the' – he grinned – '*police* caught. Didn't get a penny, did he? Well, none of them did.'

'Did anyone here ever wonder about the gang? We think there must have been at least four others in on it.'

He looked a little defensive, suddenly. Darac sensed an opening. '*Did* someone say something, Artur?'

'*Someone*? No, no. Nothing.'

The implication seemed clear. 'But *you* have a theory?'

Artur craned his neck in several directions. The coast clear, he dropped his voice.

'Well, I always wondered how he got together with the others. You know, where's a bloke like that going to meet a *gang*? Doesn't make sense. I can't imagine he had much of a social life outside this place.' He raised his eyebrows. 'If you catch me.'

'So you believe the others probably also worked here?'

'No, I didn't say that.' Quieter still. 'But I must admit, I have wondered it.'

'Who did he work with, mainly?'

'The alarm team, theoretically.' Artur scrawled his signature on the sheet, completing it with an extravagant flourish. 'But he worked on his own, really.'

'How many in the alarm team?'

'There's five... six guys in it now. In his day there were four but most of them aren't here any more. In two cases, literally.'

'Oh?'

'You know that big smash they had on the *voie rapide* up behind Gare Thiers a few years back? A couple of them were killed in that. Sad. Not that I cared, to be honest with you. Couldn't stick either of them.'

'The other two?'

'One runs the place, nowadays.'

'Leroux?'

'Yes. Big-headed bastard. The other one, Thierry Artaud – he retired. Lives over in Riquier. Haven't seen him in a long time.'

'Thierry Artaud?' Darac said, underlining the name on his list.

'Yeah. He'll be in his late sixties now. Nice fella. But who knows? Maybe he was the brains behind the whole thing.'

'Artur!'

The supervisor's voice was loud and insistent and it brought an end to proceedings. Darac left the building but, needing a moment to disentangle his day, he decided not to drive away immediately. As if observing the miracle of flight might enable his own thoughts to take wing, he crossed the boulevard and stood gazing through the airport's perimeter fence. His eye was taken by a private jet taxiing for take-off. He watched as it turned away from him, and then, framed in a single cell of the chain link, sped down the runway trailing twin vortices of heat in its slipstream. The nose tilted and cell by cell, the jet climbed free of the mesh into clear air. As it carved a wide arc over the Baie des Anges, Darac wondered if a Geneva-bound Vincent Leroux was on board. And whether he knew as little about Pierre Delmas as he had claimed.

It was remarkable that the case files, witness statements, and photos sitting in piles around the squad room were only part of the cache of documents Archive held on the 2003 So-Pro bank robbery. Wearing a rapt expression, Darac was coming to the denouement of a particularly meaty-looking report.

'Typical Agnès.' He smiled, closing the cover. 'When it comes to lateral thinking, there is no one to touch her.' He picked up a spill of photos. 'Let's go through these, Flak. I'll bring them over.'

The photos recorded the concrete-walled vault, the tunnel the gang had excavated between the vault and an abandoned brick-lined culvert, and the shaft that rose from the culvert via a manhole to a short service road. At her desk, Flaco squared them into a neat stack and set the topmost shot down in front of her.

'The site is right in the centre of the city. So how was it no one heard anything? How was it no one noticed all the gear and the vehicles?'

'I know you weren't on the force then.'

'In 2003? I was still at school back in Guadeloupe.'

'Of course. The first thing to bear in mind is that the bank abuts the Rue Lamora complex, one of the biggest redevelopments in the city's history. At the time of the robbery, the block was one giant building site. Noise, constant activity – it was perfect cover.'

'Ah, I see.' Scowling in concentration, she flipped to the next photo. And the next. 'What am I looking for, Captain?'

'Things like…' He leaned over her shoulder. 'That, for example.' He pointed to a mixture of earth and brick rubble piled up outside the tunnel that was cut into the vault's rear wall. In front of it was a smaller heap of broken-up concrete and dust. 'And those.' His finger traced a series of tool marks incised on a rock wall at the opposite end of the tunnel. 'No?'

Pressing her full lips together, Flaco shook her head. 'No.'

'If the gang had followed normal practice and tunnelled out to in, that rubble is at the wrong end of the tunnel and those tool marks are back to front.'

Flaco broke into an uncharacteristically broad smile. 'So Commissaire Dantier worked out the gang didn't tunnel *into* the vault, they tunnelled *out* of it?'

'Yes, she did.'

'That's… superb.'

'Isn't it? And finding the heaviest tools the gang used lying in the culvert, rather than at the vault end of the tunnel, confirms the direction they were travelling in.'

'So the robbery began in the vault. But how did the gang manage to get in?'

'Pierre Delmas *let* them in. There were two teams. One cut into the safety deposit boxes and so on; the other excavated the tunnel. Considering the time constraints they were working under, you can see the advantage of this approach for the gang.'

'It was quicker. If they had tunnelled in, they couldn't have done both jobs simultaneously.'

'Exactly.'

'But why tunnel at all? If Delmas could let the gang into the vault, why couldn't he just let them out again?'

'Something to do with how the alarms worked at the time. I've sent the stuff over to Tech. R.O. is going to drop in and explain it to us.'

Granot lumbered in. 'Look at all those files,' he announced, giving a little grin of satisfaction. 'I feel like an author must feel walking into a bookshop.'

'I'd ask you to sign them but you already have,' Darac said. 'Co-signed, anyway.'

'I only work with the best. Present company excepted.'

Flaco was still considering the ins and outs of So-Pro. 'What they did – wasn't it dangerous?'

'Dangerous?' Granot colonised a desk next to the window. 'In what way?'

'We were just commending the gang's originality in tunnelling out, not in,' Darac said. 'And Agnès's perspicacity—'

'*And* mine.'

'And yours, in working it out.'

Flaco turned to Granot. 'Supposing they hadn't managed to complete the tunnel before the staff came in after the weekend? They would have been caught red-handed.'

Granot hauled himself up. 'Let's look at those photos,' he said, implying that it would be a definitive assessment. He sorted through them and pulled one out. It showed a metre-wide aperture cut into the centre of the steel door that connected the vault with the bank proper. 'This is the hole workmen had to cut into the vault door so staff could get into it on the Monday morning. At first, of course, they didn't realise they were dealing with a robbery. Employees turned up for work as normal, someone went down to the vault and couldn't get in. A fault with the door, they thought. When they finally cut through into the vault, they found it in a complete mess. Emptied boxes everywhere, strongroom door open, lumps of concrete and broken bricks piled up. And the famous message chalked on the wall, of course.'

'Why did workmen have to *cut* through into the vault?'

'Vis-à-vis your point about the danger of the gang being disturbed on the job, once they were inside the vault, they sealed the door behind them.' Granot ran his finger around the photo. 'Its outer edges are still welded to the inside of the frame, look.'

'I see it bought the gang time. But wasn't that even more dangerous?'

'May I?' Darac picked up the shot of the vault door.

'More dangerous, Flak?' Granot said. 'How?'

'What if the gang hadn't been able to complete the exit tunnel? They would've trapped themselves in.'

'Ah but...' Granot searched through the stack for another photo. 'One second... Here we are. That is the entire length of the tunnel. It's less than six metres. Gives into that culvert, look. And it's a shaft from there that led up into the building site.'

'That *isn't* very long. Still...'

Lips pursed, Darac pulled out a written account of the sealed door. Every so often, he compared it with the photo.

'How far above the culvert is the surface?' Flaco said.

Granot gave an approving grunt. He loved the young officer's thoroughness, her voracious appetite for discovering the how and why of things. 'I just had the shaft photo in my hand...' Turning two and three shots over at a time, Granot's thick fingers were not made for leafing but he found it. 'Here, look. The climb is no more than... five metres. Steel rungs set into the side. Push the manhole cover off and you're away. Easy.'

'I see.'

Eyebrows lowered, Darac took one more look at the vault photo, stared into space for a moment, and then picked up a phone.

'Adèle, could you send me a data file of all the So-Pro bank robbery photos?'

'I asked you if you wanted that earlier.'

'I didn't want it then. Now I do.'

'No need to get shirty, Captain.'

'Thank you, Adèle.'

'What do you want the data disc for?' Granot said.

'I just want to check something.'

Erica walked in carrying a clear plastic folder containing pages of handwritten scrawl. 'R.O. has had to go up to La Trinité so I'm delivering the great man's words.'

'No finer speaker,' Granot said, his buoyant mood persisting. 'La T – that's Agnès's stabbing, I take it?'

'Double stabbing. Bonbon's just joined her up there.' Erica sat, crossed her legs and opened the folder. 'Are we ready?'

'If you can read his handwriting,' Darac said.

'I've had long practice. I'll summarise it.' She took out Ormans' notes and read the first few sentences. 'Ten weeks or so before the robbery, Delmas set up a pattern of triggering false alarms from So-Pro at the weekends. A "fault in the system"' – she signed the inverted commas – 'caused lights to flash on a central console. Officers from the Caserne and from Foch were dispatched to the bank the first few times. Then just officers from Foch. Then just a couple of prowl cars. Then one. Then a beat officer. Until finally, it got down to, "Oh there's that flashing light on the console again – don't worry, it'll go out in a minute." Once that stage had been reached, it opened the door, so to speak, to the vault.'

'It's like nobody takes any notice of a car alarm that goes off all the time,' Flaco said. 'On a bigger scale.'

'Exactly. But there's a problem with the method, apparently.' Erica read ahead for a moment. 'Right… The way the system works, the alarm signal is sent immediately

when the door is opened in any period of activation –
which usually means overnight but in this case, it meant
the weekend. If the door remains open for any longer than
thirty seconds…' She skipped ahead once more. And then
giggled. 'R.O.'s actually written: *After thirty seconds, big
scary things happen automatically – like bars shooting out of
the walls. Best avoid!*'

'We get the picture,' Darac said.

'So that's basically it on the alarms. Delmas could get the
gang in through the vault door but he couldn't get them out
the same way.'

Granot imperiously folded his arms. 'I could've told you
that.'

Darac glanced at his watch. 'Look, we have a lot to
consider and I don't want to go much further without
Agnès and Bonbon. And Perand, come to that. Okay with
everyone?'

Erica got to her feet. 'Okay with me. I've got a date with a
couple of errant hard drives.' She lingered, her head cocked
slightly to one side. 'Have you changed your perfume,
Flak?'

Girl talk was unfamiliar terrain for Flaco. 'Uh… yes. The
captain's papa sent it over. It's one of his. One he invented
for his company, I mean.'

The humour that usually played around Darac's mouth
returned.

'Really suits you.' Erica filled her nostrils. 'What's it called?'

'Oh, uh…' The merest hint of a blush. 'Something *des
Bois.*'

'*Nymphe?*' Darac said, knowing full well it had to be.
'Woody yet—'

'Indeed,' Flaco said. 'I've got paperwork and I need to press on.'

Perand walked in. 'No one has seen Delmas and he hasn't been at the apartment.'

Darac pursed his lips. 'Have you been on to the utility companies, his bank and so on?'

'Yes. No meter readings asked for at the apartment and no applications anywhere else. No mobile contract, Internet – nothing. I reckon he's staying with someone else.'

'We'll find him.'

Officer Charvet's head appeared around the doorframe. The duty officer was wearing the deadest of deadpan expressions. 'Captain?' All eyes turned to him. He withdrew, then reappeared carrying a hard, rectangular case bearing a metal plate that read: GIBSON, INC., KALAMAZOO, MICHIGAN USA.

'Yes, yes, yes!'

Walking into a buzz of congratulation and high spirits, Charvet handed over the case. 'I've never been so popular.'

As the group gathered around Darac, Perand took the opportunity to slide in next to Erica. 'Better check it's not been pissed on or anything, Captain,' he said.

Erica gave him a look. 'What are you talking about?'

'You know – like burglars do in houses. And worse.'

'It's been cleared for explosives, anyway,' Charvet said. 'I had Roulet run it past one of his sniffer dogs.'

It was such an unlikely image, Darac tried to think of something witty to say but he was too happy in the moment. 'Thanks, Charvet.' He set the case down on a desk, paused, and then with both hands, reached for the locks. 'And now… the moment of truth.'

He flicked the catches and opened them. There it was. His faithful old Gibson SG in all its cherry-lacquered glory. 'Pristine.' He plucked the guitar from its velvet cocoon and turned it over. 'Cleaner than when I lent it to Freddy.' He sat and rested the lower bout of the instrument on his left thigh. 'Pity I don't have an amplifier here.'

Granot mugged disappointment. 'We'll get over it. In time.'

Darac played a chord, adjusted the tuning a couple of times and then let fly, swooping, soaring, and finally fluttering to earth in a series of spectacular falls.

'Show-off,' Erica said.

'Impressive.' Flaco nodded. 'Not my thing but very impressive, Captain.'

'You know, I usually play my D'Aquisto at our Thursday gigs but just this once, I think I'll take this as well. A sort of welcome home present.'

'It's what I'd do,' Granot said.

'Where did you find it, Charvet?'

'Somebody wearing a parka left it outside the gate a couple of hours ago. Would've brought it in sooner but Roulet was out on a job.'

Darac put the guitar back into its case and swiped his mobile. 'A guy in a parka? Probably some old blues man who saw it and just couldn't resist. SGs aren't used much for jazz...' The call connected. 'Freddy? Paul Darac here.'

'Captain – listen, I've been round every shop, I've—'

'It's here. I've got it back.'

'You have?'

'The amnesty I was telling you about? It worked.'

The boy shrieked something that began with 'Shit!'

Holding the mobile away from his ear, Darac shared a grin
with the others.

'And is it alright, Captain? Not damaged or anything?'

'Just the opposite,' Darac said. 'I can't wait to play it
for real.'

19

Julie Issert snuggled into Martin Darac's chest. 'I haven't got off to the best of starts with Paul, have I?'

His hand drifted across her flank and drifted back again. 'He'll come around. I'm sure of it.'

'He's right, though. It was reckless. I do too many things without thinking.'

'I'm glad you do. Or I probably wouldn't be here with you now.'

'He obviously loved his mother very much.'

Martin's hand came to a stop.

Julie propped herself on one elbow. 'I don't *have* to have Paul's acceptance. But it would be so much nicer for everyone if he got on with me.'

'He will.' Martin returned her look. 'He just needs time.'

Her auburn hair splashed over his chest as she snuggled back into him.

'You see, it's not you he's unsure about in this, Julie. It's me.'

'What do you mean?'

'I've been looking for so long… Can you take this?'

'Of course.'

'I adored Sandrine and I suppose I've tried again and again to find that same feeling with someone and never have. Until now.'

'What happened? To Sandrine, I mean.'

His hand drifted away.

'You don't have to talk about it.'

'She… had a brain tumour.'

Julie listened intently as Martin continued, his voice no more than a murmur.

'She had no idea. None of us did. It was a Saturday. Except that I was away for the company, it began like any weekend day. The carnival down in Nice was nearly over and we hadn't managed to get to any of it. Sandrine loved things like that and she'd promised Paul she'd take him to the Parade of Lights. Mother and son out together – great fun. But she started to feel unwell in the afternoon. Not terrible, just headachy, a little queasy. If I'd been around, I would've taken Paul myself but I was in London. He made a fuss: "You said we could go," all that. So she took him. They watched the whole thing and enjoyed it. But by the time they came away, Sandrine felt much worse. She got them both back here. And then… half an hour or so later, she suffered a massive brain haemorrhage. And was gone.'

'I'm so sorry.'

'It was a black time. And perhaps especially so for Paul. You see, he…' Martin exhaled deeply. And got no further.

'He what? Blamed himself?'

'Uh-huh. Even though it was explained to him time and time again that Sandrine would not have survived the day under any circumstances, part of him still feels responsible.'

'I can understand that.'

'I don't mean he thinks about it constantly. Even when we talk about her, he doesn't. Carnival season is not a good time for him, though. That's one of the reasons I—'

'I know.'

Nothing was said for some moments.

'I lost someone, too, actually. Someone dear to me. My brother, Sebastien. Died in a motorcycle accident. He was only twenty-five. I still have some of his things. It's silly but I don't want to part with them.'

'Now it's my turn to be sorry. Life can be really…'

Julie was no longer listening. She was thinking about Sebastien's things and feeling gladder than ever that she still had them.

20

Darac appeared at Frankie's office door, holding two porcelain cups. He raised the larger one invitingly. 'Got a minute?'

'If that's a mint tea with two sugars, the answer's yes.'

He entered, closing the door behind him.

'So I'm in conference, am I?'

'I lied about the minute.' He handed over the cup and drew up a chair next to her. 'Be more like twenty.' He reached into the breast pocket of his denim shirt.

'Not baklava, as well? You can call again.'

'Something more interesting. So-Pro photos. All of them.'

'The Delmas case?' She slotted the disc he gave her into the drive. 'It's a hot ticket, this one.'

'Something's come up and I need to discuss it with you.'

She gave him a look. 'I never really did leave your team, did I?'

'I wish you never *had* left it – you know that. You're *au fait* with everything about this case?'

Cradling her tea in both hands, she swung her chair around to face him. 'Probably not everything. Give me a summary.'

'Right… First we have Pierre Delmas serving a ten-year term for the So-Pro robbery of 2003. A model prisoner, he gets out a couple of years early. He was the only gang member caught. That's important, we think. He suffers from a condition called NCL which is fatal in every case. Deanna says that the vast majority of sufferers are dead by Delmas's age. I'm beginning to think that that may be important also. On the first day of his release, his encounter with a man named Michel Fouste leads directly, though accidentally, to the latter's death. We're looking into that again in the light of recent developments. On the second day of his release, Delmas is the target of a shooting by the seemingly innocuous Carl Halevy.'

In lieu of a free hand, Frankie touched her knee against Darac's.

'We're all fine,' he said and smiled. 'The question is, what was Halevy up to? What do you think?'

Frankie took a sip of tea. 'As unlikely as it might seem, Halevy must have been a member of, or closely allied to, the So-Pro gang. As might Fouste. Fearing a freed Delmas would have a score to settle with the gang, or that he might simply expose them, Halevy seeks to remove the problem at source. That's the Crime 101 answer, anyway.'

'Sure, but if Delmas was going to shop the gang, why didn't he do it when he was in prison? Despite repeated threats and, more impressively, inducements that would have made his life inside easier, he kept quiet. And then there's the fact that the gang earned not one penny from the robbery. Famously, everything of value was recovered.'

'So it's not as if poor, sick Monsieur Delmas was rotting away in prison while the other members of the gang were living high on the hog somewhere.'

Darac drained his espresso. 'Exactly. On the revenge

front, there seems to be no compelling reason for him to go looking for the others when he came out. And no reason, therefore, why the gang should be sufficiently worried about him to want to kill him.'

'On the other hand, although the gang earned nothing from the robbery, they did at least retain their liberty. From Delmas's prison cell, anywhere on the outside might have looked like paradise after a year or two.'

'Could be the case, certainly. But consider the significance of how Delmas was caught. He wasn't grassed up by the gang. It was Agnès working out some esoteric stuff that led to his arrest. And that, remember, did not lead to the recovery of the money. Delmas gave her no help whatsoever on that. It was the bank's offer of a two-million-euro reward that was the catalyst. A member of the public saw something, phoned it in, and it was *that* that directly led to the recovery of the nineteen-million-plus haul.'

Frankie took another sip of her tea and set down the cup. 'That member of the public wasn't Carl Halevy, was it?'

'Nice idea but it wasn't.' Darac took out his notebook. 'It was a Monsieur Jean Aureuil who lives near Cannes, now. I'm going over to see him first thing tomorrow. The name was never released so Delmas couldn't have gone looking for him, anyway.'

Frankie brought up the disc menu. 'Just what did this Aureuil see?'

'You won't find it there, Frankie. It's on a different disc. I haven't had time to look into the recovery side of it yet but basically, three days after the robbery was discovered, Aureuil came across the gang's base, a farmhouse up by Coaraze. The haul, intact, was inside.'

'So far, the cemetery shooting appears to make little sense. And yet it happened.'

'Delmas's daughter, Sylvie, is one of the key players. A shop girl living in straitened circumstances, she dies of the NCL she inherited from the father she never knew while he is still in prison. In poor health for many years and probably knowing what was coming, she had paid for her funeral herself – a very basic affair. Yet a bank statement shows 400,000 euros had been paid into her account a few years before. It hadn't – the statement was a forgery. Strangest of all, some years later, her remains are reburied in a grave costing 25,000 euros, paid for in cash by an anonymous "friend".'

'You're going for an exhumation, I imagine?'

'It's tomorrow. Perand isn't alone in thinking that some of the gang are buried in Sylvie's grave along with her.'

'So from prison, Delmas orchestrated a multiple hit?'

'It's a possibility.'

'And Halevy, a fellow gang member or close associate, found out about it and tried to kill Delmas out of revenge or before he was next?'

'According to that theory – yes.'

'On a less sinister level, could it have been Delmas who paid for the new grave for Sylvie? Out of love or regret or remorse at never having been there for her?'

'Granot's looked at Delmas's accounts already. He couldn't see how he could have been the source of the money. Besides, why should he mask his identity? The daughter who knew nothing of his existence was dead, obviously, so he wasn't protecting her. No, I think someone else paid. Delmas had no idea which grave was Sylvie's in the cemetery. I wonder if he even knew Sylvie had died until he was released.'

'What makes you think that?'

Darac gave a rueful grin. 'This is the kind of thing we usually disregard but my Aunt Sophie is a very reliable witness. She saw only Delmas's back as he stood at the grave, but his shoulders were really shaking, she says. He was sobbing. Well, you can weep at any time at a graveside, of course. But this had a rawness to it, she said. That awful initial feeling of devastation. You know?'

'Yes, I do… I take it Perand's man in Villeneuve-Loubet hasn't seen Delmas?'

'No, he hasn't shown at his apartment. In fact, no one has seen him in the area at all. Nevertheless, I've had a notice of Sylvie's exhumation put through his letterbox and newspapers, TV and radio have all referred to it. It might just pull Delmas back to the cemetery. Or other interested parties.'

'Exhumation.' Frankie gave a little shiver. 'Let's hope for a nice clean skeleton.'

'Rotting remains don't do much for me, either.'

'You're attending?'

'Yes but I'm leaving it to them. Unless it proves necessary to view the body. Or bodies.'

Frankie nodded. 'The reburial certainly is suspicious. And then when you factor in the false bank statements, it seems clear that deception is at the heart of the case.'

'Agreed.'

'But who is deceiving whom and why?'

'I think we may be able to get closer to that by looking at some aspects of the robbery in detail. And there's something else here, Frankie.' He ran a hand through his hair. 'Something I *really* need your advice on.'

Frankie picked up her tea cup. 'I'm intrigued. Flattered. And suckered.'

'Oh, the power I have over *le belle donne*,' he said, mimicking Armani.

Frankie gave him a look but said nothing.

'Alright – So-Pro. The received wisdom is that it was a case of sharp criminals coming up against an even sharper *flic* in the form of Agnès. She reasoned the gang had tunnelled out of the vault, not into it. Combined with other evidence, it led to the arrest of the security man, Pierre Delmas, as the inside man on the job. He confessed, confirming that Agnès was right.'

'As usual.'

'I think the criminals were sharper than she was on this one.'

'You're not serious.' Her smile faded. 'You are serious.'

'I know it seems weird but…'

Frankie took a moment to get used to the idea. 'Well, she has never claimed to be infallible.'

'No, of course not, but she hardly ever makes mistakes. On the more important cases, I would say never. And it is tempting to say that the So-Pro mistakes don't matter – everything was recovered at the time, after all, and I still think Delmas was the inside man. But they have a bearing on the *current* case and so there'll be no way of avoiding bringing it up in meetings. The last thing I want to do is stick the boot in, but it will have to come out.'

'Let's not get ahead of ourselves. Go through the evidence first.'

'Okay.' Sitting forward, he scanned the list of file numbers. 'Open V23.'

The shot was of the breached vault door taken from inside the disaster area that was the vault itself.

'Breached from the inside, you see?'

'Yes, I'm with you,' Frankie said. 'Go on.'

'That door is steel-clad concrete. Really tough and heavy.'

'And the large hole in the centre of it was cut by the authorities on the Monday morning following the robbery?'

'So they could gain access to the vault, yes. See those little twisted shards of metal lying directly under the hole? It's debris from torching through the steel casing of the door, right?'

'Ri-ight?'

'Now look at those differently shaped shards lying well apart from them on either side. Under the line of the doorframe, in fact.' He pointed to them. 'That's torch debris of a different kind. When he finally broke down under questioning, Delmas said he had first let the gang into the vault through that door. Then, before they did anything else, the gang welded the door to the frame. Sealing themselves off from the bank itself gave them a safety margin should they still have been hard at it come Monday morning. Are you with me on shards one and two?'

'Uh-huh. The ones in the middle are *cutting* debris made by the bank people *after* the robbery had happened and the gang had all gone; the widely spaced ones are *welding* debris made by the gang *before* they got started.'

'Exactly. Except – it's not what happened, is it? If the gang had welded the door shut before they started ripping everything out of the strongroom, tunnelling out, and so

on, we wouldn't be able to see any welding shards at all –
they'd be buried under all those discarded boxes, piles of
rubble and other stuff. Instead, they're sitting on top of it,
just like the cutting shards that were produced long after
the gang had gone.'

'Ah, yes.' Frankie took another sip of her tea. 'But
whether the gang sealed off the door early or late into the
weekend doesn't seem all that crucial. Is that it for the
shards of destiny?'

Darac grinned. 'For the time being, yes. But it was those
little bits of metal that got me thinking about the tunnelling,
the handling of spoil, and so on.' He consulted his notebook.
'Let's have T65 and T9. Split-screen them.'

They were the shots he had shown to Flaco earlier. T65
showed the tunnel-opening in the rear wall of the vault.
Around it was a pile of earth and brick rubble, in front of
which was a smaller pile of broken-up concrete.

'The story as accepted is that once Delmas let the gang
members into the vault they divided into two teams. While
one team started opening the safety deposit boxes and so
on, the other began drilling, cutting and bashing a very
large hole through the concrete rear wall of the vault. That
team then excavated what was effectively a tunnel through
the compacted earth and rock that lay behind it until they
emerged in the brick-lined culvert beyond.' He traced the
direction with his finger. 'Above that was the shaft that
rose, via a manhole, into the chaos of the giant building site
that was Rue Lamora. Based on the simple principle that
tunnellers get rid of spoil behind them, shots like T65 seem
initially to support Agnès's theory.'

'Because if the gang had tunnelled into the vault from

outside, the spoil is at the wrong end of the tunnel.'

'Exactly. T9 shows some of the tool cuts made on the rock wall lining the culvert end of the tunnel. The direction of the cuts appears to further support the inside-to-outside theory.'

'Ye-es?'

'I think both of these things are red herrings.'

'Why?'

'Ultimately, because I believe the gang *did* tunnel into the vault.'

Frankie raised one eyebrow. 'You begin to interest me, Mr Bond.' She took a final sip of tea. 'Go on.'

'Split screen V67 and C25.'

The shots were of the tunnel-opening in the bank vault wall and the tunnel-opening at the culvert end.

'Ah,' Frankie said. 'I see what you are getting at. The tunnel entrance in the vault wall is quite high up; at the culvert end, it's bang level with the walkway flanking it. If you were tunnelling from inside to outside, it's not very likely that you would choose to start at an awkward height and then arrive slap on Position A at the other end. But that's exactly what would happen if you started tunnelling at the culvert end.'

'The vault *is* lower than the culvert so the hole in the wall would have to be *somewhere* above the floor. But that's just too precise, Frankie. As for the direction of the tool cuts on the wall – it would be easy to trick those up.'

'Agreed. But how did all the spoil from the—?' She interrupted herself. 'They shovelled it through into the vault after completing the tunnel.'

'I think they did. And you say *all* the spoil. There wasn't *that* much, really. The average height of the tunnel is 1.7 metres but it's less than a metre wide and only 5.4 metres long. They had wheelbarrows, or something similar – you can see tyre tracks on the tunnel floor. And while we're on the subject of tracks, bring up T87. They're not the focus of the shot but if you look, you can make them out.' He ran his finger along two V-shaped grooves about five centimetres wide that ran the length of the tunnel floor. At the vault end, the grooves began cleanly; at the culvert end, both terminated in a miniature slagheap of earth. 'See?'

'They're grooves, alright…' Frankie shook her head. 'Help me.'

'C107 will give you the answer.'

The shot was of one of the two heavyweight rock drills found in the culvert. At the business end, the bit was chevron-shaped and appeared to be about five centimetres wide.

Frankie pursed her lips. 'Hmm. Tools being found in the culvert was one of the reasons Agnès believed the gang had tunnelled inside to outside, wasn't it?'

'It was one of them, yes.'

'But these photos suggest the opposite. The drillers were clearly working *away* from the culvert end of the tunnel, not toward it. After they had got through into the vault, they must have dragged the drills back along the tunnel floor, the bits gouging out those grooves.'

'And now we can see that the vault door wasn't welded to the frame *before* anything else happened in there.'

'Those little shards of metal – I missed them. But I agree: having broken through into the vault, the strongroom team must have started ripping out the safety deposit boxes and so on while the tunnellers still had the spoil to shift, perhaps the tunnel to shore up – whatever. By the time they got around to sealing the vault door, the floor in there was already knee-deep in rubble.'

'It had to be that way.' He glanced at his notes. 'Almost done… Can we move on to the haul itself?'

Frankie's soft green eyes clouded over. 'There's more vis-à-vis Agnès?'

'Afraid so. It's to do with those safety deposit boxes you mentioned.'

'Some of the haul will have come off the shelf, won't it? Loose, as it were.'

'Indeed, but it still left quite an amount of cash and other valuables in the boxes. I only mention this because I think it could be important in what we're doing now. Delmas said in court that he'd opened all the boxes electronically using codes he'd pre-generated himself. Then, he said, in order to "throw the police off the scent", one of the gang lasered the boxes to make it appear that they'd been opened in the normal way. However, when Agnès and the team got in, they found one box lying there open but completely pristine. It bore no laser marks at all. Bring up… V45, I think it is.'

'V45?'

'Yes, this is it. Box 328. *How could it be open if no one opened it?* Agnès asked herself. It must have been opened some other way. Added to all the other stuff she was thinking, she reasoned it had been opened by an inside man and all the other boxes doctored to look as if they'd been lasered open.'

'But if Delmas could get into the vault and open the boxes

himself, didn't anyone wonder why he needed a tunnelling gang at all? He could have just got in, helped himself and left, surely?'

'The gang was quite clever here. And it was all part of their strategy to mask what they really did. It's to do with alarms. A signal is sent the moment the vault door is opened out of hours. If it's still open thirty seconds later, a second signal is sent and all kinds of things happen automatically. Agnès got part of the way down the line. She correctly worked out that Delmas arranged things so staff got used to ignoring the first signal; the second one he couldn't do anything about. But then she went off beam because she hadn't understood how the tunnelling had really gone.'

'Did she really believe that Delmas and the gang could have got themselves and all their equipment into the vault in a window of just thirty seconds?'

'She came to believe it, yes. Delmas said that they had practised the move hundreds of times. Stopwatches, military precision – all that.'

'How did Delmas account for the opened box – the one without laser burns?'

'He said that he'd opened it at the very last moment – just before the gang abandoned the vault. Everything had taken longer than they thought and there was a certain amount of panic. That led to a breakdown in communication and the laser guy didn't do his stuff on box 328 as he had on all the rest.'

'Sounds plausible.'

'Does, doesn't it? It was another red herring, I think. I've just had a chat with a Monsieur Mizzi from A1 Security. He believes Delmas could have opened no more than one or two boxes with the "pre-generated codes" he said he'd devised. They were *all* lasered open, he reckons – apart from 328 and *maybe* one other.'

'He obviously didn't say that in court. Why not?'

'Mizzi didn't work for A1 back then.'

'Any other leads there?'

'We've been through a list of all those who were there at the same time as Delmas. No criminal records for any of them before or since. I went to see one Thierry Artaud earlier. It seems he was the closest to Delmas but it's a relative term. He did work with him on the odd occasion, though.'

'On So-Pro?'

'He said not. I checked the job logs anyway just to be sure. They confirmed it. "I knew him but I didn't know him," he said about Delmas. They nearly all say that.'

'You obviously don't have the feeling that Artaud was a gang member.'

'I really don't.' He looked into Frankie's eyes. 'But what I'm getting at here is this: if the gang did what you and I think they did – tunnelled from outside to inside – why did they rig clues to be picked up by the police that suggest the opposite? Why did they rig clues that ultimately pointed the finger at Delmas? And – this is the interesting part – with his total complicity?'

'I don't know. It seems that Agnès did ultimately believe what the gang wanted her to believe. But why did they want her to believe it?'

Darac nodded. 'Indeed. At first sight, it looks like a straightforward fall guy ploy that went wrong, doesn't it? Delmas draws the short straw or even volunteers for the role, serves his time and out he comes to pick up his share of the gang's ill-gotten gains. Except that we beat them to it and there were no gains to be got.'

'But why the necessity for a fall guy at all? If the gang had put all their energies into just getting away with the robbery, they might well have.'

'Ye-es.' Darac stared at the floor. 'Whatever it was, it's obviously behind what's happening now and that's our main focus.'

'I see that. On the other question, I doubt if there's any need to stress about Agnès, you know. When has the floor around those bare feet of hers ever been littered with eggshells?'

'Never.'

'Exactly. Just go and talk to her. She's always reasonable. Super reasonable with you.'

'She's certainly fought my corner enough times.'

'I think you may have more of a problem with Granot. He's always been very protective of his work.'

'That's true.'

Darac's mobile rang. 'Lieutenant Malraux here.'

'*Lieutenant* Malraux,' Darac said, for Frankie's benefit. She rolled her eyes. 'Yes?'

'I hear on the grapevine, Captain, that you're giving my patch a visit tomorrow morning?'

'By the grapevine, you mean your boss?'

'Well, he calls himself that. I thought I'd go along with you to interview the man who got the So-Pro reward, one Jean Aureuil.'

'Did you?' Spending time with the former riot squad bully boy was the last thing Darac wanted to do but he felt he owed the man. 'Alright.'

The arrangements were made and Darac hung up.

'Malraux gets promoted.' Frankie's face was a mask of tragedy. 'He gets transferred.' Delight. 'But only as far as Cannes.' Her face fell once more.

'I'll give him your love.'

'You'll do no such thing.' She smiled, going to a happier thought, suddenly. 'Completely forgot – you got your guitar back. I'm delighted.'

'Thanks, yes, I am too. Haven't had time to play it yet. Not properly.'

'Beats me how you find the time to play at all.'

'Bunking off work regularly helps.' He got to his feet. 'Thanks for the advice. And everything.'

She ejected the data disc. 'Don't forget this.'

Her fingers brushed his as she handed it over. Quite suddenly, he felt an impulse not to trill out one of his routine goodbyes. He wanted to say something less flippant. He looked into her eyes and smiled.

'What would I do without you, Frankie?'

Her reply was a little behind the beat. 'You'd go into a terminal decline, obviously.'

'You're right,' he said, taking his leave. 'I would.'

21

Turning away from Cannes, Darac picked up the N98 coast road as it followed the tightening arc of the Golfe de la Napoule. With Orchestra Baobab along for the ride, he was bound for La Bocca, a diverse suburb a couple of kilometres to the west of the city.

It was a spectacularly bright, hazy morning. Away to his left, sea and sky merged in a seamless azure continuum; ahead, the Esterel Massif jutted between them in a blur of burnt orange tones. Blue-orange-blue. A Rothko come to life.

Malraux was waiting for Darac in the parking area of L'Hippocampe, a six-storey apartment block facing the gulf. 'I saw you turning in,' he said, squinting into the light. 'What did you take the coast road for?'

'Morning, Malraux.'

'Should've taken the A8 all the way. Then you could've come off at the Stade—'

'Something wrong with your eyes?'

'It's nothing.'

'You've got shades, haven't you?'

'They don't work for me.'

They rode the lift to the top floor of the building and pressed the bell of apartment three. A cheery, fresh-faced man in his early fifties answered the door. Showing them in, he paused at an old-fashioned sideboard. On it was an e-photo frame displaying a shot of a cheery, fresh-faced woman in her early fifties.

'That's my wife, Paulette,' Jean Aureuil said. 'She's out walking Domino at the moment. Our dog.'

Domino was a cheery, fresh-faced Labrador in his early fifties, Darac imagined.

'Either of you fancy a drink? I can do anything from iced tea to hot chocolate. Including beers.'

'I'm fine, thanks,' Darac said.

'Pastis?'

Malraux seemed affronted by the offer. 'It's nine o'clock in the morning.'

'Let's go and sit out, then.'

As they followed Aureuil on to the terrace, a series of metallic clinks and squeals rose up to meet them.

'How about that eh, gentlemen?' Aureuil indicated the view as if it were his alone. 'We love it here. Can't beat La Bocca for value.'

'What, you like living on top of railway marshalling yards, do you?' Malraux said.

'Where do *you* live, mate? The Carlton?'

'The Golfe de la Napoule...' Darac smiled, re-establishing the rapport. 'Beautiful.'

'We think so.' Aureuil directed them to a trio of chairs set back in the shade. 'So, what do you want to know?'

'What we want to know—'

'I'll take it for the moment, Lieutenant.' As he sat down, Darac noticed that Malraux's fingernails were chewed practically to the quick and there were eczema patches on his hands; a young man, literally unhappy in his own skin.

'What we would like to talk to you about is your part in the Société Provençale Bank Robbery of 2003.'

Aureuil gave an amused little snort. 'I think you'd better rephrase that, Captain.'

Darac grinned, sharing the joke. 'I meant your part in securing all the money and so on that had been stolen.'

Aureuil sat forward in his seat, the life returning to his face. Darac couldn't guess how many times the man had recited the tale that had been the defining moment of his life. But however many it was, he clearly hadn't tired of telling it.

'We were living on Rue Cluvier in Nice then. Do you know it?'

'No view of the sea there,' Darac said.

'Or much else. And talk about noise. Traffic thundering overhead all bloody day and night. Not that *I* was around much to hear it but it practically put Paulette in the loony bin. I had two jobs at the time. I drove a dump truck at the Rue Lamora site by day and then at night, I was on the taxis. On the Monday the robbery was discovered, I got laid off the site for several days – a lot of us were – so I went on to doing full days in the taxi. Same old, same old. Early on the Thursday morning, I picked up this fare at the airport. A middle-aged American couple just flown in from Paris. Lovely people. And but for them, my friend, Paulette and I would still be living under four lanes of traffic back in Nice.'

'Really? How come?'

'I'll tell you. I took the couple to the Negresco, right? I was getting their bags out of the boot and the wife says: "Do you know where Coaraze is?" I said, "I should do, I used to have a girlfriend up there." Then she says, "Do you know where the famous sundials are?" I told them if you get up there before lunchtime, you can get a map from the Info place that shows where all of them are and more besides. "Right, stay there," he says. "We want to hire you for the rest of the day." Half an hour later, off we go. You've never seen so many cameras, lenses. All sorts of stuff, they had. So we get there and park. I walk with them into the village and take them to the Info. They get their map and go off sundial spotting. I go for a bit of a stroll and head back to the taxi. That's when I see this truck. A newish mid-sized Iveco Eurocargo, sleep-over cab, twelve tonner.'

'The lorry was parked?'

'Yeah.'

'Where?'

'On a hardstanding by an old farm cottage – not an abandoned place but not one obviously lived in either, if you know what I mean. It was off the Avenue Théophile Gilli, the road that winds up to the Blue Chapel?'

Beneath them, a lone goods wagon shuddered as it rolled into the buffers at the end of its track.

'Yes, I know the chapel.' Darac could picture its cool, pastel walls; its weathervane in the form of the village's lizard emblem. The place was one of his former lover Angeline's favourite spots in the area. 'Were there other vehicles parked nearby?'

'It was on its own.'

'Why did you pay attention to it?'

'To begin with, I just thought a truck that size looked out of place in Coaraze. And especially parked where it was.' He smiled, reliving the moment. 'Then I spotted this faded old AS Roma football pennant hanging in the cab and I remembered it. The week before, I'd seen the very same truck at the construction site.'

The answer begged an obvious question. 'Malraux, do you have anything?'

'I can speak now, can I?'

Aureuil gave Darac a look. 'You've got a right one here, Captain, haven't you?'

'Malraux?'

'Alright, you identified the lorry as one of the hundreds of trucks you'd seen at Rue Lamora, and the site was right next door to the Société Provençale Bank. But what made you think that particular one had been used in the robbery?'

'Good question,' Darac said, quite genuinely.

'I didn't. But there was a two-million-euro reward out, right? So I went up and first of all, I looked through the windows of the farmhouse it was parked next to. Couldn't see anything. Then I went up to the lorry and had a closer look in the cab. There were a couple of paper wrappers on the floor – the sort banks use for wads of notes. That got me thinking a bit. So I went off to the café to mull things over and they had the TV news on. That's when I nearly had a heart attack. They flashed up a picture of the guy they'd arrested, you know – Delmas. I knew what the score was then, alright.' Sitting forward, he lowered his voice. 'The day before the robbery, I'd seen that very same man getting into the cab of that very same truck.' Triumphant all over again, Aureuil sat back. 'I called you lot. You came running. I sat in my taxi and watched the whole thing. By the time the American couple got back, it was all over.'

'What a photo opportunity *they* missed,' Darac said, amusing Aureuil all the more. 'Did you have the farmhouse in view the whole time you were waiting for the police?'

'I nipped off to get a bottle of wine. Gone ten minutes max. If the gang had been in the place and driven away, they would've gone past me. I didn't see anyone.'

'A house with nineteen million euros sitting in it? There must've been someone there, you'd think.'

'If there was, they must have got away on foot.'

'When you saw Delmas get into the truck back at the Rue Lamora site – what was he doing exactly?'

'Dunno. But I definitely remembered him. Big witless-looking fella.'

'Did you see anyone else?'

'No, he was the only one.'

'Think about this.' Darac looked into the man's light-brown eyes. 'Did he see you?'

Aureuil didn't need to give it any thought. 'It's dusty work on a dump truck, mate. I was wearing a mask. And a hard hat.'

'That makes sense… And then in due course, you picked up the reward.'

'All two million lovely euros of it. The happiest day of my life. By some distance.'

'Fantastic.' Darac smiled, sharing the moment. 'What did you do with it? If you don't mind me asking.'

'You can see what we did with some of it. And I bought the cab company I was working for, too. That was *really* sweet. And I've never worked since. Well, not what you'd call work.'

'Alright for some. Which company is yours?'

'Pro Cars, we called it. Well, I say *we*. Paulette came up with it. Neat touch, eh?'

'Very appropriate.' Darac rose. 'Well I think we've detained you for quite long enough, Monsieur Aureuil.'

'I'll see you out. Pity you missed Paulette.'

The e-photo frame was showing a different image of Madame. She looked just as cheery, fresh-faced and in her early fifties as in the earlier shot.

Darac and Malraux rode the lift in silence and maintained it as far as the car park. In the rail yards beyond, rakes of wagons were moving to and fro on separate tracks.

'I'm getting back to the office,' Malraux said.

'Are you free this afternoon?'

'Might be.'

'We're exhuming Sylvie Galvin's grave. If you can make the cemetery in Vence by four o'clock, come along.'

'Four?' He ran his fingertips across the backs of his hands in turn. 'No, I can't. I've got something on.'

'Okay. All the best, Lieutenant.'

'Yeah.'

Darac walked to his car feeling something remarkable. He felt sorry for Malraux.

22

'Your back appears to be doing well at the moment, Agnès?'

'It's much better. If you ever need an osteopath, I've got a name.'

Darac made a little amused sound in his throat. 'Do you remember the time your feet were aching and I found you trying to massage them? In this very office, it was. You could hardly bend so I massaged them for you. Nearly causing the greatest scandal in the history of the Caserne.'

Agnès's smile was at her most feline when there was sass in the air. '"Foot-Gate?" Never forget it. You know, there was scarcely a woman in the place who didn't ask me "what was it like?" afterwards. It was like being back at school after my first… encounter.'

'School?' Darac said, essaying shock.

Agnès gave a little shrug. 'Well, you know…' She sat back in her chair. 'Why do you bring that up?'

'I was thinking about feet.'

'Uh-huh?'

'And reflecting that you are one person I never have to worry about treading on eggshells around.'

'What?'

'I put that really clumsily and it's a tired metaphor, anyway.' He took a deep breath. 'Uh… I've been re-examining So-Pro, trying to get a handle on what's going on with Delmas and co. and I found some problems.' Darac had scarcely blushed in his life but he could feel his face flushing as he continued. 'Problems in the interpretation of events.'

'*My* interpretation of events, you mean?'

'Well, yours and… yes, yours.'

Agnès stiffened. 'Go on.'

'I only mention this—'

'Paul. Just get on with it.'

He took a stack of photos from his bag and began his analysis. She listened in near silence as he built his case point by point. However much he sugared the argument with disclaimers and with references to other triumphs, it still amounted to a demolition.

When he had finished, Agnès put her glasses on the desk and like a slowly deflating balloon, shrank back in her chair.

'In just an hour or two of looking at secondary materials, you've wrecked what I took days to put together working on the spot.'

No, no, no! *Anything* but this.

'Agnès, please…'

She slipped on her shoes. 'Excuse me,' she said, with the smallest, politest of smiles.

And walked out of the room.

23

The officer looked only a year or so older than young Freddy. He reached for the cordon tape. 'Would you like a moment alone, sir?'

Although his mother's graveside provided a focus for contemplation, Darac rarely felt closer to her there than he did elsewhere. Less so, in fact. 'You are Officer…?'

'Marquand, Roger.'

'It's fine. I was just wondering if the flowers and so on had been cleared away.'

'I see.'

Darac looked at the bullet-pocked headstone. The travestied forename. The pieces missing.

'We're all really sorry about what happened, sir.' Marquand's young face lightened. 'I always say hello to her when I come on. And goodbye. We all do, I think.'

Darac couldn't say anything for a moment. 'Thanks, man.' He gave the boy a pat on the arm. 'Thank everyone.'

Darac walked away, taking Carl Halevy's firing line. Some twenty-five metres ahead, Sylvie Galvin's tomb was surrounded by a green canvas screen. The girl had finally attracted quite a crowd to her graveside: a priest, two court officials, a forensic anthropologist, funeral directors Marvais *père et fils*, cemetery labourers and their manager – it was a good turnout. There was no sign of Pierre Delmas.

And there had been no sign of a rapprochement with Agnès. An exchange just before Darac had left the Caserne had been conducted in an atmosphere of aching cordiality, references to their earlier meeting studiously avoided.

He looked back at the cemetery gates. Beyond them, a couple of men were in conversation over the opened bonnet of a Fiat Punto. One of them gave Darac a discreet shake of the head. Still no sign of Delmas.

A tall, raw-boned black man was standing a little apart from the exhumation party. Djibril Mpensa, the pathologist, was a welcome sight.

'Alright, Map?'

'More to the point, how are you?'

'I'm fine. Glad you're here.'

'I'm just observing. A courtesy, really. But I'll be able to interpret stuff for you. If there's any need.'

'Good.'

Behind them, Benoit Marvais was buttonholed by one of the cemetery staff. As they exchanged a few words, old Monsieur Marvais took the opportunity to slip his leash. 'Everything will be as it should be,' he said to Darac. 'You'll see.'

'I sincerely hope so.'

'And I have to tell you, Captain, that I am frankly dismayed that this desperate performance should have been deemed necessary.'

'And I am frankly dismayed that your son has taken it upon himself to withdraw from sale some of your finer coffin handles.'

'I beg your pardon?'

'Coffin handles. Are you aware that your establishment no longer offers B3?'

'The *Malmaison*?' The old man's mourning-black eyes widened in astonishment. 'But it's—'

'A classic – absolutely.' Darac clicked his tongue. 'That's progress, I suppose.'

Benoit Marvais intervened at the double. Escorting his father to a neutral corner, he gave Darac a poker-hard stare as the recriminations began.

'What on earth was that about?' Mpensa asked.

'Just a bit of nonsense.'

Standing nearest the entrance to the screen, the senior court official looked at her watch and nodded to a couple of men in overalls. At their feet was a selection of masonry tools.

'What I'm really worried about, Map, is what may emerge from Sylvie's grave.'

'What are you hoping for?'

'That's a difficult question. Have you read the file?'

'Yes.'

All was not well at the screen. The priest, a preternaturally solemn figure in full regalia, halted the masons before they had taken a step. He indicated his watch as he spoke to the court officials, and pointed in the general direction of the old town.

'Let's say the tomb contains only Sylvie, and everything is as normal as old Monsieur Marvais just assured me it would be. What kind of state might she be in?'

'From what point of view?'

'From the point of view of the squeamish bystander.'

Mpensa performed a double-take. 'This from the man

who once found three decapitated heads in a kitchen cupboard and didn't throw up?'

'Consistency is an overrated virtue, don't you think? Some of the time.'

Mpensa smiled. 'In science, we kind of depend on it, you know. But there are so many factors in play, it's almost impossible to predict what the body will look like.'

'Take a stab at it.'

'She's three years dead?'

'Yes. She died in hospital and was presumably attended to promptly.'

'That's obviously crucial. Embalmed?'

'No.'

'Wooden coffin?'

'What else would it be?'

'Cardboard. Metal. Cloth bag, even.'

'Cardboard and cloth, bad; metal, good? From the appearance point of view, I mean.'

'Not necessarily. In fact, with a sealed metal casket, you can get what we call the… you don't want to know.'

'It was wood for the first two years. Wood-effect, anyway. Above-ground interment.'

'We-ell… there'll be the skeleton and skull, obviously, complete with teeth, hair and nails. There *could* be tendons, sinews and similar tissues. Perhaps some adhering skin. As she died of a diagnosed condition, there was probably no autopsy, but if there was, there'll be some redistribution and bagging. But we'll just have to wait and see.'

The answer wouldn't be long in coming. In the old town, the church bell sounded four times. Satisfied that the appointed hour had finally arrived, the priest intoned something pious and led a small procession into the screened-off area.

'I'm on,' Mpensa said, falling in behind them.

At the Fiat, the guys closed the bonnet and looked up and down the street. Darac met the gaze of one of them. He shook his head.

24

Wherever Jacques Telonne looked in the city, he saw something he'd built or developed in one way or another.

'What does *that* feel like?' the reporter asked him in the site office of his latest project, a hotel complex in the 'up and coming' area of Pont Michel.

Telonne could tell him exactly what it felt like. A couple of months before, he had been flying over Nice in the company helicopter with his wife, Elise. 'I could get a hard-on the size of the Eiffel Tower looking down on all this,' he'd said.

'What does it feel like?' he said to the reporter as site foreman Walter Picot handed him a clipboard. 'I don't know. I've never thought about it.' He began running an eye over the topmost sheet. 'Humbling, I suppose would be the word.'

Telonne's PA, Véronique Savart, bolted on a smile. 'Just one more,' she said, unbolting it just as efficiently.

'Monsieur Telonne,' the reporter began, essaying a *faux* grin of his own. 'Although we're still only halfway through the current term, a question on the mayoral race? An opinion poll yesterday puts you, for the first time, trailing both the incumbent and your principal rival to replace him at the next election.' Telonne looked up from the sheet. 'The reason, it seems, lies in your performance as chair of the carnival committee. Many believe your handling of the fatal incident four days ago showed immaturity, arrogance and even a sense of disconnection from the general public. And without *its* initial support at the ballot boxes, your perceived advantage with the councillors themselves would never, of course, be put to the test. You would remain plain Monsieur Jacques Telonne.' His grin gone, the reporter eyeballed his victim. '*Monsieur*, plain and simple.'

Véronique stepped in with the speed of a stricken boxer's corner man. 'Enough! We are not going to dignify such a—'

Looking as if he'd like to throw a punch anyway, Telonne laid a restraining hand on Véronique's forearm instead. 'No, no – it's a fair question.' He turned to his inquisitor. 'I would ask you to note, monsieur, that the source of that poll, Radio Côte 415, is one of the many media holdings of my "principal rival", as you call him. Now if you'll excuse me, some of us have real work to do. Walter?'

Telonne and Picot left the journalist to Véronique. They pushed through the site office door into a maelstrom of cranes, diggers, drills and trucks.

'I've never been behind in *any* poll before.' He slapped the costings clipboard against Picot's chest. 'Never! Not even on that fucking little nonentity's phone-in.'

'Opinion polls don't matter.' Picot launched a gobbet of spit into the dust. 'Nobody will vote for an arse-wipe like him, come the day. But I tell you what does matter. Setting straight a little blond piece by the name of Yvette Halevy.'

Telonne came to a dead halt. His index finger jabbed the air in front of Picot's nose. 'I shouldn't be having to give even a second's thought to any of this! I ought to—'

Picot knocked Telonne's finger away. 'You ought to what, Jacques? You think Fouste going under the truck was a vote loser? That's nothing. Is it?'

Their eyes bored into one another.

'The costings stink,' Telonne said. 'Get them done again.'

25

Flaco followed Darac into Pierre Delmas's apartment and closed the door quietly behind her. Uppermost on the mat was the notice of exhumation. Beneath it was a loose pile of circulars and junk mail.

'Untouched, Captain. And nothing among the rest.'

'The super said he hasn't seen a personal letter for years.'

An atmosphere of suspended animation hung over the long-empty apartment, an effect given ghostly connotations by the white sheets that had been thrown over the furniture.

'Why do I have an urge to remove *all* these sheets, Captain?'

The remark, uncharacteristically relaxed and personal, took Darac by surprise. Maybe it was his father's *Nymphe des Bois* talking.

'It's the completist in you,' he said. 'A good thing in a *flic*. But we can leave the sofas and things.' Darac went to a bureau shape in the corner of the room and pulled off its cover. 'There shouldn't really be anything of interest but things get missed.'

It took them just five minutes to sort through Delmas's sparse collection of documents and personal items. They left his photos until last, setting them out on a coffee table.

'No shot of Delmas in a group,' Flaco said, scanning them. 'So no clues to the gang's identity there.'

'Nor at the exhumation, earlier.'

'Did you really expect to find others alongside Sylvie in the grave, Captain?'

'Under the circumstances, anything was possible. I wasn't even sure Sylvie's remains would be there.' He shook his head at the scant pickings before them. 'These pictures are all of Delmas himself, alone.'

Flaco swiped her mobile and, bringing up Sylvie's tomb photo, held it next to a photo of her father. 'Strikingly similar, aren't they?'

'That same soft, forlorn expression, too.'

'Did you see her? In her coffin, I mean.'

Another slightly *hors-piste* remark, Darac reflected. 'I didn't see her, Flak; I saw *it* – what was left of the body. The *him* and the *her* disappear the moment you die, don't you think?'

Boldness vied with discomfort in Flaco's large, dark eyes. 'They don't so much disappear as go on, I think.'

He looked at her. 'You're a believer? That surprises me.'

'Because you take me for a "no-nonsense character".' Bolder and bolder. 'Right from *maternelle* back in Guadeloupe, people have thought of me like that. And I am, I suppose, in a lot of ways.'

Darac felt strangely moved that after eighteen months with the Brigade, Flaco was finally opening up to him. 'In my book, no nonsense trumps nonsense every time.'

'It explains why I *am* a believer, actually.'

'Yes?'

'To me, life makes no sense unless there's something more to it. What that something more *is*, though, I have no conception.'

He collected up the photos. 'So you don't buy the whole package?'

'The whole *Catholic* package?' She grinned. 'Too much voodoo in my background for that.'

'Seriously?'

'Seriously.'

'Well, there's very little voodoo in my background but I tell you what *I* believe in, Flak. I believe in your abilities as a police officer. We all do.'

Her eyes swam. Her mouth widened the merest scintilla. 'Thank you.'

He went to an armchair and grabbed a handful of cloth. 'Shall we, after all?'

A search of the soft furnishings revealed that nothing had been hidden in a cushion or a frame lining. The pair put the room back as they had found it.

'Nothing of interest in the entire apartment,' he said, closing his notebook. 'And there's no sign Delmas has been here since he got out.'

There was a loud knock at the door. The pair exchanged a look.

'Cover me,' Darac whispered. 'Just in case Carl Halevy Two is standing there.'

Flaco drew her SIG, stood firm and aimed it into the doorway. Darac drew his and concealed it behind the door as he opened it a crack and then wide. Carl Halevy Two proved to be an intelligent-looking elderly lady with wide-set cheekbones and downy white hair. With the quickness of conjurers, Darac and Flaco holstered their weapons.

'I… heard voices,' the woman said. 'I wondered if it was Monsieur Delmas.'

'You are Madame Otaphu, I believe?' Darac said. 'Monsieur Delmas's next-door neighbour? We're with the Brigade Criminelle.' He showed her his ID. 'And this is Officer Yvonne Flaco.'

'I see.'

'We were just about to knock on your door but we could talk here, if you prefer. It will only take a moment.'

'Alright.' Tentatively, as if she were trespassing, she stepped inside. 'I've never been in this room before.' She looked around. 'It's unfair to judge in its present state, I suppose. But drab, isn't it?'

'Our understanding is that Monsieur Delmas was a rather understated individual.' Darac went to remove a cover from the sofa. 'Please, sit down.'

'I'll stand, thank you. Yes, he was understated.'

'I know the other officer asked everyone in the building to contact us should Monsieur Delmas appear. To your knowledge, has anyone else been here looking for him?'

Her eyes took on a provocative glint. 'Apart from the officer who sits outside in his car all day? Apart from him, you mean?'

'Ah, but there's another one around the corner you haven't spotted.'

A throaty laugh turned into a brief coughing fit.

'Some water, madame? The supply's switched off but...' Flaco reached into her bag. The bottle was half full. 'I have Vittel.'

'*No* thank you,' she said, conveying that the prospect was an unappealing one.

'I could pour it into a cup,' Flaco said, her hackles rising, 'if you prefer.'

'No, no. I'm…' She coughed once more. 'I'm perfectly alright now.'

'I'll have a swig, if I may.' Darac held out his hand. 'I'm a little dehydrated this afternoon. Too much espresso.' He put the bottle unceremoniously to his lips and took a good mouthful. 'Thanks, Flak.'

The demonstration cut no ice with Madame. 'You ask if there has been anyone else looking for Delmas?'

'I did, yes.'

'There has. Yesterday, I heard a knock on Monsieur's door.'

'At what time would that be?'

'About five o'clock. I popped my head out to see if there was anything I could help with. But the man walked away just as I spoke.'

'Did he pass you?'

'No, he went toward the stairs rather than the lift. I didn't see his face.'

'It was definitely a *he*?'

She pursed her lips. 'I assumed so. But not necessarily when I think about it.'

'Height? Build?' asked Flaco.

'Shortish for a man; taller than average for a woman. One seventy to one seventy-five, I would say. Something like that. Of slim build.'

'What was the person wearing?'

'This is why I'm hesitating as to the gender. He or she was wearing motorcycle leathers. Or probably not leathers nowadays, are they? A two-piece riding suit, anyhow. And a helmet.'

Flaco shared a look with Darac.

'Wearing a helmet?' he said. 'On a third-floor landing?'

'Yes.'

'Colour?'

'Black, navy blue, brown – something dark.'

'Any insignia or distinguishing marks?'

'Yes, there was. At the back of the helmet, two initials I suppose it was. They were quite large but I couldn't be absolutely certain what they were.'

'Think, madame,' Darac said, a touch of impatience propelling the voice. But then he remembered his own dismal performance as an eyewitness. 'I'm sorry. If you could picture it, we would be most grateful.'

'It was either BL, RL, BI or RI. I think.'

'Thank you. That may be of great help to us.'

Darac ended the interview moments later and the pair closed up the apartment. In the subsequent door-to-door, a second resident corroborated Madame Otaphu's sighting of the mystery motorcyclist but could add nothing to her description. As they left the building, Darac and Flaco ran through the names of everyone connected with the Delmas case so far. None matched the motorcyclist's suggested initials. But at the wheel of an unmarked Renault parked opposite, the surveillance officer, Walter Peyresourde, still had his contribution to make.

First, the pair had to wake him.

26

The *petit train touristique* snaked on to Villefranche's Quai Amiral Courbet and slowed to a stop. An anomalous yet familiar sight locally, the white-painted locomotive, complete with smokestack and cowcatcher, was a pastiche of a Wild West steam engine. Things were a little more indigenous behind: its three open coaches bore destination boards reading: Porte de la Santé – Place de la Paix – Citadelle – Porte de la Santé.

The train driver's mike resembled a silver goose neck. He pulled it toward him and cleared his throat. 'Okay, folks, we've stopped right on the edge of the quay so I hope you can all swim. If you can't, my lovely assistant will dive in and save you.' The ticket girl struck a presentation pose. 'At no extra cost.'

A couple of passengers alighted; a couple boarded. It was no surprise that trade had slowed over the past hour: another Parade of Lights was due to start in the city shortly.

The driver put the engine in gear. 'I'm Alain; the young lady demanding money with menaces is Danielle. And so, taking your lives in my hands – let's go.'

One passenger seemed to enjoy the gag, anyway. Alain switched on the recorded commentary and pulled away.

On the quayside, waiters were already laying places for dinner, scurrying between tables that clung like clusters of barnacles outside each of the restaurants. Alain bantered with a couple of them as he trundled sedately past.

'*The Rade de Villefranche is considered by many to be the most beautiful bay in France*,' the commentary announced. The punters needed no such encouragement. Every face was turned toward it already.

Every face except one. Sitting at the rear of the front coach, Pierre Delmas was engrossed in a *Nice-Matin* article headlined VENCE CEMETERY SHOOTING. The page carried two police artist sketches of him: one balding with goatee, the other balding and clean-shaven. He concluded that in his disguise of the day, he looked insufficiently like either to cause him any trouble. And that was good because he had things to do and kicking his heels in police custody was not an option.

He set the paper down on the seat next to him. Ahead, a Menton-bound TGV powered easily along the embankment that described a perfect arc around the bay. All that speed. All that ease. All that freedom.

'*The Eglise St Michel boasts one of the finest tiled cupolas on the whole Côte d'Azur...*'

Prompted by the turning heads, Delmas, too, cast a glance inland. What they were looking at in particular, he wasn't quite sure. When he turned back, the ticket girl was standing in front of him, smiling and mouthing something.

'I'm sorry,' he said, taking out his earphones. 'I didn't catch that.'

'I said, "Good idea to bring an MP3 player." The recorded commentary is terrible.'

'Oh dear.' He smiled back. 'And you have to listen to it all day.'

'There are worse things.' Her eyes scudded across Delmas's newspaper. 'It's ten euros, please. But for that you can hop on and off as many times as you like.'

Delmas made no attempt to cover up the sketches as he reached into his jacket. But he kept his palm over his wallet photo of Sylvie as he took out a note. 'I have only twenty,' he said. 'Apologies.'

'That's fine.' Her eyes met his as she gave a ten in change. Her smile returned undiminished. 'Thank you and have a nice trip.'

'As atmospheric as it is beautiful, the quayside has featured in several movies…'

Putting his earphones back in, Delmas caught sight of his reflection in the driver's rear-view mirror. Once again, he rode the moment. He had no intention of making himself known. Not yet.

27

Stepping off the loft ladder brought it all back. For some moments, Julie Issert just stood breathing it in, as if the air still bore traces of the things that had happened there.

It had been one of the happiest days of her life when the purchase went through on the Saint-Sylvestre villa. Not that there had been any doubt about it. She had bought it from her cousin Liliane, who had wanted to keep the property in the family. Julie was delighted because she had known and loved the villa since she was a child. Loved it despite some unhappy times spent there.

Converted into a den-cum-playroom, the loft had been one of the key sites of her childhood, a magic faraway place just a ladder-climb away. Or it should have been. It should at least have been a place in which she, her cousin and her friends bonded. But on most occasions, it hadn't worked out that way. They played board-game marathons that Julie always won, until she'd started losing on purpose. They mounted elaborate fashion shows in which Julie, fleshily ill at ease on the catwalk, had been the butt of their whispered asides. They acted out episodes of *Charlie's Angels* in which Julie had never been allowed to play anyone but Sabrina, the part they deemed the least glamorous. After each of these humiliations, she had gone home knowing that Liliane and the others merely tolerated her. Perhaps she had been included in the first place only at the insistence of her sweet Aunt Josephine.

But now here she was. A successful businesswoman. She'd shown *them*.

It had always irritated her parents that Julie never quite seemed to fit in. Wherever she went, whatever she became part of, the girl seemed to generate a sort of centrifugal force that always propelled her to the periphery of things. Having her first period a full twelve months before any of her peers hadn't helped in this process; it had just added to the sense of her difference, her otherness. A lone butterfly circling the pupae.

Slight in stature, her brother Sebastien had nevertheless been a tower of strength during those years.

'So the little tossers went to the cinema without you. Screw them. It's their loss.'

'But Mama and Papa said…'

'Yeah, well I've got news for you. Mama and Papa don't always know best.'

Julie stepped away from the hatch entrance and started exploring. Like any family, the Isserts had acquired all manner of paraphernalia over the years. Julie had kept nothing but Sebastien's stuff. Things that reflected their shared passion for motorcycles were divided into two parts. Practical things like clothing, spare bike parts and manuals, Julie was putting to good use already. Magazines, books, memorabilia and the like were stored in the loft. Seeing it all again was a double-edged experience for her. At the time of Sebastien's death, she had been unsure if she wanted to keep it. Her feeling lately was that she ought to set aside some time for going through it all and then let it go to a collector or a club or something. Which is probably what Bastien would have wanted.

But the motorbike memorabilia wasn't the reason Julie had taken on the climb and the cobwebs. She was almost certain that she had kept... Yes, there it was. She smiled. What a card it was to play. A card that, one way or another, was sure to change things.

28

At last, the head of the parade appeared at the entrance to Place Masséna. Behind it, the heads of giants receded into the darkness. In the dignitaries' box, Laure Telonne leaned in cosily to her stepmother. 'The guy that got splatted under the float the other night? His head looked like a burst melon, they say.'

Elise Telonne stirred uncomfortably in her seat. 'The one time you sit with us… I might have known there would be a price to pay for the pleasure of your company.'

'His eyes stuck in the tyre treads. They had to scrape them out.'

Elise turned to her. 'Do you get pleasure from being so wicked, Laure?'

'That's what wickedness is for, isn't it?' A buzz went through the crowd at the roadside. She felt a pang of nostalgia. 'It's nowhere near as much fun stuck in here as it is out there.'

Flanking Laure on her other side, Jacques Telonne kept the smile on maximum as he canted his head toward her. 'I want you here where I can see you.'

Laure smiled back, mimicking him. 'Does *she* know?'

Still the smile. 'Shut up.'

'Do I know what?'

'Nothing, Mama. I'm looking forward to the music,

aren't you? I'm into guitars now, by the way.'

Laure began to laugh. At that moment, a Steadicam operator scanning the crowd appeared in front of them. Jacques Telonne joined in the laughter suddenly, giving Laure's shoulder a playful slap. What a witty girl she was! What an asset! Laure stopped laughing immediately.

To a rising crescendo of noise, the parade began to move forward. Laure could see the dragon, lolling and rearing, shaking itself and blowing smoke. Fuck that. It was the samba band she wanted to see. Years of headphone abuse had taken the edge off her hearing and she cupped her hand around her better ear to listen for a guitar she knew wouldn't be her Gibson. But she was intrigued by the boy, the one who'd gone charging off after the fat prick who'd fallen off the float. And left the SG right there under her nose. And it wasn't even his. At last, she picked up the sound of a guitar. And then she saw him. He was playing some cheapo copy. You win some, you lose some. How old was the little angel? A couple of years younger than she was. Pity. He was cute.

Oye como va, mi ritmo, Bueno pa gozar – mulata…

The dignitaries' enclosure allowed just enough space in front of the seats for dancing. If, that is, you were sufficiently intimate with your partner. Rolling his hips, Jacques Telonne stood and archly held out his hand. Elise's white-out smile matched his as she stood and took it. The self-made man and the ex-model – a moment or two of moving to the music was expected of them. Beneath the rainbow of their outstretched arms, Laure sank into her seat. The couple took a step forward and Elise started to move spectacularly around her flat-footed husband. A cheer went up from the Great and the Good. Dazzled by Elise's mastery of her art, or maybe just fooled by Jacques's hard-on persona, hardly any of them seemed to notice that only she was actually dancing.

'I want to be there,' Laure said to herself, almost throwing up with the pain of it. 'I want to be there when that *flic* plugs in his guitar.'

29

There were two phones on Darac's desk: black for internal calls, beige for outside lines. At first, he didn't hear the black phone ring. He was lost in thought. Lost and not lost – he could at last see a way into the Delmas case. A light indicated the call was from the commissaire's office.

'Got a second?' Agnès said.

Less formal. A good sign, perhaps.

As so often, he found her sitting barefoot at her desk, reading glasses halfway down her nose. Parking them over her ash-blond bob, she sat back in her chair and gestured him to sit. As he did so, she swung around and began stamping lightly on the tiles.

'Crunch, crunch, crunch – if eggshells do crunch when you tread on them. It's more of a thack, thack sound, really, isn't it?' Her eyes met his. 'There. All gone.'

Darac exhaled deeply, and ran a hand through his hair. Twice. 'Thank God. I thought I'd really—'

'The problem was all mine.'

'No, no.'

'Yes.'

'I had to point out what the gang had done.'

'Absolutely. They had a ploy and I fell for it. But it wasn't you pointing it out that got to me. Not so much, anyway.' She gave a little shrug. 'And if we hadn't got on to Delmas

immediately and retrieved the haul so quickly, I may well
have rethought the thing and put it right.'

'I'm sure you would have.'

'It was the ease with which you spotted it. That's what
got to me.'

He waited until her eyes met his. 'You taught me too
well,' he said.

Her eyes lowered. 'I suppose I've got rather used
to being thought well of over the years. By my team,
I mean. I don't care a fig what a string of *commissaires
divisionnaires* have made of me. Or a pompous oaf like
Frènes, or even a decent man like Examining Magistrate
Reboux. But if I were to lose *your* respect… I would find
that very difficult.'

'You haven't. Not for a second.'

'I know. I've just seen Frankie.'

He sat forward, keeping a straight face as he reached
for her hand. 'Agnès, I don't just respect you –' he ignored
the sound of someone tapping at the door – 'I adore you.
Almost as much as I adore Sonny Rollins.'

Half-laughing, Agnès's free hand went to her forehead.
'Oh no, no.'

'What?'

'Bé just popped her head round the door at exactly the
wrong moment. You know what that means? It's Foot-
Gate all over again.'

He thought about it. 'But I put Sonny Rollins in the
punchline.'

'She didn't hear it. She'd already scooted off.'

His mobile rang. 'Word's got round already?'

'Charvet, Captain. I've just had Villefranche on. They

thought there had been an accident but now they're saying it's one for us.'

'What happened?'

'You know the *petit train touristique* they have over there? It's gone into the harbour.'

30

The Parade of Lights may have been going full swing in the city but just a few kilometres to the east, the *petit train* disaster was drawing a fair crowd of its own. Darac nosed his Peugeot toward the quayside, tapping the horn on the off-beats to Bobby Watson's 'Love Remains'. As a dispersal measure, it was signally ineffective. Holding the horn down would probably have worked better but he'd refrained out of respect — respect for the Watson tune. He swiped his mobile. 'Who's attending, Patricia?'

'Dr Barrau, Captain.'

'Wrong answer.'

'Where are you now?'

'Almost at the Cocteau Chapel. With these crowds, I can only go at walking speed.'

'Got your roof siren?'

'Last time I put it on in a situation like this, somebody nicked it.'

It got a laugh, at least. 'You're only about forty metres away from our cordon now.'

A uniform appeared through the squeeze. He turned, and walking in front of the car, began clearing the way ahead.

'I've picked up some help, Patricia. Any problems with the quayside diners over there?'

'Some people are still dining. But they've been cleared right back. It's a good job it's not summer. They'd be right on top of us.'

'Absolutely. See you shortly.'

He restored Bobby Watson to his rightful volume and followed the uniform toward a group of officers policing the cordon. In the cleared area beyond them, Darac counted four, five, six tents – one standing alone, the other five clustered together. He could already picture tomorrow's headline: CARNAGE ON THE QUAY.

Reaching the cordon, Darac had a word for his guide. 'Thanks for the snowplough job.'

'You're welcome, Captain.'

Darac indicated the tents. 'It's *that* bad?'

'Bad enough.' The officer followed his gaze. 'Oh, I see what you mean. No, the tents grouped together is just a craft fair. We've evacuated the people.'

'Thank God for hand-thrown pots.'

The officer waved Darac through into the safe haven of the crime scene. The floodlit area was a teeming hive of activity: officers, technicians, equipment and vehicles – the *cirque du meurtre* was in town, alright.

Ahead, Darac saw the white-clad figure of Patricia signing a couple of technicians out of the red zone. At its heart stood a cube of breeze-ruffled nylon – Barrau's pathology exam tent. Darac shook his head. One minute, people were trundling around Villefranche enjoying a bit of innocent fun, the next they were being zipped into body bags. Sometimes he hated his job.

Parking as the haunting lilt of 'Love Remains' faded into silence, Darac slipped on his police armband and got out of the car. Radio messages crackled on and off around him. Darac made for the quay where the winch crew appeared to be almost ready to go, aware that all the heads in the restaurants and the apartment houses above were turned toward the action.

A voice shouted from the edge of the quay. 'Chains are on!'

'Okay. Stand by!'

Sporadic shouts and counter-shouts.

'Haul it!'

Raul Ormans joined Darac as the winch's engine faltered and then coughed into gear. The steel cable began wrapping back around its drum.

'Put those' – Ormans indicated Darac's index fingers – 'into those.' He pointed to his ears. The cable straightened above the water. 'Now.'

Having learned the hard way that it was folly to ignore Ormans' advice at such times, Darac did as he was told. A moment later, the winch engine emitted an ear-splitting screech as it took the strain and began hauling up the load. Spouting like a giant colander, the *petit train* locomotive slowly emerged from the water. Once clear, it hung for a moment and then, following another interplay of shouts, swung inexorably into position over a low-loader waiting on the quay. The loader driver started its engine, reversed a little and the docking phase of the process began. It took three attempts, but the loco was finally lowered safely into position. The winch engine relaxed.

'Safe?' Darac said, tentatively unplugging his ears.

'Safe.'

More shouts and the crew set about unhooking the chains.

Ormans indicated the locomotive 'Exhibit A. I must go and impress that fact upon the boys.'

'Hang on one second, R.O. Before I learn absolutely nothing from Barrau, what happened, roughly?'

'Bonbon's in the tent. He'll give you chapter and verse.'

'How many dead?' he called to Ormans' retreating back. 'Just one.'

Darac met Bonbon, the crime-scene photographer and several technicians coming the other way. Bonbon did not look his usual happy self.

'The wrong people die. Have you ever noticed that, chief?' His hand went to the copper frizz that was his hair. 'Mate – what a time to come out with that.'

'Hey.' He gave Bonbon's cheek a pat. 'Mama would've been the first to have agreed with you.'

'It's Barrau. He's getting worse.' Bonbon mugged the man's Dracula-like mien. '"My preliminary report will be ready within an hour of returning to the lab…"'

Darac joined in the recital: '"A full report will follow once the autopsy itself has taken place." I know. I've had just about enough of it.'

His tawny eyes round with indignation, Bonbon wasn't finished yet. 'Deanna, a world-renowned genius, *she'll* speculate at the scene – within reason. Map – he'll give you opinions you haven't even asked for. *This* bastard' – Bonbon pointed toward the tent – '*nada*. It doesn't usually get to me but today, it bloody well has.'

'This is a first, isn't it? *Me* calming *you* down.'

'Ai, ai, ai.' Bonbon produced a notebook and a striped paper bag from inside his overalls. 'Sherbet Doodah?'

'Pass. So what have we got?'

As Bonbon stuffed in the sweet and opened his notebook, Darac began scanning the cordoned-off area. It was an evocative sight. In the glare of the floodlights, officers going about their business had the look of a movie crew working on a night shoot.

'Okay – the *petit train* had finished its stint for the evening. The driver, one Alain Saxe, dropped off his ticket girl, Danielle Veron, backed the coaches into their shed behind the Gare Maritime, unhooked the loco and set off in it to Avenue Gallieni where he was going to garage it for the night. That's where he lived, also. Alone, divorced, no children.'

'Parking something like that at home? Unusual, isn't it?'

'Saxe held the franchise for the service *and* he owned the vehicle. He didn't just work for the Mairie.'

'I see.'

In a strong cross light, a shadow moved massively across the gable end of an apartment house. 'Granot's here. Go on, Bonbon.'

'A few people report seeing someone in the cab with Saxe. No description, sex unspecified. You see the biggest of those five tents? The one nearest the water?'

Darac turned. 'Yes?'

'The loco, with two aboard, passed behind it. When it emerged a moment later, there was only one aboard. Then – splash! People come running. A couple of them – a waiter and one of the diners – jump in, manage to free Saxe from the submerged wreckage, get him into that rubber dinghy, paddle it to the steps and get him back on the quay.'

A shadow fell over them.

'Alright, Granot?'

A grunted greeting.

'Was Saxe alive at that point, Bonbon?'

'Who knows? Thanks to that arsehole—'

Granot cast an eye over the exam tent. 'Barrau's on the job, then?'

'Oh yes. Thanks to him, the only pathology I can give you is what the two rescuers have already told us.'

'Which is?'

'That they thought Saxe "looked" dead. Once back on the quay, they tried to revive him anyway.'

'They felt for a pulse?'

'After a fashion. They weren't exactly on top form themselves, by then. Although it's only a few metres deep where the loco went in, it still must have been quite a production number for them.'

'I certainly couldn't have done it. Where are they now?'

'We sent them home.' Bonbon shook his head. 'There's a lot of questions here, aren't there? Did the other person in the cab with Saxe kill him before he hit the water? Did he drown—'

'You'd think that just once,' Granot said, raising an accusing finger. 'Just once, that mental midget Barrau might actually help us at the scene.'

'Fuck this, guys.' Darac strode off toward the exam tent. 'Enough is enough.'

Darac found Barrau completing a form over the dead body of the victim. The rest of the pathology team had already left.

'At last.' Barrau scrawled a signature. 'Trolley!' A couple of cheerful-looking men in whites stepped forward. 'You can take him.'

'We know within a minute or two when Saxe was killed,' Darac said. 'What killed him?'

'My preliminary report will be—'

Darac moved in close. 'We've taken this shit long enough, Barrau. You are a fucking disgrace. Give. Me. An. Opinion!'

The morgue boys froze.

Barrau looked so shocked that for a second, Darac thought he might just spill. Instead, he fixed the statues at his feet with a wide-eyed stare.

'You… you are a witness to what he just said. So are you.'

'No, I didn't catch it, sir,' the older one said.

'Me neither.'

Unzipping a body bag, the older man looked enquiringly at Darac. '*Can* we have him now – Monsieur Saxe here? Only, my wife will be getting aerated. I'm not really supposed to be on tonight.'

Barrau gave a sour little grin. 'Alright. I see.' He turned to leave. 'But you have not heard the last of this.'

Darac grabbed his arm and stopped him. 'Dr Carl Barrau, I'm placing you under arrest.'

'What?! Don't be ridiculous.'

'Captain – no!' the older man said.

Yanking his arm, Barrau tried to move off. He made no progress. 'You are making such a mistake.'

'I am placing you under arrest for refusing to assist a police officer in the course of an investigation when instructed to do so.'

Barrau's lancet-sharp eyes began to swim with uncertainty.

'Further, Doctor, I am arresting you for obstructing—'

'It was… a blow with a blunt instrument – possibly a

cosh which fractured cervical vertebra C2. Breathing and heart would have stopped almost immediately.'

'Thank you. This is how it is going to be from now on, Barrau. Understand? When I or any of my officers ask you for an opinion, you will give it. And if you run to Frènes over this, remember that I too have grounds for an official complaint.' Finally, Darac released him. 'And believe me, I will lodge it.'

Rubbing his forearm, Barrau stormed out of the tent like a reprimanded child.

Silence. The morgue boys looked at each other and then at Darac.

'Captain? That was un-fucking-believable.'

'Could you *really* have arrested him?' the younger one said.

'I could, though it wouldn't have stuck for a second and he'll realise that, I'm sure. But it would've made a stink and he must know that this stonewall approach he's been getting away with… it's not best practice, put it that way.'

'You've had your moments, Captain. We all know that. But "I'm placing you under arrest!"' He gave his younger colleague a slap on the arm. 'Brilliant!'

'Thanks for the selective hearing, guys. I owe you both one.'

'Pah,' the older one said. 'I would have paid to see that.'

Darac looked down at the body. 'Broken neck… Did Lami log Monsieur Saxe's effects in, by the way?'

'Yeah. He gave everything to Officer Lartigue.'

'Chief?'

Bonbon was standing just inside the tent entrance.

Conveying that he had only a second or two's grace, he performed an ecstatic fist pump. Then, checking behind, he calmed himself and laid an index finger over his lips.

'You should've seen it, Lieutenant...' the older man called out. A dig in the ribs from his mate made the penny drop. 'Oh, yeah. Later.'

'Mademoiselle Veron is here,' Bonbon announced. 'The young lady who worked with Monsieur Saxe on the train. She has kindly offered to identify his body for us. And she would rather do it here.'

'Just a second, Bonbon.'

No order needed to be given. As the younger one swapped a body bag for a sheet, the other readjusted the lie of Saxe's head and quickly combed his hair. The sheet in position, the boys retreated into a corner. 'Alright, Lieutenant.'

Bonbon took a pace back and smiling into the wings like a stage MC, held out an arm. Danielle Veron appeared, took his arm and looking anywhere but at the sheet, walked unsteadily forward.

A cool onshore breeze was blowing and Danielle seemed glad of the police blanket someone had draped around her shoulders.

'Let's get into my car,' Darac said. 'It's got a good heater. Would you like an espresso or something?'

'No, thanks.'

As he switched on the engine, the CD player launched into Bobby Watson's 'Blues For Alto'. Darac reached to turn it off.

'Could you leave it on, please?'

He lowered the volume a couple of notches. 'You like jazz?'

'I like music. I need something normal.'

'I know. This is weird, isn't it?'

'I can't believe it.'

He turned on the overhead light. Danielle was about twenty, with short dark hair and a lean, broad frame. Under the blanket, she was wearing a zipped jacket bearing an insignia embossed with initials.

'What does FFN stand for?'

'Oh, it's the National Swimming Federation.'

'You're a swimmer? You can see I'm a brilliant detective, can't you?'

She gave the slightest of smiles. 'I'm ranked fourth in the eight-hundred free. If you can call that being a swimmer.'

'Fourth in…?'

'The country.'

'Fourth in the whole of France? That's fantastic.'

She stopped staring at the fascia for a moment. 'The girl ranked third is only fifteen.'

'Well, good for her.'

'That's what my sponsors thought as well.'

'Ouch.'

'Exactly. I was working for Alain just while I got something sorted.'

'I can't swim at all so I'm still in awe.'

'You can't swim?'

'Not a stroke.'

She gave him a look and for a moment, Darac sensed she might offer to teach him. 'You should learn,' she said, returning her gaze to the fascia.

'Let's talk about Alain.'

Danielle told him that she'd known Saxe since she was a child. She found him a nice enough guy and a decent employer. She didn't hold it against him that he'd tried it on with her a couple of times since she'd gone to work for him – she could look after herself. She knew of no next of kin except a frail and somewhat fearful aunt. It was to save the old lady a visit to the morgue that Danielle had volunteered to identify the body.

'Where did Saxe drop you this evening?'

'By the steps under the station. I went into Nice. To the Parade of Lights.'

'The dragon up and running?'

'I think so but I left before it really got going. Somebody had a radio and once I heard what had happened here, I came straight back.'

'Please don't take this wrongly…'

Anticipating the question, she reached into the slanted pocket of her jacket and without any sort of rancour, handed him a train ticket.

'There's no barrier or anything and I hadn't thrown it away. Fortunately.'

Assuming it was hers, the time stamped on it at Nice's Gare Thiers put her out of the frame as the person who was in the cab with Saxe and then wasn't.

He handed it back. 'Thank you. Did you see anyone who knows you, by any chance? On the train?'

'Yes, I met a couple I know on the platform in Nice. We rode back together.'

He took their names. 'Did Saxe often give other people lifts in the cab? Perhaps to drop them off on his way home?'

'Not that I know of.' She sat forward and undraped the blanket from her shoulders. 'I've warmed up, thanks. It was the shock, I think. I don't usually feel the cold at all.'

'Shock does all sorts of funny things.' He took it and tossed it on to the back seat. 'Did Saxe say he was going to meet anyone after work?'

'No, he didn't.'

'Did anything happen today or over the previous days that gave you any inkling about what ultimately took place?'

'No, nothing on that scale but something strange did happen today. A man got on and sat at the back of the first carriage. Perfectly pleasant. He rode around the whole route and got off just along there at the Porte de la Santé. Next time around, he got on and did the same thing again. The tickets are hop-on hop-off so you can do that as many times as you like. On the last circuit of the day, Alain recognised him. He called him up to the front of the carriage and started talking to him as he drove on. Things started to get a bit agitated between them. And then they proceeded to have a proper row. At this point, there were only the three of us on board. Alain dropped me off. The two of them went on and that was the last I saw of him. Until just now.'

'This man. Was he sitting alongside Alain in the cab?'

'No. He was in the front carriage.'

'Definitely not in the cab?'

'No, but as I say, he was still on board when I got off. I don't know what he might have done afterwards.'

'Can you describe him?'

'Uh… tall, quite a big man all round. Fleshy face. His

eyes – I don't know why I noticed this – but they were deep set and close together.'

'Danielle, would you open the glove compartment? And take out the photo. The one on top.'

She looked at it. 'That's him,' she said.

31

It had been a long night after a long day and it wasn't over yet. Agnès had already gone home, but not before addressing the squad room on two contentious issues. She'd gone over the various mistakes she had made on the So-Pro investigation, and she had supplied the context to her latest *in flagrante delicto* encounter with Darac. Her complete candour had eased Granot's mind in particular over the old case, and her way with a story had taken everyone's mind off the rumours about herself and Darac.

Darac scanned the faces all around him as he took over the session. Few would have made the cover of *Health and Vitality* magazine. He glanced at his watch. Twenty-one hours straight, he'd been working. Parting the high rises of espresso cups populating his desk, he parked his backside on it and yawned.

'Let's give it another half-hour, shall we? And then we can stagger off home. Providing we can remember where home is.' Behind him, a whiteboard headed with Alain Saxe's name was set alongside those of Michel Fouste and Carl Halevy. Darac pointed to them in turn. 'All three are dead. Dead within three days of Pierre Delmas's release from prison. So all three were members of the So-Pro gang with him. Discuss.'

Settling in for one last push, Bonbon sat sideways in his chair and draped his legs over the arm. 'On the deaths themselves, the first one looks like a classic see-what-you-expect-to-see thing, right? Because Fouste was blind drunk and belligerent, no one suspected he'd only started to barge into people because he'd spotted someone he was desperate to get away from: the very pleasant and polite gentleman we now know as Pierre Delmas. Fouste made it as far as the front float in the parade.' Bonbon put his hands together in the manner of a diver. 'Whoooosh! And that was the end of him. Carl Halevy we've discussed at length and we know how he died. And now tonight, thanks partly to an eyewitness account by the wonderful Mademoiselle Danielle Veron, Delmas is squarely in the frame for the murder of Alain Saxe. And that's a definite escalation because the first two deaths were accidental, fundamentally.'

'Indeed.' Darac got to his feet. He wrote the name Artur Rigaud on a flipchart headed AI SECURITY and sank back on his desk. 'Artur's the maintenance man at the firm's HQ. When I interviewed him, he posed an interesting question: "Where would someone like Pierre Delmas meet a *gang*?" he said. Granot, you've spoken to Artur, as well. What do you reckon?'

'The trouble is that we know so little about Delmas.' On the desk in front of him was a stack of files, mostly thin. 'Until So-Pro, he seems to be one of these people who just ghosts through life.'

Perand was sitting slumped forward on his desk as if waiting for a back massage. 'That's implied in Artur's question, isn't it?'

'Partly, yes.' Granot closed one file and opened another. 'Take the child, Sylvie. Delmas fathers her with a woman who gives her up to the Sisters of Mercy at birth and then the mother dies not long after. Sylvie has no other relatives. According to the convent, Delmas never once visited or wrote to the girl. It looks as if she, like the authorities, had no idea who her father was. Neighbours at his apartment building have very little to say about Delmas except Madame Otaphu, who doesn't really know him but has an opinion on everything, it seems. Then, there's A1, the company for which he worked for twenty years. Apart from Artur, no one has anything significant to report. Vis-à-vis his idea that the gang may also have worked at the firm – a plausible idea on the face of it – we've moved on from that now we have Fouste, Halevy and Saxe, none of whom have ever worked for A1.'

'We *may* have moved on from A1,' Darac said. 'But I'm assigning it to the back burner rather than forgetting about it altogether. There's something about that set-up I don't like.'

Granot sniffed. 'Up to you. Prior to his release, I've got nothing that links Delmas to Fouste, Halevy and Saxe. But I have come up with something that links *them*. It's a bit...' Granot made a so-so gesture with his hand. 'But all three have worked in construction at one time or another. The jobs they did might have fitted them for tunnelling, digging and so on.'

Her head propped on the heel of her hand, Flaco looked up from her note-taking. 'So Halevy wasn't always an accounts manager for a lift company?'

'No, he'd done all sorts.'

Darac gave him a look. 'They ever work for the same outfit?'

'Loosely – different parts of the Telonne empire. I'm checking but it seems they may well have worked at the Rue Lamora site at the same time. I know a lot of the city's hard hats *did*. But it would be something.'

While the debate continued around him, Darac sat back in his chair, ideas chasing one another around his head like a series of chord progressions. After several stalled choruses, one of them took flight and kept going. He was about to run it past the team when a junkie wearing torn jeans hustled into the room.

'Out on the prowl in a minute, guys.' Armani winked at Bonbon and sat down. 'But I couldn't hit the streets without catching the latest instalment of "Captain Busy Hands and the Delmas Case".'

'Sorry, mate.' Darac gave him a rueful look. 'There's only Delmas left. We've been all through the other thing already.'

'Already?' Armani bore the expression of a dog who's just seen its dinner whisked away. 'It's no fun here any more.'

'Want to stay?'

'I'll give it ten minutes. Excite me.'

'I just might be able to. I *think* I've got something.'

Like a magnet passing under iron filings, these words made everyone in the room sit up. Even Perand.

'It takes us only part of the way but what do we think of this? Pierre Delmas suffers from NCL, a terminal condition that has usually proved fatal by the age he is now. One of the few things people have had to say about him is that he's quiet, respectful, even proper. We don't know the how and why of his fathering of Sylvie—'

'I'll tell you all about that later,' Armani said. 'It's catching on, they say.'

'Shhh!' Flaco said, before she'd thought about it.

Amused at her uncharacteristic cheek, Armani made a *mea culpa* gesture. 'I humbly apologise, ma'am. Carry on, Darac.'

'We don't know at what point Delmas knew of Sylvie's existence. You'd imagine it might have been the moment her mother knew she was pregnant, but it could have been years later. Sylvie might even have been in her teens by then. Whatever, let's say Delmas wanted to make amends for missing out on her childhood.' Eyebrows raised, he looked from face to face. 'Make amends in the little time he thought he had left. Can you see where this might lead and what sense it makes of some of the other things we know?'

Bonbon clicked his fingers. 'I can see where it starts.'

The half-smile that so often played around Darac's lips widened a little. 'Go on, Bonbon.'

'To set up his neglected daughter with a trust fund, Delmas dreams up a scheme to rob A1's biggest banking client, So-Pro. Or perhaps someone comes to him with the scheme. Either way, he's vital to it and he's in. Three members of the gang that eventually pull the robbery are Fouste, Halevy and Saxe. All the stuff you've shown about the direction of tunnelling et cetera is there to convince Agnès of Delmas's part in it. He was the willing fall guy…'

The sound of pennies dropping all around the room heralded a free-for-all.

'Bonbon's got the floor,' Darac called out, quietening the hubbub. 'Carry on.'

'Delmas is the willing fall guy because he expects to live only a short time in prison. All that matters to him is that his share of the haul goes to Sylvie. In the end, the haul was seized so she never got it.' As he warmed to his theme, the rapid Catalan clatter of Bonbon's Perpignan accent became more and more extreme. 'That's Variation From The Plan Number One. Variation Number Two is that, defying all expectation, Delmas doesn't die shortly after going to prison. He serves his term and out he comes. So he naturally seeks out the gang. Now *we*... Hang on, let me get this straight.' Bonbon stared at the ceiling for a moment. When he continued, his delivery gave way to something more *adagio* and deliberate. 'Yes – we originally thought there was no connection between Halevy and Fouste because Halevy had been waiting at the cemetery for Delmas the morning *before* he met up with Fouste at the Parade of Lights. Therefore Halevy's attempted shooting of Delmas couldn't have been a case of revenge. Maybe Halevy, who everyone has described as a nervous individual, went along on that first morning simply to check on Delmas. But maybe, fearing exposure, he'd intended to kill him all along. Hearing of Fouste's death at the carnival can only have strengthened his resolve.'

Flaco held up her hand. 'But as the captain said, Delmas could've shopped the gang at any time while he was in prison.'

Perand gave an almost Granot-like grunt. 'Yeah, he could've *shopped* them. But he couldn't have *iced* them from his cell, could he? Not personally, anyway.'

'I think we've all been forgetting something,' Darac said. 'Ask yourselves why Delmas might *want* to kill the members of the gang.'

Tapping his watch, Granot mugged, *It's obvious now, isn't it?*

'Because of what they did to Sylvie,' Bonbon said. 'And didn't do.'

Darac nodded. 'Exactly. What we were failing to grasp is the significance of the false bank statement and the double burial.'

Granot hauled himself on to his feet. 'And that kind of oversight is a sure sign we're too tired to carry on and should all go home to bed. Preferably separately.'

'Well, we've got squads out looking for Delmas,' Darac said. 'We've got media up and running. We've got Lartou and co. looking at CCTV and stuff from tourists' cameras.' He stood, stretching out his back. 'That can all go on without us. Let's call it a day, a night, or whatever it is.'

Around the room, computers were shut down, shoulder bags and rucksacks were dragged out from under desks, chairs were scraped back. Everyone was on the move except Armani. He'd had his dinner whisked away. Now he saw his nightcap following it.

'You can't leave it there. It was just getting good. What did the gang do to Sylvie? Or not do?'

'They cheated her out of four hundred thousand euros. Delmas goes to jail, believing he's not going to come out, happy in the knowledge that he's finally done something right by his daughter. I think we got so fixated on the idea of the gang not being able to divide up the spoils of the robbery that we didn't consider other possibilities. One is that Delmas might have negotiated a flat fee with them beforehand – to get them into the vault and out again. And it was *that* sum that was earmarked for Sylvie. But it never reached her.'

Granot paused in the doorway. As bleary-eyed as he felt, he couldn't resist putting in a last two cents' worth.

'The agreement was that Delmas alone would go down for the robbery, and he stuck to his side of it. Delmas knew he couldn't run the four hundred thousand through his own bank account before transferring it to Sylvie's or the State would have seized it. So he asked the gang, who were completely unknown to the police, to pass on the fee for him. They didn't, as we've seen, but they tricked up a bank statement bearing her name in order to convince Delmas they had.' Granot gave the squad room a ceremonial wave. 'And now I bid you all goodnight.'

'And the trickery didn't end there, did it?' Bonbon said. 'But you tell them about that, chief. I'm going to escort my young friend here off the premises.'

Granot harrumphed. 'I think I can just about make it to the exit myself.'

'Don't want you collapsing with fatigue, though, do we? If *you* block a gangway, none of us is going home.'

'See you tomorrow, boys.' Darac turned to Flaco, Armani and Perand as he picked up his bag. 'Sure you three have got it?'

Flaco switched off her desk lamp. 'Think so, Captain.'

Perand nodded. 'Yeah, yeah.'

'Armani?'

'Go for it.'

'Alright. Someone with four hundred grand in the bank

isn't likely to have had the sort of funeral referred to by the undertaker as a "plywood and niche job". The gang believed that the terminally ill Delmas would die in prison and never discover what they had done. It wasn't until they learned that, against all the odds, Delmas was going to serve out his prison term, and therefore might well discover the truth, that they dragged the poor girl's remains off her shelf and reburied them in the Arc du Triomphe. And it might have worked but for the intervention of Carl Halevy.'

Armani put his arm around Darac's shoulder as they filed out into the corridor. 'Know something? I don't blame Delmas. Wanting to kill them, I mean. So would I.' His face a mask of outrage, he pressed the thumb and fingertips of his free hand together and shook it. 'Halevy was a nervous one, right? He didn't want to take any chances the reburial scam wouldn't work. If that arsehole hadn't tried to kill Delmas, the man might never have realised the bastards had cheated him. And now three of them are dead. Good! Let's hope he gets the others!'

Darac gave him a look. 'But how many more of them are there? Two? Five? Ten? And maybe some of them didn't go for this part of the plan.'

'A gang is a gang.'

Without waiting for a response, Armani kissed Darac and Flaco on the cheek, shook Perand's hand, and then, talking animatedly to himself, hustled away to his night shift in the city.

Perand looked a little slighted. 'It's a story of cheats, this case. Cheats and deception. Delmas and the gang deceive Agnès, the gang cheat Delmas and Sylvie, Delmas cheats death…'

Flaco seemed unimpressed. 'Isn't that the nature of all crime?'

They had reached Darac's office.

'I'll leave you two to continue that one,' he said. 'Good work today.'

The pair carried on the debate as they headed off home.

Darac felt exhausted by the time he finally took the steps down into the compound. It was a spectacularly starry night. Or was he just seeing stars? He closed his eyes. And could still see them. Lungfuls of cool night air failed to revive him and his mind began to wander as he headed for the parking lot, wander almost as if in a dream.

'Night, Captain.'

'Oh – night, Mireille.'

People were criss-crossing the compound: coming on shift, going off shift; sweeping headlights, flaring tail-lights; it was a busy, blurry scene. And then he saw Frankie walking ahead of him, held like a stage performer in a cone of following light. She looked as tired as he felt and she lived in La Turbie, a good twenty-minute drive over dark, precipitous roads. It was not a terrain in which to fall asleep at the wheel. He resolved to catch up with her in the parking lot.

'Hi, Captain.'

'Oh, hi, Cabriet.'

'You playing tonight?'

'What day is it?'

'Thursday.'

'We're playing.'

'Might see you at the club.'

'Thanks, man.'

Darac continued, his tiredness increasing with every leaden step. Ahead, Frankie disappeared into a patch of shadow. Disappeared to the point of invisibility. His mind was not so much wandering now as galloping, galloping far and wide and further still. Frankie may appear to be invisible… Could you *appear* to be invisible? But she would still *be* beautiful. Wouldn't she? Yes. It had been proven that reality existed independently of the observer. What did they call that? There was a name for it. In any case, Frankie would always be beautiful because her looks were only part of the story. There was a name for that, too.

He paused, took a deep breath and then another. He began to come round a little.

Frankie…

He had always felt more than everyday friendship for her. But during the four years he'd lived with Angeline, seeking an illicit love affair with anyone was the last thing on his mind. Lately, he'd been wondering if Frankie had ever felt more than just friendship for him. If he were being honest, he'd never detected any real sign of it.

Beauty…

If they worked together long enough, detectives got to know almost everything about their closest colleagues. Traditionally, the bigger revelations happened during overnight stakeouts. Sitting side by side for hours in the dark lent itself to sharing confidences like few situations in life. It was on one such night that Darac learned Frankie didn't think she was at all beautiful. She saw herself as too short, too broad in the hips, too heavy in the breasts. After a couple of hopelessly bland rebuttals, Darac had been on the verge of saying: *Look, Frankie, you're gorgeous, alright?*

when shots rang out and the topic had been shelved.

Perceptions…

Angeline had once asked him to describe his colleagues using just one word. The purpose, although he hadn't tumbled to it at the time, wasn't only to gain meaningful insights into *them*; it was to expose the underpinnings of *his* assumptions and attitudes.

'Okay – in one word, give me… Granot.'

'Gruff. Painstaking—'

'No, no. Just one word. The distilled essence of the man.'

'Indomitable.'

'Bonbon?'

'Bonbon in just one word? Impossible.'

'Indulge me.'

'Alright… Sweet.'

'Frankie?'

'Beautiful.'

What a faux pas. Answering 'womanly' would scarcely have triggered a more searching examination of his attitudes. Adding that he'd meant it in a complete sense had only made matters worse. But that was then.

Finally, he reached the parking lot. 'Hey, Frankie.'

Frankie turned. And yawned. 'Excuse me… Hey, yourself.'

'You're not going to drive all the way to La Turbie in that state, are you?'

'No, I was thinking of taking a room at the Negresco.' Making combs of her hands, she drew her hair back from her forehead and kept them in place. 'Or perhaps a suite.'

'I've got a spare bed, you know.'

'Which, following a fumbling exchange, we'll naturally both climb into.'

The scripted response was, 'Naturally.' Regulation kisses of parting would then follow and they would go their separate ways. An alternate play was to enquire after her husband, Christophe, a designer who was often away on business. Christophe was a bright man. A good man. A man who deserved consideration. A man, Darac felt quite suddenly, who had been given quite enough consideration over the years.

'Yes, Frankie.' He looked into her eyes. 'I would love you to come home and sleep with me.'

She looked fully awake, suddenly. 'What?'

'Come home with me,' he said. 'To bed.'

One hand went to her forehead, the other to her hip. 'God, after all this time, you come out with this *now*?'

'Well, I… The time just seems right, somehow.'

She stared away, shaking her head. 'I don't believe it.'

'What don't you believe? That I have feelings for you? And have done for some time?'

'Feelings for me?' She bit her lip. 'Why do you think I left your team four years ago? Huh?'

The question perplexed him. 'I thought it was to take on a new challenge. That's what you said.'

She moved in close, her eyes wide. 'Well, I lied! Okay? I left because my feelings for *you* were getting out of control.'

The words exploded like a stun bomb between them.

It was Darac who finally spoke. 'I wish I had realised that.'

'You are a great detective, I must say…' She exhaled as if the breath had been held in ever since that time. She took his hand. 'Paul, back then, I would have given anything to have heard you say these things. But now, it's…'

His turn to exhale deeply. 'All too late?'

'Yes.' Her brow lowered. 'Perhaps.' She shook her head. 'Perhaps not. I don't know.'

'Keep that thought, will you?'

'Which one?'

'The one that says there may be hope.'

'I will keep it. But in any case…' She closed her eyes. 'What am I trying to say?' She had it. 'If somehow our circumstances changed and we found ourselves in a different place, I wouldn't want it to begin like *this*. At the end of a ridiculous day when we're both dog tired and our judgement is all to—'

'Cock?'

She laughed. 'Yes.'

He kissed her hand, and held her for a moment. 'You alright to drive now?'

'Believe me, my eyes closing for a second on the way home is no longer an option. Or even when I *get* home, come to—' Her brows rose, propelled, it seemed, by a horribly disconcerting thought. 'What just happened. That wasn't your way of ensuring I wouldn't go off the road?'

'No, Frankie. It wasn't.'

They embraced, and went in for regulation kisses of parting. But they didn't part and after a moment, there was nothing regulation about it.

32

For the past eight years, a buzzer had roused Pierre Delmas from sleep. The crowing of a solitary cockerel was proving a far more agreeable alarm. Or it had, until today.

With shaking hands, he eased down the volume on his MP3 player and lay back on the pillow. The bedroom ceiling was Artexed. It wasn't the kind of thing that would normally be considered fascinating but as the minutes ticked by, it came to command Delmas's entire attention. He knew he had to snap out of it, that he had to sit up, take notice, and then swing his legs out of bed. But for the moment, it was beyond him. All he could manage was to stare up at the infinite ice floes of low-relief ripples drifting in and out of focus above him. It was like floating in an endless, timeless waste. It was an inhospitable place but as long as Delmas kept thinking that, he was safe.

He'd had bouts of depression in prison. There was never any warning. He would go to bed feeling no more than frustrated, guilty and anxious, but it was as if the condition stole into his cell like an overnight fog and refused to lift with the light of day. It presaged feelings of numbness and flatness, a relatively lively state compared to the world of non-feeling that lay beyond.

The fog had rolled in again last night. He knew that if he didn't fight it, it would slowly and surely erase his world until nothing of any substance remained. Nothing left to react to. Nothing to connect with.

The ceiling was disappearing.

A dagger twisted in his temple. Jolted sickeningly into life, images of Sylvie's grave came to him, releasing a stream of increasingly powerful feelings. Sector by sector, the ice world of the ceiling began to reappear as the depression lifted. Thanking God for pain and for anger, Delmas got out of bed. For the time being, he was alright. That was good. Because there was still a lot to get through.

33

Yvette Halevy peered around the frame of her living-room window. On the hill, the toy-like fort of Haut-de-Cagnes was picking up the morning's first fingers of sun.

'I need protection,' she said into the phone. 'But I can't go to the police, can I? I'm not supposed to know anything.'

'You won't have to go to the police, sweetie.' The voice was playing hide and seek with the metallic blurt of pneumatic drills. 'They'll come to you.'

'I am not your sweetie. What am I supposed to tell them?'

All she heard of the reply was a threadbare crackle of odd syllables. 'I can't hear a thing. Where are you?'

'Where I've been most of my life, darling,' Walter Picot said. 'At the bottom of a big fucking hole. Hang on.'

Yvette took a brisk drag of her Gauloise. And another. Picot came back on the line.

'Can you hear me now?'

'Yes. What am I supposed to say to them?'

'Tell them the truth. You don't know anything about it. Full stop.'

Yvette filled her lungs with the last of the cigarette and ground it into an ashtray.

'Look, it was easy on that first day – I *didn't* know what Carl, the imbecile, had been up to. But since you passed on your suspicions, I cannot un-know them, can I? I'm no actress.'

'No? Let me tell you something. Every woman's an actress. There isn't one…'

Yvette opened her fingers and the handset dropped like a hanged man to the floor. Watching it turn on the end of its cord, she felt like kicking it. *What have I done to deserve this? What have I done to have to listen to this garbage?* She took a moment to recover, then locking her eyes on the toy fort on the hill, prepared to do battle once more.

'…In fact, Yvette, you could be acting now. I wouldn't put it past you to have been part of the So-Pro gang yourself. Probably as the brains.'

'Don't be ridiculous.'

'Is it so ridiculous? You've got bigger balls than Carl ever had. And you're a lot cleverer.'

'So is a worm. On both counts.' She swiped the air. 'Look – forget this rubbish. Tell me what to say to the police.'

'Have it your way. I would tell them that as the widow of Carl Halevy, the man who tried to kill this Pierre Delmas guy, you're concerned he may come after you.'

Yvette withdrew from the window. 'Why would the police believe Delmas would come after me? I had nothing to do with the shooting.'

'Delmas's not right in the head, is he? Haven't you read the paper? He might do anything. Tell the police that.'

'Well, it's something, I suppose.'

The doorbell rang. Her hand went to her throat. 'Someone's here. At the door.'

'Well, go and see who it is.'

'Yes – "go and see". I'm not used to this!'

'*Don't* go, then.'

She padded quietly up to the door and put her eye to the spy-hole. A pig-faced individual with a shaved scalp was holding up an ID. She dropped her voice to a whisper. 'It's the police.'

'Better than a nut job with a sawn-off. Just remember what I told you the other day and what I said just now and you'll be fine. Sweetie.'

Setting her chin, Yvette Halevy cursed the man all the way to the door.

34

It was a cool, bright morning as Darac took the up-ramp and nosed into Boulevard Risso. In the car, Satie's 'Gnossiennes' drifted from Richard Galliano's accordion like slowly vaporising breath.

Rush-hour traffic sometimes moved with reasonable speed along the boulevard. Today, it was pouring like molasses from a narrow-necked bottle. But Darac was in no hurry. He had the beauty of local boy Galliano's playing to listen to. And he had Frankie to think about. Yes, everything was on hold between them. Yes, it was possible, even probable, that it would stay that way. But he had kissed her and she had kissed him back and that had felt very, very good.

In the cold light of day, thinking about her husband, Christophe, felt far less good. As he slowed to a halt behind the Renault in front of him, further reflection was interrupted by his mobile.

'Marco. How are you feeling, man?'

'Fine. All the more so for hearing from Sticks last night.'

Rama 'Sticks' N'Pata was a former drum student of Marco's, and for a short time in his absence, his deputy in the Didier Musso Quintet.

'Sticks? How's he doing?'

A full-scale row was starting to develop in the Renault. Darac kept an eye on the two men as he listened.

'Brilliantly. Touring Canada with the septet at the moment. And they've got a couple of New York gigs coming up. Iridium and ker-tish! The Blue Note.'

Darac's smile was broad. He had a special place in his heart for the young drummer. 'He had a good teacher, they tell me.'

'The best. So you got the Gibbo back?'

It was turning ugly in front.

'Just a second, Marco.'

Still stopped in the traffic, Darac got out of his Peugeot and walked forward. He knocked hard on the Renault's nearside window.

'What do *you* want?'

'To arrest you two if you give me any more concerns.' He showed his ID. 'Everything alright here?'

'Course it fucking is,' the passenger said. He shared a look with the driver. 'Jesus.'

The traffic began to move. Horns blared behind. Having given the men a common enemy, Darac assessed he'd taken the heat sufficiently out of the row. 'I'll be watching.' He got back into the Peugeot. 'Sorry about that, Marco. Yeah, I got the SG back.'

'I tell you, Freddy was so relieved.'

'Sweet kid. Really promising player, too. From the little I heard.'

'Would you consider taking him under your wing?'

'He's got a teacher already, surely?'

All seemed harmonious in the Renault as it took the turn for the Palais des Sports.

'We use a couple of guitar guys at JAMCA. Both are good but one's only a kid himself, more or less, and the other has a couple of weak spots. One of them is improvisation and that's your strongest.'

'Thanks for asking, Marco, but I really can't. I can barely find the time to play, myself.'

'Understood. Shame, though. There's nothing so rewarding as nurturing talent. And the kids are great, you know. Most of them.'

'Besides, I don't know what I could pass on to Freddy. Or to any student, come to that. When I play, I just do everything I can think of. Not much of an approach for a teacher.'

'You know more core stuff than you realise. A lot more. For instance…'

Marco spent a good couple of minutes highlighting Darac's skills as an all-round player and his potential as a tutor. He made a pretty good case.

'Thanks, man, but I just can't see it.'

'I'll get you on board yet.'

Reaching the Caserne, he exchanged nods with the barrier man and rolled into the compound. 'I've decided to use the SG at tonight's gig, by the way. On a couple of numbers, anyway.'

'I loved the sound of the thing at the Parade. Before I took a header off the float.'

'I'd abandon plans to reprise that this evening. There'll be no Erica to tend your wounds this time.'

'Erica! Oh, my Lord. What a sweet… technician.'

Darac could almost see Marco's expression – eyes on stalks as in a cartoon.

'Yes, she is.'

'You haven't got her phone number, have you? Having a bit of a software issue with my MacBook.'

'She doesn't make house calls.' Darac pulled into his space. 'Especially to play around with horny old drummers' laptops.'

'Pity. And less of the old.'

'Got to go now, Marco. See you tonight.'

'Bring Erica, anyway.'

Darac caught up with Granot outside Building D. The man seemed to be in one of his less expansive moods.

'Will you co-ordinate things this morning, Granot?' They started up the steps. 'I've got a load of stuff for the Palais to deal with first.'

The big man gave a shrug only a degree or two into the affirmative.

'Thanks. I had nothing in overnight, by the way.'

'I'm pleased to hear *that*.'

'Alright, Granot – let's hear it. What's up?'

'I called in at the canteen on my way home last night. Just briefly. When I got to my car, I saw you. And Frankie.'

They paused on the landing.

'Did you?'

'Joking around about rubbing Agnès's feet, holding her hand and so on – that's funny. And it's good for morale.'

Darac stared out toward the street. A lecture was the last thing he needed.

'Having an affair with a fellow officer?' Granot shook his head. 'Doesn't work. Particularly when one of the pair is spoken for.'

'Have you finished?'

'Don't worry, I won't tell anyone. But it's better to stop it, believe me.'

'There's nothing to stop. For the foreseeable future, at least.'

'That's not what it looked like. If you two go any further, it'll be Pandora's box time. Anything and everything could come out.'

'You're a friend, Granot.' Darac punched in the door code. 'But one more comment and I'm going to have to tell you to mind your own damn business.'

Bzzzzzzzut!

Granot's expression remained fixed as they entered the building.

Darac went to his desk recalling the conversation he'd had with his father in the hotel bar. He knew he'd been arsey with him about his relationship with Julie Issert. Darac understood Martin's reaction better, now. The three of them were having dinner soon. He'd already made his mind up to cut them both some slack; now, he felt inclined to go a little further. Above all else, he knew his mother would never have wished a life without love on anyone, especially Martin.

Halfway to his espresso machine, the black desk phone rang.

'Charvet, Captain. I've got Monsieur Jacques I-want-to-be-mayor Telonne on the line. Well, his PA, but he's waiting to talk to you.'

'What the hell does he want?'

Bonbon walked into the office. Darac raised an invisible cup to his lips and pointed at the machine. Bonbon nodded.

'Shall I tell her you're in, Captain?'

'Yes, go for it.'

'I think it's lovely,' Bonbon said, as Darac waited for the connection. He picked up a couple of cups. 'You and Frankie.'

'Captain Darac? Jacques Telonne. How are you today?'

'Fine. Could you just hang on one second, monsieur?'

'Of course.'

Darac smothered the mouthpiece. 'How do you—?'

'Saw you in the car park. About time. The two of you are made for each other.'

'Granot saw us, too. He's revolted at the thought.'

'I'll tell you why some other time.' Bonbon began grinding the beans for two espressos. 'Of course, it's a shame about Christophe. Nice man. Kind. Bit safe, though, isn't he? Secure. Unlikely to stop a bullet designing a new font or a food mixer.'

'So you don't approve, either?'

Whether Bonbon was genuinely affronted or just feigning it, Darac couldn't tell.

'Of course I approve. On a personal level, that is. On a *practical* level…' Pressing his lips together, he canted his head almost to the horizontal. 'Tricky.'

'Look, there's nothing really going on.'

'No?'

'I should get back to this call. It's Jacques Telonne.'

Bonbon's mouth formed an upside-down U. 'What does he want? Put it on speaker.'

Darac flicked the switch. 'Sorry, monsieur. Go on.'

'Not at all, Captain. Principally in my role as chairman – oh, don't tell my wife I called myself that – my role as *chair* of the carnival committee, I was just ringing to express

my pleasure at the return of your instrument. Your amnesty
idea worked perfectly, I hear.'

'Yes, we were lucky.'

'So did you really have no cameras running or anything?
When the guitar was handed in?'

'No, nothing.'

'A man of your word. I like that. And the guitar was
undamaged, I hope?'

'It was.'

'The case, too?'

'You seem inordinately interested in this thing,
monsieur?'

'Well, I was blamed for its theft, indirectly. If you recall
my on-the-spot interview on TV.'

'We've been watching it over and over,' Bonbon said,
sotto voce.

'A drunk falls under a float and who is responsible for
the subsequent crime wave? Jacques Telonne, that's who.'

'It's a shame.'

'It is absolutely a shame. But my main concern, obviously,
was that you got your instrument back and in good
condition.'

Darac shared a look with Bonbon but then he had a
pleasingly wicked thought. 'Actually, I'll be playing the very
same guitar at the Blue Devil club tonight. Why not come
along? You'll love it and you'll be able to see for yourself all
is well.'

'Uh… Ye-es.'

Darac grinned. He could practically hear Telonne's heart
sinking into his flat feet. 'Well, I never have been to the
Blue Devil.'

'Then you should! But just to warn you – there won't be much in it for you campaign-wise.' Bonbon gave Darac a thumbs-up. 'Not many votes in the jazz audience.'

'Captain Darac.' The voice was full of pain. 'That is an unjust accusation.'

'I'm deeply sorry. So – eight-thirty, then?'

'Yes. Definitely.' A politician's promise. 'It's a date.'

Darac hung up. 'I'll lay you two to one he doesn't show.'

'No bet here.'

Darac's eyes met Granot's as he waded into the room and stayed on them as he beached in his usual chair. 'So do we need to clear the air?'

'I stand by what I said but that's an end to it as far as I'm concerned.'

'Alright with me.'

'Is that coffee I see, hear and smell?'

'Yeah, yeah,' Bonbon said. 'I'll do another.'

'Updates.' Granot flipped open his notebook. 'One: no one's seen Delmas. Two: Lartou has found nothing useful on CCTV or on punters' cameras from last night. Three: there's no sign of Alain Saxe's mobile.'

'The diver's report in yet?'

'Yes, she didn't come up with anything. Neither did the house search team. Nor did they find anything obviously linking Saxe to So-Pro or to any other criminal activity, come to that. Erica's taken delivery of his home computer just now. She might turn up something.'

Darac ran a hand through his hair. 'I might go over to Saxe's place later.'

'And finally – ' Granot's notebook made a little slapping sound as he snapped it shut – 'Madame Halevy's been interviewed again. Genuinely doesn't know anything about hubby's likely membership of the So-Pro gang.' He essayed a smile. 'According to that brilliant interrogator, *Lieutenant* Christian Malraux.'

Bonbon handed Darac his espresso. 'You assigned *him*?'

'I thought my front-liners had seen quite enough action with Madame. Besides, Cagnes is Malraux's territory, strictly speaking.'

'Doing things by the book now?' Bonbon shrugged as he wrapped himself around a chair. 'Well, it's worth a try, I suppose. Nothing else is working.'

The beige desk phone rang. Darac reached over and picked up.

'Is that Captain Darac?'

'Speaking.'

'This is Pierre Delmas.'

'Monsieur Delmas?' Darac clicked his fingers at Bonbon. 'Uh… we've been looking forward to talking to you.' Bonbon was already on his mobile. 'You wouldn't be a hoax caller, would you, monsieur? We do get them from time to time.'

'I'll give you my social security number.'

Darac picked up a pen. Where was his notebook? Moving with surprising speed, Granot opened his own and set it in front of him.

Darac took down the number. 'The line isn't great – let me repeat that back to you.' It was a delaying tactic, of course, but the caller listened patiently.

'That is correct, Captain.'

Granot pointed to an entry in his notebook. The number tallied.

'Well, how have you been, Monsieur Delmas?'

'Not too well, lately.'

The techniques of keeping suspects talking on the phone varied according to the situation. On hearing Delmas's voice, Darac concluded that chatting slightly off-piste might offer the best way forward. 'I'm sorry to hear that. NCL is horrible, I know. By a strange coincidence, my niece has the condition, too – Ella.' It was as good a name as any. 'You perhaps know her from the Marseille clinic? She's a patient of Dr Scalette. Poor kid. I don't need to tell you how excruciating the headaches can be.'

Keeping his mobile to his ear, Bonbon tapped Darac on the shoulder and nodded – the trace request was in. Darac put his phone on speaker. 'And all the other aches and pains, of course.'

'It can be unpleasant, Captain, but I won't have to endure it for much longer.'

Granot shared a look with Bonbon. A wanted man phoning in unhurriedly, revealingly? It wasn't the usual pattern.

'We have the same worries about Ella, of course,' Darac continued. 'Very difficult.'

'Actually, Captain, I didn't call to give you an update on my condition or to discuss your niece's. And I need to be brief.'

Darac caught Bonbon's eye. He shook his head – no lead on the trace as yet. 'May I just say that all of us here understand completely why you killed Saxe. The gang cheated you, didn't they? There isn't an officer here who wouldn't have done the same. Killed Alain Saxe, I mean.'

'Is that what you think?'

'You must admit that everything seems to point to it.

For one thing, you were seen talking to Saxe on the *petit train* moments before he was killed. But I think we should talk about this in person, don't you? We've been over to Villeneuve-Loubet a couple of times but we haven't been able to…' Down the line, he heard a sound in the background. Faint at first, it built into a thunderous roar as he continued. 'Sorry, yes, we haven't been able to find you in.' He made an emphatic face at Granot, alerting him. 'So where are you flying off to? Somewhere exotic?'

'You have sharp ears, Captain.'

Mouthing 'I'm on it', Granot swiped his mobile and bustled out into the corridor.

Darac smothered the mouthpiece and called to his retreating back. 'One unit to the airport, one to A1 Security – their HQ is directly opposite.' He continued to Delmas. 'I enjoy city breaks, myself. In three or four days, you don't really get to know a place but you can do more than just scratch the surface. So where are you going?'

'Do you think I would actually try such a thing at the moment?'

'You of all people know how slack airport security can be. I bet you'd find a way.'

'Captain, I may not be functioning at my best but I am not an idiot.'

'I know you're not, monsieur. Did you have any problems getting there, by the way? Traffic's always slow around Terminal One.' Delmas didn't fall for it but he stayed on the line. 'And Terminal Two can be just as bad.' Ditto. 'Giving yourself plenty of time is the key. Unless you're staying nearby, of course.'

'Captain, I said I'm not an idiot.'

'And I said, I know you're not.'

'I am ringing to tell you quite straightforwardly that I didn't kill Alain Saxe. And I have to correct you. The gang didn't cheat me. They cheated Sylvie.'

Darac heard a voice in the background. A voice reciting a list. And then the acoustic on the line changed.

'Please give my regards to Commissaire Dantier.'

'I will.'

The sound of closing doors.

'But going back to the question of… Shit!'

Delmas had rung off.

'He's not at the airport or A1. He's next door – Saint-Augustin rail station. He's just boarded a Nice-bound train. I heard the announcement.' Darac went to make another call on the landline, then thought better of it and keyed in a number on his mobile as Granot hurried back in.

'All systems go for the airport.'

'Nix that, Granot. He's on a train bound for Gare Thiers.'

Granot nodded, turned and began the process again.

'Hang on.' Bonbon held up a hand – the message he was waiting for was coming in. 'Trace is on to it. That call was from a mobile. And, chief, he's left it switched on.'

'Keep them on the line. I'm ringing Foch.' Darac's call connected. 'Hi, yes, Darac at the Caserne. Detail a squad to Gare Thiers immediately.' Getting to his feet, he began edging toward the door. 'Wanted murder suspect Pierre Delmas is on a train coming in from Saint-Augustin. We *might* get there in time to intercept him but you're much nearer.'

'Will do, Captain. Want me to contact UCSTC, too?'

'Who the hell are they?'

'The new body co-ordinating the SNPF rail police.'

'There's no time for more links in the chain. Besides, SNPF are just a bunch of glorified border guards. I need you guys.'

'Alright.'

Darac could hear the desk officer's misgivings but he didn't care. 'Listen, we've got Trace talking to us on another mobile. Keep me *au fait* with your progress on this one, Okay? I'll stay on it.'

'Right, Captain. Over and out.'

He gave Bonbon a look. 'Coming?'

'Looks like it.'

'Sorry, Granot – fleet feet needed. See if you can get a message to the train crew. Tell them to keep the doors closed when Delmas's train pulls into Nice.'

'For that, I *will* need UCSTC.'

Darac and Bonbon were already running along the corridor. They passed Frankie at the top of the stairs. Sometimes, a split second was all it took to convey a world of meaning. The lovebirds fluffed it, barely looking at one another.

Darac and Bonbon took the steps three at a time.

'My car or yours?'

'Yours is faster, chief.'

In the compound, they ran, almost literally, into Officer Wanda Korneliuk's prowl car.

'What a break.' Darac's words emerged in a breathless blur. 'Forget my car.'

'You got a death wish? The woman's a lunatic.'

Darac's reflection ballooned in Wanda's mirror shades as she rolled her window. He gave her the score and told her what he needed.

Wanda's nostrils flared. 'Get in,' she said, hitting the siren and lights.

Darac slid into the front, Bonbon into the back, and both had barely touched the seats before the car lurched toward the perimeter gate.

'Belts on, please.'

Going into almost comic fast-forward, the officer on duty raised the barrier just in time. Power sliding into Rue Roquebillière, Wanda looked in complete control as she hammered the throttle toward the junction with Maréchal Vauban.

'Jesus! Anything from Trace, Bonbon?'

The turn was accomplished with no discernible loss of speed.

'Just relax, gentlemen.'

'*Bonbon!* Anything from Trace?'

'Uh…Watch the— Shiiiit!' A message was coming in. 'Getting something!' His skinny frame thrown around in his seatbelt, he put the phone tighter up against his ear. 'The train's still some way off. Must be a speed restriction. We may just make it!'

Place Armée du Rhin came and went in a zigzag, mostly on the wrong side of the road. Wanda accelerated hard on to the *voie rapide*. 'We'll take the first exit after the tunnel.'

Its mouth was a black dot; a second later, they were in a black world; another second and they were powering through space, an asteroid shower of lights flaring past them.

They screamed out of darkness into daylight.

'Trace?'

'Still okay. Foch there yet?'

'No.'

A bad break. Their exit was blocked and the *voie rapide* ahead was at a standstill. Darac knew the siren would eventually part the jam but there wasn't time for that. He looked across. Wanda was running her eye along the reservation that divided the east and westbound carriageways. For the next fifty metres, cones stood in for a removed section of crash barrier. She jetted a glance at the entry ramp curving on to the opposite carriageway. If it offered a way on, it offered a way off. It was a single lane with no room to dodge oncoming traffic but there was none at the moment. The traffic on the carriageway itself was sparse but moving fast.

'We're coming off. Hold on.'

Bonbon closed his eyes.

Hands and feet moving with co-ordinated precision, Wanda jagged the wheel hard left. Sideswiping cones like ice-hockey pucks, the car lurched through one-eighty and finished in line with the oncoming traffic. Behind, horns blared; brakes squealed; cars snaked. But none crashed as Wanda straightened and, trailing clouds of tyre smoke, zoomed away from them. She glanced over her shoulder at the on-ramp. Nothing was coming around the curve. The grassy kerbsides gave some bail-out room but they were studded with trees and lampposts.

'And again, gentlemen.'

A power slide to the right. Another one-eighty. Wanda squeezed the nose between the kerbs and shot up the ramp. The siren still screaming, she floored it, her eyes fixed ahead as the bend unfurled. 'If anything's coming,' she said, calmly, 'let's hope the driver's eyes and ears are open.'

Still nothing came toward them. Darac's knuckles were white. Bonbon offered up a prayer. The curve was almost paid out. But then a tin can on wheels trundled into view just beyond their exit point. If it advanced another few metres, a head-on crash was all but inevitable.

'Get it off the road, darling…'

The 2CV could abort if its driver acted decisively.

'Come on…'

The jalopy bounced incrementally on to the verge.

'Good boy.'

Missing him by millimetres, Wanda kept the power on as she jagged into Boulevard de Cimiez. Darac felt like cheering but all he could do was let out the breath he hadn't realised he'd been holding. He put the phone back against his ear. Nothing. He'd lost the line to Foch. Wanda made another hard turn, sprinted between two lines of parked cars and jinked in front of a tram on Jean Médecin. Just Avenue Thiers to go. Ahead, a police van came to a sharp stop in the station forecourt and a quartet of officers piled out.

'Shit – have they only just got here? Kill the siren now, Wanda.'

'How's the train doing?' she said, flying past the van.

Darac turned. Bonbon was ashen. But he still had his phone to his ear.

'Still a couple of hundred metres away,' he said as if in a trance.

Darac's face broke into a broad grin. 'Fucking incredible, Wanda, you did it.'

They screeched to a halt.

'Any time you want a lift, gentlemen.'

'We'll call someone else!' Darac said, giving her arm a

squeeze as he got out of the car. In the back seat, Bonbon
didn't move. 'You staying there?'

'No!'

'Still got your running legs on?'

'No idea.'

They managed to sprint toward the booking hall.

'Which platform, Bonbon? Say A.'

'It's D.'

'Maybe we can hop across the tracks.'

Delmas's train was threading its way through the station
approaches as the pair ran through the concourse. Spotting
them, one of the Foch uniforms shouted at the ticket barrier
officials.

'They're *La Crim'* – let them through!'

Dodging passengers and pull-cases, Darac and Bonbon
ran out on to Platform A. Impasse – a stopped TGV was
taking up its whole length. Beyond, the Delmas train was
already nosing into Platform D.

'Stairs!'

Leaving the lofty airiness of the train shed, they skipped
down into the vaguely toilet-like atmosphere of the
underpass and tore along it as fast as they could. Overhead,
the rumble had almost stopped as they reached the slope
up to Platform D. Darac pounded heavy-legged up it
wondering if any other officers had beaten them to it. As the
panorama opened up, he would have heaved a sigh of relief
if he'd had the energy – a small contingent of uniforms had
gathered.

A PA announcement reverberated through the sun-
shafted air. 'The service arriving at Platform D terminates
here.'

The sergeant in charge hurried across to them as they dragged themselves up on to the platform. 'This is where we need to be, sirs. According to the signal, our man should be somewhere in the first four carriages. Any further orders?'

Lungs bursting, Darac was standing hands on knees. 'Ever done… this before?'

'Used to be in the SNPF.'

Darac took that as a *yes*.

The train squealed to a stop. All over the station, bored travellers became interested spectators. Another message rang out over the PA: 'Due to a technical problem, detraining from this service will be phased.'

Bonbon's breath was returning quicker than Darac's. 'Granot came through for us. So how's this going to work, Sergeant?'

'We'll funnel the passengers through just one or two doors, Lieutenant. We know what Delmas looks like.'

'He wears disguises. Or at least alters his appearance.'

'Can't alter his size,' Darac said. 'Or that fleshy face… or the set of his eyes.'

'We're on it.'

Doors opened only at the rear of the fourth coach. Immediately, officers boarded to establish a bridgehead and to screen those getting off. A second line of defence was waiting on the platform itself. Passengers were cleared from the rear of the train first. Inevitably, irritation levels grew as the procedure dragged on.

'So this is a technical problem, is it? Bollocks!'

'I'm going to miss my connection, thanks to this.'

'Who are you looking for? Me? My wife? Fucking disgrace!'

'Where were you lot when I was mugged?'

'Is it a terrorist? It had better be.'

Darac scanned every face. Now and then, he took closer order as a possible candidate stepped out on to the platform. None of them proved to be Delmas.

The rear of the train empty, it was time to vet the front four coaches.

'Still got a fix on Delmas?' Bonbon said to a uniform.

'He's in the front coach, we think. If he's using an old phone, the overhead wires sometimes interfere with the signal. Twenty-five kVs in those babies. That's one hell of a current.'

More faces still. But no sign yet of Delmas. Coaches four, three and two emptied and each of the toilets was checked. Nothing. Darac looked through a window into coach one as possible candidates filed slowly out until no one appeared to be left but uniforms.

'Let's get on board, Bonbon.'

'Where the hell is he, chief?'

They looked into spaces a man the size of Delmas could not possibly have squeezed into. And then, quite suddenly, Darac found him. 'Here he is.' He was lying in a waste bin about halfway along the carriage. Darac slipped on a pair of gloves and reached in.

'If this had been stuck down the back of a seat,' he said, unpeeling a hummus-slathered wrapper from Delmas's mobile, 'we might've thought he'd just mislaid it.'

'Playing games with us? Hadn't pegged him as that sort.'

'Neither had I.'

His eyes trained incredulously on the mobile, the sergeant in charge put in an appearance. 'So…?'

'Delmas dropped it in the bin at Saint-Augustin, then got off the train before it departed. And kept it switched on in the hope we'd follow it.'

The sergeant nailed on a grin. 'Well, he got his wish.'

'Listen,' Darac said. 'Thanks for everything and sorry it worked out like this.'

'That's just the way it goes sometimes, Captain. We'll take our leave.'

Muttering not quite *sotto voce* that the next time the Caserne needed Foch's help, it could fucking whistle, the sergeant led his contingent off the train.

'You can't blame him,' Bonbon said. 'A greasy phone isn't much to show for all this. And was it worth risking our necks for? And the necks of half the car drivers in the city?'

Having removed most of the goo, Darac started to scroll through screens. 'Wanda was brilliant but you're right. It was my call and I got it wrong.'

Bonbon pressed his lips together. 'No one actually crashed, to be fair. And we haven't caused *that* much disruption here.'

They risked a glance around. Angry knots of passengers were remonstrating with anyone wearing a uniform.

'I'll remember to tell Frènes that.'

'Did Delmas get this phone specifically to pull this stunt, do you think?'

'Perhaps.' Darac's eyebrows rose. 'But not in the way you mean. Look who it belongs to.' He held it out.

'Alain Saxe at Bouygues dot com. Well, well.' Bonbon made an extravagant moue. 'Delmas having the victim's mobile in his possession? Pretty incriminating.'

'He denied killing him, though. In fact, he rang expressly

to tell us that. And then he leaves us a direct link to the man. Strange.'

'He is terminally ill, remember. Maybe he never has been able to think straight. Who knows?'

'I'll let Erica have the phone. And we should get info from the provider shortly.'

A man who had the bearing of a senior official hailed them through the open carriage door. He bolted on a smile so false, it might just have been genuine.

'Would it be alright to have my train, my platform and my station back now?'

'Certainly,' Darac smiled but he knew further flannel was needed. 'I want to thank you for your kind co-operation, monsieur. It's much appreciated.'

'Is it? You do realise that the rail authority has its own police force, Captain?'

'Sorry. Forgot.'

The official gave a grunt of Granot-like proportions. '*Forgot...* And that miserable little object you're holding. I understand that it is all you have to show for this charade?'

'This miserable little object is actually a vital piece of evidence in a murder case, monsieur. Goodbye.'

They left the man to contemplate the vicissitudes of his lot and headed for the steps.

'He'll be dining out on this story for years,' Bonbon said.

They descended into the half-light of the underpass.

'Why do you reckon Delmas chose Saint-Augustin to ring us from, Bonbon?'

'Maybe he had been at the airport. Maybe in Arrivals, not Departures as we assumed.'

'Meeting someone? Interesting thought. CCTV should be able to confirm that.'

'Or maybe he's living around there.'

'Unlikely to ring from there, in that case. I wonder if he'd been visiting someone at A1 Security. Let's go and see.'

'We'll have to call the Caserne. We've got no car.'

'Maybe Wanda's still here.'

Blood drained from Bonbon's face. 'If she is, you're on your own, mate.' He pointed to the coppery frizz that was his hair. 'Look at what all that shock has done.'

'Bonbon, it always looks like that.'

'Is it any wonder?'

There was no sign of Wanda in the car park. Bonbon took out his mobile but it rang before he could make the call.

'Okay, sure… Right away? I'll get a cab back to the Caserne and meet you up there.' He turned to Darac. 'Agnès. Developments in her stabbing case.'

'Okay. I'll see you later, Bonbon.'

Darac called for his car, repaired to the coffee stall and took a double espresso to one of the stone benches facing the avenue. Traffic formed a backdrop in muted shades of grey and beige as he sat and sipped. He found himself wondering why the current fashion was for such drab colours. Where were the Bugatti blues of old? The Facel Vega reds?

Motorcycles seemed to be an exception to the rule. And if he hadn't turned away at that moment, he would have picked up the brilliant yellow of a 750cc Suzuki gliding toward Avenue Jean Médecin.

Riding it was someone wearing two-piece leathers and a black crash hat.

35

The male receptionist at A1 appeared to have been sucking lemons. He had no record of anyone named Delmas calling in person, or on the phone, today, or yesterday.

'Is Monsieur Leroux in, Fabrice?'

'He's in Milan until tomorrow.'

'When did he go?'

Fabrice whipped back a page of his agenda. 'Yesterday morning. Eight o'clock.'

'Was that so hard? How about Monsieur Mizzi.'

'He's not here. Paris – since, before you ask, the day *before* yesterday.'

'My, the cupboard *is* bare. How about Monsieur Rigaud?'

'Who?'

'Artur. The maintenance man.'

An absurd smirk on his face, Fabrice closed his agenda. There had been a contest and he'd won, somehow. 'Try the toilets. In the basement.'

'I will.' Darac indicated the CCTV camera covering the entrance. 'In the meantime, I want a copy of today's footage from that. And don't give me any bullshit about how long it will take. You're a security firm. Right?'

Darac found Artur tiling an awkward space under a washbasin.

'Alright, Captain… don't tell me – Darac? Mind if I carry on?'

'Go ahead.' He continued to the back of the man's head. 'Tell me – is there any way into this building except the front door?'

'There's a fire *exit*, of course. But no, we all come in that way. Even the likes of me.'

'*Liberté, fraternité* and *egalité* at its finest. Have you been in the basement all morning?'

'No, just come down.' He laid a tile into a cutting frame. 'Why?'

'Don't suppose you've seen anything of Pierre Delmas, have you?'

'He's gone and done it now, hasn't he? Still haven't got used to the idea of him robbing a bank and now he's… how did that Annie Provin put it? "Wanted for questioning in connection with the mysterious death" of that poor sod in Villefranche. That means you think he did it. Right?'

The tile snapped clean and true.

'Have you seen Delmas this morning?'

'*We ask the questions*, I get it. No, I haven't seen him. Should I have?'

'He was at Saint-Augustin station earlier. I wondered if he'd been here.'

'That fairy on the door should be able to help you with that.'

'When you guys have breaks, lunch and so on, where do you go?'

'Personally, I favour a table at Maxim's.'

Darac was rapidly developing a soft spot for Artur. 'Seriously.'

'Depends what day it is.' He buttered the cut tile and pressed it into place on the wall. 'Camembert, grapes and stuffed courgette flowers it'll be today. And if I'm lucky, a nice slice of *tarte aux pommes*.'

'Lovely. The others?'

'The brass go all over the shop. Some of the lesser lights go to Café Grinda. On the avenue of the same name.'

'Did Delmas used to go there?'

Artur stopped what he was doing for the moment. 'I see what you're getting at. He may have done. Mainly, he used to eat at his desk if he was in the office.'

Darac resolved to pay the café a visit. Delmas may not have frequented it but he now knew that others did.

'Thanks, Artur.' He gave him a card from his wallet. 'You will let me know if you do run into Delmas at any time?'

'Will do.'

Darac turned to leave. 'Oh, Thierry Artaud sends his regards, by the way.'

'That's nice. Was he on good form?'

'Seemed to be.'

'Excellent.' He pressed another tile into place. 'See you.'

A simple spot offering limited seating and an even more limited menu, everything about Café Grinda looked right to Darac. Too early for lunch, he ordered a double espresso and sat at a table near the window. As he waited, his thoughts turned to Frankie. And Christophe. And back to Frankie.

The coffee was brought over by Max, the café's ox-armed patron. It went dark briefly as he delicately set the cup on the table. Darac showed him his ID. 'People from A1 Security come in here, I understand?'

'Looking for Pierre Delmas, are you? Nasty business, that. Think he did it?'

Max pulled a chair away from an adjoining table and settled massively upon it. An arm wrestle between him and Granot would make some contest, Darac reflected idly.

'The A1 people come in now and again, yes. Pierre Delmas did a couple of times when he worked there.'

A phone rang behind the counter. A girl with a mane of black wavy hair appeared from the kitchen and picked up.

'You knew Delmas?'

'Well, I *knew* him—'

'But you didn't know him?'

The big man chuckled. 'I see you've heard that before. That's what he was like, though.'

'You haven't seen him today, by any chance?'

'Haven't seen him in years.'

Darac took a sip of coffee. 'I may come and live around here – this is superb.'

'You wouldn't put that on Tripadvisor, would you? It all helps.'

'Sure.'

'Max?' The girl at the counter was holding the phone. 'A gentleman wants to know if we've got *caille au thym* on the menu tonight?'

'Tell him yes.' Max rolled his eyes as he turned back to Darac. 'I don't know what she thinks all them quails are doing in the kitchen. Perhaps she thinks I collect the little buggers for fun.'

Darac grinned but his mouth was watering at the thought. In the right hands, the dish was a poem. And his father thought so, too, he remembered. Perhaps he should think again about his dinner plans for Julie.

'Listen – you haven't got a table for three tomorrow evening, have you?'

Max looked blank. But then the penny dropped. 'Oh! You threw me there for a minute. Tomorrow night? Bit short notice, mate.'

'Yes – forget it. It was just—'

'Hang on – Jade? Got the reservations book there?'

'Yes.'

'*Did* that four cancel, in the end?'

She ran a finger down the page. 'They… did.'

Max turned to Darac. 'Eight o'clock okay for you?'

'That would be perfect.'

He could always cancel if the arrangement didn't suit his guests.

'Jade – put a three in that slot. Name of Darac.'

'Right.'

'Thanks for that. How did you know my name?'

He gave a sly-looking grin. 'You showed me your ID, didn't you?'

Darac nodded, impressed. 'If I ever need a good eyewitness, I'll know where I can find one. When Delmas came in here, did he talk to anyone in particular?'

As he thought about it, Max lowered his head, compressing the roll of fat around his neck. 'There was a woman once. Don't know her name and I never saw her before or since. But I thought it was odd because she was nice-looking, I think. Younger than him.'

'Describe her.'

Max looked a little uncomfortable, suddenly. 'I can't.'

'No?'

'I was drinking then, you see. Heavily.'

'Uh-huh?'

'I was never ratted by lunchtime or anything like that. But come the evening – it wasn't pretty. How I got through it all without screwing up dishes or burning the place down, I don't know.'

'But you remember this woman was young and good-looking.'

Shifting his weight forward, Max's expression took on a new earnestness. 'To be really honest, all those evenings are lost to me. What I remember is just the *impression* of Delmas with this woman; the memory of it, if you like. But I really couldn't describe her. At all.'

'So theirs must have been a dinner engagement.'

'Yes – if it had been lunchtime, I would have remembered her, no problem.' He gave his forearm a scratch. 'Dinner – that's even stranger, isn't it? Considering Delmas isn't exactly Alain Delon.'

Darac took out his mobile – the odds seemed long but it was worth a try. 'Okay, you can't describe her but if you saw her again, would you recognise her?'

'Why, have you got someone in mind?'

Darac didn't usually answer questions. But Max liked to roast quail. With thyme. 'Not as yet,' he said. '*Would* you recognise her?'

'There's no point saying I would.'

'Take a look at this photo.'

Max slipped a pair of glasses out of the breast pocket of

his shirt. 'Who's this – his long-lost daughter?'

'Yes.'

'Really? I was just joking. I had no idea.'

'So you don't think she could have been the younger woman.'

'No – but only because my impression is of somebody, well… better-looking.'

At the counter, Jade cast him a filthy look.

'Was the young lady behind the bar working here then?' Darac said.

'Doing bits and pieces in the background, yeah.' He gave her a beckoning nod. 'Got a minute? I know you have so there's no use fibbing.'

Jade came over. Darac showed her Sylvie's photo.

'I've never seen her.' She eyeballed Max. 'But I think she looks gorgeous.'

Max hauled himself off the chair. 'I tell you what, though, my head waitress, Justine, will have served Delmas and his lady friend. She was with me all through that period.'

'Justine live nearby?'

'Upstairs close enough for you? She's my wife.'

'Yes she is,' a woman said, emerging through the arch at the rear of the café. 'For her sins.'

Justine was a short, strong-looking woman in her late forties. Louise Brooks-style black bob; full mouth glossed in a matching shade – she seemed an unlikely partner for Max. She must also have been a forgiving soul to have stuck by him through his drinking.

'This is Captain Darac from the PJ. He's interested in Pierre Delmas and that woman he was with that time. You remember?'

'Perhaps.' She came over to the table. 'Why, after all this time?'

Darac shook her hand as she sat. 'We have a number of questions about Monsieur Delmas. Especially after last night's incident in Villefranche.' He outlined as much of it as he thought appropriate.

'And the good captain has booked a table for three for tomorrow evening so be careful what you say. Coffee, dear?'

Her look said: *What do you think?*

'A noisette, Jade,' Max called out, sitting down once more.

'He looks after my every need.' Justine gave Darac a look. 'So… Pierre Delmas and the younger woman. What do you want to know?'

'When were they here?'

'That's difficult. And we don't keep our reservation books from one year to the next so we couldn't look it up, either. When was the robbery – the one he went down for?'

'2003. End of May.'

She pursed her lips. Full, dark and glistening, they looked like slugs made of chocolate ganache. 'I would say it was the previous autumn.'

'Can you remember the name attached to the booking?'

'Delmas. I think.'

'Can you describe her?'

She gave a throaty little laugh. 'Oh yes. Mid-thirties, slim, attractive. She had reddish, shoulder-length hair. Nice complexion.'

'From eight years ago, you remember all that?'

Her eyes slid to Max. 'Old babe magnet there's got a thing for redheads.'

'*Had*,' he said. 'Had.'

'Especially when he was drinking. I had to watch him. And as I say, it was out of the ordinary – Delmas and a woman.'

'How were they with one another?'

'How do you mean?'

'Did they seem close? Distant? Cordial? In love? Argumentative?'

Jade delivered the coffee.

'Thanks, darling. *Cordial*, I suppose is the word. She did most of the talking. I remember that.'

'A woman doing most of the talking?' Max said, getting to his feet. 'Who'd have thought it? Right. To work.'

'He's a genius,' Justine said as Max headed for the kitchen. 'You wouldn't think it, would you? But wait until you've tasted the food.'

'I'm looking forward to it. If I sent a sketch artist over here, do you think you could come up with a likeness of the mysterious woman?'

'I could give it a try.'

Darac got to his feet. 'Thank you. She'll ring beforehand. And I'll see you tomorrow evening.'

36

The black desk phone to his ear, Darac got to his feet and gazed out over the compound. It was only then that he realised Frankie was standing immediately below his window. She seemed to be talking to the wall – the person she was with was hidden in the lee of the building. He tried to work out by Frankie's mien and by her body language who it might be.

His call connected. 'Hi, Erica – listen, have you found anything on Saxe's mobile?'

'Lots of things. But nothing links directly or indirectly to any of our other principals.'

'You've been around R.O. too long. That's the kind of thing he says.'

'A little bit of his genius probably has rubbed off.'

'He's there, isn't he?'

'Sitting right next to me.'

Darac's habitual half-smile gave way to a full grin. 'Saxe's computer?'

'Looking at it now. Nothing in a saved file of much note. But among the deleted stuff, I've just come across some figures that got us thinking.'

'What's so special about them?'

'There's a column here headed €400,000.'

Darac turned away from the window. '*Is* there?'

'That's the pay-off on the faked bank statement to the cent, isn't it?'

'It is indeed.' The worn patch by the desk leg was looking particularly threadbare this afternoon. 'I'll come over.'

En route, he discovered that Agnès was Frankie's invisible friend. 'I thought you were talking to the wall.'

'Once a Jew, always a Jew.'

'Right, I'm off to La Trinité,' Agnès said, hitching her bag on to her shoulder. 'A second witness to the stabbing has come forward.' She smiled at them both. 'See you.'

'Bye,' they said in unison.

'That smile,' Darac said, as Agnès took her leave. 'She's heard, hasn't she?'

'Perhaps.'

A uniform walked by and glanced at them. '*He* knows.'

Frankie clicked her tongue. 'I doubt it.'

Checking no one was within earshot, Darac came in a little closer. 'I rub Agnès's feet and it's all anyone talks about for days. I share a passionate moment with you and no one says a thing – except Granot and Bonbon and they're family.'

'You know why, don't you?'

'No – tell me.'

'Because this isn't just a bit of harmless fun, an opportunity to rib you. It's serious.'

Darac looked into her eyes. 'Is it?'

'Uh-huh,' she said softly, meeting his gaze.

He was within the thickness of a top E-string of kissing her all over again.

'But I still think' – she brushed her fringe away – 'that we should keep everything on hold.'

'Hold. Absolutely. Of course.'

Her mobile rang and she took the call. A van had been held at the toll booths on the A8 beneath Cime de la Forna. A man and six tearful young women from Eastern Europe were on board. The gendarme at the scene didn't believe their story that they were bound for a stint of lemon-picking at Cap Martin.

'I'm needed.'

'Me too,' Darac said. 'I think we should go for the regulation kiss goodbye, this time.'

'Or even a handshake.'

'Handshake is good. Anyone looking?'

They exchanged regulation kisses of parting and went their separate ways.

Erica was tapping figures into a calculator when Darac walked into the crime lab with a new spring in his step. On Erica's bench, Alain Saxe's computer was displaying the spreadsheet that was the source of all the interest.

'The column is headed four hundred grand exactly? Bit of a coincidence, Erica.'

'Indeed.'

'Don't you believe in them?' Raul Ormans said, on his way out. 'Coincidences?'

'Yes, I do. But only rarely.'

'That's a coincidence – it's just what I think. I'm off to fire some guns.'

'Have fun.' He turned to Saxe's computer. 'Confusing spreadsheet, isn't it? Looks as if a four-year-old child has done it. When was this created, Erica?'

She selected the file menu. '28 May 2003.'

'Okay, the odds on this being a coincidence have just gone through the roof. That date is two days after the robbery was discovered – one before the haul was recovered.'

'I told you I'd got something. So we know the four hundred thousand was never paid in to Sylvie's account. But it looks as if the gang had at least earmarked the sum. Maybe they *intended* to pass it on to her, after all.'

'I wonder…'

'See those smaller amounts listed under the principal?' A slender fingertip pointed to the screen. 'I was wondering if they represented deductions.'

He peered at the figures. 'Difficult to tell, isn't it? There's no running total or anything.'

'If there were, it would leave €312,487.'

Folding his arms, Darac set his weight back against the work bench. 'An eighty-eight grand or so shortfall… Whatever this means, we're following money again so I'll get Granot on it.' He tapped the computer screen. 'Very well found, Erica.'

'Thanks.' There was a ballpoint pen on the bench, a promo item from a rugby club. Erica picked it up, absently pressed the end cap and clicked out the tip. And clicked it back again.

'I hear you and Frankie…' Her search for an appropriate conclusion ended in a concise little shrug. 'You and Frankie.'

It was the moment to play things down. 'Okay – me and Frankie. At the end of a ridiculously long day, we fell into each other's arms and enjoyed a big, sloppy kiss. End of story.'

The pen clicked in and out. 'It's not, though, is it? I know you've always adored her.'

'Everyone does. She's adorable.'

Adorable – another good word for Angeline's list.

'She is, yes.'

'What's that sad little smile about?'

Erica tossed the pen on to the desk. 'Nothing. Nothing at all.'

Another colleague concerned about Christophe, Darac concluded as he took his leave. And then he took a call from Frènes.

37

Pierre Delmas smiled as he switched off *France Info* and retuned to his regular listening. It seemed that leaving Saxe's mobile on the train had achieved exactly what he'd hoped. Yet he felt a certain pity for the man he'd so easily duped. Captain Whateverhisnameis's efforts had been rewarded by a severe reprimand from the Palais de Justice, they had said. His recklessness had created disorder, danger to the public and inconvenience at the station. He'd been lucky not to earn a lengthy suspension.

'That's the powers that be, for you,' Delmas said aloud. Powers that *be*? It sounded wrong to him. With some difficulty, he pressed the record button on his player. 'Look up whether it's powers that *be* or *are*,' he said into the mike. Now all he had to do was remember to play the message back sometime.

The image razor sharp in the lenses of his Leica binoculars, he scanned the scene once more. Still no sign of his subject. He retrained them on the door.

A battle had gone his way, but the war was still very much to be won. The police had infinite resources and he had almost nothing. But there were things in his favour. Most importantly, they didn't know what he knew, and they had no idea where he was staying. Also, his technical expertise was second to none. There was nothing he didn't know about surveillance and security.

But then, there was his condition. In some respects, NCL was an out and out hindrance. No man on a mission would choose to suffer headaches, depression and diminishing physical co-ordination. But it had one saving grace. The ultimate deterrent – the prospect of losing one's life – simply didn't apply to him. He was a dead man walking, anyway. Just a few more days. That was all he needed. His faith in God had been severely tested over the past few days but He would grant him this, he was sure.

At last, there was activity at the house. The door opened. A swelling shadow appeared. And then someone stepped quickly into the light, exiting the narrow field of view of his lenses before Delmas could identify who it was. He panned, rolling the focus wheel with a trembling finger. The image blurred. He tried again. Worse. And again. He kept trying. Just when it seemed that the identity of the figure would remain a mystery, the scene snapped into sharp focus. 'Yes,' Delmas said aloud. 'It *is* you.'

38

On Quintet nights, Darac liked to walk to the Blue Devil, part of a pre-performance routine that rarely changed. Many found it a paradoxical or even perverse approach for a man who loved to improvise but it made perfect sense to him. If you want to fly, first you need the ground.

At the foot of the steep stone steps that led into the club, he paused to honour his talisman – a poster entitled *Blown Away by the Brass Section*. It was his practice to reach up and touch it before crossing the threshold but, carrying two guitar cases this evening, he blew a kiss, instead. Feeling slightly transgressive, he passed underneath it and backed through the twin red-painted doors into the lobby.

Pascal the doorman was sitting at the pay table, scribbling something down on the back of a flyer. Whatever he was putting together, it was giving him trouble. The page was a muddle of arrows, underlining and crossings-out.

'Two axes?' He crossed out another line. 'One was enough for Django.'

'I need all the help I can get.' Darac indicated the smaller of the two cases. 'Got the SG back – going to give it some blues tonight.' He glanced into the takings tin. 'Not a bad crowd in, by the look of it. See you later, Pas.'

'Wait a minute.' He put down his pen. 'I've got something to run by you.' He cleared his throat and scanned the page for a way in. 'Check it.' He started up a little mouth music.

'*My name is Pas, I sit on my ass, on an old drum stool, in the vestibule. You can't pass my table, unless you are able to drop it in the can, for the...*' He ground to a halt. 'That's as far as I got. What do you think?'

Darac had maintained for years that, muzak excepted, there was no genre of music that didn't have merit. But he had a tin ear for rap.

'That's as good as I've heard,' he said. 'Truly.'

'Yeah?' Pascal beamed, primping the lapels of his jacket. 'I got it. I got the juice.'

'Certainly have, man. Ridge around?'

'Upstairs.'

In the concert room, Dexter Gordon's *Our Man in Paris* album was entertaining a buzzy crowd. Jacques Telonne, Darac was amused to note, was not among them. Swapping greetings with some of the regulars, he ran an eye over the bandstand. The club's much-loved Steinway was in position; Marco's drums were set up; chairs, music stands and mikes were all ready to go. And, its stand-by light aglow, Darac's amp was warming its valves in its time-honoured spot, stage left. It didn't matter how many times he'd seen a bandstand dressed for a performance, the sense that magic might happen *right there* was a feeling Darac loved.

In the kitchen, he found Khara, the club's waitress, hat check girl, barmaid and everything in between, in an unfamiliar position. She was sitting down. Standing over her, the chef Roger was administering a glass of something steaming.

'Hot lemon and ginger,' he said, answering Darac's enquiring look as he headed back to his bench. 'Head cold. Flu, maybe.'

Khara wrapped her long, tapering fingers around the glass. 'No greeting kisses tonight, Darac.' Her voice was a threadbare wheeze. 'I've got a razor where my throat used to be.' She coughed. 'Ow.'

'I never thought I'd say this, Roger, but your wife looks terrible.'

'Came on just like that.' He started feeding a cut of meat into a mincer. 'Ridge has called Fama and Carole in early.'

'How are you getting…?' Watching Khara massage her throat, Darac redirected the question. 'How is she getting home? Cab?'

'A cab is no good – we live on the top floor of our block. I'm going to run her back after I've prepped everything.'

'One call and I could get you a ride straight away. The Caserne's only just around the corner and the driver will escort Khara right to your door.'

'A police escort?' she said. 'That's all' – a sneeze – 'I need.'

'He or she will be in plain clothes, and the cars are unmarked – don't worry.'

Roger left the meat to disgorge by itself. 'Don't send that stuntwoman who nearly killed everybody today. Including you and your partner.'

'That stuntwoman is the best driver you'll ever come across.' He glanced at the mincer. 'Your meat's running over.'

'I don't care who it is.' Khara took a sip of her drink, swallowing as if it contained broken glass. 'Just get them here quickly.'

Carole, a large, cheery Englishwoman, appeared in the doorway. 'My, look at you!'

As Carole went into full nursing mode, Darac rang the Caserne and arranged the lift.

'Car will be here in five minutes, guys.' He headed for the archway into the stairwell. 'Unmarked ZX with a nice young man at the wheel – Fabien.'

'Not too nice, I hope,' Carole said, grinning. 'Eh, Roger?'

'*Bof!*' It was going to be a long evening. 'Thanks, Darac.'

'It's nothing. Get well, Khara.'

'She says, "Thank you!" Now, what you need, sweetheart…'

Abandoning the patient to Carole's ministrations, Darac climbed the stairs that led to the first-floor dressing room. If he were ever brought to this spot blindfolded, he would have been able to identify the location immediately. The smell, a melange in which damp plasterwork and drains were the principal notes, was not quite like any other.

A voice that was also not quite like any other greeted him from the landing. Born and raised in the South Bronx, NYC, the club owner Ridge Clay spoke in a strange, hybridised argot – standard French laced with words and expressions from the black neighbourhoods of home.

Darac had neither touched the poster nor kissed Khara – an ominous precedent. As he set down his guitar cases, he wondered if anything might derail his usual bi-play with Ridge.

'Garfield – kick anybody's ass today?'

The world saved, Darac slapped his palm into the big man's. 'Not today, Ridge. Carole's arrived, by the way. And a car's coming for Khara.'

'That's good.' Looking Darac in the eye, Ridge nodded, gravely. 'Some week, huh?'

'You could say that.'

'It was in *Nice-Matin*, you know – what happened in the cemetery.' He shook his large head. 'Pictures, too.'

'Annie Provin rang me. Did I "want to do an interview for TV?" I declined.'

'Reporters have no respect for anything except a good story. Death and destruction? They'll splash that every time.'

Death… The subject was never far from Darac's thoughts at the moment. He knew Ridge would have his own very particular thoughts on it. But did he want to hear them *now*? Maybe now was the perfect time.

'You grew up in the church, didn't you, Ridge? Gospel choirs and all that.'

'Yes, sir. East 149th Street Baptist. And every so often, I feel those ever-loving arms around me, still.'

Ridge had a way of imbuing even the most trivial statement with significance. When matters were weighty, the effect could be overpowering.

'You believe?' Darac decided to leave out 'despite everything'. 'Believe in something beyond this veil of whatever it is, I mean?'

As if a DJ with a penchant for corn were looking on, Dexter's 'Stairway to the Stars' drifted in from the concert room.

'I tell you one thing I believe: you don't play the same at Carnival time as you do the rest of the year. You don't realise it, I know, but just for a few days, your solos work in a different way. Now that must mean something.'

He shouldn't have started this. But there was no going

back now. 'And that something is what, do you think?'

Ridge turned away, trusting the banister rail with his weight. When he spoke, his words rumbled around the stairwell like a downtown subway train.

'Most of the time, you're a player who takes a solo to the edge, right? And once there, you jump off. And you fly around getting further away, making it harder to find a way back. And then you take one flight too many. Now you're really in trouble. But then you hit on something. And it points you in the right direction. You follow it. And you do make it back.'

'That's what a jazz solo is, isn't it? It's what everyone does.'

Ridge shook his head. 'No. Most cats head back before they hit trouble. You don't.' He tramlined his forehead. 'You love those remote places. This is when you're playing at your best, I'm talking about.'

'And around carnival time, I don't do that?'

'You get out to the edge, alright. You tip a toe over… and you bring it right back.'

'And you infer what from that?'

Still resting his weight on his forearms, Ridge turned to him. 'When my mother passed, I really felt a sense of the vastness of the place she had gone to.' He shook his head. 'I didn't think of it as Heaven or Eternity, *per se*. It was just this… endless space I'd never even really thought about before. Then, at age nineteen, there I was – standing on the edge looking right into it.'

Carole bustled into the space below. 'Ridge? Khara's gone home, bless her. Fama just rang – she'll be here in five minutes.'

'I'll be right down.' Straightening, he looked Darac squarely in the eye. 'We can fight over whether that vast space is all there is. Whether it all ends there. But whatever we think, I know you're standing on that same edge now, as you do every year at this time. So all those remote places you love? Just now, they don't seem so lovable.'

With everything he knew about Ridge, Darac could see where the man was coming from. Maybe he even had a point.

'And there's me thinking that when I'm soloing, I'm just bending a tune out of shape and trying to bend it back again.'

'There's a couple more stops on that journey. And you know it.'

'I'll make you a promise, Ridge,' Darac grinned as he picked up the SG case. 'If I somehow do glimpse the void tonight, I'll do my best to jump right out into it.'

39

Julie Issert pulled the Suzuki back on to its stand and took off her helmet as she strode to the door. It opened before her gloved hand reached the bell.

Martin stood, breathing in the moment. 'An Amazon in leathers? I don't recall sending for one.'

'Special delivery.' Julie shook out her auburn hair. 'But if you don't want me, I could always go away.'

'I suppose you may as well come in.' He closed the door behind her. 'Do you have any idea just how aroused I am?'

She slowly pulled down the zip of her jacket. 'Prove it.'

In his younger days, Martin Darac would have been capable of spending the next couple of hours proving it. But at fifty-six, half an hour was probably all he was good for. He'd understood from the first moment they had started making love that the flame of Julie's libido burned hotter than his. But perhaps tonight…

Le Citronnier had become Martin's favourite restaurant in Vence. A swish place around the corner from Place du Grand Jardin, it was the classic-with-a-twist cooking of young chef Marie Frémault that was the draw. He and Julie were shown to a table presided over by a framed still from *La Grande Illusion.*

'Are you partial to *caille au thym*?'

'I love it. Why are you whispering?'

'Because we're having it in a different establishment tomorrow night.'

'Excellent. And you say Paul is a capable cook?'

'He's quite good with chicken in various forms but we've decided to dine out instead. He's discovered a little place down in Saint-Augustin. Café Grinda. Do you know it?'

Julie's face fell. She set down her menu, almost knocking over an empty wine glass.

'I don't know it.' She picked up her napkin. 'And neither do I want to get to know it just at the moment.'

Martin smiled, slightly taken aback. It wasn't like Julie to be defensive or demanding. 'It comes highly recommended. Funnily enough, one of my assistants went there a few months back and—'

The napkin slapped the air as she opened it with a sharp flick of the wrist. 'Martin, I don't want to go there.'

'Uh… alright.'

She gave an apologetic little smile and reached for his hand. 'I'm not being difficult but I could go there anytime. I want to see Paul's place – I've always loved the Babazouk. And a roof terrace? It sounds wonderful.'

'I'm sure there will be many other opportunities to go there.'

'But there may not.'

She withdrew her hand. An awkward silence. Their first. It was Martin who broke it. 'Alright, if it matters to you so much. I'll ring him later.'

She smiled. 'Thank you. I'll make it worth your while. After dinner.'

Martin could feel his sap rising once more. 'Julie,' he said, taking her hand, 'you might just be the death of me.'

40

The Telonne party had requested table number twenty, a corner banquette nearest the bar and furthest from the bandstand.

'You are to be congratulated, Monsieur Clay.' Jacques Telonne gave Ridge's hand a pump as he beamed into the camera. A flashgun went off. 'This is a fine club.'

'You know what would make it finer?' Ridge maintained his grave mien. 'The city owns the building, right? We need renovation here. And we need action on the rent. If you get into office, will you promise to do that?'

'I promise we'll look into it.' The smile morphing into a look of earnest authority, Telonne turned to his PA. 'Make a note of that, Véronique.'

'Yes, sir.' She wrote something on her pad. 'Got it.'

The woman had scribbled 'blah, blah, blah'.

'Excuse me. I need to go wash,' Ridge said. 'Spent the last couple of hours unblocking the dressing-room toilet.'

Laure Telonne grinned. 'I've never seen a proper dressing room,' she said.

'And you're not going to see this one, young lady.'

Jacques Telonne's face hardened. Who was this old black boho to talk to his daughter like that? Laure was his to command. Not that she needed much commanding this evening – he'd seldom seen her so engaged.

'Monsieur Clay?' Elise called out. 'How long before the show starts?'

'Couple of minutes – jazz time.'

'And in real time?'

'Maybe fifteen.'

Jules Frènes made an extraordinarily disdainful moue. He hated jazz. He hated Darac. He hated squalor. But he loved power and he knew that it was sometimes necessary to bite the shittiest of bullets to court it. He'd even had his wife buy him a black poloneck for the occasion.

Nodding to his photographer, Telonne stood.

'Everyone?' he called out to the crowd, his voice competing with Sonny Rollins's *The Bridge* album. Few heads turned. The smile took a well-earned rest as he looked around for assistance. The bar was bookended by a dough-faced white woman and a younger black woman wearing an exotic head wrap. 'Turn the music down, will you?' he said to her. 'I'm trying to make an announcement here.'

Fama Ousmane took her time over giving change and stared back at him. 'Carole?' she said, her eyes holding Telonne's. 'Could I trouble you?'

'Of course, darling.'

'Would you be kind enough to fade the track? Monsieur here wants to tell everyone that the next round of drinks is on him and that he is going to help taxi them around the floor. Along with Monsieur Retro, the other gentleman.'

'No, no, no…' Palms outwards, Frènes wiped the pane of air in front of him. 'Enough is enough. Impossible!'

Telonne's smile stayed on Fama like a death ray as Carole reached into the alcove next to her. The track faded.

'You read my mind. What's your name?'

'Miriam Makeba, sir.'

Véronique whispered something in Telonne's ear.

'Well, I'll call you Miriam anyway.' He turned back to the crowd. 'Everyone? Before our local favourites, the Didier Musso Quintet, strut their stuff for us, the next round of drinks is on me.'

A little wave of approbation broke around the tables.

'And to prove that serving the community really is…' He was already totting up the likely cost in his head. 'Really is…'

'*Where we're at*,' Laure whispered, giving him the idiom. Elise looked on astonished. The girl was actually being helpful.

'To prove that serving the community is where we're at, I and my esteemed colleague from the Palais de Justice, Monsieur Jules Frènes here, will help our beautiful waitresses with your orders.'

No one bought the shtick but they didn't care – a free drink was a free drink. All around the room, half-empty glasses were raised.

Producing the tightest of tight-lipped smiles, Frènes straightened his poloneck and prepared to serve the community.

Telonne put a hand on his shoulder. 'Later – find out that bitch's real name and have her papers checked.' He was still smiling. 'The one at the bar.'

'That's not so straightforward, monsieur.'

Telonne's grip was threatening to leave marks on the cashmere. 'I don't forget my friends. Do it!'

Dispatching Frènes with a dismissive push, Telonne turned to the adjoining table. 'Now who's first? You, monsieur – that's cognac? Let's make it a double.' A flashgun popped as the man shook Telonne's hand. 'Doubles for everyone!'

On the floor above, the shabby space of the dressing room was alive with what Ridge called the Thursday Night Sound: a high-octane mix of talk and laughter, shot through with flurries of notes. He'd known professional bands that barely said a word to each other during warm-ups and then coasted through the subsequent performance. There was nothing jaded about the Didier Musso Quintet. Whether they went out as a trio or a twelve-piece big band, the outfit always gave it everything they had.

As befitted his status as bandleader, pianist Didier Musso was occupying the most comfortable seat in the room, a reclaimed porcelain hip bath lined with cushions. Using his knees as a writing slope, he was scribbling a set list – his third of the evening. The two earlier attempts sat obliterated on the upended crate next to him.

'You look like a jazz *Marat Assassiné*,' Luc the bass player said, emerging from the toilet. 'The painting by Jacques-Louis David.' He picked up a towel and began wiping down the strings of his instrument. 'Louvre. Room 54. Or 53. No – 54.'

'Marat was pockmarked.' Didier put three question marks by the opening number on his list. 'I'm more the petal-soft baby-faced type.'

'Didier Musso – baby-faced assassin,' Dave Blackstock said, slipping his tenor sax neckstrap over his pink pate.

'Marat wasn't the assassin, you idiot.' Marco stopped

laying down beats on his practice pad. 'It was Charlotte somebody or other. You English don't know shit about anything.'

'Best sparkling wine? English. Best cheese? English. And do you know France's sixth biggest city by population? London.' He tossed Marco the day's *Libération*. 'It's all in there.'

'You can't believe everything you read.'

'What makes you think that?'

'Read it in *Nice-Matin*.'

'Okay,' Didier said. 'I've changed my mind. How's the tongue tonight, Charlie?'

Trudi 'Charlie' Pachelberg adjusted the mouthpiece of her alto sax and blew a slow and shaky take on 'Happy Birthday'.

'Lightning,' she said.

'Fabulous. So…'

As usual, everyone was talking at once.

'Guys? Be so kind as to shut the fuck up! Thank you. I want to open with 'A Night in Tunisia'. We've got exactly the right line-up for the Parker Septet '46 Dial version. You take the first solo, Charlie.'

'You want the full Bird?'

'I want the full Pachelberg.'

'Fame at last.' She grinned at Darac. 'You going to use the SG on it?'

'Maybe.' He laid the cherry-red plank back into its case. 'I'm going to play it by ear.' He waited theatrically. 'What – no gag?'

'Too obvious.'

Ridge lashed through the bead curtain. 'Okay, guys.

Let's go.' He turned to Darac on the stairs. 'We got royalty in tonight.'

'Telonne actually came?'

'And some.'

The band took the stand to a warm hand from the crowd. Smiles. Nods. Waves. Darac took his arch-topped D'Aquisto out of its case. Didier hit A natural on the piano and the band re-set their tuning.

In the audience, Jacques Telonne leaned into his PA's ear. 'We'll leave at the interval.'

'Alright.'

'All of us, I mean.'

Laure was sitting forward in her seat, eyes glued on the stand. 'Sshhh!'

Elise almost choked on her Perrier. 'You're a jazz fan all of a sudden, Laure? And your back is dripping with sweat. I think you're sickening. For something.' She turned to her husband. 'And I'll stay as long as I like, thank you, Jacques.'

Telonne holstered the smile. 'You'll go when I go.'

On the stand, Darac was still undecided which instrument to open with. He had to prepare both, anyway. He plucked the SG from its case and set the tuning with his meter. The guitar's neck felt good all the way up. Clean. Fast. But the true test would be playing the thing through the amp. He hadn't had that particular pleasure since it had been returned.

Ridge joined the band on stage and turned on his radio mike. 'These Thursday nights come around, don't they? It's going to be a good one, people. But first, I've got to do the small print…'

With only a minor dip in volume, the audience continued

276 BOX OF BONES

to enjoy their meals and drinks as Ridge ran through the routine announcements they had heard a thousand times before. Then finally, he got to the new stuff. 'So, yes it's Thursday at the Blue Devil and that means the Didier Musso Quintet.'

Applause. A few whistles. Calls of 'Yes!'

'Just before I introduce the band, we got special guests in the house tonight.' Ridge raised an arm. 'Stand up, please – Monsieur Jacques Telonne, the man who builds Nice. And buys drinks. Jacques Telonne, everybody.'

Led by Ridge, a few clapped Telonne as he stood long enough to perform a drop-handed wave that said, *No – hey, I'm just doing my job. Let's get on with the entertainment.*

'The good monsieur has already promised to look into looking after us should he be elected next time. And we also have Madame Elise Telonne. We've got no catwalk but stand up anyway, honey.'

Elise didn't need a catwalk to show herself off. She stood and smiled.

'Hey *now*,' Ridge said, making a show of his own smile. 'A man can dream, you know.'

The former model laughed as if it were the funniest thing she'd heard that day. Maybe it was.

'Next, we have Véronique, Monsieur Telonne's personal assistant. She knows how to spell "blah" so well she can do it three times over.'

Darac shared a look with Marco and the others. What was *that* about?

'And now we got another man who's no stranger to the limelight. Mister Swingin' Good Times himself – Public Prosecutor Jules Frènes. Stand up, brother.'

Frènes bobbed up and down.

What? Darac was too appalled to hear what Ridge said next. Frènes was so far up Telonne's arse, he'd even followed him here? Frènes at the Blue Devil? It was just plain wrong.

On the stand, Ridge couldn't resist a smile. 'Alright, people. That's enough of that shit…'

As if they were one instrument, piano, bass and drums set off at a loose-limbed walking pace under Ridge as he continued:

'Let's say hi to the fellas… Leading the band on piano, from Nice: Didier Musso. On bass, from Lille: Luc Gabron. On drums, from Nice: Marco Portami. On trumpet, from Fort-de-France, Martinique: Jacques Quille. On tenor, from Canterbury, England: Dave Blackstock. On alto and flute from Berlin, Germany: Charlie Pachelberg. And on guitar, from Vence: Paul Darac. When does seven go into five? When it's the Didier Musso Quintet. Put your hands together.'

It was only as Ridge left the stage that Darac decided which guitar to go with on 'Tunisia'. Out in the audience, he saw a young woman stand up momentarily as he picked up the free end of his amp lead… and went with the D'Aquisto. The young woman sat down.

The rhythm section's walking theme sauntered off into the distance. More nods and smiles. Breaths in. All set to go, Didier counted the number in.

'Um-aah, um-ah-um-ah-ah…'

Piano and guitar began together, a Latin-style repeating arpeggio: *do, do, do, dee-dee; do, do, do, dah-dah…* After four bars, a little trembling figure in the horns came in on the off beat. Another four bars saw the introduction of the main theme on muted trumpet. Now the whole band was playing, a living, breathing thing.

Charlie Pachelberg's opening solo was so nimble, so sure-footed and yet so extraordinarily explorative that Darac forgot all about Frènes, Telonne and co. As the moment to begin his solo approached, the only thing on his mind was where he could go with it. His conversation with Ridge came back to him just as he took off. Listening intently to what everyone else was playing, he kept going – too far and too fast. After just a few bars, he found himself orbiting the tune in deep space. This was the territory that normally inspired him; the cusp between two worlds, a trajectory in which one wrong move would mean there could be no way back home. Images crowded in, obscuring the various ways ahead. He searched for a moment but finding nothing, resorted to the safe way out. He turned the phrase he was playing around and retraced his steps. It lacked all originality and inspiration but at least, eight bars later, he docked seamlessly with the band where he had come in – the number's Latin head: *do, do, do, dee-dee; do, do, do, dah-dah...*

He'd played faultlessly through the solo. He hadn't missed a beat. He'd demonstrated a certain mastery of the craft. But craft and art were two different things and he felt a little sheepish as he acknowledged the crowd's appreciation. A second sensational solo by Charlie followed and the number built to a dynamic climax.

The crowd erupted. Everyone loved it. Especially Jacques and Elise Telonne, or so it appeared.

'Thank you,' Didier said into his mike. 'That wasn't

Charlie Parker you heard there.' He threw out a hand. 'That was Charlie Pachelberg. Give it up, come on.'

More applause. Charlie took another bow.

'Okay we're going to play some blues now.'

As Darac unplugged the D'Aquisto and set it on its stand, out in the audience, Laure Telonne sat forward once more.

'I see you are a particular aficionado of the blues, mademoiselle,' Frènes said to her, oilier than a grease monkey's rag.

'Oh yes.' A sweet smile. 'You never know what might happen.'

Her father gave her a quizzical look. The girl was behaving so far out of character, it was beginning to worry him.

'Is Laure on something?' he whispered to Elise.

'If she is, I hope she keeps taking it.'

As Didier started a droll routine on the theme of the over-commercialisation of music, Darac took the SG off its stand. It was second nature to him to check that the guitar's pick-up volume controls were set to zero before he connected it to the amp – failing to do so created a loud grating buzz that no one wanted to hear. The controls on zero, he sat down and picked up the lead. The jack plug stabbed blindly around the socket on the guitar as he tried to catch Charlie's eye.

'Hey! That was fabulous. Super hot.'

'I want that in writing.' Charlie's eyebrows rose, making ledger lines high up on her forehead. 'And how about that return you played? It was amazing.'

Her assessment catching Darac off guard, he held on to the jack plug for a moment. 'Amazingly boring, you mean.'

'No – it was… monumental. I haven't heard you do anything like that for a long time.'

At the mike, Didier was nearing his punchline. 'So don't line *their* pockets, everyone – line ours.' A ripple ran around the audience, even though most of them had heard variants of it before. 'Yes, our CDs are on sale at the desk, reasonably priced at ten euros. And we'll sign them at no extra cost.' He looked across at Darac. 'Ready?'

'Almost.'

'Okay this is "Blues For Philly Joe". And it's going to feature two of our very hottest hotshots: drummer Marco Portami… and guitarist Paul Darac.'

Applause. Jacques Telonne smiled to the room and glanced at his watch. Frènes yawned behind his well-manicured hand. Laure's cheeks flushed. She craned forward.

Darac finally inserted the lead into the SG's socket. Click. His hand went to the neck pick-up volume control.

'Chief?'

He turned. 'Bonbon? What…?'

'I'm really sorry, mate.'

41

It was 9.30 and the streets were practically deserted. Buffeting wind and lashing rain will do that even to a place as beautiful as Villefranche-sur-Mer.

Windscreen wipers barely coping with the deluge, Bonbon turned toward the foot of a high, buttressed wall. In his rear-view mirror, the blurred mass of the Citadelle Saint-Elme sank into the darkness like a whale going down in the ocean.

'Thought it better to stop you before you got started, chief. Examining Magistrate Reboux asked for you personally. Didn't think I could say no.'

'It's fine. In fact, you saved me. I'm playing in a whole new style at the moment – shit with a monumental twist.'

Bonbon slowed, the dripping stonework blooming brighter in his headlights as he drew tight in to the wall. 'It's better than monumental shit, I suppose.'

'I suppose it is.' Darac slipped on his police armband. 'Where are we going?'

'Around to the other side of the Citadelle. The body is either on the paved walkway that runs alongside the water, or it might be on the rocks below it. The guy that phoned in on his mobile had a really bad signal. They could hardly make out a word he said.'

Darac glanced at the fortress-like structure morphing

into abstract shapes on the rain-streaked rear screen. 'All that masonry in the way, I guess.'

'Yes. Perand's with him. Or should be by now.'

Bonbon reached for his police-issue cap. Using the peak for leverage, he ratcheted it hard down on to his skull. The bird's nest of copper wire that was his hair had other ideas. The cap immediately began to rise.

'You need a chin strap.'

Bonbon kept his hand firmly on the crown of the cap as he got out of the car. 'This hair of mine. Talk about a blessing and a curse.'

'What's the blessing part?'

'Piss off.'

Leaning into stinging spits of rain, the pair set off along the void between the buttressed outer and inner walls of the Citadelle. It was like walking through a wind tunnel.

'One good thing about a filthy night,' Bonbon shouted. 'No rubberneckers.'

'We're not at the scene yet.'

Pulling the lapels of his leather jacket together, Darac glanced up at the sloping inner walls of the Citadelle. He wondered how many poor sods had been hurled to their deaths off its battlements over the centuries. Maybe that was what they would find waiting for them around the other side.

The walls extended to a narrow, turret-capped corner. Walking beneath it was like rounding the prow of a stone battleship. With every step, the wind tunnel effect eased but it was still a wild night. Ahead, lights danced on the choppy Rade de Villefranche like tinsel scattered on black satin. Black satin bounded by red cordon tape. The waterside walkway began at a wrought-iron gate. Next to it, a soft-walled shelter the size of a sentry box had been set up. Standing in it was a familiar figure wearing white hooded overalls.

'Hi, Patricia.'

'How'd you like my new on-site accommodation?' She struck a pose like a trade-show model. 'White. One-person. Strong but lightweight material. Good, huh?'

'Lovely.' Darac signed in and held the clipboard for Bonbon. 'White-clad gatekeeper; white walls; a stack of white garments waiting to be dispensed to new arrivals. All you're missing is St Peter.'

'He's gone for coffees.' She took back the clipboard. 'If by St Peter you mean the big, burly officer who's meant to be guarding me.'

Darac scanned the terrain. 'You're vulnerable here. He shouldn't have left you.'

'He'll be back in a minute. Besides, I'm armed.'

'Who's stationed at the other end of the walkway?'

'Emil. And he's not happy. No nice new shelter for *him*.'

Darac grinned at the pleasure in her voice. 'You're a wicked woman. So what have we got, Patricia?'

'A hanging. That's all I know.'

'The person who found the body around?'

'He lives back that way.' To her left, a flight of steps descended away from the Citadelle toward the Port de la Darse. Halfway down, a landing gave on to a lane. 'Perand's with him.'

'Okay. We'll take a look at the body first.'

A sudden gust lashed Patricia's shelter but it remained anchored to the spot.

'You warm enough in that thing?' Bonbon said.

'Only because of my thermals.' She dispensed a couple of sets of overalls. 'You didn't need to know that but I've stopped caring.'

Bonbon handed her a paper bag in exchange. 'Keep them. Aniseed twists.'

She unwrapped one immediately. 'You married, Bonbon?'

'Twenty years, nearly.'

'Pity.' She gave Darac a most unholy grin. 'It's one revelation after another this evening, isn't it?'

Another gust ripping through, Bonbon shivered like a Chihuahua whose owner had forgotten its waistcoat. 'Hang on – you're married as well, aren't you?'

'Twenty-*two* years. Slipped my mind for a moment.'

'Ai, ai, ai.'

Darac clocked a uniform with outstretched arms emerging at the top of the steps.

'St Peter's back. We'd better get to it.'

He glanced at the first signature on Patricia's sheet. It belonged to pathologist Carl Barrau.

'He's a new man since you tore him off a strip, Captain. He's even more obnoxious.'

'We'll see about that. Stay warm, sweetheart.'

The walkway under the seaward wall of the Citadelle was too narrow for a proper pathology tent so the team had set up a structure of screens and breaks instead. As Darac and Bonbon drew close, a flashgun fired a shadow-play of forms on to the rippling fabric. Downwind of the entrance, a pair of jocular figures were enjoying a crafty smoke. Darac recognised them as the two morgue boys from the Alain Saxe murder.

'Alright, guys? How's your hearing tonight?'

'Better wait and see, Captain.'

'So it's a hanging?'

'A bloke. Middle-aged. Fully clothed.'

'Dressed for outdoors?'

'Yeah but that's about all we know, really. Only just got here.'

'See you later.'

'We'll be in directly, Captain. If *he* wants to know.'

Its face to the wall, the body was hanging from a lantern bracket cast in the form of an anchor. Peering intently at the corpse's neck, the thin-limbed figure of Carl Barrau was clinging anxiously to a ladder set up alongside it.

Exuding his usual bonhomie, pathology lab assistant Lami Toto stepped pleasantly forward. 'Hello, Captain. Lieutenant.'

'Good to see you.'

Lami took a breath but Darac stopped him – Barrau using an assistant as a shield was a thing of the past.

'A moment, Lami.' Darac turned to the wall. 'Good evening, Dr Barrau.'

No response. But the man *was* hanging off a ladder all of a half-metre from the floor.

'Who? How? When? Any preliminary thoughts, Doctor?'

The morgue boys came back in at that moment. Excluding Barrau and the corpse, there were now five people at the scene. All eyes turned to the ladder. As if the four rungs he had to descend constituted a *Man on Wire*-style challenge, Barrau clung on for dear life as he went for it. After a dodgy moment on rung two, he made it. It took a special sort of person to metamorphose from quivering jelly to arrogant stuffed shirt but in the blink of an eye, Barrau aced it.

'Follow me, Captain,' he said, walking away. 'You also, Busquet. We'll need three more sets of overalls, Lami.'

'Yes, Doctor.'

Once out of earshot of the others, Barrau turned, a duellist ready to fire. 'After your unprofessional, unwarranted and ungrateful outburst, Darac, *I*, nevertheless, have been asked to effect certain changes in *my* approach – to wit, offering of preliminary opinions at the scene. Although I stress once again that the value of such opinions is limited by so many factors as to be virtually useless.'

'Not at all. You were spot-on with Alain Saxe.'

'That was an unusual case.'

'It was an excellent piece of analysis that was scarcely revised subsequently.'

Something as rare as hen's teeth appeared on Barrau's face. A smile. 'Don't try to curry favour with me, Darac.'

'No favour sought. You do good work, Barrau. Usually. We'll have no problems with each other if you implement' – he almost said 'Deanna's instructions' – 'the recommendation you mentioned.'

Barrau was clearly seething with righteous injustice yet there was an oddly positive look in his eyes. Something was giving him comfort. Darac understood right away what it was. Somewhere down the line, the pathologist expected Darac not just to bend regulations at some crime scene, but break them. That would be when Barrau exacted *his* revenge. And Darac suspected it would lead to far more than a ticking-off.

'Very well,' Barrau said. 'Let us return.'

Darac gazed along the path. 'It seems unlikely that a man would come out here to hang himself.'

'You have never known anything unlikely happen?'

Out of Barrau's eyeline, Bonbon performed 'Arrogant Masturbator' from his repertoire of character vignettes.

'Yes I have. Do you think the man hanged himself?'

'I… suspect he may have been strangled with a cord of some sort and then strung up.'

'What leads you to that conclusion?'

Barrau's lips tightened. 'There appear to be two ligature furrows around the neck: one a clear narrow lateral at the larynx; the other, a wider inverted V-shape. We'll get him down presently, at which point we will know more.' They slipped on fresh overalls. 'But even the sainted Professor Bianchi would tell you, Captain, that we won't know *exactly* what happened until we examine the body properly in the lab.'

Darac hated 'sainted'. 'I understand that.'

Familiar voices fought their way along the path. One was the delicately enunciated Ghanaian-accented French of Lartou, the officer responsible for collecting and logging evidence. The other was the booming delivery of Raul Ormans. 'Anything for me to look at?' Ormans said to no one in particular.

'The rocks abutting the path directly outside.'

'Who said that?' Ormans looked around theatrically – he knew perfectly well the words had been Barrau's. 'So what's good on the rocks? Apart from a dry Martini?'

'The doctor believes the man was killed before he was strung up,' Bonbon said, amused. He turned to Barrau. 'You're wondering if it happened out there, or if the body was brought there from elsewhere?'

As if fielding a question from a lowly lieutenant were a bridge too far, Barrau remained silent for a moment. 'Yes,' he said, finally. 'I do wonder that.'

Ormans looked astonished. 'Wondering at the scene? Well done, that man.'

Lartou opened a metal evidence case. 'Can we log the deceased's effects first, Lami? If that's alright with you.'

'Can't, I'm afraid. There are none. Pockets empty. No ID. No mobile. Nothing.'

Darac gave Ormans a look. 'Do you want to dust up there before we get him down, R.O.? Or after?'

'After will be fine.' He gave a nod to the morgue boys. 'As long as our brawny friends give it their feather-fingered best.'

'Don't let the body down on the rope,' Barrau cautioned them. 'Lift it up and support its weight.'

'Yes, Doctor,' the older man trilled, but his expression said: *We always do that, you prat.*

As the younger one hopped up the ladder, the older man positioned a trolley and locked its brakes. Taking a deep breath, he put his arms around the corpse's thighs.

'Don't loosen the running knot', Ormans said, 'until he's down. Happy with that, Barrau?' Barrau raised an eyebrow by way of agreement. 'He's happy.'

'Maybe there's a name tag in his clothes,' Lartou said, as the men took the strain.

'Heave!'

The move was accomplished with the minimum of fuss. But it was with the utmost care that they laid the body on to its back on the trolley. Discolouration, swelling, lingual protrusion, blood spotting – the face exhibited signs of both strangulation and hanging. And then Darac saw it.

'We won't need to check the clothes for an ID. I know who this man is.'

And knowing who he was had broken the case.

42

Good news travelled fast: Darac could hear the buzz in the squad room from way down the corridor.

'I've got tickets for the match,' a uniform called out. 'Tickets for the big game!'

Darac hoped that the celebrations weren't premature. He may have broken the case but whether it would bring a speedy end to the murder-by-murder liquidation of the So-Pro gang was still open to question. He tossed his bag on to the front centre desk and for the moment, just stood taking in the scene.

From Agnès on down, officers from several divisions had made it in. A group had gathered around the seated figure of Wanda Korneliuk. The patrol car ace was either demonstrating how to perform a drum solo or a handbrake turn. Probably the latter, he decided. Flaco seemed particularly fascinated, he noticed. He made a mental note not to accept a lift with her for a while.

Over by the water cooler, strapping beat officer Serge Paulin was sharing a joke with Bonbon and sketch artist Astrid Pireque. The talented young rugby player was making the story live, judging by their helpless reactions.

A motley assortment of photocopiers and other electronica lived in the far corner of the room. Lartou Lartigue appeared to be giving a seminar on the subject of the exposed cabling that hung like thrown spaghetti from the ceiling above it. He alone, it seemed, knew what went where and why.

As Flaco took a turn in the driver's seat, another peal of laughter rang out from Serge's corner. The whole atmosphere put Darac in mind of the Blue Devil's dressing room before a DMQ gig. Since looking into So-Pro, he'd been thinking about his year-long secondment with the Brigade in Paris, the cause of his absence during the investigation. He'd found it a sobering experience. Yes, the workload had been huge. Yes, the problems they faced had sometimes proved intractable. But his team in Paris would have fared much better, he believed, if they had gone about things less like a dysfunctional family and more like a united group. It had been a team in name only. It was thanks to Agnès's stewardship that a culture of true teamwork thrived in the Nice Brigade; teamwork in which individuals, even mavericks like him, were given scope to express themselves.

His mobile rang. Parking his backside on the desk, he took the call.

'Paul,' his father said, 'I was expecting to leave a message. Are you on a break or something?'

'No, I had to abandon the club. Called out on a case.'

'You got to play your beloved old guitar first, I hope?'

'Still awaiting that pleasure.'

Granot entered the room, pausing to whisper, 'Just had a thought,' in Darac's ear. He gave the big man a thumbs-up as he joined the throng. Granot's 'just had' thoughts were usually invaluable.

'Ah, pity,' Darac *père* went on. 'Anyway, is this convenient? Only take a second.'

'Yes, go ahead. Things are still being set up here.' He smothered the mouthpiece as he opened his bag. 'Anyone bringing me a double espresso will be promoted immediately.'

Serge Paulin volunteered to run what he must have known was a fool's errand. Within a couple of paces, he was taking orders from all around the room. Darac caught Erica's smile as her man called on the spurned Perand, of all people, to help him.

'So basically, Paul,' Martin went on, 'Julie would love to stick to our original plan for tomorrow night.'

'You're marrying someone who doesn't like *caille au thym*?'

'That would be unconscionable, I agree. No, it's the café idea she's not keen on.'

'The place may be humble but the chef is a genius, I've heard.'

'It's not that. She's got her heart set on us eating at your place, that's all. Seeing where you live. Experiencing the roof terrace and everything. I think it's sweet.'

'Well, alright, but if we have a storm like we did earlier, we won't be venturing out on to the terrace.'

'Thanks, Paul. So what will you make?'

'Uh… I could do my *poulet à l'estragon*, I suppose.'

Frankie caught his eye and shook her head.

'Or my *poulet au citron*, perhaps?'

'Wonderful. Julie will be delighted.'

'She does realise—'

'I've told her you may have to leave suddenly or even cancel at the last minute.'

'And it didn't deter her?'

'Nothing deters Julie. She thinks your job is utterly fascinating, anyway.'

The first of the espressos was on its way.

'Listen, will you ring the café to cancel? I'm on in a minute.' He ran a hand through his hair. 'I mean, I'll be busy.'

'I'll do it straight away.'

'And tell them it is just a postponement. We ought to go soon – Chef Max looks as if he might succumb to a coronary at any moment. Just the two of us. How's that?'

'Excellent idea.'

'Until tomorrow.'

'Indeed. Oh, one last thing. Is it alright if Julie gives you a ring tomorrow morning? She has a favour to ask. Well, she called it a favour. Actually she has something for you.'

'Uh… yes, I suppose so.'

'Good. And, Paul? Thank you again. For everything.'

'Sure.'

Darac gave Perand a sympathetic smile as he took his espresso. He'd tasted the bitterness of unrequited love himself. But he'd never been dragooned into domesticity by the woman's lover into the bargain.

As drinks were dispensed and Frankie helped Erica set up an array of visual aids, Darac went to share a few thoughts with Agnès. Their conversation flowed as easily and amusingly as normal but at moments he wondered if he detected a new note, a subtle new scent in the atmosphere between them. There could only be one cause: the rumour of his burgeoning relationship with Frankie. He tried to assess Agnès's feelings about it. Not flat-out disapproval, certainly. Nor distance or disappointment. But there was something.

A call came in on the hot-desk phone. A light indicated it was from the duty officer's desk along the corridor. Bonbon took it and handed Agnès the receiver.

'Go ahead, Bé.' She listened for a moment and responded, 'Tell them no comment on the Villefranche hanging for now.' Agnès handed back the phone. 'My, it's taxing being commissaire.' She slipped off her shoes. 'Alright. Ready, Erica?'

'All set, Agnès.'

'Paul? Dazzle us.'

'Well I'll start, anyway. This is what Bonbon and I found at the scene.' He gave Erica a nod. A shot of the hanged man, face to the Citadelle wall, filled one of the screens. 'We'll go into the "how?" of this murder later but let's start with the "who?" because it's significant. Next one, please.'

Erica brought up the desperate face of a man whose life had been squeezed out of him. Studying it, Darac wasn't alone in filling his lungs for the sheer pleasure of breathing.

'He looks vaguely familiar,' she said. 'Who is it?'

'None other than Monsieur Jean Aureuil. The man who earned the two-million-euro So-Pro reward.'

Voices rose in the air like startled pigeons. Flaco seemed especially exercised at the news. 'It's too great a coincidence that the murder isn't the work of Pierre Delmas, but how could it be?' she said. 'Aureuil's name was never released.'

'Anyone have a theory on that?' Darac asked the room. 'No? What if Delmas knew Aureuil's name already?'

Around the room, brows were still furrowed. And then Agnès clicked her fingers. Eight years too late, she realised what the gang had actually done.

Clocking that she had the whole thing down, Darac gave her a look. 'Like to—?'

'No, no.' She shook her head in frustration. 'You outline it.'

'Alright.' He shifted his weight on the desk. 'From the beginning, we focussed on the fact that the robbery, although executed with panache, was ultimately unsuccessful. Everything was returned, there were no ill-gotten gains to divide up between the thieves. We were left considering that Pierre Delmas may have negotiated a separate deal with the others beforehand. And it was *that* sum, earmarked for his daughter Sylvie, that he was cheated out of subsequently. We got that wrong.' He raised both hands. 'In fact, *I* got that wrong. Delmas didn't need to negotiate such a deal because there *were* ill-gotten gains to divide.'

'The reward itself!' Perand said, sounding as if he admired both the concept and his own perspicacity.

'Exactly. With Jean Aureuil's murder and other developments, I'm sure that the reward was what the gang was after from the start.'

Flaco raised a hand. 'Isn't there a problem with that? From the gang's point of view, I mean. The reward was two million euros and the haul was... how much, again?'

'Nineteen million-plus in cash,' Granot said, twisting the end of his moustache. 'And there was jewellery and other stuff.'

'So the gang beat the alarms,' Flaco went on. 'They dug a tunnel. They set up the elaborate scenario to confuse us. They also broke into the safety deposit boxes. And more besides. That's a lot of work to put in, unnecessarily. And on top of all that, they got away. Got away without having to resort to violence, hate, weapons, et cetera. So they wind up getting two million when they actually had got clean away with more than nineteen million. That doesn't add up.'

'*Clean* away?' Darac said.

'Well they did, didn't they, Captain? To start with.'

Granot stopped playing with his moustache. It was time for him to speak and Darac recognised it.

'Go on, mate.'

'The original So-Gén gang of '76 got clean away, too,' he said. 'From the bank itself, that is. But that's only the start of your problems as a bank robber. What do you do with the traceable loot, like the jewels? Fence it? Barter it for drugs? Do you launder just the cash? It sounds straightforward enough but there are a number of problems. First, the return from illegal laundering or selling on the black market is always lower than the value of the original stash. Then there's the fact that setting up the deals inevitably brings more people into the equation and that hugely multiplies the risk of someone talking, or being made to talk, to us. And before all that happens, there's the problem of maintaining the integrity of the haul itself. My experience is that one or more of the gang invariably keeps something back. They see a watch, a ring or a necklace they like the look of and pocket it. And then they give it to a girlfriend who goes and wears it to the policemen's ball.'

Laughter all round.

'Or they use some of the stolen cash to buy a car or whatever and the notes are subsequently traced by some poor sweat like me.' Winding up to the finish, he took on a more serious mien. 'It's absolutely in this *après*-robbery phase that over ninety per cent of' – he supplied airborne speech marks – '*successful* robberies fail and the brilliant and daring gang members get caught. Set against those odds, our So-Pro boys made a terrific bet. A guaranteed two million euro payout? Fantastic.'

'Beautifully summarised,' Agnès said. She gave Flaco a look. 'Alright?'

'I see it, yes.'

Bonbon was wrapped around his chair in a knot of Gordian complexity. But there was nothing tangled about his thinking.

'Going for the reward *is* the percentage play, when you think about it – providing there aren't hundreds of people in the gang.'

It was hardly necessary, but Frankie raised a finger to attract Darac's attention. He felt like answering, 'Yes, darling?' but decided against it. They were under scrutiny as it was.

'So Jean Aureuil, solely, scooped the two million euro reward.' She turned to Granot. 'How did they divide it up, do you suppose?'

'He couldn't write cheques for the amounts, clearly. I think when I follow the money, I'll find a trail of share deals, small business purchases and so on that involve the others. But there's an obvious point here we haven't touched on. So obvious, I only thought of it just before the meeting.' Granot's expression was one of imperious certainty. 'We've got Jean Aureuil – dead. We've got Michel Fouste, Carl Halevy and Alain Saxe – dead. All within a few days of each other. And on Saxe, thanks to Erica's way with a hard drive we have this column of figures.' He brandished a computer printout. 'It's headed "400,000"; the rows below it are subtractions from that principal. This is the second reference we've come across to the number four hundred thousand; the other was on Sylvie's fake bank statement. So assuming equal shares, which now seems probable, we know how many were in the gang, don't we? Two million divided by four hundred thousand equals five. Four dead plus Delmas, in other words. And that, my friends, means Aureuil's death will be the last. The killings have stopped.'

It was a cogent argument and all around the room, what had been strained minds and bodies until an hour or so ago began to relax even more. Whether they were criminals or not, corpses piling up all over the city was something every officer abhorred.

'So, chief,' Granot went on. 'You can shelve your concerns about A1 Security and other parties.'

'Good work, Granot,' Darac said. 'I sense there's more to come on this aspect but whether there is or not, our primary goal remains the same: catch Pierre Delmas.'

Frankie looked up from her notes. 'I take it he's still made no application to the utilities? Internet provider, phone, housing people?'

'Nor to a medical practice, interestingly.' His eyes locked on hers. 'Be interesting to see what happens next, won't it?'

'Yes. It will.'

Granot's gaze joined the traffic streaming on to the Darac–Frankie freeway. Trading coded messages? The pair had forgotten their audience.

'Yes,' the big man said, bristling. 'What *Delmas* will do next is interesting. It's of paramount interest, in fact.'

'He might give himself up now,' Flaco said.

'"My work is done here?"' Perand gave her a sideways

look. 'So why didn't he turn himself in right after killing Aureuil?'

'Could be a lot of reasons.'

'On the hanging,' Agnès said. 'Let's rewind to the "how" you mentioned, Paul.'

'Perand interviewed the man who found the body.'

'Okay... Can we have the next slide?' Perand asked Erica.

A paved waterside walkway came up on the screen.

'Despite the weather, it was on this path that at about 8.45 p.m., one Monsieur Patrice Feilleu was walking his dog.' He checked his notes. 'Fifi. A poodle.'

'God bless the dog walkers of this world,' Bonbon said.

'Yeah, let's hear it for them. Feilleu's head was down against the wind and rain and he says he may even have passed by the body without spotting it. Fifi went ape, though. Erica?'

The shot of Aureuil hanging once more appeared on the screen.

'Feilleu called in on his mobile straight away and then waited until we got there. No one else came in the meantime and he saw no one else on or near the path beforehand.'

'8.45,' Agnès said. 'Has the new improved Barrau been of any help establishing the time of death?'

Still wrapped around his chair, Bonbon somehow fished his notebook from his pocket.

'He reckoned... sometime between 8.30 a.m. and 8.30 p.m.'

Agnès made a sound in her throat. 'Not exactly pinpoint, considering the circumstances. The bugger's punishing us. Did he offer *anything* useful, Bonbon?'

'To be fair, he did. Aureuil was strangled from behind with a ligature of some sort' – Erica brought up a close-up shot of Aureuil's neck – 'and then was laid on his back for an unspecified time.'

'There was lividity staining?'

'Indeed there was.'

Erica showed a montage of Aureuil's back and legs. Purplish patches had formed where pooled blood had leaked into the tissues. There were also abrasions on the skin.

Anticipating Agnès's next question, Raul Ormans riffled the pages of his notebook.

'Ye-es, those abrasions correspond to tears in the man's jacket.' He swivelled his glasses up on to his pate. 'Erica, I believe we have that slide as well?'

The shot came up.

'At great personal peril, I found a patch of material on the slippery rocks below the walkway.' He looked expectantly at the screen. 'Rocks below? Do we have a shot of that?'

'Sorry. No rocks.'

'Alright – you'll just have to picture it. I haven't had time to run the test yet but I think the patch will match Aureuil's jacket.'

'So the body was laid on the rocks, initially? How did it arrive there? Have you anything to show us, Lartou?'

'I'm afraid not.'

A groan went up.

'But the fact I have nothing is significant. The CCTV cameras covering the ends of the walkway are working perfectly and there's no sign of a hanging party in the footage.'

'Not being caught on CCTV fits Delmas's security background.' Agnès shared a look with Darac. 'So how did the body get on to the walkway?'

'Unless Delmas abseiled down the Citadelle wall, which, let's face it, is unlikely, he must have arrived at the scene by boat. A small, shallow-draft one. A motorboat, say.'

'With the victim lying on deck. Or somewhere horizontally, anyway. A few seconds lying on the rocks wouldn't have given all that lividity.'

'Then he strung up the body, clambered back on to the boat and left as he had come.'

Agnès gave Perand a look. 'It's a long shot but better get on to Maritime.'

He made a note of it. 'Okay.'

'Now?'

'Oh, right.'

As Perand picked up the phone, Agnès took things forward again. 'If you wanted to disguise a strangling as a suicide by hanging, you wouldn't do any of this, obviously. So what other reason could there be for stringing up a strangled body? And why do it in such a public place?'

Granot gave a very convinced nod. 'Delmas is displaying the final gang member's body as a kind of trophy. He's saying: "Look, everybody – I've won."'

'It's one interpretation, certainly,' Darac said. 'I don't want to burst our bubble but let's just speculate for a moment that Aureuil *isn't* the final victim—'

'He *is*, I'm telling you.'

Darac saw Granot's irritation and raised it. 'Just as speculation, if that's alright with you? Displaying a body like that could also act as a warning to others, couldn't it?'

Granot shrugged.

'Let's rewind a little,' Agnès said. 'Whether it was an act of triumphalism or to serve as a warning, I'm exercised by the venue. Yes, the walkway is well-frequented and the killer knew a hanging corpse would soon be discovered. But how was it that *he* wasn't discovered hanging it? What he did must have taken quite some time.'

Darac nodded. 'It may be a popular spot for a stroll in normal weather but in heavy rain and with a gale blowing? I think Delmas simply assumed no one would be around.'

'Vis-à-vis our dog walker, he got that part wrong,' Bonbon said. 'But happily for him, not when he was actually performing his hangman routine.'

Perand put down his phone. 'Maritime have nothing. Large vessels? Yes, they're all over them. Small fry? Not so much.'

'Thank you.' Agnès sat back, her forehead creased in fine, almost exactly parallel lines. 'Physically strong, isn't he? Pierre Delmas. For a dying man.'

The thought hadn't occurred to Darac. 'Think he had help?'

'I wonder.'

'Not that this woman looks the type to help string up dead bodies,' Astrid said, retrieving her sketch pad from her bag. 'But as we're on the subject of Delmas's possible pals, I've got one here.' She flicked through pages. 'I did it at Café Grinda... Good call on the quail, by the way, Darac.'

'I thought you were a vegetarian,' Granot said, perplexed.

'Because the thought of munching slaughtered songbirds doesn't do it for me?'

'Meat's meat.'

'Thanks for that. Anyway, here we go.' She held up a page showing a watercolour sketch of a pleasant-looking red-headed woman. 'This is the woman the staff at the café saw having dinner with Delmas shortly before the So-Pro job.'

'Let me see that,' Darac said, reaching. It couldn't be. Could it?

'Know her?' Agnès said.

'I… I'm not sure.'

But he made a mental note to ask Bonbon and Flaco back to his office afterwards. He had something he wanted to run by them.

He didn't have long to wait. The meeting broke up ten minutes later with no further progress having being made.

'Okay, you're going to think I'm crazy,' he said, back in his office.

'Bit late for that, mate,' Bonbon said.

Darac held up Astrid's watercolour. 'She look familiar?'

'N-no.'

'Flak?'

'Who do you think it is, Captain?'

'Answering a question with a question?' He propped up the sketch on his desk and went to sit behind it. 'You've been in the Brigade too long.'

She smiled. 'No, I don't recognise her.'

'Think back to the shooting at the cemetery. Except for Delmas and Carl Halevy, you met everyone who was at the scene.'

'The cemetery? Who could—?'

'Don't try to work out *how* anyone there could possibly be connected to Delmas. Just look at the likeness.'

The pair looked harder at the sketch. After a moment, the dawn of realisation broke on Bonbon's face.

'You don't mean your father's girlfriend – Julie Issert?'

'Yes.'

'I *do* think you're crazy.' He indicated the painting. 'This woman looks no more like Julie than any other attractive red-headed woman. Of a similar age.'

'Well, you'd have to compensate for that a bit.' Flaco closed one eye as she made the calculation. 'You'd have to add eight years.' She studied the image once more. 'Even so, Captain, I don't see it.'

'Okay – the likeness isn't working, so consider this. Since he's been out, the only party we know of who's tried to contact Delmas in person is a motorcyclist. Came to his apartment in Villeneuve-Loubet.'

Bonbon nodded. 'The one Madame Tofu or whatever she was called saw at his door?'

'Madame Otaphu, yes. Remember, Flak?'

'I do. She couldn't say whether the person was male or female.'

'*May* have been female?' Bonbon let out an involuntary breath. 'Come on, chief.'

'Wait. What else, Flak?'

'The motorcyclist was wearing a blue or black helmet with initials on it.' They appeared to be hovering somewhere above her head. 'Uh… B.L.… R.L.… B.I.… or R.I.' She lowered her gaze. 'That was what she said, I think.'

'Hey – "I" for "Issert". Got her!' Bonbon's faux-amazed expression didn't last. 'And not even *J*.I. at that.'

'Julie does ride a motorcycle, though.'

'So do lots of women.'

'Actually, they don't,' Flaco said. 'Women ride scooters and mopeds. Very few ride motorcycles.'

'It's a big one, apparently. Big and fast. Papa has refused every entreaty to get on the pillion.'

'Alright, but it's thin. Paper thin.' Bonbon proffered a bag from his pocket. 'Banana Bongo either of you?' No takers. 'And you know it is, surely.'

Darac sat back in his chair. 'It is thin – you're right. But we've had thinner, haven't we? Some very flimsy things have worked out in the end.'

Bonbon smiled his avuncular smile. 'You know what I think is happening here, chief?'

'You think I've got it in for the woman.'

'Possibly.' The sucked sweet softened the word into a sibilant slosh. 'But mainly, I think we're back to perception. You've got Julie on the brain so you see her in everything.'

Darac exhaled deeply. 'I am thinking a lot about the woman at the moment.'

'You know I just bought a new car? I thought I might have a change, this time. Go for more practicality, reliability. Something I could use on my antiques trips. I started thinking about a Toyota Estate. So the next thing that happens, everywhere I go, I see nothing *but* Toyota Estates. A couple of days later, I started to wonder if a Volvo wouldn't suit me better. No Toyotas to be seen now. It's wall-to-wall Volvos everywhere. It's just how minds work.'

'I think the lieutenant's right, Captain.'

Darac closed his eyes, tired suddenly.

'Yes. I think he probably is.'

43

Pierre Delmas had no problems getting out of bed. After the strenuous work he'd got through yesterday, he felt in need of a good breakfast. Coffee and, with any luck, croissants. But as his headache was of only average intensity, he decided to tackle his exercises first. He felt it important to keep his fitness level high. He still had a lot to accomplish and any edge he could maintain was worthwhile.

It wasn't until he was in the shower afterwards that he realised he'd forgotten part of the routine. He'd missed out the star jumps. Resolving to make up for it the next time, he stepped out of the cubicle and picked up a thick, fluffy towel from a heated rail.

'What a nice touch,' he said aloud.

Turning his MP3 player back on, he went downstairs and for some moments stood looking out of the kitchen window. It was a dismal morning, the higher ground shrouded under heavy blankets of cloud. In his earphones 'Surf Beach' shuffled to 'Falling Rain'. There was no sign of a beach outside but it started raining almost immediately.

If it were ever necessary, Delmas knew he could heave a sack of coffee on to his chest and press it clear over his head. Repeatedly. He found lifting a single spoonful altogether more difficult. Not trusting the steadiness of his hands, he positioned the Moka pot base in the sink and turned on the cold tap. Air in the pipes made a banging sound as the water poured in. He looked at his digital watch. After precisely four seconds, he turned off the tap and peered into the pot. The water level exactly bisected the valve. Perfect. Now he faced the challenge of filling the basket with a few grams of coffee. He set it on the work surface, shook the caddy above it until it overflowed, and then scraped the excess back in using a knife blade. Without further mishap, he screwed the two halves of the pot together and set it on the stove.

Three fresh croissants had been left for him in the stoneware bin. Another nice touch. He tried not to crush them as he took them out.

Delmas's MP3 player had a preset for the France Info radio station. He selected it with some difficulty and listened in. A man had been found hanged in Villefranche, the female newsreader announced. Police were making no comment as yet but observers believed a connection with a series of recent suspicious deaths in the area could not be ruled out.

'Come on, Captain…' He couldn't think of the name. 'Well come on, Commissaire Dantier, then. You can do better than that.' He pressed the record button on his player and left himself a voice message. 'Buy more croissants,' he said.

44

'People will talk,' Darac said, setting down his pen as Frankie appeared in his office doorway. 'That was a joke.'

'I've got something better. Have you seen this?' She displayed the local *St-Roch Express* newspaper, opened at an inside page. 'It's today's.'

Darac craned his neck.

'"PARISIAN'S WHITE RECYCLING BIN FOUND IN EZE." You couldn't make it up, could you?'

'Not that, you idiot.'

Marucca filled Darac's nostrils as Frankie set the paper down in front of him. A photo showed 'jazz fans' Jacques Telonne and wife Elise snapping their fingers in time with the 'Didier Masso Septet'.

'Jesus Christ… And Masso? That's *Musso*. The Didier Musso *Quin*tet!'

'There were seven of you, after all.'

'Three-strong, seven, twelve, we're *always* the Quintet.' He looked at the photos accompanying the article. 'Telonne and his wife grinning like hyenas, look.'

'I know. But my favourite thing?' She leaned forward. A wave of hair dark as midnight rolled across his cheek. 'Look at the other photo – Frènes and Telonne's daughter.' Frankie's laugh was a rich, contralto gurgle. 'I've seen people having more fun in the morgue.' Her shoulders were shaking. 'Read the piece.'

Darac couldn't have read his own name at that moment. His senses were reeling. But now was not the time to give in to them. *You're not a schoolboy,* he said to himself. *Stop being so foolish.* It was sound advice but he needed a better antidote than common sense. Granot. Nothing more effective. Granot and his Pandora's box image. Pandora's box with hanged men, drowned men and exhumed remains flying out of it. It helped but it still took a considerable effort of will to turn his attention to the paper. Shifting his focus to the page, he found his voice. '"Jacques Telonne's music-mad daughter, Laure, loved the Septet so much, she's already asked if she can visit the Blue Devil club again next Thursday." I'll bet she has. "Here we see the youngster with family friend, the *Juge de Jazz*, Jules Frènes…" What?'

He ran aground. Pandora's box as an antidote? It was a sugar pill compared to the notion of a jazzed-up Frènes. Darac's outrage made Frankie laugh all the more. He shook his head, steeling himself for the finale.

'"The *Juge de Jazz*, Jules Frènes, grooving to…" What's this? "Blues For Philly Jones." That was the number the band played immediately after Bonbon came for me. But *Philly Jones*? They can't get anything right, these people.'

'Isn't it priceless?'

Righting herself, Frankie swept her hair away from her forehead and stood gathering it at the nape of her neck. Watching her, Darac knew that not even the *Juge de Jazz* could help him now.

'"Blues For Philly Joe" is what the tune is actually called,' he found himself saying.

'Really?'

Even before she caught the look in his eyes, the bobbing cork of her levity was ebbing away on the tide. She returned the look. His pulse quickened. Despite everything they had told themselves, and each other, she must be feeling as he was.

'Though his name *was* Jones,' he said, his words drifting. Drifting low and slow. 'Philly Joe Jones. Drummer. From Philadelphia.'

'Hence the name. Philly.'

'Philly. Yes. Indeed.' Lower and slower now. 'He… wasn't the Jones of Hank, Thad or Elvin fame, of course.'

'No, no.' Their lips almost touching, she shook her head slightly. 'Of course not.'

'Brothers, they were. Nor… was he related to drummer *Jo* Jones. Strangely.'

'Oh, I thought' – her voice no more than a breath – 'that was *his* name?'

'There are two drummers called that. There's uh… Jo Jones. And Philly Joe. Jones. And then there's Elvin, as I say. Elvin—'

'Jones.'

'Yes.'

'It's confusing.'

Their eyes were swimming in each other's. The strategy was failing. Hopelessly. A phone rang. And rang again. The beige one. An outside line. A lifeline, perhaps, but one Darac was no longer sure he wanted.

'I suppose I'd…'

'Better get that?'

He nodded. 'Darac.' It didn't matter who was calling.

'Stay on the line, please. I'm putting you on hold.'

With only a moment to adjust to the change in atmosphere, he felt the sort of disorientation a diver might feel when forced back to the surface.

Frankie made it easier for him. 'I'm going,' she whispered. Picking up the newspaper, she squeezed his free hand and quietly took her leave.

I'm a free spirit, he said to himself. *An improviser. An iconoclast. Go after her!* He was also a captain of police in the middle of a murder investigation. He closed his eyes and let out a long breath.

'Yes, uh… sorry about that. Go ahead, please.'

'Paul? It's Julie. Martin mentioned I may call?'

'Yes, he did. What can I do for you?'

'First, I want to apologise for being such a demanding dinner guest. Thank you so much for changing your plans just for me.'

'Uh… not at all. It was I who changed them originally, anyway.'

'That's kind. I have another favour to ask, actually. If you have a moment.'

Julie's call was working miracles.

'Fire away.'

'Are you sure? I know how busy you must be.'

A Mont Blanc of paperwork dominated the eastern horizon of his office. But with Delmas's days of reckoning just possibly over, and with forces all over the area looking for the man, Darac was actually less stretched than usual.

'It's fine, honestly. Go ahead.'

'Thank you. I don't know if Martin has mentioned my late brother to you – Sebastien?'

If his father had mentioned him, he couldn't recall it. He sounded important to her. 'I think he did say something.'

'That's nice. We were very close, he and I. He died in a motorcycle accident.'

'I'm sorry.' He gave it a beat. 'Papa tells me you ride, also. It hasn't deterred you.'

'You only live once, don't you?'

'I'm inclined to think so, yes.'

'Besides…'

Bonbon entered, pointed at the espresso machine, and raised both eyebrows.

Darac nodded and then smothered the mouthpiece. 'It's Julie.'

Bonbon's brows lowered accusingly.

'*She* rang *me*,' Darac said, and then uncovered the mouthpiece. 'Sorry, I didn't catch that last bit.'

'I said, besides, I have a talisman with me whenever I ride.'

A here-and-now rationalist with an irrational, sentimental streak? His kinship with the woman was growing. 'A talisman?'

'Yes, I wear one of Sebastien's old helmets.'

Other considerations were put on hold. Darac was back with Delmas's neighbour, Madame Otaphu. Sebastien Issert… Initials S.I. Pretty close to the alternatives the woman had come up with. 'You always wear it?' He gave Bonbon a look. 'Whenever you're out on the bike?'

'Always. And if Sebastien had done, he'd be with us now. He was squirting round to the local Monop' when it happened. He'd ridden all over Europe and North Africa, tens of thousands of kilometres, without any real mishap. He runs out of milk and he's killed.'

'Awful. And very tough for you.'

'But this is all by the by. Listen, I know you're a gifted jazz player but Martin tells me you're into the blues, also.'

Into the blues? It sounded odd coming from a girlfriend of Martin's. And where was this going? 'Yes I am into the blues. In fact, it was through it that I got into jazz.'

'Sebastien was a huge blues fan.'

'Uh-huh?'

'Tell me if this is of no interest but I still have a lot of his stuff. Mainly records – you know, vinyl LPs.'

'And you want to know where you could sell them, or something?'

'No, not that, although some of them are pretty rare, I think.'

If Julie hadn't pricked Darac's interest before, she was warming up the needle now. '*Are* they?'

'Obscure labels, things like that. Martin says you still own a record deck?'

'Absolutely.'

'Well, why don't you come and look at what there is? Borrow them if you'd like to. I'm never going to play them. Haven't got a record player now, anyway.'

'Thank you. So who were your brother's heroes?'

'All sorts of people. But his favourite was Little Somebody or other.'

'There are a lot of Littles.'

She laughed. 'I like that.'

Bonbon looked on from the Gaggia, increasingly intrigued by the exchange.

'I would love to look through them, Julie.'

'Good. They're just sitting here in a box.'

'Here?'

'I'm calling from home. I've been thinking for a while that Bastien's records ought to go where they would be listened to and enjoyed. You can have them on permanent loan.'

Bastien, Darac repeated to himself. Her brother's pet name. That made the initials B.I. And that *was* one of Madame Otaphu's alternatives. 'Uh, you must let me pay for anything—'

'No, no. Certainly not.'

'Very kind of you. Truly. Look, things can suddenly get ridiculous here so if it would be convenient, may I come over now?'

'Perfect. I'm meeting some clients to start planning their round-the-world trip shortly so I'm going to be up against it for a while, myself.'

'I haven't got your address. It's Saint-Sylvestre, isn't it?'

'Just off Boulevard de Cessole at the top – Boulevard Jean Behra. I have a small villa. Very small, actually, but it stands on its own.'

She gave the address and told him where he could park. They ended the conversation on a cordial, even upbeat note.

'There you go.' Bonbon handed Darac a double espresso. 'You're going to be one big happy family, aren't you? By the sound of it.'

'Bit early to say that.' Especially as he had just put Julie back in the frame as Delmas's visitor. 'But there is nothing like a shared experience of pain and suffering to bring people together. And that, Bonbon, is the power of the blues. Part of it, anyway.'

On his way out of the building, Darac realised that whatever he discovered at Julie's, there was something bluesy he could put out on permanent loan himself. He swiped his mobile.

'Freddy?'

'Captain Darac?'

'When do you get home from school?'

45

It was a curiously nightmarish sight. Blackened by the rain, the pollarded plane trees lining Boulevard de Cessole resembled nothing so much as charred, skeletal hands thrusting up out of the ground. What were they reaching for? Darac wondered. The light? Truth? Maybe just for an umbrella.

Following Julie's instructions, he turned into Boulevard Jean Behra and kept going until he found the concrete shoebox that was the church of St Francis. Splashing between puddles, he parked and went the rest of the way on foot. It had finally stopped raining but the shoulders of the surrounding Collines de Pessicart were drowned in gloom.

With its clean apricot-washed walls and crisp powder-blue shutters, Julie's villa presented a smart, attractive face to the street; a feminine, even girlish face. In the side entry, a 750cc Suzuki sat on its stand like a crouching cheetah.

'Paul.' Julie held the door wide open. 'What terrible weather.'

'The kind that people from elsewhere think we never have.'

'Indeed.'

The hallway smelled of orange blossom. Orange blossom and something woody.

She smiled prettily. 'Coffee? Croissants?' She indicated the kitchen, glimpsed through an open door at the end of the hall. 'I think there should be a couple left.'

'No thanks. And I'd better not stay too long, I guess.'

'Of course.'

She held out her hand for his leather jacket. He gave it to her.

'There's no tag. Just plonk it on the peg.'

She hung it on the stand next to her own. On the shelf below, her black crash hat was sitting with its back hidden against the wall.

'So this is the helmet you mentioned?' he said, hoping she might pick it up.

'Silly to keep it, really.'

'Not at all.' Not wishing to overdo things, he decided to leave it at that for the moment. He would be leaving that way, after all. 'I've really been thinking about who Sebastien's favourite Little might have been. How about Little Walter?'

'No, I don't think it was that. Come through.'

'Little Milton?'

He followed her down the hallway.

'Definitely wasn't that. Give me some others.'

'Little Joe Washington?'

'No, it was different. More whimsical.'

He hardly noticed that she was leading him upstairs.

'Little Smokey Smothers? That's fairly whimsical.'

They passed under the loft hatch on the landing...

'No, not that. Oh, what was it?'

...and entered her bedroom.

'Not Little Junior's Blue Flames? Songs like "Sittin', Drinkin' and Thinkin'"?'

Orange blossom, wood and fresh laundry.

'No, not that either. But I'll soon be able to put you out of your misery.'

A fitted wardrobe occupied the entire wall opposite the bed. She pulled open a louvre door, revealing a large cardboard box sitting at one end.

'Here it is.' She kneeled and began dragging it out.

Living with Angeline had taught Darac never to assume control in such situations. But Julie was shaking with the effort.

'Here, let me do that.'

She stood and took a pace back as he kneeled and pulled out the box. There must have been forty or so LPs and even a few 78s stacked vertically inside. The frontmost album, *Texas Blues Guitar*, brought a nod of recognition.

'Ah, here's your Little – Little Hat Jones.' Another Jones for Frankie, he thought. 'Your brother had good taste.'

'Yes, that's the name.' Standing directly over him, Julie reached behind her.

Darac picked up the album but then discovered a greater treasure underneath.

'This is really something. "The Blues of Alabama" on Yazoo but with the original Belzona label.'

She found her zip.

'It's incredibly rare.' Still on his knees, Darac was smiling as he turned to face her.

'You were right,' she said, stepping naked out of her dress. 'I am reckless. And so are you. You ran toward the gunfire.' She moved forward, her eyes on his. 'No one need know. No one need find out. Ever.'

She was in close. Darac stepped back, his foot skidding on the slick surface of the Belzona record. Instinctively, he bent down to put it back into its sleeve. Off balance, he was a pushover. She straddled him, enveloping him in her nakedness. He felt her hand search for his zip.

'Stop this!' Shoving her aside, he scrambled quickly to his feet. 'What do you think—'

'Don't be mean to me, sweetie.' She stood, advancing toward him so seductively, it was almost like parody. 'I want you. Come on—'

'Julie, listen to me—'

'No, you listen to me.'

He pushed past her and strode out on to the landing. Ignoring a torrent of entreaties, Darac ran quickly down the stairs, grabbed his jacket from the hall stand and jetted a glance back up to the landing. No Julie. He picked up Bastien's crash hat and turned it around in his hands. There was no B.I. nor any other initials on it. As he put it back, she appeared on the landing, still naked and looking curiously tranquil.

'You'll be back,' she said. 'Sometime. I know you will.'

Darac turned and closed the door behind him.

46

'I've heard from Julie, Paul.'

Darac braced himself. 'Papa.'

'She's so glad you loved the hoard.'

'Yes... there were some remarkable things. She didn't say anything else?'

'About what?'

He gazed out of the window. People were moving around the compound as normal. Beyond the barrier, life on Rue de Roquebillière looked the same as always. 'Papa, this may seem... Have you actually proposed to Julie yet?'

'I was thinking of doing it tomorrow, actually. By then we will have spent the evening with you, and so... Why?'

'Don't.'

'What?'

'I don't think Julie is quite the person you think she is.'

'Nonsense. Look, I can't really talk now but it's clear we need—'

'Papa, something happened at Julie's place. Something in her bedroom.'

'I can't imagine what you—'

'Papa! She threw herself at me. Naked.' Laughter from below. He moved away from the window. 'For God's sake, say something.'

When his father finally spoke, his voice had a hard, unfamiliar edge. 'I am finding it very difficult to say anything. It's never occurred to me that you could stoop this low.'

Darac sank back on to his desk, toppling a stack of files. One by one, they began to flutter slowly to the floor. 'Surely you believe what I'm saying?'

'I do not. It's sick. You are lying to prevent what is an entirely natural—'

'No. I'm not.' Like egg-timer sand, the files continued to fall. Darac pictured Julie's nakedness. He could describe it to his father. Describe her breasts, her sex – even its particular scent. Now *that* would convince him. 'Papa, listen to me…' He couldn't bring himself to go any further. But then he realised he shouldn't have to. 'You don't believe me but you believe a woman you've known for four months?'

The sands of time continued to run out. As the final file fell, it seemed the pair had nothing left to say to one another.

47

Steady rain did nothing for the marshalling yards at La Bocca, except slightly muffle the clinks and squeals of the rolling stock as Darac got out of his car and jogged across the parking lot to Granot.

'Malraux joining us?'

'He's off sick. Psoriasis.'

'I noticed the odd patch on his hands when he was working with us.'

Granot gave Darac a sideways glance. 'He'll come round, you know. Your papa.'

'Ah, yes?'

'Don't make out you don't care.'

They entered L'Hippocampe and crossed the lobby to the lift. The doors closed behind them.

'I *do* care. But I'll tell you this: even if he does come round, I may not.'

'What would that achieve?'

Darac turned to him. 'Do you believe what I said about Julie?'

'Yes.'

'So should he.'

'He should. But you can see why he wouldn't *want* to believe it, can't you?'

'Let's leave it there.'

Nothing more was said until the doors opened at the top floor.

'So why do you think Paulette Aureuil wants to see us, Granot? To tell us she's glad she doesn't have to live a lie any longer?'

Granot made a huffing noise in his throat. 'And risk a lawsuit from the bank to get the reward back? I doubt it.'

'Have you had time to go through their papers?'

'Haven't had time to have a shave, a shit or a haircut.' Granot looked nostalgic suddenly. 'As my old grandmother used to say.'

'Colourful lady.'

'It was grandpa, really, but it's a better gag with her.' He indicated a door. 'This it?'

'Uh-huh.'

Granot rang the bell. 'Erica find anything on their computer?'

'Not as yet.'

The door opened. Paulette Aureuil's eyes were red with grief. Barely glancing at their IDs, she said nothing as she let them in. Wiping his feet, Darac noticed a broad damp patch just above the knee of her navy-blue dress. He gave Granot a look. Perhaps they should leave immediately, and let Paulette sob in peace.

'She sent for us, remember,' Granot whispered, as they followed her into the apartment.

'Well, let's see how she holds up.'

A Labrador scampered solicitously around her as she led the pair into the living room.

The patio doors were closed, framing the Golfe de la Napoule in flat tones of grey.

Directing them to a cushion-strewn sofa, Paulette
subsided onto a stiff-backed armchair. The dog sat on the
floor next to her and keeping a weather eye on the visitors,
settled his chops over the wet patch on her dress.

'We understand what a terribly difficult time this must
be, madame.'

'Oh, do you?'

Paulette patently didn't believe Darac. But her sarcasm
encouraged him. Perhaps her face, swollen as a flooded
field, had absorbed all the outpouring it was going to.

'We can empathise, at least.'

'Have you made any progress? That's what I want to know.'

'We have strong suspicions about who may have
murdered Jean. And we are currently doing all we can to
apprehend that person. But before we get on to that, we'd
like to show you some faces. Is that alright?'

'I suppose so.'

Granot fired up his laptop. 'Clearer image than on my
mobile. Some of these names have been in the news but it's
only your possible *personal* connection with these people
that we're interested in.'

'Uh-huh.'

'This is Michel Fouste.' Granot angled the screen toward
her. 'Is he personally known to you?'

'No.'

'As far as you know, was he known to Jean?'

A shake of the head.

'This is Alain Saxe.' He waited. 'No? Okay… What
about Carl Halevy?'

More head shaking. There was just one image left to
show.

'This photo has been all over the media,' Darac said. 'So I'm sure you recognise it as Pierre Delmas. He was the only gang member to be sent down for the Société Provençale robbery of 2003. The robbery, I need hardly add, for which your husband subsequently earned a reward of two million euros.'

'I've seen the photo.'

'Think carefully. Have you ever—'

'I've never seen him in the flesh.'

It was perfectly possible that Paulette knew nothing of her husband's connection with Delmas but Darac had to pursue it. 'Have you ever wondered about the So-Pro robbery, madame? About the great good luck Jean enjoyed in coming across what he did up at Coaraze?'

The e-photo frame Darac recalled from his previous visit had been set down on the drinks cabinet. As if he were keen to take part in the conversation, a beaming Jean faded up on the screen.

'Enjoyed? Well, he's not enjoying it much at the moment, is he?'

'We know it's difficult,' Granot said, picking up the reins. 'But this is going to come out anyway and there probably never will be a good time to hear it.' She stiffened. Granot went on. 'We strongly believe that the So-Pro gang never intended to keep the spoils of the robbery. We believe their sole aim was to claim the reward offered for its return. We further believe that Delmas and the other names we gave you were Jean's accomplices in the scheme.'

'No. Rubbish. Complete rubbish.' A catch in the voice. 'How dare you?'

Sharing her distress, the dog whined and then barked.

'Quiet, Domino.'

Darac got to his feet. 'I'm afraid everything points to it, madame. But we can conclude this another time.'

'I didn't ask you to come here today so you could throw allegations around!'

Making an effortful noise, Granot hauled himself up from the foamy depths of the sofa. 'It's only natural that you would want to be kept updated on our search to find Jean's killer but we don't usually come out—'

'I didn't ask you here to be *updated*. I asked you here because of the burglary.'

'What burglary?'

'From our safe.'

Granot could not conceal his irritation. 'Yesterday, the officer who came to take away your computer asked where you kept your personal papers. You did not mention a safe.'

'The paperwork is kept in the bureau, and you've taken that. There's hardly anything in the safe but some jewellery and a few other odds and ends.' She rose. 'This way.'

The dog managed not to trip Paulette as he crossed and re-crossed in front of her en route to the bedroom. A sub-Dufy oil of the Baie des Anges hung on one wall. The safe, a simple affair, lived in a recess behind it. Three turns on the tumbler opened it. She took out two plastic trays and set them on a dresser.

Darac shared a look with Granot. They knew that every article of value had been recovered from So-Pro. But one or two unspecified low-value items from the inventories had not been found, nor had claims been made for them. Had Bonbon been along, he would probably have been able to put a tentative value on Paulette's jewellery collection. At first glance, it looked modest.

'Is it a piece of jewellery that's missing, madame?' Darac said.

'No.' She pointed to a space on one of the trays. 'It was there. A DVD.'

'A DVD of what?'

Paulette shook her head. 'I don't know. Not for sure.'

Granot clicked his tongue. Mourning or no mourning, the woman was continuing to annoy him. 'Madame, you've demonstrated that you know the combination to the safe. So you had access to the missing DVD.'

'Yes but Jean told me never to watch it.' She hesitated, embarrassed. 'He knew I wouldn't like it. Jean was always very considerate like that.'

'You thought it was porn?'

She looked Darac in the eyes. 'We never needed muck like that, you understand. But if it wasn't, I couldn't think what else it might be.'

Darac was already forming theories. 'So what was it doing in your safe?'

'I thought Jean must have been looking after it for someone else.' Granot gave her a look. 'Truly. Someone at the cab firm, probably.'

'How long had the DVD lived in the safe?'

Paulette shrugged as if she'd never considered the question before. 'Since we moved in, I suppose.'

Since So-Pro, in other words. 'And when did you notice it had gone missing?'

'This morning.' Her eyes welling up, she touched one of the earrings she was wearing. 'I wanted to put these on.

They were Jean's favourites.'

Darac felt sympathy for anyone who was grieving. In lieu of expressing it more directly to Paulette, he gave Domino's head a stroke. 'You used the word "burglary", madame. Were there any signs of a break-in?'

'No.'

'How do you know that Jean didn't get rid of the DVD himself?'

'It was still in the safe after he went out… for the last time. I saw it when I put a brooch back in there. I don't care that the blasted DVD is gone.' She shuddered. 'But it means *someone* has been sneaking around the apartment. *Someone* got into my bedroom. Anything could have happened.'

'We'll need to get Forensics in here, madame,' Darac said. 'Dust for prints, and so on.'

She nodded. 'I understand.'

'And we'll have to take the safe contents. We'll give you a receipt.'

'Alright.' She touched her earrings, anxiously. 'Could I—'

Granot shook his head. 'We'll need those, too.'

Darac gave him a glance as he swiped his mobile. 'We could just take photos of them.' Granot shrugged. 'Is that alright, madame?'

Paulette essayed a smile. 'And could I have a guard here, do you think? Please? Just for a day or two?'

'We'll have officers in the building and in the immediate vicinity anyway, asking questions. But I think it would be a good idea to assign someone.'

'What a relief. Thank you.' The larger crisis came crashing back into her head. 'But I have to say again that

Jean had absolutely nothing to do with that robbery.' She began to take off her earrings. 'Nothing!'

Granot pressed the button for the lift. 'Do you believe this DVD exists?'

'I don't disbelieve it. What do you reckon – footage from So-Pro?'

'I don't know. Why keep such a thing, exactly?'

'To shop the others? Or blackmail them? No – that doesn't work, Aureuil was part of it. To prevent *himself* being shopped or being blackmailed by the others? Or maybe the DVD was part of the haul – nothing to do with the gang.'

Granot's portrayal of disillusionment had been known to make examining magistrates weep. 'And I thought we'd finished with So-Pro itself.' The lift arrived. 'It was Delmas, clearly. The thief.'

Darac nodded. 'Getting into a cheap safe like that would be child's play to him.'

'Did he do it before or after he killed Jean, do you think?'

'How about during? Aureuil caught him in the act and that was that. We know Delmas moved the body.' He gave Granot a salutary look. 'If it *was* Delmas who killed him.'

Granot's mood was dropping faster than the lift. 'Alright. Let's hear it.'

'Even if Delmas did kill Aureuil, I've had a thought about the other killings. I like your idea that we could deduce the number of gang members by dividing the reward total by the amount of each share.'

'Hallelujah.'

'Four hundred thousand into two million gives us five. Five gang members altogether. But what if those shares were meant to be split more ways? What if Saxe, Fouste, Halevy and/or Aureuil were team leaders, each with people working for them? Those team members would obviously take their cut as well. Right?'

Granot shook his head, depression beginning to give way to irritation.

'I need the paperwork! Until I get that, all I've got is speculation. *Informed* speculation, but still speculation.'

'I know. And even when you've got it all, it could take weeks to sort out – longer.' He threw an arm around the big man's shoulders. 'But if you can't do it, nobody can.'

Granot acknowledged the compliment with a shrug. He looked his age, suddenly. 'One minute, we've got five gang members. Next minute, we've got any number of them. And that means...'

The lift doors opened.

'Exactly,' Darac said. 'It means the killings may not be over.'

48

Walter Picot put down the phone and rammed on his hard hat. Through the mud-spattered site-office window, he caught sight of Jacques Telonne arguing the toss with a contractor.

'Look at that. Squeezing his balls over a few euros. Cheap fucking bastard.'

'I don't think you should talk about Monsieur Telonne like that.'

Picot turned. 'How do you know I was talking about Jacques?'

Véronique looked away. Picot was a Great Dane of a man, all strapping power and unpredictable impulse, and she had no intention of taking the thing further. As if reading her lack of interest as a challenge, he moved toward her, grinning. Véronique was not intimidated.

'A building site is no place for you, darling. Why don't you go and powder your pretty little arse somewhere else?' The cabin door opened, bringing the site into the room, momentarily. 'Or would you like me to do it for you?'

Telonne sat down and began taking off his boots. 'Do what for her, Walter?'

'Nothing.' Picot gave Véronique a final leer before going over to join him. 'Seen the paper? Man found hanged. Villefranche. Weren't expecting that when you moved there, were you, Jacques? Must be like living in a fucking morgue.'

'Véronique?' Telonne called out, half-potentate, half-toddler in his stockinged feet. 'If you wouldn't mind?'

Without a moment's thought, she scanned the cabin for his loafers and went to pick them up. Picot's face collapsed in gratitude. 'That's thoughtful, darling, but I've got to go and check out the sewers.' He grabbed a couple of fat folders and opened the door. 'Come and see me later.' Giving them both a grin, he closed the door behind him and headed out on to the site.

'May I ask why you employ that man?'

'Yes.' Telonne slipped on his shoes. 'You may.' He stood and ran a comb through his hair. 'Have you booked our usual room?'

'Yes.'

'That's good.' He stroked the back of her hand with the comb. 'Isn't it.'

His mobile rang. 'It's that arse-wipe Frènes. I'll put him on speaker.'

'Jacques? Jules.'

Telonne smiled into his mobile as if he were on Skype. 'Jules! Or should I say Jules, *Juge de Jazz*?'

'Pah! Listen, I have an answer for you. On the status of waitress Fama Chinwe Ousmane.'

'Who?'

'You called her "the bitch", remember?' Véronique said. 'At the jazz club.'

'Ah yes, of course. What have you got, Jules?'

'The mademoiselle is a French citizen.'

In the yard, a group of mainly immigrant workers was

signing on for their shift. Telonne ran an eye over each and every one of their faces.

'Ah well,' he said. 'You win some, you lose some.'

49

Cranking up the volume on the Peugeot's CD player, Darac held his mobile to the speaker for a moment.

'Recognise that sound, Frankie?'

'Bit behind in my jazz homework.'

'We saw him at the Blue Devil. You and I.'

'That narrows it down. It must be the Israeli guy. The Israeli with the Palestinian point of view.'

A mass of frothy green leaves flounced past Darac's window. Peering somewhat anxiously through the fronds was a young woman carrying a pot.

'I never asked what you made of his political stance.'

'As a Jew? I share it. On the whole.'

On the pavement, the young woman was on a collision course with a black metal waste bin. 'Just a second, Frankie.' He opened his door to alert her but a passing jogger beat him to it and struck up a beautiful friendship on the spot. 'Panic over. Where were we before I got distracted by Gilad?'

'I was saying that your father is a very foolish man.'

'At least I won't have to buy a chicken, now. And cook it *au citron*.'

'You don't always have to be flip, Paul. You can scream or shout or cry. Or all three.'

'Actually, I am very sad about it.' He felt his hackles rising all over again. 'And mad. He didn't believe me, Frankie. I can't see much of a way back from that.'

'I'm sure there will be. Give it time.'

'And we've been closer lately. It's a shame.'

In his rear-view mirror, Darac saw a bus bound for Résidence des Baumettes draw into the stop and open its doors. A tide of teenagers flooded out. Among them was a figure carrying a shoulder bag bearing the logo of JAMCA, the Young Musicians of the Côte D'Azur. In a sea of largely sullen faces, Freddy's smiling mien shone out like a beacon.

'Now that you're free this evening and I'm off as well, why don't you come over?'

Darac's gaze drifted from Freddy like a panning camera. 'Come over? To… your place? In La Turbie?'

'It's the only place I have.'

'Yes, of course it is. Uh, will—?'

'Christophe is out of town. Rome. But I think we need to talk, Paul. *Just* talk.'

'Just talk. Absolutely.' Darac refocussed. Freddy was still chatting with his schoolfriends. 'And it has to be away from the Caserne, doesn't it?'

'Definitely. I'll cook something.'

'We'll talk and eat.'

'Preferably not at the same time.'

'Eight o'clock, Frankie?'

'Aim for that and we'll see how we go.'

'Well… see you later,' Darac said, imaginatively, and got out of the car.

'Freddy!'

'Oh, sorry, Captain, I didn't see you. I thought you were coming up to the apartment?'

They shook hands.

'Running a bit behind.'

'Shame. Mama wants to meet you.' The grin widened. 'I told her it wasn't worth it but—'

Darac feigned a punch.

'Are you sure you can't come up? I burned a couple of discs – JAMCA rehearsal stuff from Salle Pou.'

Darac's eyebrows rose.

'Salle Poulenc? That where you guys rehearse?'

'Cool, huh? Marco got us the funding in the first place; then he insisted that only the Salle was good enough for us.'

Darac laughed. 'That's Marco, alright. I'm looking forward to hearing your stuff. But next time?'

'I could email it to you.'

'Perfect.' He gave his address. 'Come here a second.' He stepped around to the rear of the car. 'I lose track of all Marco's projects but when you guys next get together at the Salle…'

'We're meeting tonight. Do you want me to pass something on to him?'

Darac opened the boot. 'No. I want to pass something on to you.' He took out the SG case and handed it to Freddy. 'Providing you promise not to leave it lying around anywhere, you can keep it for as long as you like.'

The boy's jaw dropped. 'But—'

'Just enjoy it.' Darac got back into his car. 'And maybe I'll come over and we can work on a couple of things sometime, huh? See you.'

Leaving Freddy standing like a cardboard cut-out, Darac drove away, reflecting that handing over the SG was the second positive thing to have happened in the day. But then, quite out of the blue, another one happened almost immediately. As he joined a long queue of traffic held at a red light on François Grosso, a motorcycle rolled past him and threaded its way toward the stop line. The back of the rider's navy-blue helmet bore two initials in white. A.L., it looked like. Close. Close enough.

Darac assessed the road conditions: dual carriageway, surface wet. Not ideal. Traffic: heavy. A useful thing, potentially. Or it might have been if the vehicle he was tailing was another car. He radioed Mobile Control, gave his position and outlined what he wanted. As the lights changed, he crept forward.

'I'll set the link up, Captain. Sirens?'

'No sirens. No lights. I don't want the rider spooked or it might be me that winds up chasing him and I'm no Wanda Korneliuk.'

'They'll start hooking up with you in a minute. Out.'

The lights changed back to red. The blue helmet was about twenty-five metres ahead. Nothing was moving. What was his best chance here? Twenty-five short metres… He switched off his engine, snatched the key and threw open the door. His shoes kicking up spray, he ran as fast as he could along the pavement. The traffic alongside began to move. Cars trapped in the lane behind his car blared their horns. He kept running. The motorcycle crept forward. The traffic speeded up and went away from him.

'Shit!'

He ran back to his car. He received a warm welcome.

'Yeah? *You* go fuck yourself! I'm going, I'm going! Jesus…' He got in and powered forward but traffic in the adjacent lane was already filtering across in front of him.

He slammed on his brakes, almost rear-ending a VW Dormobile. Now he couldn't see the helmet at all. He hit the horn, pointlessly. 'Control – where is everybody? I'm stuck in traffic.'

'We've got relay problems to you, Captain. But I've got several units homing in. They know what they're looking for.'

'Bikes among them?'

'Two.'

'Good – they're the best hope. Keep me posted.'

'Affirmative. Out.'

There was space on the pavement next to him. He checked in his mirrors. No pedestrians. What would Wanda do now? She certainly wouldn't strike out on foot. He looked over his shoulder. Still no pedestrians. And none ahead. He bounced the car over the kerb and throttled forward. He overtook the Dormobile; a car; another; several cars. But then pedestrians, a loose group of them, wandered out of a shop ahead. He braked hard, alarming them, but that was the only harm done. The plan had worked – he caught sight of the helmet. The rider still seemed oblivious of what was playing out behind.

A space opened up on the road. Darac bumped down into it and started making stealthier progress. After a few judicious moves, just one vehicle, a panel van, separated him from the target. There was an intersection ahead. More traffic lights and they were changing to red. The helmet beat them and turned right into a side street. The van stopped in front of Darac. He was blocked.

But there was a chance. The lead vehicle in the adjacent lane went through the lights on red. The car behind it was some way back. Darac jagged out behind the Fiat and floored the pedal into the gap. On the damp surface, he overshot into the middle of the intersection, facing the wrong way. Now was the perfect time to execute a handbrake turn. Picturing Wanda's lesson at the Caserne, he went for it.

Cradling a mint tea, Frankie drew her legs up underneath her and settled back into the sofa. 'And then you stalled?'

'Brilliantly. Pure textbook.' Darac took a sip of cognac. 'Meanwhile, the motorcyclist got away. Control didn't even spot him let alone catch him. But Lartou is pretty sure CCTV will come to the rescue for once.'

'You'd think there was enough street coverage. In the city.'

'A make on the plate is all we need.' He set down his glass on the coffee table. Made of bits of driftwood, it was one of many unusual pieces in the room. 'It's nice here. Different.'

'Living with a designer has its plus points.'

'What's Christophe working on at the moment?'

'A new take on the intrauterine device.'

Darac gave the coffee table a second look.

'It's a transferable skill,' she said. 'I hope.'

He laughed, and took another sip of cognac. 'It was a delicious supper, Frankie.'

'Thank you.' Setting her full lips into a modest pout, she blew a cooling draft of air across her tea. 'You know, I never dreamed that one day I'd turn into this domestic—'

'Goddess?'

She gave him a look. 'Are we still on message here? This is *just* talk, remember?'

'It's an expression,' he protested. 'Like... wage slave or left-wing intellectual.'

'I'm being oversensitive. It's the situation.'

'I think so. Anyway, you've turned into this domestic...?'

'"Nut job" probably says it. For instance, yesterday I caught myself saying: "I *love* my little béchamel pan."' She shrugged one shoulder. 'Fancy it, yes. But "love"?'

Darac's smile was the first to fade. 'Let's have that talk, Frankie.'

'Yes.' She set down her cup, her gaze falling on a framed photo of her and Christophe at some glitzy function. She kept her eyes on it. 'You and I are mature adults, Paul. And French mature adults at that, supposedly.'

'Supposedly? I'm as French as they come. Both sides.'

'Yes? I've got all sorts of non-blue blood in me. Egyptian. Greek. Even some English.'

'I never realised. And that all adds up to?'

'I can't be unfaithful to Christophe.'

'Ah. I see.'

'That's my intention, anyway. Will you help me keep to it?'

Looking into Frankie's soft green eyes didn't make it any easier. 'If you want that. Yes, I will.'

'Thank you.'

A huge wave of sadness broke over him. So that was it. There would be no deepening of their relationship. He'd missed his chance. Missed it some years ago, the blind idiot that he was. 'Could you *ever* envisage a time when your relationship with Christophe might mean less to you than it does now?'

It took a moment for Frankie to gather herself. 'You know, in a way, entering into a full-on affair with you

seems less of a betrayal of Christophe than acknowledging
that things aren't perhaps as they could be with him. So I
don't quite know how to answer.'

'I understand.'

'Except to say… let's wait and see what happens over
time. No one can predict—'

Darac's mobile rang.

'Yes, ruin my big scene, why don't you?' Frankie's
attempt to lighten the mood lacked conviction. 'Did I ever
tell you I was Jewish?'

'Did I ever tell you I'm wildly—' He'd forgotten their
pact already. 'I'd better take this.'

Clocking the caller's ID, he put the phone on speaker.

'Chief?'

'I'll save you the trouble, Bonbon. From a wonderfully
sharp CCTV image, Lartou read the registration of the
motorcycle, and the rider in question is already in custody,
spilling the beans about his or her ongoing relationship
with Pierre Delmas.'

'No, they're still checking through the footage.' Bonbon's
voice was slab-flat. 'I'm calling about something else. We've
got a homicide.'

'He doesn't sound himself,' Frankie whispered.

'I was thinking Jean Aureuil mightn't be the last.'

'It has nothing to do with the Delmas case.'

Still no give in the voice. Darac shared a concerned look
with Frankie.

'What's all this about, Bonbon?'

'Mate… I'm calling from Salle Poulenc.'

51

The stage was littered with abandoned instruments. Lying dismantled on an opened-out sheet was a cherry-red Gibson SG, its bridge and pick-ups bearing a thin crust of char. Hovering over it was the unusually solemn figure of Raul Ormans. Darac and Frankie suited up and went over to him.

'We've just seen Bonbon, R.O.,' he said, relieved to be getting on with it, finding some succour in the procedure. Nevertheless, shards of ice turned in his stomach as he studied the murder weapon. 'But talk me through it, technically. Assume I know nothing.'

'Alright… An electric guitar is basically a passive device deploying electro-magnetic transducers. These things.' He pointed to the pick-ups. 'Their job is to turn the physical vibrations of the strings into electrical energy. That energy passes through wires via the jack socket to an amplifier. We're talking current at minute forces – microvolts only. If everything in the chain is properly earthed, a plugged-in electric guitar is a very safe piece of tech. The first thing the killer did was to bypass the guitar's own earth wire.'

'I got as far as plugging it into an amp, myself. There was no loud hum. No hum at all, in fact.'

'I'll come to that.' Ormans pointed to a row of components arranged on a poly-bag. 'After de-earthing it, the killer packed all these capacitors and other bits into the various cavities and routing paths in the instrument.'

Darac's gaze was steady. His voice was even. 'And that racked the voltage up to a lethal level?'

'It did, but on its own high voltage isn't the killer. Think of a Taser kicking fifty thousand volts into someone and doing them no real harm. It's not so much the speed of the current, it's how much of it there is – the amperage – that's the crucial element.' He picked up a couple of rogue components. 'That's where things like this come in. As you say, there should have been a hum on plug-in. But everything was wired to the volume controls. As soon as they were turned up, a high-amperage, high-voltage, unearthed current was generated.'

'Right.'

Frankie's hand went to her forehead. 'My God, Paul. One turn of that control and—'

'Is this the work of a genius, R.O.?' Darac needed to move the thing on. 'Or just an everyday hobbyist?'

'Nearer the former. The business with the volume controls is just plain evil, though. A loud hum is an alert, isn't it? They didn't want to give the victim a chance.'

'Prints, R.O.?' Darac said, acknowledging Bonbon as he rejoined them.

'No prints on the components. Several on the instrument. Including yours, of course. I've got people working on them.'

Darac laid a gloved hand on his shoulder. 'Thank you.'

'You're welcome, my old friend.'

Darac turned to Bonbon. 'Is it possible to hold the body?'

'It's still here. But, chief, I really don't think…' Shaking his head, he took a breath. No words emerging on the exhalation, he gave Frankie a look.

'Paul? Bonbon's right.'

'It's alright, Frankie.'

'I'll stay here.'

Bonbon led the way. 'He's in one of the anterooms. And it's Deanna attending, by the way. She swapped her shift when she heard.'

Darac nodded. 'Flak and Perand?'

'They're getting on well, considering they're talking to people made of tears.'

'What are the witnesses saying?'

'They were setting all the instruments out, he picked up the guitar… and then it happened as R.O. said. Most of them saw it. And they're all saying the same thing.'

'Right.'

'So our next step is clear. We find the guy who handed in the guitar at the Caserne. The guy with the parka. Had time to set anything up yet?'

'I've ordered our CCTV of the Roquebillière and Maréchal Vauban entrances to the Caserne. Plus all the street footage in the area. I've sent out a slog squad door to door. I've got TV, press and radio on it. That's it so far.'

'Tomorrow, we'll circulate anything we have to guitar shops, electronics places and so on. See if we can trace the provenance of the components.'

'You watch – someone will complain about our violating the sanctity of the amnesty.'

'Well they can fuck off. This is a murder investigation now.'

'At least we know you weren't the intended victim. It

was never stated whose instrument had gone missing.'

Deanna intercepted them at the door to the side room. 'Hey.'

'Thank you for being here, Deanna. Listen, uh…'

In one glance, she read his mind. 'He didn't suffer. The current across his heart caused a cardiac arrhythmia. He died instantaneously.'

'May I see him? May I see the body, I mean.'

'Of course.'

'Alone.'

'He's through there. Go ahead.'

He took a breath and stepped toward the door.

The doorknob. The light switch. The floor. The walls. The trolley. The sheet. Another breath. And then the face… Darac shuddered. For a full five minutes he stood trying to make sense of it. He couldn't. It was pointless, he knew, talking to a corpse. But so was just standing and looking. He pulled off a glove and laid his hand on the side of the face. And then rejoined Deanna and Bonbon.

'Thank you. I guess no one has identified the body yet? Formally.'

'Not as yet but—'

'Let's do it now.'

'Very well.'

Deanna took a form from her case.

'There's no need to go back in. Are you ready?'

'Yes.'

'Do you recognize Marco Luciano Portami?'

'Yes. It's Marco.'

It was then that Darac wept.

52

Agnès Dantier had just slipped on her shoes when the phone rang.

'Commissaire? Jules Frènes.'

'Could we make this brief, monsieur? I'm due in the AV suite.'

'I can assure you that I too am busy, madame.'

'All the more reason.'

'Very well. The murder victim, Marco... Portami—'

'Spit it out,' she said, tapping her desk pad with a pencil.

'I think you mean "spell it out", don't you? Are you aware of any issues between him and Captain Darac?'

There wasn't time to count to ten. 'No.' On the pad, she began absently spelling out a word of her own. 'Of course not.'

'Issues of a disputatious nature.'

'Do you actually think... In fact, I can answer that question for you. You *don't* think.'

'Darac must be questioned! He may have doctored the guitar himself. Have *you* thought of *that*?'

'Captain Darac was about to play the instrument in question at the Blue Devil club, an occasion on which you and your pal Telonne were present, if you recall. And only didn't play it when a call to duty intervened.'

'He could have interfered with the instrument *after* that.'

One, two, three… 'And the motive, monsieur?'

'Darac and Portami may have been deadly enemies for all you know. And you never will know until you question him!'

'Captain Darac has already made a full statement. He didn't hand over the guitar to Portami, by the way. It went through several pairs of hands first.'

'The fact remains—'

Agnès heard a thin snapping sound. The point of her pencil had broken off.

'Just read my report, Frènes.'

Agnès slammed down the phone. On her pad, the words 'stupid' and 'little arsehole' were deeply gouged into the paper.

In the hours that followed, Darac's grief came in waves; periods of near forgetting alternating with inescapable pain. When it swamped him, the cold shock of it was unbearable: he was investigating the murder of one of his closest friends. A man he'd played alongside for twelve years. A man with whom he'd experienced some of the most fulfilling moments of his life.

It was en route to the AV suite that the latest breaker slammed into him. He rode it as he stopped off at the duty officer's counter. Behind it, there were three work stations, all of them occupied.

'Any further eyewitnesses to the handover, Charvet?'

'Still only the barrier man, so far.' Charvet's second-in-command, Béatrice, kept her eyes on her screen as she handed him a clipboard. He slid it across the counter. 'The page on top.'

Charvet's headset beeped. He took the call as Darac read the officer's statement:

The guitar case was left by a stocky man wearing a hooded parka and a scarf. I couldn't see his face at all. No other distinguishing features.

On the page below was an alphabetised list of names, initials A to D from the handover day's work roster. Columns headed 'Contacted', 'Responded' and 'ID' were set out in a table alongside. Ticks, crosses and the letters 'P' for personal, 'T' for telephone or 'E' for email appeared in different handwriting in the relevant squares.

Charvet's call ended. 'Pass me the list for a second, Captain? We've just got the one so that nothing gets missed.' Turning a couple of pages, he entered a 'T' in the 'Responded' column and then put a cross under 'ID'. He handed the list back.

'Everyone contacted,' Darac said, riffling pages. 'Impressive.'

'The list again, please,' Béatrice said, taking it. 'Email response. Another negative.'

'What about the various ancillaries and visitors?'

'Their names are on the list too – back pages. *Anyone* who was here, or who was coming on or going off site within fifteen minutes of the guitar being left, has been contacted. Most, like your team, have responded already.'

'How many haven't?'

'Just a handful, but it only takes one, Captain. And Lartou does have a sighting on CCTV.'

'I'm going down there now. It's not a very positive one, he says. But still…' He gave Charvet's counter a conclusive rap. 'Thanks. Let me know if you get anything.'

Bzzzzzzzut!

'Hold the door, Paul?'

Agnès threaded her arm through his as they took the steps. 'Want to talk about him?'

'Can't.' His body felt lifeless against hers, as if the emotions that were weighing him down had physically flattened him. 'I'm meeting the guys at the club later. That will be enough talk for one night.'

'It will do you all good. The boy – Freddy? It must be particularly difficult for him.'

'Some heap of shit turns a beautiful thing into a lethal weapon and now Freddy is sobbing his heart out. He blames himself. And if I know anything about it, he'll still be blaming himself twenty years down the line.'

Nothing galvanised Darac like his sense of injustice. And nobody knew that better than Agnès. 'While the real culprit doesn't feel a scintilla of guilt, you can bet.'

'I tell you, Agnes, when I—'

'My arm, Paul?'

Her strategy was working too well. He relaxed his grip. 'Sorry.' Then he rumbled her. 'Skilfully done.'

'It's better, isn't it? Feeling empowered rather than hopeless?'

He put his arm around her shoulder, and he didn't care who was looking.

The AV suite was a static-charged room little larger than a walk-in wardrobe. Beneath its bank of screens, Lartou Lartigue was sitting at the console with the air of a projectionist who'd run too many bad movies. Behind him, it was standing room only.

'Sorry to keep you waiting, everyone,' Agnès said, as she and Darac crammed themselves in. 'Thank you, Lartou.'

Standing shoulder to shoulder with his teammates, Darac felt a surge of feelings as the screens fizzed into life; the sort of impregnable confidence he felt when the DMQ was playing at its best. And then another wave of despair swept over him.

'Each is showing the same clip,' Lartou said. 'And here he is… the man in the parka.'

Seeing the figure gave Darac a new resolve. 'Well built,' he said. 'Strutting gait even though his head is down. Face shaded by the parka. Scarf around his neck.'

Granot's eyes bored into the man. 'Look up, you bastard.'

Lartou shook his large, bald head. 'He doesn't. I've run the sequence several times.'

'Zoomed in?' Frankie said.

'Yes. His face just turns into a bigger shadow.'

Perand spotted something. 'Look how he's carrying the guitar case.'

'In his left hand? I often do that and I'm right-handed.'

'Ah.'

They watched the man calmly set down the case, turn around and go back the way he had come.

Bonbon was tapping his chin, a sign that something was gnawing at him. And then he stopped. 'Cool, isn't he, when you consider he came to the Caserne of all places to leave the guitar? He could have left it far more safely elsewhere. Alright, he's wearing a parka with the hood up but it tells us something, doesn't it? He doesn't know what he's carrying.'

On the screens, the faceless man went through the routine all over again.

Darac nodded. 'Yes, he's not returning just a *stolen* item, is he? What he's got there is a ticking time bomb and he doesn't realise it.'

'Indeed,' Agnès said. 'Parka Man *may* prove to be the bomb maker, as it were, but I agree, the odds are that he's just an errand boy. We still need to find him, of course. Any further sequences, Lartou?'

'Two more.' He pressed a second button. 'This is the corner of Fornero Menei and Antoine Albin, as you can see. Timed ninety seconds before the other sequence. Still no identifiable face.'

'He's walked down Menei by the look of it,' Granot said. 'Where's he parked? Outside the sports hall?'

Frankie had a different thought. 'If he *has* parked. He may live around here. Or have taken a bus. The other sequence?'

'The return journey – same set-up. Back view. It goes on for some time, this clip. I let it run in case he suddenly appears in a vehicle coming down the road. He doesn't.'

They watched it anyway.

'Dead end. Anything from the slog squad, Bonbon?'

'Nothing as yet, chief.'

Darac exchanged a little eyebrow semaphore with Agnès. 'Okay, I think we'll continue in the squad room. Thanks, Lartou.'

The session may have been over, but for Darac, the night shift was only just beginning.

53

The story had made the morning edition.

'What the fuck were you playing at?' Picot slapped it against Jacques Telonne's chest. 'Sending me off to the pigs with a fucking murder weapon in my hand? Eh? You arsehole!'

'I didn't know what the little bitch had done!' Telonne was shaking, every part of him pulsing, twitching. 'Look at what I've given her.' He turned slowly on the spot, looking in awe at the perfect little palace he had built. 'Everything top of the range. Everything!' Suddenly aware of the paper at his feet, he kicked it apart, the pages falling sedately around him like snow in a paperweight globe. 'The little bitch!'

'What about me? After everything I've done for this fucking family, the police are going to be looking for me now. Me! For doing nothing!'

Framed in the window behind them, a Porsche appeared at the top of the drive. His face a mask of pained astonishment, Telonne grabbed Picot's jacket collar.

'Why does she hate me? Why does she want to stop me?' He shook his head. 'I can't have this any more. I am not going to let her ruin everything I've worked for.'

Picot thrust his forearms up, breaking the hold. 'Listen! If the police start investigating me, *you* are going down. Got that? You!'

Telonne looked childlike, suddenly. 'But I haven't done anything.'

The sound of grinding gravel drew their eyes to the window. Elise got out of the Porsche and bent to retrieve a collection of ribboned boxes from the back seat.

'Laure is deranged, Picot. A danger to me and to others. She ought to be put away somewhere. Somewhere she can be cured.'

A door opened behind them. Wearing a thigh-length T-shirt, Laure padded barefoot into the room. The men looked at each other. Had she overheard? A page bearing Marco's story stuck to her foot as she crossed nonchalantly in front of them and opened the fridge.

'Still here, Papa?' She kicked off the page as she scavenged the shelves for breakfast. 'How lovely.'

Elise paraded in. 'What's the paper doing strewn everywhere?' Her face coloured as she saw Picot. 'Walter.'

'Madame.'

He helped her collect up the pages.

'Laure – get some clothes on, for goodness' sake.'

'Been up all night. Going back to bed. You can come with me if you like, Walter.'

'I do apologise for her,' Elise said to him, purposefully following the girl into the hall. 'Laure!'

Fit to explode, Telonne went to push past Picot but he grabbed his arm. 'Let her go,' he said, as raised voices turned to shouts and doors slammed. 'You're right, Jacques. Laure ought to be put somewhere. Somewhere for good.' His eyes bored into him. 'And you know someone who'll do it, don't you?'

54

Darac woke in a pool of sunlight. And with a colossal hangover. For one glorious moment, he forgot all the reasons why, and then one by one, they came back to him. Dragging a pillow on to his forehead took care of the light. Dealing with the rest of it was not going to be so easy.

At least today would see the end of Carnival. At nine o'clock in the evening, crowds would gather for the final three events: the illusionistic burning of the hillside around Château Park; the immolation of the king; and a grand firework display. The immolation was a maritime affair, the royal barge being towed into position off the Promenade des Anglais. Enthroned on a bonfire invisible under his full-length robes, the king would go up in smoke and, as rockets exploded overhead, that would be that for another year.

Darac patted around on the bedside table for his mobile and somehow managed to avoid knocking it on to the floor. Jettisoning the pillow, he rang the duty office's number.

'Charvet?'

'It's Bé, Captain.'

Seeking the shady side of the bed, he crabbed slowly sideways. 'Bé. Any developments overnight?'

'We would have called if there had been anything important.'

'I thought I heard Agnès telling you not to.'

Silence. The young woman was arrow straight. Not to say unimaginative.

'Bé – it's fine. So nothing?'

'No, Captain.'

'I'll be in shortly.'

A cool shower and an *hors catégorie*-sized espresso worked wonders. By the time he got to his desk, he was still as depressed as hell but at least he'd lost the jackhammer in his skull. He thought about calling his father. He wondered if *he* had thought about calling *him*. He decided to leave it for the day.

Erica appeared in the doorway. 'Hello.'

There was usually something of the silky exuberance of an Afghan hound in the way Erica pranced into a room, but not this morning. She was carrying the morning edition.

'I'm so sorry.' They shared greeting kisses. She sat down opposite him. 'Are you alright?'

'So-so.'

Shamefaced was another unfamiliar look for her.

'I… said some unpleasant things about Marco at the parade. I wish I hadn't, now.'

Darac managed a grin. 'No, no – you were spot-on. Marco was a very… *human* being.'

'Have you seen the paper, though?' She held it up. 'I had no idea he was such a renowned teacher. Dedicated. Respected. There are some glowing tributes to him.'

'I'm sure there are. He really… cared.' No. Not now. He took a deep breath, lowering his head. 'Uh… Listen…'

Erica stood. The sight of a strong man fighting back tears was something she couldn't handle. 'I'll go. This isn't the time. I'm sorry. I'll see you later.'

Darac didn't look up. Suddenly, he felt that too many people had got away from him in his life. A phone rang, an outside line. He composed himself.

'Darac.'

'It's Jacques Telonne, *Paul* – if I may?'

'You may not. What can I do for you, monsieur?'

'I've seen the morning paper.' Telonne's voice stiffened. 'And I felt the need…'

Darac held the phone away from his ear.

'…of your loss. Marco Portami was a tireless educator…'

Darac waited until the noise stopped. 'I repeat. What can I do for you?'

'It is more what I can do for you. Having been there at the start of this whole guitar business, and at the jazz club with my family, I feel a responsibility to help in any way I can. I am proposing to come in—'

'The time for cheap publicity stunts is over, Telonne. Goodbye.'

He hung up.

'Chief!'

Lartou was standing in the doorway, holding up an enlarged, time-tagged photo.

Darac sat forward. The shot was a three-quarter rear view of a motorcycle negotiating a rain-washed street. Riding it was a figure wearing a crash hat bearing a familiar set of initials.

'Have we…?'

Lartou shuffled out a second photo: a blown-up shot of the bike's registration plate.

'And last but not least.'

Brandishing a printed form, Lartou came in and set it

down on the desk. News of the breakthrough spreading along the corridor, Bonbon led a posse in behind him. Darac began to feel some energy return as he read the bike owner's name and address. Shaking his head in irritation, he held up the form to the others.

'Anyone free to come up to Levens with me?' he said.

55

Backed by the higher peaks of the Férion range, Levens was a full twenty-five kilometres north of the city. From its tree-lined approaches, the *village perché* looked typical of the genre: a warm-toned spiral of masonry winding around a cone of rock surmounted by a church tower. It was the landscape at its foot that gave the place its unique character: a vast plateau of pan-flat meadows.

'The Prix du Jockey Club is going on over there, look,' Bonbon said.

Away to their left, horses were being galloped across a field the size of Nice airport.

'It looks more like a John Ford movie. *Stagecoach* or something.'

'You're talking my language now, chief. They used to call me *Tex* Busquet, back home, you know.'

'They called you Tex?'

'Yep.'

'In Perpignan?'

'Uh-huh. Well, one guy did.'

'Who was that? The Banyuls-sur-Mer Kid?'

'Oh, you know him?'

Bonbon kept the nonsense going all the way up into the village – anything to let a little light into Darac's darkness. He picked up his radio handset. 'Flak? You read me? Over.'

She and Perand were following immediately behind.

'Loud and clear. Over.'

'All the roads down from the village funnel into this one, so in case our phantom motorcyclist decides to make a run for it, park…' He assessed the options. '…right where you are now. We'll be in touch. Over.'

'Check. Over and out.'

Flaco faded from the rear-view mirror as Darac continued the pull uphill. Turning away from the village, the road levelled out on to a bare shelf with a view clear across to Mont Férion itself. The target address was the last property on the road – a shabby old place with a couple of rundown outbuildings to the side and chickens pecking around a dirt yard in front. A line of washing blew in a strong breeze sweet with mountain air.

'Male *and* female clothing on the line,' Darac said, *sotto voce*, as they began crossing the yard. 'No sign of the motorbike.'

Bonbon's foxy eyes were darting between the house and the outbuildings that flanked the yard to their left.

'No lookout, as far as I can see, chief.'

'Want the front door or back?'

'I'll take the back.'

'I'll knock – you hold.'

'Safeties off?'

'Safeties off.'

As they walked on, the view of the outbuildings opened out.

'There's the bike, Bonbon. And someone owns a shotgun, look.'

The machine was parked on its stand in what looked like

an old bakehouse. A brace of rabbits was hanging from a row of hooks behind it.

Bonbon nodded. 'No keys in the ignition by the look of it but they could be secreted on the frame. I'll go and disconnect the battery, then take that path into the back yard.'

'Eyes everywhere. Remember the shotgun.'

It took Bonbon a matter of seconds to immobilise the bike. Jetting glances all around, the pair set off toward their respective stations at the same pace. Arriving at the front door, Darac stood for a moment, listening. Chickens murmured busily behind him. Sheets slapped briskly on the line. There were no sounds of raised voices inside the house, or of sudden panicky movements. No one jumped through a window or peppered the step with shot. So far, so good.

The door was opened by an auburn-haired woman wearing jeans and a Breton-style top. A harassed expression put some hard edges on what was a pretty face.

'Relax, madame,' Darac said, unfolding a piece of paper, 'and you might look more like yourself.' He showed her Astrid's watercolour from Café Grinda. 'Don't you agree?'

The woman tried to slam the door but Darac put his shoulder against it, easing it gently back. He reached for his ID, and, holding it where she could see it, flipped it open.

'Darac. Brigade Criminelle.'

'Police?' She looked anxiously back down the hall. 'Why didn't you say so? I wouldn't have reacted like that. But police?' she repeated, louder this time. 'Why are you here?'

A navy-blue crash helmet was hanging from a row of coat hooks behind her. 'A1' was stencilled on its back.

'Is Artur in, Madame Rigaud?'

In the house, a door slammed loudly. And was that a shout? And then another, fainter.

'It's the wind. It does that. Artur? Uh… no. He went into…' Her eyes were everywhere. 'Why do you want to see him?'

'So he can tell me the truth about Pierre Delmas.'

In the yard, chickens began to scuttle, squawking noisily.

'Pierre Delmas?' More glances behind. And into the yard. Her eyes widened. 'You'd better come in and wait for Artur, then. Please.'

Looking past her down the hall, Darac took a step inside but went no further.

'Yes, go through into the kitchen.' She reached to pull the front door closed behind him. 'Come right in, please.'

'So now you want me indoors?' Her face fell as he stood his ground and turned. Chickens scattering ahead of him, Artur was running his bike across the yard. 'Stop there!' Darac called out, moving to intercept him. 'Stop!'

Artur jumped on to the saddle, releasing the clutch. The engine failed to catch. He hopped off and kept pushing.

'Forget it, Artur!' Darac closed in, his arms spread wide. His eyes on the man, he didn't notice madame creeping up behind him. 'Your bike's not going anywhere.'

'Don't even think about it!' Bonbon warned her, hobbling through the front door.

She didn't think about it. She acted, throwing herself over Darac like a fire blanket. Artur seized his chance. Letting go of the bike, he escaped Darac's blind flailing and ran toward the lane. A gunshot rang out. All at once, the chickens stopped squawking, and Artur stopped running.

'Alright. Alright,' he shouted, raising his hands. He looked across at his wife. 'It's over, sweetheart.'

Darac pulled sweetheart up out of the dust, taking a kick on the shin for his pains.

'This thing can fire just as well horizontally,' Bonbon said, waving his automatic. 'Get inside. Both of you.' Bonbon winced as he flexed his arm. 'And by the way, you'll need to re-hang that cellar door, Artur.'

'I'm sorry about shoving you down there, mate. I panicked.'

'You in one piece, Bonbon?' Darac said.

'Just about.' He made a shepherding gesture with his automatic. 'Move!'

'Hold it a second, Bonbon. Train it on the house.' Darac drew his own weapon. 'Where's your shotgun, Artur?'

'Inside, mate.' The situation seemed not to have blunted the man's bonhomie. 'But there's no one in there with it.'

'I'm scanning the upper storey.' Bonbon took aim. 'You take the lower.'

'Is there an exit out of the back yard?'

'No. If anyone else is here, they're in the house.'

Darac glanced behind him. A short section of chest-high wall was all that was left of the right-hand boundary to the property. 'Let's get behind there.' Sights trained on the house, he began backing toward it. 'You two as well. Come on. Back!'

Reaching the wall, they took cover behind it.

Artur shook his head. 'This is pointless. There's no one in there. Is there, Odette?'

'No.'

'So Pierre Delmas is not at home, then?'

'What?' Artur's look of astonishment was comically false.

'If he isn't, Artur, why were you trying to lead us away from the house?'

At last, the man seemed discomfited. 'Look, I don't know why I tried to run off like that. I panicked. But there's no need for guns.'

'Pierre? You in there?' Darac shouted. 'If you are, come out with your hands up. We don't want any accidents, do we? Just come out nice and easily and everything will be fine.'

Artur clicked his tongue in exasperation. 'I'm telling you, there's no one—'

'Shut up.'

Darac kept his eyes on the windows and the rear corner wall of the house. Looking for a shape, movement, shadows – any sign of Delmas or the shotgun. In the no-man's land of the yard, the motorbike lay jagged in the dust like a slaughtered animal.

No sign coming, Darac took out his mobile. 'Flak? We've apprehended the Rigauds. There's just a chance Delmas is in the house and he could be armed. If you don't hear from me in the next five minutes, get back-up.'

'Check.'

He outlined what he wanted. 'Have you had anything from Erica?'

'There have been three calls since the tap went in. Two in, one out. Just routine stuff.'

'Thanks. Out.' Darac eyeballed Artur. 'Alright, you go in first. Then you, madame. We'll be right behind you.'

'Oh God,' Odette said, looking less and less happy with the situation.

Artur smiled at her. 'You did great, sweetheart.'

'And you didn't. You should never have told *him*' – she stabbed a finger in Darac's direction – 'about Café Grinda.'

'Look, guys, before we go in, you're right.' Artur was talking as if the concession were somehow a gift. 'Pierre has been here. And I know we've done wrong. But somebody had to extend the hand of friendship to the poor bloke, didn't they?'

'Where is he?'

'Dunno. He left this morning. You'd never know he'd been here. Cleaned his room and everything.'

'You've got a lot of ground to make up with me, Artur, so just do as you're told. Get in the house. We'll talk more when we're sure the coast is clear.'

Darac went through every room in the place including the cellar and loft. Delmas was nowhere to be seen. Darac updated Flaco and Perand, then joined the others in the living room.

'At one end of the scale, Artur, you and your wife have obstructed a police enquiry. At the other end, we could charge you with complicity in murder. We know you're guilty of the first. How are you doing on the second?'

Muttering that it was the worst day of her life, Odette closed her eyes. Perhaps she was running a loop of all the other days of her marriage. They had little to recommend them, it appeared.

Artur gripped the sides of his chair. 'We are not guilty. For one thing, Pierre hasn't committed any murders. He's as gentle as a kitten, isn't he, Odette?'

She opened her eyes. 'Yes.'

'Where is Delmas now?'

'I told you – I don't know. That's the truth.'

'Madame?'

She shrugged.

'How did Delmas come to stay here in the first place?'

'What with everything he was up against, I felt sorry for the guy. I always did but this was beyond anything. So I asked him if he'd like to come up here. He said he would.'

'When was that?'

'The day he got out.'

'Uh-huh. How did he strike you? What kind of a guest was he?'

'No trouble. Quiet. Quieter than before, if anything.' As if there were a sudden need for confidentiality, Artur dropped his voice. 'He hasn't got long, you know.'

'It's by no means impossible that he *could* live for several more years.'

Artur was struck dumb, momentarily. 'Well, that's good because he's innocent of these murders, I'm sure of it.'

'And you, madame? Are you so convinced?'

'Yes. I am.'

'And did you find him an easy guest, also?'

'I'll be honest with you, Captain…'

Artur's earnest round eyes narrowed anxiously.

'I didn't enjoy having him here. In fact, I hated it.'

'Odette!'

'It was alright for you, you were at work during the day. Most of the time. I got so fed up with it yesterday evening, I told him I wanted him to leave. Immediately.'

'He was still here this morning,' Bonbon said.

Artur had been quiet for all of ten seconds. 'I said we

couldn't chuck him out just like that. We had words over it, actually.'

'But Madame held sway.'

'We compromised. In the end, we decided to tell Pierre he could stay until tonight. But he'd made up his mind to go, anyway. And so off he went. He didn't say where he was going.'

Bonbon's pen was poised over his notebook. 'We need a description of what he was wearing and what he took with him.'

Odette gave it in some detail.

'Did he go out much when he was here?'

Artur nodded in the same amiable manner he seemed to adopt for everything. 'Occasionally.'

'Did you take him out?'

'On the bike? Sometimes.' His forehead creased in concern. 'Well, the guy had been in prison for seven years plus. He pays his debt to society, comes out and has to bloody hide. Is that fair? I don't think so.'

'Did he ever wear a disguise when you were out?'

'He had a couple of joke-shop beards. That's all I saw.'

'Madame?'

'We don't know what he had in that holdall of his. Who knows?'

'When did he leave, exactly?' Darac said. 'And how? On the back of your bike?'

'No, no, on foot. Then maybe he got the bus. Or cadged a lift. Or nicked a push bike. Dunno.' He glanced at his watch. 'Two hours ago, it was. More or less on the dot.'

'In a place like this, someone is bound to have seen him. We'll check that timing, Artur.'

'Mate, there's no need to use that tone. We *know* you'll check what we tell you. Check away! We *want* you to check because we know it'll help Pierre.'

Bonbon was still taking notes. 'What did you do after he'd gone?'

'Just started going about our normal day. Until you got here.'

'Go out anywhere?'

'No.'

'Then why was your bike engine warm?'

The question threw Artur, for the moment. And then he slapped his forehead. 'I tell you – if it weren't screwed on... I nipped down into the village. Just for bread.'

'Sure you didn't drop Pierre Delmas off somewhere at the same time?'

'No. I told you.'

If the man was lying, he was an expert in the art.

'Let's rewind a bit, Artur,' Darac said. 'How did you get in contact with Delmas following his release?'

'I went round to his apartment and he asked me if he could come to my place. We got back here and that's when he told us about the gang.' He gave Darac a stare heavy with outrage. 'Do you know they cheated his daughter?'

Darac made no reply.

'He was so mad about that. Wasn't he, Odette? Spitting, he was.'

Odette had a sweet face. But it was capable of an excoriating look.

'Oh yeah,' Artur said, taking his foot out of his mouth. 'Well, I say *mad*. I don't mean he was mad enough to do anything about it or anything. A gentle giant, he is. But I tell you what – I don't know how *I* would've reacted in the circumstances. Do you?'

'Did he name them – the gang?'

'No, and I didn't want to know who they were.'

'Madame?'

'No, he didn't.'

'Many years before this, you had dinner at Café Grinda with Delmas, madame. How did that come about?'

Odette's features twisted disagreeably. 'It was a *treat* for us. To say thank you for some little thing Artur had done.'

'But I had a migraine – a blinder – and couldn't go. I was going to cancel but then I thought – why? I trust the bloke. And I trust the wife – you've seen how loyal *she* is.'

Darac felt a sudden twinge in his shin.

'So they went, just the two of them. Had a lovely time.'

Odette stirred in her seat. 'Lovely? I was bored stupid.'

As the questioning continued, Darac began to develop an uneasy feeling about Monsieur and Madame Rigaud. Odette was pluckily supportive of her husband one minute, utterly dismissive of him the next. It was a pattern he'd encountered before but there seemed something a little forced about it.

'Returning to the murders of Messieurs Saxe and Aureuil: although you concede Delmas had a strong revenge motive, Artur, you say you're certain he's innocent?'

'Definitely.'

Odette nodded.

'Pierre is a big man but he's a gentle giant.' He dropped his voice. 'Actually, he's a wimp if I'm being really honest. Isn't he, Odette?' No response. 'Take it from me.'

'Okay,' Darac said. 'You're both convinced of Pierre's

innocence and you want to help us prove that, right?'

'Absolutely, mate.' Artur seemed to particularly relish the idea. 'I keep telling you.'

'Got a pad of paper handy?'

The couple spent the next fifteen minutes constructing a timetable of Pierre Delmas's movements as they themselves had witnessed them. Leaving them under Bonbon's watchful eye, Darac went into the yard and made some calls. Throughout, he watched the chickens pecking away at the earth, intent only on what was in front of them. It seemed a life of enviable simplicity. The final call was to the duty officer's desk at the Caserne.

'Charvet – any developments in the hunt for the man in the parka?'

'Tech have come up with *something*, Captain. But not enough to trouble you with at this stage.'

Darac had been leaning back against the house wall. He eased his weight forward.

'No, no – go on.'

'It seems that some of the components the perpetrator had built into your guitar had unusually high values. Only one shop in the area stocks them – a place in Riquier. R.O. has gone over there to see if he can find out more.'

The news buoyed Darac. For every case solved by a piece of inspiration, he knew a hundred more were solved by painstaking checking and slog. Unusually high-value components... If it worked out in the end, it wouldn't be the first time that overkill had proved a killer's undoing.

His jaw set in a determined jut, Darac headed back into the living room. The couple had already finished their timetable task. Bonbon was running an eye over the first page.

'Artur – at about five o'clock on the Monday, you were seen outside Pierre's apartment.'

'I haven't put that because he wasn't around.'

'Indeed not.' He handed the timetable to Darac. 'But what were you doing there?'

'Went to pick up his shaving kit. I was coming out into the corridor when I heard the neighbour's door open. So I knocked on Pierre's to make it look as if I hadn't been inside. Then I left.'

'That was quick thinking,' Darac said. 'Quick as a criminal.'

Artur looked disappointed. 'Parking tickets. Speeding. That's my lot, Captain.'

Darac fixed him with a look. 'Until now.'

The questioning went on for another hour. At the end of it, Darac decided it was more useful to leave the couple where they were than to take them into custody. As he and Bonbon began spiralling their way down through the village, he updated him on Raul Ormans' possible lead.

'Cases have been broken on a lot less, chief. Want to ring him?'

Darac shook his head. 'Best to leave R.O. He'll call if he comes up with anything.'

The centre of the village was milling with Saturday crowds and the car came to a dead stop in Place de la République. Outside the post office, the slog squad was already showing photos to groups of head shakers. Bonbon indicated the wrought-iron sign hanging over the entrance. 'See that – the dog chasing the postman? Cute, isn't it? I tried to buy it once. Without success, clearly.'

'Where would you have put it?'

'That's what Julieta said.'

The traffic began to move.

'Artur and Odette…' Darac mused, canting his head as if the change of angle might give his thoughts a new perspective. 'There's something odd about them.'

'I think you're right but that doesn't mean they're lying.'

'Though Odette did signal our arrival by announcing "Police?" as loudly as she could to alert Artur. And then she tried to hustle me inside once he emerged.'

'His attempted getaway – what sense did that make if it wasn't to lead us away from the house? Yet neither Delmas nor his stuff was there. He *had* packed up and left as they said.'

'Is it possible that he *was* still there?'

'When you were bashing your way out of the cellar, he slipped quietly along the hall and out into the back yard?'

'If he did, where did he go then? The only way was towards you. I tell you something, though. I'm glad it was Artur and not big old Delmas I had my fling with. Wimp or not.'

As low as he was feeling, Darac couldn't resist a smile. 'By which you mean he flung you through the cellar door and then threw away the key?'

'Exactly.'

He gave Bonbon's knee a squeeze. 'Listen, you got out of there quickly enough. For a skinny bugger.'

'"Bonbon Busquet – Human Wrecking Ball." He gave his shoulder a rub. 'That'll be sore for a while.' He delved in his pocket. 'Luckily, I have something to ease the pain.'

'Advil?'

'Kola Kube.' He proffered the bag. 'From Cours Saleya, before you ask.'

Darac took one. 'So… We've got people out quizzing the locals on Delmas. We've got phone records being checked. Better still, we've got the Rigauds' phones being tapped. We've got surveillance on the house. And a decent couple of tails in place.'

'So let's hope the Rigauds and Delmas try and get in touch. One way or another.'

56

Darac was working through the Rigauds' timetable when his mobile rang.

'Didier. How are you doing, man?'

'Sorting out the memorial gig is helping, I guess. But next Thursday, when we go out to play that final number? I've no idea what state I'll be in then.'

Darac swivelled in his chair and looked out over the compound. He pictured the bandstand set up with Marco's kit. 'Me neither.'

'I'm dropping the bandleader bit for this. What should we play? I'm taking a consensus.'

'Tricky.' He gave an involuntary laugh. 'Hardly says it, does it?'

'Well listen, Marco loved Shelly Manne above all, probably. Right? The Blackhawk albums, particularly.'

'True.'

Frankie appeared below, heading for the car park with a couple of her Vice team.

'There's a feeling we should open with "I Am In Love" from Volume Three. What do you think?'

'Yes. Perfect.' He turned away from the window. 'Have you put it to Luc?'

'He suggested it initially.' Grief tore at his voice. 'The rhythm section union, you know.' And then it took on an edge Darac had never heard before. 'Are you any nearer getting the bastard who did it?'

'We're throwing everything we have at it, Didi. Believe me.'

'I do. We all do.' He tried to rally. 'How lucky to have a detective in the band, eh?'

'If you say so.'

'I'm going to see Freddy, later.'

'I rang him again this morning. I warn you, he's not doing all that well.'

'Marco would have to show off his one flash riff to the kid, wouldn't he? If he hadn't, he'd still be alive and so it's a double thing for Freddy. He's devastated at what happened to Marco; and he realises that but for that, it would have been him who was killed. And he blames himself for the guitar's theft in the first place.'

Granot walked in, carrying a report. He set it down in front of Darac and subsided into the seat opposite.

'I know... Listen, I'd better go now, Didi.'

As the call ended, Darac picked up Granot's offering. It was the post-mortem report on Jean Aureuil.

'Just heard from R.O., by the way.' He gave a sad shake of the head. 'No go on the guitar components yet. And the slog squad haven't found anyone who saw the man wearing the parka.'

Darac exhaled deeply as he opened the report. 'Right.'

'You'll notice Barrau's guesses at the scene all proved right,' Granot said. 'The cause, the moving of the body, etcetera. He could do it all along, couldn't he? The arsehole.'

'These timings look interesting.' Darac cross-referenced

them with the Rigaud timetable. 'Allowing the usual margins for error, Barrau says the strangling happened about four hours before the body was found; about three before it was strung up.'

'You mean it's interesting that the body was hanging there for possibly a whole hour before anyone saw it?'

'Not so much that...'

Darac sat back, staring into the framed absence of the doorway, an unpromising space in which to see a vision. But see it he did. A vision of a tall, strongly built man wearing a pair of earphones.

'In you go,' Flaco said.

His eyes trained on the apparition, Darac put the timetable away and got slowly to his feet. 'Good to meet you, Monsieur Delmas.'

Turning, Granot performed his impression of an astonished walrus.

'Good morning, Captain. Lieutenant.'

'A uniform out of Foch, Officer Laurence Filliol, picked him up, Captain,' Flaco said. 'At Pont St Michel near the tram stop. There was no struggle.' She raised her eyebrows. 'And no arrest.'

Darac nodded – he'd picked up the inference. Had Delmas been arrested, he would have been entitled to a thirty-minute meeting with a lawyer down the line.

'And then Officer Filliol put him in his car and drove him here.' She set down Delmas's holdall. 'I've checked it. No weapons.' Her eyes slid to the corridor. 'Is this a good moment to bring up my overtime, by the way?'

Darac made a show of irritation. 'Now? Oh, alright then. Excuse me, monsieur.'

'Needs must.' He adjusted a control on his earphones. 'As long as it doesn't take long.'

Granot got to his feet. 'So, Pierre – long time no see. How have you been keeping?'

As the pair renewed their acquaintanceship, Flaco and Darac convened in the corridor.

'Using the pretext of the weapons check, I had a quick look for other stuff. There's no mobile, no car keys, no other keys except the ones to his apartment.'

'Letters, diaries, notebooks?'

She shook her head.

'There are paperbacks and things but nothing like that. It's mainly clothes.'

'A DVD, by any chance?'

'Several. Monsieur enjoys movies starring someone called Cary Grant.'

'You've never heard of—?' There wasn't time. 'We'll examine those later.'

'Might have to arrest him first. I don't think he would fall for it a second time.'

'We'll see.' He recalled Artur's earlier account of his visit to Delmas's apartment. 'Was there a shaving kit?'

'Electric razor only.'

'Okay. What was he doing at Pont St Michel?'

'Walking briskly. It's part of a circuit he's been doing every day for his health, he says. The exercise does him good.'

'Better than usual, today – he was carting his holdall around.' He gave her shoulder a pat. 'Let's go back in.'

'You've lost a little weight,' Delmas was saying to Granot. 'But you need to lose a lot more.' He saw Darac had returned. 'May I sit down, Captain?'

'Please.'

His grin at its foxiest, Bonbon swept into the room, pulling Perand and Lartou along in his slipstream. 'Well, well, well,' he said. 'Jesus.' Perand circled Delmas as if he were the prize exhibit in a cabinet of curiosities. 'It *is* him.' He gave Flaco a look. 'The dragnet actually worked.'

Caught in a crossfire of gazes, Delmas maintained an almost serene calm. And the mood didn't appear to leave him when he removed his earphones. As the leads fell loosely around his neck, Darac pictured the cheery face of Jean Aureuil, the twin ligature marks bitten deep into his throat.

'Won't be a minute, Monsieur Delmas. Just need to get organised.'

'Don't be long about it, please.'

Darac's thoughts once more returned to the Rigauds' timetable of Delmas's movements. One thought led to another. And another still. A scenario he hadn't envisaged began to suggest itself. But would it play? At least they could test it now.

'Get a secretary in here, would you, someone?'

'Sabrina Fabre is in, chief.' Perand gave Flaco a grin as he loped to the door; Darac's antipathy to the woman was well known. 'Will she do?'

'Just wait in the corridor a second.' He joined him. 'Yes, ask her to come in. First though, get on to Surveillance. Update them about Delmas but tell them to stay on the Rigaud house. They're not to stand down.'

'But…' The order seemed to mystify the young man. 'Delmas is sitting right there.'

'Just do it. I'll explain later.' Perand shrugged and

headed off. Darac beckoned Bonbon out of the office. 'Four's company, seven's a crowd, don't you think? For the interview.'

'We can't use the squad room, obviously. And last time I looked, we don't have a two-way mirror anywhere. Unless you want to decamp all the way over to Joinel.'

'No, no, we'll stay in my office.'

'There'll be a mutiny if you banish Flak, Perand and Lartou and we'll only have to update them later.'

'So when we get underway, I'll put the interview through into the squad room on the phone mike. It's not ideal, but it'll do.' They went back into the office. 'Tell Flak.'

'Right.'

Darac picked up the internal phone.

'If you're calling Agnès, she's out. Examining magistrates' meeting at the Palais.'

'That's right.' Darac glanced at his watch. 'Shouldn't be long before she's back.' He picked up the landline phone and left a neutral-sounding update on Agnès's mobile.

'Still using the two-phone system?' Delmas said, matter-of-factly. 'Surprising.'

'Ah, yes?'

Darac cleared a space on the front edge of his desk and sat there. A casual atmosphere had its advantages. A relaxed suspect was easier to catch off guard. 'So what do you listen to on your personal stereo, monsieur?'

'Just then, it was "Summer Rain". I have severe tinnitus. Most people only listen at night but I have it on during the day as well. Usually.'

For the first time, Darac noticed the tremor in Delmas's hands and the dead look in his small, deep-set eyes. He was a big man, bigger than Darac remembered from their brief encounter at the cemetery. But could Delmas have carried the body of Jean Aureuil across the rocks on to the walkway at Villefranche? And then hoisted his dead weight aloft? All by himself?

'Just waiting for someone to take down what we say. Won't be a second.'

'Good. The sooner we start, the sooner we can finish.'

Granot gave a derisive grunt. 'You in a hurry to get somewhere?'

'My time is short. Perhaps that's the best way to put it.'

Darac nodded sympathetically. 'I understand.'

'And how is your… niece, wasn't it?'

'My niece?'

'Yes, the girl who shares my condition. You mentioned her when I talked to you on the phone some days ago. What is her name?'

It seemed Delmas had not guessed she was a fiction, a ruse to keep him talking.

'He means Ella, chief,' Bonbon said, his memory ever reliable.

'Ella, of course. I hesitated because she's not really my niece – just the daughter of a family friend. But happily, she's doing much better, thank you.'

'That's good.'

Darac glanced at the doorway. Where had Perand got to with Sabrina Fabre?

'I really would like to get the interview underway, Captain.'

'Monsieur, you do understand that we can hold you here for forty-eight hours? In the first instance.'

'And then for another forty-eight upon application. But only, in both cases, if I am formally placed in custody. True?'

'True.' Delmas may have been slow on the uptake, Darac reflected, but there seemed nothing muddled in his thinking, per se. 'Got somewhere nice to stay, by the way?'

'Quite nice. My apartment.'

Escorted by Perand, the human sphinx that was Sabrina Fabre rolled into the room as if on castors. As she readied her pad and pens, Bonbon gave Flaco the nod to scoop up Perand and Lartou. The trio trooped out of the office with the air of theatregoers banished to the worst seats in the house.

Darac waited a moment and then rang the squad room. As the call was taken, he returned the handset to its cradle. 'Hear me alright, Flak?'

'Loud and clear.'

'Monsieur Delmas, would you say something?'

A request to sing 'La Marseillaise' backwards could not have presented a greater challenge. Delmas remained mute.

'Anything at all,' Darac said. Still no response. 'Just tell me your name.'

'Delmas. Pierre Henri.'

'Heard that, too,' Flaco said.

'Good.' Darac turned to Sabrina Fabre. 'Ready?'

Her pen poised, the woman inclined her head the slightest degree. The room fell silent.

'So, monsieur – where to begin? It's difficult to avoid clichés, isn't it?'

'It is?'

'Certainly. "We meet at last"; "You've led us a merry dance."'

'Yes, we meet at last. But I don't know anything about dancing.'

'Actually, apart from our little chat on the phone, we had already met, hadn't we? Or at least come across one another.'

'Had we? Where?'

'At the cemetery in Vence. Where your daughter and my mother are buried.'

'Yes, of course. That idiot Carl Halevy. I am more than happy to pay for the damage he caused to your mother's grave, Captain…?'

'Darac.'

'Darac – that's right. Desecration like that – appalling. I'm more than happy to pay.'

Disarmed, Darac lost his next point, momentarily. 'Thanks but that won't be necessary.' With a sinking feeling, he realised what *would* soon be necessary. He would have to commune with his father at the ceremony to consecrate his mother's new grave; commune with him despite the growing silence between them. 'Monsieur, I think we could save time here. We know a lot about the So-Pro robbery.'

'Do you? Commissaire Dantier and this gentleman' – he waved a shaking hand at Granot – 'thought they did, too.'

'We know it was planned from the outset that you would take the fall for the gang; that you expected to die during your term of imprisonment; that your unacknowledged daughter Sylvie was to benefit from your share of the proceeds; that she was subsequently cheated out of that sum; that she then died from a terminal condition inherited from you; and that her grand, final resting place was an afterthought designed to fool you into thinking she *had* been paid her share.'

Fabre's pen was already in pause mode.

'An effective summary. And I *would* have been fooled had Halevy not panicked and tried to make sure I never would find out the truth. A stupid, stupid man.'

'The other gang members must have been furious with him. Alerting you, like that.'

'Indeed so. You mentioned the proceeds of the robbery being divided up.'

Bonbon gave Granot a look.

'Yes.'

'But the haul was all recovered, Captain.'

'The haul was the two-million-euro reward earned by Jean Aureuil. He was part of the gang, also.'

Whatever emotions were passing through Delmas, his facial expression had remained blank until that moment. 'Two million is a poor substitute for nineteen million.'

'Not when you weigh up the relative risks. Bank robbers always get caught in the end, don't they? On this occasion, until the gang tried to cheat…' He remembered Delmas's earlier insistence on the point. '…tried to cheat *Sylvie*, everyone involved in So-Pro was a winner.'

'You're a clever man, Captain… I'm sorry but my short-term memory isn't all it should be these days. It's *Darac*, that's it. Captain Darac.'

'We're well aware of your health problems. Would you like some water, by the way? Or coffee?'

'Does either improve short-term memory?'

'I was just wondering if you would like some.'

'I see. Water.'

Bonbon moved to the cooler.

'Would you not use the cardboard cups?' Delmas shook his head. 'My hands are not what they were, either.'

'I'm afraid we're going to remain on the recent past, monsieur,' Darac said. 'You and I had an earlier encounter than that at the cemetery. I'm thinking of the Parade of Lights.'

'I didn't see you there.'

'But I saw you. Pursuing Michel Fouste. Where did he fit into the gang?'

'He didn't.'

Silence.

'Fouste, the man who fell right under the float? And was killed?'

Bonbon handed Delmas a half-full porcelain cup.

'Fouste – yes. He was drunk.' He gave Bonbon a nod. 'Thank you.'

'But he knew Halevy, Saxe and Aureuil,' Darac said. 'He'd worked with all three.'

'He was a friend of theirs and that's why I wanted to see him. I knew he would know where they all were. Of course, I didn't know then what they had done to Sylvie. I just wanted to see them. Talk to them. He took fright when he saw me. Tried to get away.'

'Just to get this absolutely straight – Fouste was *not* a member of the gang?'

'No.'

Darac shared a look with the others. If Fouste was out of the frame, it meant that at least one more gang member was yet to be identified. 'So Fouste never earned a €400,000 share of the reward?'

'Of course not. You were doing well, Captain. But now—'

Granot stirred like a prodded bull. 'How many were in the gang, Delmas?'

'You'll have to work that out for yourself.'

'Pah!'

Darac still felt a deal of sympathy for Delmas but his patience was not endless. 'You know, monsieur, I don't know how I would have reacted in your situation. I think we all feel that. The gang trusted you not to divulge their identities to us. And you didn't. How did they reward that loyalty? By dividing up your share of the reward among themselves. So it's hardly surprising that you've killed two of them and are looking to kill—'

'I haven't killed anyone.'

'No? Let me take you back to last Wednesday. Early evening. Do you remember where you were when Alain Saxe was killed? We know, so there's no point in lying.'

'When was that?'

'It was seven-thirty. Take your time.'

'I don't need to. I was on my way back from Villefranche. With a friend.'

'We know you met up with Saxe because somehow or other you had his mobile, didn't you? And we have an eyewitness, anyway.'

'The ticket girl, presumably. We chatted. A lovely young person.'

'What did you talk about with Saxe?'

'Eventually, we talked about Sylvie. And why they did what they did. Alain said he had never intended to cheat her. But one of the others said it was too good an opportunity to miss and convinced the rest. And so Alain had to go along with them.'

'Whose idea was it to cheat Sylvie?'

'He said it was Carl Halevy's.'

'Who was conveniently dead then as he is now. You didn't believe Saxe. You thought it was all his idea. You quarrelled violently.'

'I did believe him. But I called him a coward, and that led to the set-to. It wasn't a violent quarrel. I grabbed his lapels and we had a scuffle. His mobile fell out of his pocket and landed on the street. He didn't notice. I picked it up later.'

'And if you hadn't believed him?' Darac looked hard into Delmas's eyes. 'What would you have done then?'

Delmas closed his eyes as if he were trying to picture it. 'But I did believe him.'

'You would have killed him, wouldn't you? Many would in your position. Especially as the question of paying the penalty for it hardly arises.'

'I am not a violent man.'

'Yet you quarrelled violently.'

'I've already said it wasn't violent.'

'Then the two of you were left alone on the *petit train*. Shortly afterwards—'

'Shortly afterwards, I got off *before* Alain was killed and it went into the water. I couldn't have done that. But I must say that when I read about it, I wasn't sorry. He wasn't a good man, Captain. And Sylvie was short of a good man in her life.' His expressionless eyes conveyed just a scintilla of emotion. 'Someone to be on her side when she really needed it.'

'Alright, let's say you did get off before Saxe was killed.

Then, monsieur, you made your way back to Levens where you were staying with Artur Rigaud, his wife Odette and a bunch of chickens. Right?'

Delmas's eyes lowered. 'It's a brood,' he said, at length. 'A brood of chickens.'

For a moment, Darac was back at the cemetery gates. Back with the old lady and her charm of edible goldfinches.

'You know about the Rigauds, Captain? How do you know?'

Granot's hackles were rising once more. 'We don't *always* get things wrong. However many lies people tell us.'

Delmas took a sip of water, holding the cup in both hands.

'How did you get back to Levens?' Darac said.

'On the pillion seat of Artur's bike. He's been a brick, that man. And Odette. They are the only ones who have.'

'Were either or both of them in the So-Pro gang with you?'

'No,' he said definitively. 'Of course not.'

Still exercised by questions arising from the timetable, Darac ran a hand through his hair while he thought through his next move. Sometimes, the obvious line was the one to play.

'You could have killed Saxe and *then* accepted the lift.'

'But I didn't. When I left Alain, he was angry, yes. But he was alive and well.'

'Did you see anyone board the train after you got off?'

'Yes. A man got in the cab with Alain and they went off together. He's the one who killed him, of course.'

Darac nodded as if he bought the story. 'Of course. And who was that man?'

His expression giving nothing away, Delmas didn't answer immediately. 'I don't know.'

Darac was concerned about the way Delmas had had to think about these answers. It was often a sign of lying. Or might his condition be responsible? He felt a change in the character of the questioning was called for; a change of tempo, a different point of attack. He pursed his lips, building the moment. 'Madame Fabre, would you read the last exchange back, please?'

'"Question: And who was that man? Answer: I don't know."'

'That's not true, is it, monsieur? You knew very well who it was.'

'I... It wasn't a lie. I didn't know for certain who it was.'

'Who was it? Come on, you know.'

'I don't. What point is there in my lying about it?'

'I don't know.' Time to open the questioning to the others. 'Bonbon?'

'You said you weren't certain who it was,' he said, not missing a beat. 'Who did you *think* it was?'

'I...'

Granot now: 'You're supposed to be in a hurry. Come on – answer!'

'I would never implicate anyone I wasn't certain about. Especially in a murder case.'

Darac nodded. 'Admirable. But you should name him and let us determine his guilt.'

'Oh? I thought that was the responsibility of the courts?'

Darac exhaled deeply. One minute, he was making allowances for the man, the next, he was walking into his sucker punches. 'Let's turn our attention to Jean Aureuil, the man who earned and then split the reward between you all. Or that was the original plan, at least. Right?'

'That's right.'

'You strangled Aureuil because he cheated Sylvie. And you strung him up from the sea wall of the citadel in Villefranche. Right again?'

'I did no such thing. I wasn't even in Villefranche. I was with Artur and Odette all evening.'

Granot was unable to hold back. 'Rubbish. You hung Aureuil up like a piece of meat in a butcher's shop.'

'No. I didn't.'

'And you did it as a warning to the one remaining member of the gang,' Darac said. 'You want that man to suffer, to cower, to be scared of his own shadow. Because it is *that* man, and not the conveniently dead Carl Halevy, that you believe ultimately responsible for cheating Sylvie. That is why you are in a hurry to get out of here. You want to find that man and kill him before it's too late.'

Another hiatus. But this time, there was a certain conviction in the way Delmas gathered himself before answering. 'I can't know for certain whose idea it was, can I? I wasn't there. I was in prison at the time that decision was made. But that doesn't stop me from *wanting* to know.'

Another change of tack was needed. 'On the day Aureuil was murdered, the safe in his apartment was robbed. Do you know anything about that?'

Delmas played the hesitation card once more. 'She reported it, did she?' He nodded slightly. 'The wife.'

'So you do know something about it.'

'I should. I carried out the robbery. Although robbery is not really the right word. Removal is more accurate.'

The three officers shared a look.

'You admit it?'

'Yes. But what are you going to do about it, Captain? Send me for trial? I don't think so. And the prospect of imprisonment is an entirely academic one, as we've said. I will be dead long before then.'

Granot looked unconvinced. 'You weren't supposed to survive your first prison term but you did.'

'Pity you didn't lose some of that gracelessness along with the weight, Lieutenant.'

'Yes? Let me tell you something – I didn't abandon any of *my*—'

Bonbon put a restraining hand on the big man's arm. This wasn't the moment to get drawn into meaningless clashes.

'So you *removed* a DVD,' Darac said. 'What else?'

'Nothing.'

'And what is so special about this thing?'

Delmas reached down to the holdall, and with a halting hand, pulled back the zip. 'Why don't you play it and see?'

Darac turned his computer screen around to face the room. 'Get Erica,' he said.

With progress files on a variety of cases, including the Delmas investigation itself, displayed all over the squad room, Darac had no alternative but to ask Flaco, Perand and Lartou to rejoin them in the office to watch the DVD. Including Delmas and Sabrina Fabre, that meant there were nine in the room to see the show. He loaded the disc.

A casually dressed man of about sixty appeared on the screen, staring back at the camera in what was obviously a home movie. He was a dilapidated figure, flesh sagging like deckchair cloth from his bony frame. Cheeks blushed the colour of lobster claws suggested a history of excess or illness or both.

'Who is he, monsieur?'

'I have no idea.'

No one else recognised the man. He was standing over the grill of an unlit, brick-built barbecue. On it was a rolled piece of white paper tied with a blue ribbon.

'*Where* is he?'

'Again, I have no idea.'

The red-faced man on the screen smiled into the camera. 'Congratulations. It was tough going, wasn't it?' The voice was threadbare. 'But you made it in the end.' He indicated the rolled-up paper. 'So here is your diploma.' After a moment, he reached into his pocket and pulled out a cigarette lighter. His smile broadened as he held the flame close to it. 'Now I know what you're thinking.' His features collapsed into mock disbelief. "That isn't the photo, is it? Surely he's not going to destroy it? Surely everything we've done wasn't in vain?"' The smile returned. 'It's better than that.' He extinguished the flame and unrolled the paper. It was blank. 'Yes, my friend – I lied. There never *was* a photo.' He reignited the flame. And started to laugh. 'You did it *all* for nothing. I'm only sorry I won't be around to see... your face.'

As the lit paper crumpled into ash, the laugh became a shuddering, uproarious quaking that turned into a shuddering, uproarious coughing fit.

'This isn't a snuff movie, is it?' Perand said.

The red-faced man was still alive as the screen faded to black. *Fin*.

Bonbon had scarcely had time to get uncomfortable in his seat. 'What was *that* about?'

'Thirty seconds of rubbish,' Granot said, turning to Delmas. 'You risked a lot robbing Aureuil's safe for that. Why did you? And don't play around with us.'

'Because I didn't know until I viewed it that it was thirty seconds of rubbish.'

Darac ran a hand into his hair. 'Okay, monsieur – who was the man addressing? And don't say you have no idea about *that*. You've had over seven years to ponder what the robbery was really all about, haven't you?'

'I shall disappoint you, Captain. I have no idea who the man was, or whom he was addressing.'

'Let's roll it again.'

They watched it three more times. At the end of it, Darac turned to Erica. 'Could you get a still of the man off the disc and run it through the databases?'

'I'll do it now,' she said, rising.

'Lartou? Email the still to Archive, the papers, TV – anyone you can think of.'

'Right, chief. I'll put the player back in the squad room.'

Anchoring curtains of her fine blond hair behind her ears, Erica bent to remove the disc.

'Nice to meet you, young lady,' Delmas said, pleasantly, as she straightened. 'There aren't enough women in technical roles in this country of ours. There isn't one I can think of in security, for example.'

It was all Erica could do not to reply, 'Tell me about it.'

Instead, she said, 'Oh?' and, casting a quizzical look at Darac, left with Lartou.

Flaco spotted Darac staring hard at the floor. 'Could we stay in here now, Captain?'

Darac didn't surface until a moment or two later. 'If this DVD existed in isolation, we wouldn't know where to start, would we? But the So-Pro context pushes us well down the road. "You did it all for nothing," the man said. I think we can all guess what the "it" refers to, can't we?'

Flaco nodded. 'The robbery itself.'

'Absolutely.' Darac performed a double take. 'What are you—' The penny dropped. 'Alright, you can stay, both of you.'

'I wouldn't call four hundred grand each "nothing",' Perand said.

'By doing the robbery "for nothing" Red Face meant doing it *unnecessarily*, did he not, Monsieur Delmas?'

'I... don't know.'

Darac nodded, eyebrows high. 'You don't know.' He opened his notebook. 'Well let's look at what you do know – what actually happened at the time.'

In for the long haul, Bonbon twisted sideways in his seat.

Darac found the entry he was looking for.

'Stop me if I get any of this wrong, monsieur. Contrary to what we believed initially, the gang tunnelled *into* the bank. Right?'

Delmas seemed to conclude that there was now nothing to be gained by denying it. 'Yes.'

'The members went about their allotted tasks – lasering open the safety deposit boxes, breaking into the strongroom and so on. However, at the trial, you maintained that the boxes had all been opened with codes and then lasered to make it appear that *that* is how they had been opened. This was all part of the strategy to direct the investigation at you, the inside man. Box 328 had been left undoctored, you said, because it was the last one to be opened and as time ran out, it was forgotten. I don't think that is what happened. I think box 328 had been earmarked from the start. You opened it with a code so as not to risk burning the contents, as lasers are prone to do. Obviously, those contents must have been deemed especially important.'

'I thought box 328 had been chosen completely at random. I had no idea what was in it beforehand.'

'But the DVD we have just seen was in that box. Was it not?'

'It was.'

'And you still think it was a random choice? Having seen the footage?'

Delmas's eyes seemed to sink even further back into his skull. 'No.'

'In fact, your suspicions were already raised – or why crack Aureuil's safe to retrieve it?'

Delmas made no comment.

'Box 328, specifically – whose choice was that at the time?'

'It was Aureuil's.'

Granot was looking more engaged by the second. 'How did he make that choice?'

'Somebody asked, "Which box shall we leave for them?" He replied, "I don't know. How about 328? Always been lucky, those numbers." Something like that.'

'You said you don't know the identity of the red-faced man?'

'I don't.'

'But we can work it out, can't we? He was the keyholder to box 328. What was the name on the keyholders' list opposite that number?'

'It was a false name.'

'How do you know that?'

'Because it was listed as "Monsieur Hulot".'

Laughter.

'Alright, alright…' Darac was anxious not to lose his rhythm. 'When you opened 328, what else was in it apart from the DVD?'

'Nothing.'

He brandished the empty DVD case, the Cary Grant and Ingrid Bergman picture *Notorious*. 'I take it this wasn't the original case?'

'No.'

'Was the original case labelled?'

'There was something written on it. But I never saw what it was.'

'Alright, box 328 was opened. What happened next?'

'The contents of the other boxes were tipped out and put into bags. But I saw Aureuil pocket the DVD when he thought no one was looking.'

'Why did he do that? What did you think at the time?'

'I don't want to speak ill of the dead. But Aureuil was a… common sort of a man.'

Flaco scowled, uncomprehending. Granot caught her eye. 'Porn,' he explained. 'There was a load of homemade stuff stashed away in the So-Gén vault back in '76. Local dignitaries screwing each other, en masse, in some cases. Maybe Aureuil was hoping for some of the same, thirty years later. Is that what you assumed, Delmas?'

'I must confess it was. And I thought no more about it at the time.'

'But later,' Darac said, 'in those long, long hours in prison, you did begin to wonder about it.'

'Why did I?'

'Because you had nothing else to do,' Perand said, redundantly.

'That was only part of the reason.'

Bonbon exhaled deeply. 'Presumably, Aureuil showed no interest in pocketing any *other* DVDs. Right? And there *were* some – I remember seeing entries for them on the claimants' inventories.'

Delmas nodded. 'That is the correct answer.'

'Look, monsieur.' Darac's patience was beginning to wear thin. 'This isn't a guessing game. You're in serious trouble. Just answer our questions. All of them.'

Delmas looked at his watch, holding his wrist with his free hand to steady it. 'Then get on with it, please.'

'Alright, I will. Let's call the person who commissioned So-Pro... Monsieur X. He has a guilty secret, something so heinous it must never under any circumstances be discovered. But Red Face knows about it. Judging by his state of health, and the reference he makes to "not being around" to see his gag pay off, I think it's safe to infer he was dying. He contacts Monsieur X, tells him he has an incriminating photo and that he's stashed it in a safety deposit box that will be opened at the time of his death. It's interesting that Monsieur X believes him, isn't it?'

'He must have known him,' Bonbon said, his wiry frame twisted into an elaborate contrapposto in his chair. 'Perhaps he was part of the guilty secret itself.'

'Possibly. So now, there's only one course of action Monsieur X can take that would retrieve the photo without alerting everyone to the fact. He has to mount a bank robbery in which *everything* is taken. A gang is hired. It seems that no one but Aureuil knows it is a smokescreen. He finesses the opening of the deposit box that he understands contains the photo. As we've seen, the cupboard was bare. But there is a DVD and Aureuil pockets it. He may then have made a copy and hands over the original. At which point, Monsieur X, after all that effort, has a good laugh and toasts Red Face for having played such a brilliant practical joke on him.'

Delmas shook his head. 'I don't believe he would have laughed, Captain. After all that planning and hard work?'

Darac didn't bother explaining that he was being facetious. 'Are you sticking to your story that you don't know the identity of the person who commissioned the robbery?'

'Yes.'

'Do you have a suspicion who it is?'

'No.'

'You're not telling the whole truth. Who do you think it is?'

No response.

Granot hauled himself on to his feet. 'Tell us, you arsehole!'

Perand got in close. 'Or you'll regret it!'

Clad in the armour of his illness, Delmas allowed the threats to bounce harmlessly off. Once again, he clamped his left wrist with his right hand and looked at his watch. 'Really, I must insist—'

Darac neither raised his voice nor moved toward him. 'You won't be going anywhere but the cells unless you co-operate, monsieur.'

'Alright. I don't know who commissioned the robbery. But I know it wasn't Aureuil, Halevy or Alain Saxe.'

'Which gang member approached you with the idea?'

Hesitation once more. As tells went, it seemed a pretty obvious one. 'It was Saxe. We... knew each other from a long time before.' Delmas winced suddenly, bending forward. His hand went to his temple. It didn't look like a ploy.

'Are you alright, monsieur?'

'Need... to take my pills.' He reached into his jacket and with shaking hands, fished out a blister strip of tablets.

'Water, Perand?' Darac said. 'Proper cup.'

'Yes, yes.' He rolled his eyes at Granot as he went to the cooler. For once, the big man shared the moment with him. 'And only half fill it, right?'

Darac got to his feet. 'May I, monsieur?' He relieved Delmas of the tablet strip.

'Thank you. I tend to drop them. The lighter the load, the harder it is to carry.'

Darac pressed the tablets squarely into the centre of Delmas's palm and then stood by with the water. 'You're happier with heavier weights?'

'Much.'

'Like Jean Aureuil's dead body?'

'What? Oh... I keep telling you. I didn't kill him or anyone else.'

As Darac helped Delmas haltingly complete the task, he wondered how accurately the man's life expectancy could be determined. And if it turned out to be just a couple of days, he wondered what would be the most effective, and also the most humane, way of proceeding with the investigation. 'I could have a doctor here in five minutes,' he said.

'To what end?'

'Don't be coy.'

'I do not want to see a doctor.'

Darac made a mental note to call Deanna. Even just a guideline would help. 'So, alright to continue, monsieur?'

'Yes, yes.'

'You've told us who made the pitch to you. What was the pitch?'

'He asked if I wanted to earn some serious money. I said I did. For Sylvie. I explained my health situation and the scheme gradually took shape. I *was* concerned about the risk of discovery – not because of what might happen to me, of course, but what it might mean for Sylvie. I knew she wouldn't be able to keep the sum if it was shown to be profit from a crime.'

'How did Saxe sell you the idea?'

'As you said – it's distributing the haul after a robbery that causes most of the problems. But that was never part of the plan. I felt encouraged by that and I was more than happy to play my part in the deception. Also in our favour was the fact that none of the gang was a criminal.'

Granot's shaggy eyebrows rose as if on springs. 'Listen to him!'

'None of the others had a criminal record, I mean – so that was also a safer position than usual. Is that not true?'

'Up to a point,' Darac said.

'I thought so.'

'Monsieur – why don't you tell us who the remaining gang member is?'

'I have my reasons.'

'I'm going to have *my* reasons in a minute,' Granot said. 'For giving you a kick up the arse.'

Darac wasn't listening. He was back with Artur Rigaud. 'Monsieur, did Artur know you'd robbed Aureuil's safe?'

'No. I thought it best not to burden him with that.'

'So he doesn't know about the existence of the DVD?'

'No. How could he?'

Darac wasn't sure what Artur knew. But his connections to So-Pro went beyond offering a shoulder and a bed to the one man to have been punished for the job. Of that, he was becoming surer all the time. 'Why did you leave the Rigauds earlier?'

'I thought I'd imposed on them long enough.'

'Particularly on Odette?'

'No. I think she enjoyed having me around. She's always liked me, for some reason.'

'She didn't ask you to leave?'

'No,' he said, without hesitation.

Darac shared a look with Bonbon. 'You had dinner with her once. Some time before the robbery, it was. Café Grinda. Just the two of you because Artur was ill and couldn't make it. Yes?'

Long hesitation. 'Yes.'

'It was your treat, to thank them for some kindness they had done you.'

'No. It was their treat.'

More and more possibilities were piling into Darac's head, all of them outlandish. 'Let's go back to your parting

company with the Rigauds this morning. Was the decision
to leave entirely your own?'

'In the end. Artur had asked me if I thought the time was
right to leave. He said he was sorry but the strain of having
a wanted man in the house was just too much for him. I
understood perfectly.'

'And when was that said?'

'On the Thursday evening after dinner.'

'But you weren't there for dinner on Thursday. You
were out killing Jean Aureuil and stringing up his body on
a walkway in Villefranche.'

'I was not.'

'What did you have for dinner that night?'

'Uh… was that the *loup de mer en papillote* evening? No.
It was *lapin à la cocotte*. Artur shoots them. Delicious dish.
And Odette is a superb cook.'

'You were asked to leave on the Thursday evening. But
you didn't leave until today.'

'Artur said it would be fine to leave it until the morning.
But when it came to it, he suddenly had a change of heart.
They felt bad about asking me to go, he said, and begged
me to stay. Begged me until they were blue in the face. Stay
for another week, they said.'

'Did you think it odd? Changing their minds like that?'

'Not really. Artur is a kind man but he is an up-and-
down sort of character.'

Darac got up and went over to the water cooler. '*How*
did you leave?'

'I walked down through the village and got the bus. I
thought Artur had come after me, at one stage. Perhaps
to have one last try at getting me to change my mind. But

when I looked round, he was just going shopping.'

'"For bread,"' Bonbon said, absently reprising Artur's line.

'No, he went into the Bouygues Telecom place.'

Darac shared another look with Bonbon as he went to sit down.

'*Did* he?'

A figure appeared in the doorway. 'Hello, monsieur.'

Delmas rose as if in the presence of royalty. 'Commissaire Dantier,' he said, eyes lowered, 'May I express—'

'Of course you may but not just at the moment.' She slid her eyes toward her office. 'When you can, Paul.'

'I won't be long.' As Agnès spun on her heel and left, Darac picked up a desk phone. 'Charvet? Send a couple of dogs up to my office, please.'

'Dogs?' Delmas's voice was riven with anxiety. 'Why do you ask for dogs?'

'It's just our word for guards. They're going to escort you to the cell block. As promised.'

'Am I under arrest?'

'Perish the thought,' Granot said to no one in particular.

'You're not under arrest. Yet. But you are failing to co-operate fully. And I also think you look tired. Exhausted, in fact. Go and have a lie-down and think about things.'

'I'll come and tuck you in later,' Granot said, smiling horribly. 'I don't believe this.'

'I ought to be going, really, but a nap would do me good.'

'Granot, Bonbon?' Darac retrieved the Rigauds' timetable from his desk. 'Let's go.' Once out of earshot, he took out his mobile. 'I'm ringing Proux up in Levens,' he said, answering Bonbon's questioning look.

'To check out Bouygues Telecom?'

'Uh-huh.'

'Interesting variation on good cop, bad cop, by the way,' Bonbon said to Granot. 'Good cop, grumpy cop.'

'Well, I ask you.'

'You mean it wasn't an act?'

Agnès was already behind her desk when they walked into her office. Bringing up chairs, they arranged them into a rough semi-circle opposite her.

'Now this is what I call a turn-up for the books.' She slipped off her shoes. 'I saw Erica on my way in. Yet another layer to So-Pro – interesting. What do you think we should do with him?'

'Buy him a nice pair of slippers?' Granot said.

'Before we do anything, I want to show you this. I was working on it when Flak brought Delmas in.' Darac unfolded the timetable. 'It's a plan of his movements during his stay with Artur and Odette Rigaud.' He set it on the desk in front of Agnès. 'Made by the couple.'

'Come around,' she said, swivelling her reading glasses on to her nose. 'I've never had a thing about people looking over my shoulder.'

Darac said nothing as the trio studied it.

'It could be pure fiction,' Granot said, at length.

'That's just the point. I think it is.' He pointed in turn to a couple of entries. 'But not in the way you might expect. Artur's not quite the big-hearted friend of the downtrodden that we thought, is he?'

'Nor Odette,' Bonbon said. 'Although, the jury was always out on her, I guess.'

Agnès replaced her glasses and sat back. 'Every five

minutes of Delmas's time seems to be accounted for, except around the times of the murders.'

Granot subsided back into his chair. 'Yet they were insistent Delmas wouldn't hurt a fly, you said, didn't you?'

Bonbon gave him a look. 'Oh yes – while also dropping into the mix that the man was spitting mad at the gang for cheating Sylvie.'

Darac ran a hand through his hair. 'It's not just that they're unwilling. Anyone might shy away from providing an alibi in a murder case if they weren't sure. But there's nothing shy or unsure about the Rigauds.'

Granot shrugged. 'That may be true—'

'What *is* true is how precise these timings are. Precisely incriminating.'

Bonbon pressed his lips together. 'The Rigauds couldn't have made a better job of fingering Delmas if they'd been paid to do it.'

'And consider this.' Darac opened his notebook and handed it to Granot. 'It's not just a case of gaps, omissions and discrepancies. The timings the Rigauds assert directly contradict Delmas's statements. He says he was with them at the times of the murders. And his account of how he came to leave Levens this morning is quite different from theirs. Who do you believe?'

Granot checked the statements. 'Ye-es. At last, you've put something intelligent together. But it's as thin as a Spaniard's wallet. You'd never convince a judge with it.'

'I know.'

'And if it came down to the Rigauds' word against Delmas, who has the most credibility, do you think?'

'I know the word of a convicted criminal isn't worth much—'

'It's worth nothing,' Granot said. 'Especially in court.'

'Yet I'm inclined to believe Delmas's version of events.'

'So am I,' Bonbon said. 'Or he's the greatest actor since Philippe Noiret.'

'There *was* a naturalness in the way he talked about being given the bum's rush by the Rigauds,' Granot conceded. 'But I haven't heard their version.'

'I haven't heard either of them,' Agnès said.

Darac summarised both.

'Interesting. So we come back to whom to believe.'

'I've come to doubt that Delmas has the imagination, or perhaps the energy, to lie,' Darac said. 'Effectively, I mean.'

'He seemed to have little difficulty back in 2003.' Agnès gave Granot a look. 'He lied most convincingly, didn't he?'

Granot folded his arms as if forming a bulwark against the memory. 'He did. And once an arsehole, always an arsehole, in my book.'

Darac didn't buy it. 'There could have been a lot of deterioration in seven years. Seven prison years, at that.'

Bonbon nodded. 'He's very literal, isn't he? In fact, he's got little imagination even for telling the truth. He couldn't think of a single thing to say when you asked him to test the phone mike, for instance. All he could do was give his name. When you prompted him to do it.'

'And it shows in those hesitations, as well, I think. He's done that once or twice before answering, as if he needed time to work out what he could afford to tell us. But there was no hesitation when he told us about what he was doing around the time of the killings. And he's always said straight out that he has never killed anyone.'

'He hesitated at what he'd had for dinner the evening of Jean Aureuil's murder,' Granot said.

'Just momentarily and then it was only a question of sorting out which dinner he'd had on which evening.'

Granot gave the slightest of nods, conceding if not the point, then at least the possibility. 'Alright but what about his other stock response? Silence. He just refuses point blank to answer some questions.'

'Which questions?' Agnès said.

'According to him, Fouste wasn't in the gang and so that leaves one member unaccounted for. He refuses to name him.'

'Refuses, note,' Darac said. 'A liar would have come up with a name. Probably.'

Granot grunted. 'Don't forget Delmas deceived us with Saxe's mobile. He had you and Bonbon tearing around the place like maniacs.'

'Yes, he did. But that's slightly different.'

Agnès sat forward, her hazel eyes locked on Darac's. 'With the revenge motive so well established, do you really believe Delmas is innocent of these murders?'

Darac pursed his lips. 'I'm inclined to believe it. And I suspect the Rigauds are part of a conspiracy to make us think otherwise.'

'Is Artur's "forgetfulness" about not going into the village part of that suspicion?'

'Potentially, yes. I'm awaiting a call from Proux on that one.'

'Proux? So when Delmas came in, Paul, you didn't

stand down the surveillance team watching the Rigaud house?'

'No, I expressly kept them on.'

The corners of Agnès's mouth curled into a smile that conveyed just the slightest suggestion of pride. It seemed mentoring Darac over the years had been time well spent.

'Good.' Slipping an arm of her glasses into her mouth, she sat back and stared into space. 'So what does all this imply?'

'Okay…' Darac ran a hand into his hair. 'How's this? The Rigauds are keeping tabs on Delmas on behalf of the true killer of Saxe and Aureuil. It's their job to ensure he's with them at the time the killer goes to work. If you're trying to frame someone for murder, a solid alibi – say Delmas lying in a hospital bed at the time – would obviously screw the whole thing up.'

'Why frame Delmas?' Granot tramlined his forehead. 'I'll answer my own question: because he's fresh out of prison, with a powerful grudge against the gang members, and so made-to-order for the rap.'

'Exactly.'

'It seems significant that Artur told Delmas to leave immediately after Aureuil had been killed. It suggests the killer no longer needed to keep tabs on him. Why? Because there was no one else left in the gang to kill. But vis-à-vis Fouste and the share-out, we believe that there *is* one person left. Ergo, *that* person must be the killer.'

'It has appeal, this theory, Paul. It gives us a part motive for why the murderer is killing off the other members of the gang *now*. The question is – why is he or she killing them off *at all*?'

'The DVD comes in there, doesn't it?' Bonbon said. 'Turned out to be a big joke. But jokes are only funny when they're real.'

Darac's hand was still in his hair. 'Whatever that guilty secret is, it's at the heart of this thing. And the final gang member, the killer, knows all about it.'

Granot held up his hands, palms outwards. 'One step at a time. One step at a time.'

Darac finally ran his hand out of his hair. 'Let's go back to Delmas's departure from Levens. The killer, having finished his work, tells the Rigauds that they can get rid of their guest now. Arrangements are made for him to leave the next day. Arrangements which may well have included tipping us off about Delmas's whereabouts. But then, something happens, doesn't it? The call comes in from the killer to keep Delmas there at all costs. Personally, I believed him when he said the Rigauds argued until they were "blue in the face" to get him to stay. But why? What's happened to change the killer's plans?'

'To make sure of the tip-off, perhaps?' Agnès said. 'The killer says to the Rigauds, "I've changed my mind, let's not let Delmas go – he may evade the police for ever. Keep him there and call them. Say you've been a very silly couple to harbour an old friend who's in trouble but now you've had enough of the tension so come and get him."'

Darac pressed his lips together. 'Several things mitigate against that, though – one being that the Rigauds didn't call us the second Delmas left. My feeling is that the killer is planning to kill again and still needs Delmas as the fall guy. But who could the target be if there's no one else left in the gang except the killer and Delmas himself?'

'Good point,' Agnès said. 'Bonbon – you're tapping your chin.'

'Ye-es. I was thinking about Delmas's hesitations. Two of the more telling were when he was asked who had approached him initially about the robbery, and what had prompted his dinner date with Odette.

'I like this Bonbon. Go on.'

'Delmas says *they* planned it, they say *he* did. He says Odette seemed fond of him, she says she couldn't stand him. Yet she did go to dinner with him. Alone. Which, let's face it, may just have constituted the most glamorous evening of the guy's life. Remembering his hesitation about who it was who approached him about the robbery, and adding in our suspicions about the Rigauds working for the remaining gang member, I'm wondering if it was Odette who approached him.'

'*Odette* the link to the gang?' Darac stared at the floor. 'Interesting idea. The what-ifs are piling up nicely.'

'They are indeed.' Agnès picked up her notepad. 'Let's get practical. What do we do next? First – Delmas.'

Darac knew exactly what they should do. But it was risky. 'Delmas knows who the remaining gang member is, right? If we let him go, he may well lead us to him.'

Agnès's feline eyes widened. 'The remaining gang member aka the killer?'

'It's not without its risks, certainly. But I can't see Delmas revealing the name to us. And we haven't got for ever.'

Bonbon seemed to like the idea but he had a rider. 'Delmas has no car or mobile to doctor so the tail would have to be a pavement-artist job.'

Agnès wrote: *Delmas tail: Terrevaste's team from Foch?* on

her pad. 'Agreed, if we do go ahead, but we need to think carefully about this. The timing of the swoop would be pretty crucial.'

Darac nodded. 'Indeed. And let's hope the tail doesn't lose Delmas, or we may find ourselves dealing with the opposite problem. Even if we're right about Delmas's innocent, non-violent ways, should he discover that the remaining guy is the one who dreamed up the plan to cheat Sylvie, he may well lose it and kill him.'

'We need the killer alive,' Bonbon said. 'For a number of reasons.'

Darac gave Agnès as neutral a look as he could manage. 'It's your call.'

'It would be tremendously useful to know if the Rigauds had been able to tell their man that Delmas has slipped the leash. If he does know, whatever he was planning will presumably have gone on hold; if he doesn't…' She let the implication speak for itself.

'Come on, Proux – ring,' Bonbon said, taking a paper bag from his pocket. Nestling stickily inside was a collection of ball-shaped blobs on sticks. 'Lolli-plop, anyone?'

Granot plumped for a fat pink one. 'Here's a thought. We could always go in for a bit of good old-fashioned policing. We could arrest the Rigauds and scare the shit out of them to find out who they're working for. Malraux's back at work, I hear. He'd do it and thank you for the job.'

Darac's mobile rang. Sharing a look with the others, he put it on speaker.

'Proux here, Captain. Delmas was telling the truth. Rigaud did indeed go to the shop. He bought a pre-paid SIM card. And he's bought others recently.'

'*Hop là,*' Bonbon said, giving the air a punch.

'Proux? We need that SIM card.'

'It's probably just a burner, Captain. One call and dumped.'

'I know but we can find out the number it called.'

'If that was to a prepaid as well, it won't help us much.'

'Get it anyway. And arrest the Rigauds and bring them in. Impound their computer while you're at it.'

'Arrest them on what charge?'

Darac kept his eyes on Agnès. 'Accessory before and after—' She shook her head.

'Complicity with a person or persons unknown...' She nodded. '...to commit murder.'

'Check. I'll have them at the Caserne in about... forty-five minutes.'

'Good man.'

Agnès picked up a desk phone. 'Let's get really active. I'm releasing Delmas.'

57

Laure was barely awake when the door flew open.

'You think I was just going to let you ruin everything I've worked for?' Her father stomped toward her. 'Get out of that pit. Now!'

Laure scrambled up, jagging her feet against the duvet, backing herself into a corner. But he stood flailing, suddenly, snagged on leads bridging two stacks of equipment. They fell like demolished tower blocks as he came at her again, dragging the wreckage behind him.

Laure ducked under his arm as he made a grab for her. She tried to spring forward but the mattress was like quicksand under her feet. He grabbed a handful of T-shirt and slammed her back hard against the wall. Winded, her guard went down. It was then that she saw he was carrying a newspaper.

'Read it.' He thrust it into her face. 'Read about who you killed!'

She punched through the paper and looked into her father's eyes. For the first time in her life, she felt scared. He wanted her dead. She could see it. Wanted her dead just to keep his campaign sweet. Those hating eyes... She thrust her fingers into them, making him yelp and stagger back. There was a chance. Using the wall as a springboard, she pushed off and dived headlong on to the floor. She got to her feet, her father pawing the air behind her like a tormented bear. It was then she saw a figure leaning casually against the doorframe, watching.

'How far do you think you would've got dressed like that?' Walter Picot's eyes slid to her groin. 'Just a T-shirt?'

Laure was her father's daughter in everything. She weighed her options.

'Tie him up,' she said. 'And you can have me. Knock him out. Kill him – anything. I don't care. He wants me dead.'

He smirked. 'Why do you think I'm here?'

'Listen, you can…' The realisation began to dawn. 'You can fuck me.'

'I wouldn't fuck a skank like you to save my life.'

'I've… I've got money. Lots of it. And I can get it.' She spun around frantically, as if the cash were lying there in plain sight. 'You can have it. All.'

Finally disentangled, her father walked past her. 'Goodbye, Laure.'

'No! Papa! I'll change! Stop! I won't do anything like that again! You can't… Please!'

Without looking back, Telonne closed the door slowly behind him.

58

The marketing people had assured Martin that 'Julie' was a potentially strong brand name. It was a complex scent, citrus top notes emerging from its spice base in ever-surprising combinations as it warmed and then faded on the skin. For the time being, it existed only in prototype form and so its dedicatee would have to make do with a sample vial and design sketches in lieu of the all-important packaging. But it still made a special gift. Together with a diamond solitaire ring, it was extra special.

The whole thing was a surprise. He'd told her he wouldn't be able to make it this evening and so she had decided to spend a quiet night in. It was with some relief that he'd spotted her motorcycle in the side entry as he'd driven past. It would have been like her to have taken off somewhere on a whim. That's why he was early. That, and to give her time to dress for Le Chantecler for dinner.

It should have been one of the happiest moments of his life. But as he parked his car and walked down the avenue to her villa, a profound ache of sadness tempered the thrill. He'd wanted more than anything for Paul to warm to Julie, to welcome her or, at the very least, accept her. He still couldn't fathom how low the boy had sunk. To lie in the way he had... Julie had been magnanimous about it. 'He'll come round,' she'd said. 'Eventually.' Until that happened,

Martin knew he would feel like only half a man. He needed them both.

He reached the villa and for the third time in the past half-hour mounted a paranoid search of his jacket pockets. Of course they were still there: the perfume vial in the left, the ring box in the right. He checked his shoulder bag. Yes, his portfolio of sketches hadn't been teleported into space.

And then he saw the second motorcycle, jacked up on its stand behind her big yellow Suzuki. Jet black and bigger still. He smiled. So this was how she was going to spend a 'quiet evening in' – she'd bought the second machine she'd been talking about. So that made... what? Two motorcycles, a car, a racing bike, two mountain bikes and at least one pair of rollerblades. Julie was a girl who liked to be on the move, alright. Another ten minutes and she would have been astride her new toy halfway to San Remo. Thank God he'd arrived when he had.

Passing the bikes, he took the path around to the back of the villa. With every stride, he felt a satisfying familiarity balancing the uniqueness of the occasion. To be tuned into the rhythms of another's life, to swim in the same tide; it was as essential to him as food. First, it was the sound: the strains of some rock outfit playing upstairs. Then it was the smell: water gurgling into the drain under the downpipe, notes of hibiscus and limes drifting in the steam. He didn't need to be a great detective to interpret these clues. It was just an everyday thing – Julie taking a long, hot shower to music.

Patting his pockets one last time, he put his key into the lock and entered the kitchen.

59

Darac's pan bagnat was sitting half-eaten on the dashboard.

'Had enough of that?' Bonbon said.

'Not really hungry.'

Bonbon reached across.

'You' – Darac watched it disappear – 'have it.' His mobile rang. 'It's Terrevaste.'

'About time.'

'This is Darac.'

'Delmas got off the tram at Pont St Michel.'

'That's where he was picked up this morning. Then where did he go?'

'He headed west on Pont René Coty. On foot.'

Darac pictured the bridge: wide, straight, exposed. 'That's just about as difficult as a tail job gets, isn't it?'

'For a novice, perhaps.'

Bonbon shared a look with Darac. Terrevaste was an ace tail man. He was also an ace pain in the arse. 'Where is he now?'

'Voie Romaine. I'm behind him. And I've got another man in front. I'll have a third, shortly.'

'Romaine? The Pasteur Hospital's straight ahead of you.'

'I know that.'

'What you don't know is that he hasn't got an appointment. We've checked all that.'

'Fine.'

Bonbon leaned in to Darac. 'They employ a hell of a lot of people. The final gang member may *work* there.'

Darac gave him a nod. 'Okay, Terrevaste – we may as well drive up now. And before you say it, we'll stay well back until he finally makes landfall.'

'We are perfectly capable of dealing with any confrontation that transpires.'

'Nevertheless. Keep us updated regularly now, alright? If you don't, we might blunder into the wrong spot and blow the whole thing.'

'Very well. Out.'

'People on mobiles,' Bonbon said, wiping his hands. 'Everywhere nowadays. If Delmas happened to turn around, he wouldn't have seen anything out of the ordinary.'

'You can look straight at Terrevaste and not see him, anyway. I asked Astrid to draw him once. Even she couldn't recall his face.' He waggled the gear stick. 'Right, let's get up there.'

Starting the engine scattered flurries of piano notes into the air like breeze-blown leaves. To avert the inevitable protest, Darac reached for the on/off switch.

'No, leave it on,' Bonbon said. 'That doesn't sound too bad for once. Quite nice, even.'

'I'll tell Didier. He'll be thrilled.'

'This is the Quintet?'

'Yes,' he said, the pain of losing Marco still etched deeply in his face. 'It was.'

Bonbon glanced across at him. 'One call, mate. That's all it takes.'

As if on cue, Darac's mobile rang. They shared a look. No – things like that didn't happen. Checking the caller ID, his pulse began to race. 'Erica – anything on the man wearing the parka?'

'Sorry, no. But I do have a couple of other things.'

'Ah.' He bumped the wheel with his fist. 'Go ahead.'

'Agnès and Granot are questioning the Rigauds. They haven't said anything so far. But I've made progress with Artur's mobile. There's just one call out on the new SIM. Made at 9.26 this morning. Probably to the killer, or why the subterfuge?'

'Indeed. Was he calling another prepaid? Say no.'

'It was to a prepaid.'

'Shit.'

'The call wasn't taken. But a voicemail message may have been left, presumably saying that he hadn't been able to hold on to Delmas.'

Bonbon leaned in to the phone mike. 'Was there any call *in*, Erica?' he said.

'None.'

'*That* may be why Artur made a run for it earlier. He'd tried to warn the killer that Delmas had gone but wound up having to leave a message. And then we arrive. Anxious it may not have been picked up, off he goes either to call again or maybe even to tip the guy off in person.'

'Did you hear that, Erica?'

'Yes, yes.'

'You could well be right, Bonbon, and we're in the same boat, aren't we? We don't know if the killer heard the crucial message either. Plus we have no ID for him and never will from the mobile.'

'I'm not giving up on that yet,' Erica said. 'I'm playing around with something.'

'Work your magic, Erica. And work it quickly. You said you had a couple of things?'

'I saved the best until last. I've got a positive ID on the man in the DVD. The red-faced man with the odd sense of humour.'

'Excellent.'

'His name was Stéphane Chayer.' She spelled it. 'Born 17 August 1952; died 19 May 2003 after a long illness.'

'Those dates tally with our ideas. Chayer… Chayer… Who was he?'

'Now that', Erica said, 'is the *really* interesting part.'

60

Elise unwrapped the turban from her damp hair and, turning on the lights flanking her mirror, scrutinised her neck with almost forensic intensity. 'May need a little collagen... Where's that miserable excuse for a daughter of yours got to?'

Gazing into his own mirror, Jacques Telonne smiled contentedly. Lifting the wings of his collar, he threaded the tie around his neck. 'Isn't she in her room?'

'No, she isn't. And she said she was coming with us. Perhaps she's been kidnapped. But no – that's too much to hope for.'

'If she's not back in time, we'll go without her.'

A relay from the front doorbell sounded in the room.

'I'll get it,' Telonne said. 'As you're not decent.'

'Good afternoon, Monsieur Telonne.'

Seeing Darac, Telonne shuddered as if he'd been punched. But then, like the trouper he was, he produced the broadest of smiles; a touch dry-lipped, perhaps, but broad and white and perfect.

'Captain Darac?'

'Please call me Paul, Jacques. If I may.'

'Paul, thank you – yes. And certainly, you may.' He

turned the grin on Bonbon. 'It's Lieutenant Bosco, isn't it?'

'Busquet. I'm a Catalan, not a… wherever people called "Bosco" come from.'

'Yes…' Telonne glanced at the glinting hockey puck on his wrist. 'Unfortunately, you've caught me at a bad time. As it's the final evening of Carnival, I have to be here, there and everywhere shortly.'

'We just need your help with something. Won't take a minute.'

'My help?' The concept seemed to calm him. 'A minute? Well, if I haven't got a minute for my friends in the force, I'm in the wrong business, aren't I?'

'I think you may be, yes.'

'Come in. Has there been some progress on that terrible business with your guitar?'

'Not as yet. It's a very large place you have here, Jacques. Where is everyone?'

'What – staff, you mean? We have a maid here every other day, and a gardener twice a week – but it's just the family here today.'

They crossed a marble-floored hall. In place of tigers' heads, the oak-panelled walls were hung with shots of Elise Telonne taken in her modelling heyday.

'I built all this,' Telonne said. 'Not with my bare hands. But pretty damn close.'

Bonbon nodded. 'Impressive.'

Telonne pushed open the door into the kitchen and stood aside. 'Make yourselves comfortable. I just need to tell Elise you're here. She's a big fan of yours, Paul. After the other evening at the jazz club.' He was all concern, suddenly. 'To think we could have lost you, there and then.'

Darac had run out of acting skills for the moment. 'Yes. What a thought.'

'May I set up this laptop on that counter?' Bonbon said, smiling.

'Of course. Won't be a second.'

Darac took out his mobile the moment the door closed behind Telonne.

'Like a mausoleum, this place,' Bonbon said.

'Indeed… Terrevaste?'

'Reading you.'

'Flaco's team with you yet?'

'Yes.'

'Did Delmas go into the hospital?'

'Negative. He's heading south on Avenue de Flirey now. We've got the situation well in hand. A whole new street team on. Except me.'

'Good. Should things get difficult, work to Flaco. I've put her in charge.'

'But—'

'Flaco is in charge. Got that?'

'Check. Out.'

The door opened and in plodded Telonne. He looked a little more relaxed than before. 'I'm afraid the lady of the house is still powdering her nose. But she won't be a second. Drink?'

Bonbon eyed the top-of-the-range coffee machine set up in a corner.

'Two double espressos, please.'

'Ah.'

'You don't know how to use it?'

'Elise does. Does that sort of thing, I mean.'

Darac glanced at the laptop. It was up and running. 'We won't bother with coffee, Jacques. If you'd just care to look at the screen?'

'No problem.'

'And then we'll get out of your hair.'

Darac kept his eyes firmly on him as the DVD began.

'What?' Telonne's mouth sagged open, the lips retracting over his teeth. 'What—?'

'Do you recognise this man?' *Answer no, you bastard.* 'At all?'

'Yes. Of course. It's Stéphane. Stéphane Chayer.'

'And what is he to you?'

'My former partner in the business. A long time ago, now.'

'How long?'

Telonne pointed to the screen as if what he was seeing were unimaginable. 'What the hell is he doing? What is this?'

'How long ago was he your partner?'

'We started together in '77. And went to... '92.'

'Roll it again, Bonbon.'

Telonne's face had drained of colour. 'How did you get this?'

Anticipating the question, the pair had already decided to conceal the true source.

'The man who ran the *petit train* just down in Villefranche? The one who was murdered – Alain Saxe?'

'Oh yes – murdered by that Pierre Delmas character. What about him?'

'The DVD was among Saxe's possessions.'

Telonne's mobile rang. Without checking who was

calling, he pressed the receive button and handed it straight to Darac.

'Good afternoon, Monsieur Frènes,' he said, eyeballing Telonne. 'Now, how did you know we were here?'

Less than two minutes later, Darac and Bonbon were grinding the gravel drive away from the villa. Behind them, the Rade de Villefranche stretched seamlessly to the horizon like Telonne's own personal infinity pool.

'So – "Lay off or else." It couldn't last, could it? Frènes actually helping us with the investigation.'

'Not once Telonne had phoned him to say he was being hassled. What do we do next? Bypass Frènes and go to Reboux?'

'And be under an examining magistrate's orders?' Darac blared the horn as a cat that looked as if it had been shorn of its coat wandered in front of the car. It cast them a contemptuous look and padded on at the same pace. 'A lawyer sitting in on every session? No, thank you.'

'It's better than not being able to question Telonne at all. Might be good practice, anyway, if the European Court get their way. Public prosecutor or examining magistrate, it won't matter who's handling the cases soon.'

'While we still have the old system, let's see if we can give Frènes some hard evidence.'

'It'll have to be pretty damn hard, chief. The guy is so far up Telonne's arse, he could brush his teeth from the inside.'

'Yeah, but you can imagine the sort of clever, obstructive bastard a man like Telonne could retain as a lawyer? Get you off anything, some of those people.'

Finally reaching the end of Telonne's drive, they turned into the Moyenne Corniche road and headed back into the city.

Darac's mobile rang.

'Terrevaste. We've tracked Delmas to his target destination. It's a private house on Avenue Sainte-Colette. He's just setting down his holdall at the door. And ringing the bell.'

'Street-level place?'

'Affirmative.'

'Exits?'

'Front of the house only.'

'We know he's not armed. But don't take any chances.'

'Intercept him?'

'Wait until the door's answered, jump him, then call for Flaco's team.'

Terrevaste brought a couple of his own people up, first. With his back to the house, he kept his eyes on Delmas's reflection in a car's wing mirror as he started speaking to one of them, a woman apparently out shopping.

'I'm lost. Do you know where Avenue Thérèse is?'

'No *I* don't. Do you happen to know where it is, Thierry?'

The house door opened a crack.

'I think so. It's over by—'

Terrevaste maintained his distance as the other two rushed forward, weapons drawn. He could see now that the door had been opened by a smartly dressed black woman in her thirties. Shouts, ID badges, guns waved around – the woman stood transfixed as the man standing on her doorstep was grabbed and frogmarched away to the street.

'Keep the door wide open,' the female officer said, pointing her weapon at the black woman. 'Now stand still, please.'

Terrevaste was already on his mobile to Flaco as Thierry delivered his prey for inspection.

'What's this?' Terrevaste said, astonished. 'Who the hell are you?'

Whoever the man was, he was not Pierre Delmas.

61

Showers of sparks strobed weird shadows across the quayside: a giant praying mantis; a boxer; a man begging for mercy.

The light show sputtered to an end as Walter Picot turned off his blow torch. In flat lighting, the scene looked almost as strange. Above him, the figure of the King of Harmony, garish and grinning, sat arms outstretched on his funeral pyre throne.

Using a blow torch around all that combustible material had been a risky enterprise. But events had delayed Picot and so there had been nothing else for it.

'You Telonne people are the bloody limit,' the tugboat skipper said. 'Leave everything to the last minute.'

'So what are you waiting for?' Picot took off his gloves. 'You can tow the barge out now.'

'She's secure? And everything onboard?'

'Oh yes,' Picot said. 'She's secure, alright.'

Boulevard Franck Pilatte offered a perfect overview of the quayside. This was just as well for Pierre Delmas because his binoculars were in the holdall he'd given to the man he'd met in the station toilets.

'I'll give you five hundred euros in cash right now,' he'd

said. 'Just for taking a tram ride and then walking to an address in Cimiez.' The tram ride, the same one he'd made before the police had picked him up earlier, had been a deliberate choice; the address, he'd chosen at random. The man was of similar age, build and gait as himself. And he had the look of someone to whom easy money was by far the most appealing kind.

'So have you got that? Keep this hat and coat on and don't look around until you get to the address.'

'There isn't a bomb in that bag, is there? Or weapons? Or drugs?'

'Of course not. See for yourself.'

'It looks alright. What's your game?'

'Get to the address in Cimiez the way I said, and I'll meet you there with another five hundred.'

Delmas didn't think of himself as a liar but sacrifices sometimes had to be made.

At the top of the ramp that connected the boulevard to the quayside, an illuminated signboard displayed the current time, the departure time of the next ferry to Ajaccio, and a host of other useful info. Pierre Delmas was almost level with it when he staggered, suddenly. His head started to throb in a way it hadn't before. His legs felt heavy. And then light. A searing pain shot down his spine. He stood for a moment, setting his weight against the board. Above him a line of LEDs announced that today was the feast day of John Joseph of the Cross. The saint appeared to offer scant succour as sweat began to run down Delmas's back and his vision began to cloud. But as long as he didn't feel nauseous, he was confident the attack would pass. Nausea, he'd been told, was a bad sign during an episode such as this.

Quite suddenly, he felt it, a wash of acid scouring his stomach and reaching up into his mouth. He stood like that for some moments. But then as quickly as it had come, the storm began to subside. He took a series of breaths, each slightly deeper than the one before. Little by little, he began to feel stronger, calmer. His resolve began to return.

Below him, he saw Picot's van making its way toward the foot of the ramp. Delmas had missed his chance for the moment. But he knew where the man was ultimately heading.

Darac and Bonbon were en route to Cimiez when Flaco rang with news of Delmas's escape.

'Why the hell didn't Terrevaste follow Delmas into the toilets?'

'Because there was just the one exit, Captain. He said waiting outside was "the preferred option".'

'*Delmas* preferred it, certainly.'

'I know, and now he could be anywhere. So what do you want me to do next? There's a lot of stuff to catch up on back at the Caserne.'

'You've answered your own question. See you later, Flak.' The call ended, the phone rang immediately. 'Erica? Hope you've got good news. Terrevaste's crack tail crew just lost Delmas.'

'What?'

'Let Agnès know, will you? And ask her to call me.'

'Sure.'

'And now you can tell me that it doesn't really matter

because the Rigauds just came clean and have named
the killer.'

'No, they still haven't said a word.'

Darac exhaled deeply. 'Of course they haven't.'

'So do you want to know who Artur was calling this
morning, or not?'

He shared a look with Bonbon. 'You've got an ID?'

Excitement rose like champagne bubbles in her voice.
'Yes!'

'How? Talk me through it.'

'I found the batch ID containing that SIM number; found
the store that sold that batch; had one Officer Serge Paulin
check through that store's sales receipts copies—'

'Surely the killer didn't use a credit card?'

'For a prepaid SIM? Of course he didn't. And who's
telling this?'

Picturing Erica's expression, Darac couldn't resist a grin.
'Go on.'

'The receipt was timed; the sales assistant who issued it,
identified by name. And this is where we had some luck.
The time on the receipt was 18.02 yesterday. It was the very
first item sold by Josette – a curvy little cutie with a winning
smile, according to Serge – at the start of her shift. Even
then, she says the purchaser wouldn't have stuck in her
mind if he hadn't come on to her in a really oppressive way
at the till.'

'She recognised the man?'

'No, no, she didn't. But he bought another item – a
waterproof case for a laptop costing €47. He asked for a
separate receipt. And for *that* he used a credit card.'

'That is brilliant, Erica. I could kiss you.'

'That's good because Josette is now madly in love with Serge and I may never see him again.'

'You will, believe me. Nothing is surer. What's the man's name?'

Agnès had been questioning Odette Rigaud for fifteen minutes with little success. 'First, you're desperate for Delmas to leave, then you're desperate for him to stay. Why?'

Odette was sitting legs crossed, arms folded, lips set in a sour pout, the mien of a sulky teenager, not a woman in her early forties. 'We changed our minds.'

Agnès gave a sad shake of the head. 'We know what the pair of you have been up to, and I have to say I'm surprised. At you, personally, I mean. A frisky little fellow like your husband – well, one would expect it. But I *am* surprised at you.'

Odette's expression hardened. 'Are you?' It was the first deviation from her script since the interview began. 'So what?'

Encouraged, Agnès dug the point of her probe a little further along the nerve. 'You're a bright woman. A strong woman. Artur, yes, he's a joke, obviously. Life with him over the years has been one low-comedy disaster after another, hasn't it? That's what happens when one marries beneath oneself. He's a little man, fundamentally, isn't he?'

In Odette's cheek, a muscle began beating like a quickening pulse.

Agnès's mobile rang. Untimely. But a flashing

exclamation mark accompanied Erica's ID on the screen. She decided to take the call.

'Agnès, is Odette Rigaud still in with you?'

'Yes.'

'So it's Meryl Streep time.'

'Absolutely.'

'First, Darac's just asked me to tell you that Terrevaste lost Delmas. We have no idea where he is.'

Agnès's feline features gave nothing away. 'Uh-huh?'

'But I've got much better news on Artur's SIM contact.'

Agnès kept her eyes on Odette as Erica began her update. She immediately saw the way forward. 'Just so we're clear, that means we'd know who the Rigauds have been working for, wouldn't it?'

Odette's jaw tightened.

'It was the same person who murdered Alain Saxe and Jean Aureuil – quite. Got a name? Excellent. I'll find a pen. Just a second.' Agnès took her time over it. 'I'm ready. Spell the surname first for me?'

Odette's eyes were wide.

'P for Pierre, I for Isidore…'

And then she closed them and let out a long breath.

'Date of birth?' She jotted it down. 'Let Granot and the others know.'

Concluding the call, Agnès picked up a file headed *Rigaud, Odette Françoise.* Held innocently in the embrace of a pair of brackets on the next line were two words that had just gained a great deal of significance.

'So you were *née Picot*, were you, Odette? A lot of things have just fallen into place, haven't they?'

* * *

The door was answered by a woman in a hot-pink blouse and matching blusher.

'Madame Picot?'

'Yeah?'

'Is Walter at home?' Darac showed his ID. 'Don't be perturbed, it's just a routine matter.'

'I should hope it is.'

'He reported a stolen car some time ago.'

Bonbon obligingly showed her the entry on his mobile.

'Don't tell me you've found it at last?'

'Yes, we have.' It was a lie. 'Is he in?'

'No, he isn't. It's the last night of Carnival so he's caught up with the preparations.'

'Telonne Construction is involved in that?' Darac's eyebrows rose as if in shock. 'And Jacques the chair of the committee?'

'Listen – they do all the work for nothing. *And* they don't advertise the fact.'

'Shunning publicity? That's rare, these days. I know Jacques, actually. Personally. Walter's worked for him for many years, hasn't he?'

'Walter's his right-hand man.' She smiled, a picture of smugness. 'Well, I say *hand*. Hand, arm, brains – the lot. But this car business. It's all been settled – the insurance and everything…'

Darac paid no further attention. His eyes were focussed on a point behind the woman's talking head. He pushed past her into the hall.

'Hey! Where do you think you're—'

Darac grabbed a framed photo off the wall. A snowy waste. Dog sled teams. A banner bearing the words 'Annual

Challenge'. And grinning into the camera, a man wearing a parka.

'Is that his? The thing he's wearing?'

Bonbon stepped in, smiling.

'Long day,' he said. 'Forgive us.' The smile gave way to a look of choirboy-like innocence. '*Is* that Walter's coat?'

'The parka, you mean? Well, yes it is. Or was. He lost it just yesterday.' She gave him a sideways look. 'What does that have to do with the car?'

'Where is your husband?' Darac said.

For Walter Picot, the ceremony of the Burning of the Carnival King was something of a damp squib. At close quarters, the half-scale replica of the giant parade doll looked quite something. Seen bobbing in the bay off the Promenade des Anglais, it looked as insignificant as a toy boat on a pond.

Far more impressive was the burning of the hillside beneath Château Park, the wooded hump of rock that rose between the Babazouk and the old Port of Nice. Lights, coloured smoke, burning braziers and, when conditions permitted, propane flamethrowers combined to convincing effect. To those clustered below, the whole of the hillside did indeed appear to catch fire and blaze away into the night.

The area off-limits to the public during the setting up as well as the display, Picot had to show his pass to the official at the gate as he drove in. He followed the road as it wound its way up through oaks and pines on to Terrace Nietzsche. His mobile buzzed. He read the text and smiled.

Leaving the headlights on, he got out of the van. A blast

of flame roared into the evening sky from the rocks away to his right.

'Testing the flamethrowers.' Picot's words were aimed at a dark curtain of trees. 'Good job there's no wind. We might've got singed.'

A figure moved out of the shadows. 'Did it go well? At the quayside?'

'Of course it did, Jacques. Where are you parked?'

'At the far end of the terrace.'

'Have you got my money? Two hundred grand, we said.'

'It's in the boot.'

'Get it.'

'Not until after I've joined my friends down on the Promenade.' Another blast of flame. 'And Laure's remains appear right there in front of us.'

Picot gave a sour little laugh. 'You've been working on your horrified reaction for the cameras, have you? Well you won't be needing it. Not then, anyway.'

Telonne's face took on the look of a wary animal. 'Why?'

'Because I decided not to go with the barge idea, after all.'

'What? We agreed—'

'We agreed to the principle. That's all. It's way too public down on the quayside. Someone might have seen me putting the body on board. And I wouldn't have liked that.'

'But you have killed her?'

'What do you think? In any case, you wanted the bitch cremated, right? A lump of *papier mâché* with a few sticks of wood under it isn't going to do that, Jacques.' It was his turn to be wary. 'You have got the money?'

'Yes, yes.'

'Alright. It can wait until later.' Picot nodded toward a section of low wall running around the cliff top. In its lee stood an obscure, stone-built structure bearing a plaque. 'Looks like a miniature church, doesn't it?' He pulled on gloves as he walked toward it. Telonne followed a few paces behind, saying nothing. 'Look into the apse.'

An aperture about sixty centimetres square was cut into the rounded end of the structure. Inside, a series of conjoined gutter-like chutes sloped down into its heart.

'Know what it is?'

Telonne shook his head.

'No, not a lot of call for these now. We've never had to install one, anyway. Give up?'

Telonne nodded, strangely compliant.

'It's a cannonball furnace. From the Napoleonic period. Biggest one in the country, this is. The church tower? That's the chimney.'

At that moment, massed blasts of flame roared up from the rocks below, casting a flickering orange light over the hillside. As the smell of burning propane faded, Picot shone his torch into the furnace aperture. About fifty centimetres into the down-sloping space, a stone plug served as an end stop.

'You hold the torch.'

Telonne did as he was told.

Picot reached in and pulled on two iron rings attached to the plug. Slowly, he dragged it back up the slope until the top tilted forward.

'What do the TV chefs say? Here's one I prepared earlier.' He indicated the torch. 'Shine it in the crack.'

The light found a crown of dark-brown, blood-streaked hair.

Telonne stepped back abruptly, the torch beam caroming wildly around the trees.

'Squeamish all of a sudden?' Picot began easing the plug back down the chutes. 'Good job you weren't like that back in '91. When those illegal little towel heads got flattened into pitta bread.' The plug graunched back into position. 'And then got "accidentally" built over.' He chuckled.

'You win some, you lose some,' Telonne said, absently.

'How right you are.'

Telonne was all victim, suddenly. 'The police came to see me. Somehow, Saxe had a copy of Stéphane's DVD.'

Picot's cocksure look disappeared. 'He must have copied it from Aureuil before he gave it to you.' He chewed his lip. 'But it doesn't matter. Stéphane never named you in the DVD, did he? And it's too cryptic to work out, anyway. The police are just bungling around as usual. Like they did at the time.' His face became a hideous pastiche of femininity. 'Commissaire Agnès Dantier, the Great Detective… The bitch couldn't detect her own arsehole.'

A twig snapped in the undergrowth. Both men froze.

'Could you have been followed, Jacques?'

'No. Could you?'

From the direction of the sound, a scrawny cat emerged from the shadows and scampered away down the path. As the men continued their conversation, Pierre Delmas thanked God for the animal and told himself to lie still. At the moment, the extent of his ambition was just to stay hidden and to keep listening. NCL wasn't termed a terminal illness for nothing. But what desperate luck was this? After all these years? He couldn't bear the thought that he might hit the end of the line without knowing whose idea it had been to cheat Sylvie; nor being able to do anything about Picot and Telonne. What evidence he could give to the police now! He just needed to stay alive.

'Laure never felt a thing,' Picot said. 'Just like Saxe. Aureuil? Now I admit I did make him suffer. But I never liked the guy.'

'He was a millstone. They were all millstones.'

Picot slid back the door of his van and leaned in. 'I've already started loading up the grate. No one will notice the glow or the smoke once the hillside goes up.' He grabbed two cement-spattered buckets and dragged them toward him. 'Good plan, eh?'

'Yes.' Telonne was speaking to his bent back. 'Very good.'

'She won't be reduced to ash, of course. Nothing like it. But they never are, anyway. You have to grind up the bones.' He hauled the buckets off the van floor and turned. 'If nothing else, her teeth will ID her.' His face registering the weight, Picot made for the furnace. 'Think of the votes in this, eh? Delmas frying your daughter because you wouldn't give him a job all those years ago.' He chuckled. 'The fellow must be mad.'

Picot emptied the buckets into the grate and then looked at his watch. 'That'll do.'

'Your sister was able to sweet-talk Delmas into staying up in Levens?'

'Odette...' Picot smiled, lighting a rag. 'She'll do anything to please me, that girl. And that little mouse she married will do anything to please her.'

'So she did persuade Delmas to stay?'

'He left this morning.'

'What?' Telonne indicated the furnace. 'You fucking idiot!'

'Hey, hey – there's no need to worry. When I thought about it, I realised it didn't matter. Not this time.' He stuffed the burning rag into the grate. 'The police won't be able to determine the time of death with any accuracy, will they? Besides, Odette texted me a couple of minutes ago. Delmas forgot something and had to go back to Levens. She must have laid it on thick – he's staying the night, after all.'

In the undergrowth, Delmas could hardly believe what he'd heard. Artur and Odette hadn't been his friends either? What a fool… But what did the text business mean? He hadn't even thought about going back to Levens.

At the furnace, another blast of flame from the rocks made Telonne start.

'You should do something about those nerves of yours.'

'Nerves? If you hadn't talked the others into splitting Delmas's cut between you…'

Back in the trees, Delmas felt a galvanising surge of electricity. So it was Picot. Picot was the culprit. And it was Picot who was going to be the first to pay. Delmas took a deep breath and tried to get to his feet. He could hardly move. Acid flooded his stomach. Pressure began to build in his skull. And then a blinding pain stopped him dead, taking with it all thoughts of confrontation.

Perhaps there was still hope if he could just keep still and quiet. But the pressure increased. And kept on increasing. It was agonising. His brain was being crushed, ground to dust. Images flashed in his fading consciousness: Sylvie and her two graves; Telonne's illegal workers, a pile of bodies flattened under masonry. Shorted circuits fizzed and sparked in his head. The dust ignited and exploded, and Pierre Delmas sank back on the turf, his eyes wide open.

'It'll take a while to get going,' Picot said, peering into the furnace. 'But that suits us.'

'You're absolutely sure Delmas doesn't have an alibi?'

'For the time of the killing? Totally.'

'And he's back in Levens now?'

'Yes he is.'

'That's all I needed to know, Walter.'

The blow to the back of Picot's neck was swift and sure. A nice touch, Telonne thought. The police would think it had been delivered by the same man who killed Saxe. Picot writhed. And then was still. Energy drained from Telonne's body like water from a breached dam. After all those years, the way ahead seemed clear. Clear at last. He went to Picot's van and switched off the headlights. Now he needed to make just one more move.

Above him, a broad beam of light began to rake the tops of the trees. He spun around. And then he heard the car nosing up the hill. It would soon be in sight. There was no other choice. He would have to make that move now.

Darac swung the Peugeot on to Terrace Nietzsche.

'Did you see a shadow scuttle away to the left, then, Bonbon? Toward that wall?'

'Trick of the light, I should think. The only way down that way is the cliff and it's pretty sheer.'

'Let's check it out, anyway.'

They grabbed torches and got out of the car. Bonbon hadn't taken a pace before he spotted something far more palpable.

'On the right, chief. Picot's van. Backed into the trees.'

'We'd better separate. Be careful.'

Drawing their weapons, they approached the van in a pincer movement.

'It's all clear.'

Darac's features crumpled as he sniffed the air. 'What the hell's that smell?'

'It's gas, probably. They've been testing those flame—'

And then Bonbon caught sight of something in the lee of the wall.

'There *is* someone over there, chief. Lying next to the old cannonball furnace.'

Darac turned. 'I see it.' And he saw something else. He saw the furnace was lit. He sniffed the air again. 'Shit, Bonbon. That smell isn't gas. It's scorching flesh.'

Darac ran back to the car and grabbed the extinguisher. 'Check out the man down. I'll put the fire out.'

Bonbon tried not to breathe in as he knelt. 'It's Picot. Dead. Still warm.'

Darac threw back the furnace door. 'Oh, Christ.'

The foam doused the flames in a hiss of steam. His stomach turning over, Darac peered in at the mess. The burned areas of the body were reddened and blistered, rather than blackened.

'The fire hadn't really got going,' Darac said, half into his sleeve. 'Make it easier for forensics.'

'It wasn't a shadow, was it?' Bonbon gasped. 'Somebody must be down there.'

They shone their torches over the parapet.

62

Darac's neighbour Suzanne was on duty at the hospital.

'When will we be able to talk to Monsieur Telonne?'

'Any minute now, I imagine. But I'm not working over here at the moment. And I'm no Dr Tan.'

'Do you know if the scans came back alright?' Bonbon said.

'She's just looked at them now. All fine. So physically, it's a matter of cuts and bruises.' For a moment, the sun fell below the horizon in her bright, open face. 'Mentally? That's another story entirely. After what he's been through. And what about you two? Are you alright? Must have been horrible finding the poor girl like that.' She shook her head. 'Seventeen years old. Imagine.'

Bonbon managed a smile. 'We're made of stern stuff.'

'You are made of sweets. And he's made of jazz. That's not particularly stern.'

A commotion in the corridor outside made them turn. One or two press hounds had somehow made it through security. A flashgun fired at the ceiling as a man was bundled away.

'For a moment, I thought that might be Madame Telonne arriving,' Suzanne said. 'She has been informed, hasn't she?'

'Oh yes, she has.'

'Where is she, then?'

'Telonne insisted she stayed home.'

Bonbon nodded. 'We've got a couple of officers with her. Expert hand-holders.'

Double doors opened behind them and after a moment, Jacques Telonne limped through it, flanked by a small medical team and Véronique, his PA. His right arm cradled in a sling and strips of tape pocking his ripped-up face, he did indeed look like a man who had jumped off a cliff and survived.

Bonbon gave him the once-over. 'He looks pretty good, considering. Doesn't he?'

'*There's* your stern stuff, Suzanne,' Darac said. 'Stern stuff personified.'

'For Monsieur Telonne's sake, I hope so.' She glanced at her watch. 'I've got to run. See you later, boys.'

Bonbon watched her move smartly away down the corridor. 'The girl next door.' He gave Darac a look. 'Next door to you, that is. Gorgeous woman. Don't you think?'

Despite everything, including the vision of Jacques Telonne bearing pluckily down on them, Darac couldn't resist a smile. Everyone he and Suzanne knew had tried to pair them off at one time or another, even that unlikely matchmaker, Granot. It seemed the situation with Frankie might be prompting another round.

Leaving Dr Tan until last, Telonne gave his left hand and his blessing to each member of the medical team. Darac waited for the service to be over before he stepped forward. Telonne managed a weak smile.

'Captain Darac. And Lieutenant Busquet.' More left-handed blessings. 'I must apologise about the misunderstanding at my place, earlier.'

'No apology necessary.'

'To be perfectly honest with you, I was concerned about… my Laure. We didn't know where she was and I didn't know what to do for the best. Perhaps if we had told you about it *then*—'

'Don't, Jacques,' Véronique said, touching his forearm. 'It will do no good to torture yourself.'

'The mademoiselle is right,' Darac said. 'And on behalf of the Police Judiciaire, I've been asked to thank you, Monsieur Telonne. Complying with all our various procedures is one thing; volunteering to do so, despite your physical and emotional injuries, is indeed selfless.'

Telonne accepted the remarks with a gracious nod.

Véronique's expression was a study in concern. 'Is there a crowd outside?'

'We've managed to herd them around to the front. The rear exit is quite clear.'

'Ah.' Her eyes betraying just the slightest hint of disappointment, she turned to Telonne. 'Need to make a quick call but I can't make it here. Will you be alright for a moment?'

'Of course.' He gave Darac and Bonbon a rueful shrug. 'Like a mother hen.'

A mother hen, Darac suspected, who needed to shoo some of her brood around to the back door. He called out to her. 'No need to hurry, mademoiselle. We won't be going anywhere just yet.'

'Oh?'

Essaying solicitousness, Darac spoke to Telonne. 'Because of the nature of your daughter's injuries, monsieur, Commissaire Dantier has waived the personal identification procedure.'

'My visiting the mortuary won't be necessary?'

'No. Other methods can be employed to establish her identity.'

Closing his eyes, Telonne let out a long breath. 'I appreciate that. Very much.'

'By the same token, we thought it unnecessary to decamp to the Caserne for our interview. The commissaire has had a room set aside here.'

'Most kind. Thank you. May Véronique attend?'

'Certainly. Lieutenant Busquet will accompany you. I'll just go ahead and see if they're ready for us.'

Agnès was waiting for Darac in Teaching Room One. The contingent from the Caserne had swollen to include Frankie and Raul Ormans. Deanna Bianchi had joined them from the pathology lab.

'Telonne's right behind me. Ready to go?'

'One second.' Agnès indicated a long cupboard lining the rear wall of the room. In it, a human skeleton was hanging in plain sight. 'Under the circumstances, I think we should hide the monsieur there.'

'It's a madame,' Deanna said, sliding the door shut. 'Or he's got the oddest pelvis.'

Escorted by Bonbon and Véronique, Telonne was welcomed into the room with some ceremony. Fêting the man seemed to relax him and once the introductions were over he took his seat next to Agnès without a qualm.

Darac opened the piece with the equivalent of a simple C major chord. 'Monsieur, for the benefit of the commissaire, I'm just going to reprise your account of what took place earlier. Alright?'

'Yes, of course.'

'You arrived at Château Park to check arrangements for the burning of the hillside and there you met Walter Picot. It was on Terrace Nietzsche that Pierre Delmas confronted you.'

'It was. He'd already… killed Laure although neither of us knew at that stage that she had been' – he chose the word carefully – '*stuffed*… into that contraption. Delmas taunted us about what we would find in it.' His face was a mask of pain. 'It was more awful than I could have imagined.'

'Why do you think Delmas did what he did?'

The question astonished him. 'He's a madman, obviously. He tried to join my company years ago, you know. But he failed the medical because of his condition. He bore a grudge. A grudge that became something dangerous, perverted.' Anger flared in his eyes. 'He should never have been released. Look at what he's done! He boasted of the killings.' He turned to Agnès. 'And this is so personal to me, Commissaire. Quite apart from my daughter, all of the people he killed have worked for me at one time or another.'

'Very difficult for you,' she said.

'Yes indeed.'

She smiled. 'The only problem is that it isn't true.'

Véronique's face fell. 'What?'

'Allow me to introduce our senior forensic pathologist, Professor Deanna Bianchi.' 'Delmas didn't kill Laure,' she said. 'Walter Picot was the guilty party.'

'How… What makes you think that?'

'Exchange evidence, for one thing. Your daughter put up quite a fight against Picot. Her fingernails were just one source of material from him. And his body bears reciprocal traces of her. DNA matching will confirm it.'

'I… find this very difficult but I think I can explain how that may have happened. I loved Laure but… she was a tease. She led Walter on. Things must have gone too far and by the time she changed her mind…' He looked desolate. 'Need I say more?'

'Bravo, monsieur,' Deanna said. 'However, it wasn't that kind of exchange.'

'I say again. It was Delmas who killed Laure.'

Raul Ormans shook his large, patrician head. 'No, he didn't. It was Picot who attacked your daughter.'

'No! What possible reason could he have had?'

'What reason? The same reason everything else happens around you – to protect your share of the vote.'

'That is slanderous. And in the circumstances, disgraceful!'

Ormans opened a file and slid a police evidence photo across the desk.

Telonne grabbed it. 'What is this?'

'Surely you recognise a shot of a capacitor when you see one? It's a type that only one single outlet in the area stocks. Or rather stocked. It's a chaotic place and they hadn't meant to order them in the first place.'

'So?'

'Nevertheless, they sold four of the things in a single transaction six months ago. No one working there could remember to whom they sold them. I found three of them wired into Captain Darac's stolen guitar.'

Telonne's hand went to his throat. Véronique looked as if she would gladly have followed suit.

'And what does that have to do with me?'

Ormans held up his mobile. 'This is a shot of the

remaining one. It was found just now in your daughter's room. Look.'

Telonne's face tightened as Ormans scrolled through a series of shots.

Bonbon was up next. 'We know that it was Picot who subsequently dropped the guitar off at the Caserne.'

Telonne stiffened. 'You said the handing in of the instrument would go unmonitored, Captain.'

Darac was seething but he was anxious not to do anything that would jeopardise the questioning. 'That was before we knew it had been turned into a murder weapon. It explains a lot, doesn't it? Your interest in the process of the amnesty; your sudden interest in jazz clubs. And Laure's.'

The reference seemed to jog something in Telonne's mind. 'Frènes,' he said. 'Ring him. And I want a lawyer. Now.'

'Frènes initiated this case in his capacity as public prosecutor,' Agnès said. 'Which means that except to be given a basic check on your rights, you're not entitled to the services of a lawyer. Remember the system you lectured us so enthusiastically about at the Caserne? Well, this is what that system means for the suspect.'

'Suspect? You dare to call me that?'

Agnès waved the objection away. 'Let's go back to your account of what happened on Terrace Nietzsche.'

'Yes. *That* is more like it. When Delmas told us what he'd done to Laure, I was poleaxed. I couldn't move. But Walter, bless him, went for him. Delmas may be sick but he's a big man. One blow, that's all it was. One blow and Walter fell. I ran away, falling halfway down the cliff, practically. And then—'

'You saw Delmas kill Picot? You're sure you're not mistaken?'

'Yes, I saw him kill him. Delmas! He's the murderer and I'll swear to it.'

'I think, monsieur,' Agnès said, in an even voice, 'that it was you who killed Picot.'

'I'm leaving,' Véronique said, rising.

'Stay there, please,' Bonbon said.

'This is a scandal! A scandal!' Telonne's voice burst out like a jackhammer shattering rock. 'It wasn't *me* who killed him. Why should I? It was Delmas! *And* he killed Laure.'

'No,' Agnès said.

'You will regret this, all of you.' The words came out in a growl. 'You have absolutely no grounds for making such an allegation. All you have is supposition and innuendo.'

'We also have Pierre Delmas,' Darac said. 'He was in Château Park and heard everything you and Picot said.'

Telonne gasped. 'But Delmas was up in Lev… He wasn't in the park at the time. No, no. Of course he was *in the park*. He killed Picot. I saw him.' Between the strips of tape, Telonne's face was ashen. 'Véronique – help me.'

'You're on your own, Jacques.'

'Delmas was there and he heard everything, monsieur,' Agnès repeated. 'Everything.'

'It's his word against mine.' He raised a finger, stabbing the air. 'And Delmas is a known felon. A convicted criminal. His word against mine? Me! Jacques Telonne! The king of Nice! *No one* will believe him.'

'We all believe him,' Darac said.

'*Do* you?' Ashen was giving way to crimson. 'Bring him

in, then. Let's hear what this worm has to say.'

'We can't,' Darac said. 'He's dead. Died before we could get to him, in fact.'

Telonne gave the table a triumphant rap. 'I thought so. You've been bullshitting me. Trying to intimidate and confuse me. Hot air. That's all.'

Darac took something out of his pocket. He kept his hand closed around it as he set it on the desk. 'Not quite.' His hand opened. Telonne was none the wiser. 'It's Delmas's MP3 player. Never went anywhere without it. Helped him with his tinnitus.'

'So what?'

'Let's listen, shall we?'

Darac pressed the play button.

'*Did it go well? At the quayside?*'

Telonne's mouth fell open. The recorded voice was hollow and blurred. But it was recognisably his.

'*Of course it did, Jacques. Where are you parked?*'

'*At the far end of the terrace.*'

'*Have you got my money? Two hundred grand, we said.*'

'Versatile machine, isn't it?' Darac said.

'*It's in the boot.*'

'*Get it.*'

'*Not until after I've joined my friends down on the Promenade…* Whoooosh! *And Laure's remains appear right there in front of us.*'

Darac's eyes were burning into Telonne. 'You're screwed. Delmas recorded the whole conversation.'

'No, no, no. The sound is terrible. You can't tell who it is.'

'Yes, you can. All the more after it's been cleaned up.'

'It's a trick. A trick to catch me out.'

'It is conclusive evidence,' Agnès said. 'And we have another witness. R.O.?'

Ormans waved a remote at a wall-mounted TV. All eyes were on Telonne. As the picture fizzed into life, he shuddered.

'No! You said I didn't have to...' His hand went to his mouth. 'Turn it off!'

It was Laure.

'Turn what off?' Darac said. 'Her life-support machine?'

Telonne gasped. 'She's—?'

'Alive? Oh, yes.'

'I... don't believe you. It's another trick... I was... It's a trick!'

Ormans picked up his mobile. 'Erica? Rack it back and then pan.'

The picture on the relay pulled back into a wide shot.

'That is an intensive care bed,' Deanna said, following the picture. 'That is her respirator... On the wall at the back there is a display giving the time and temperature in the room. You might like to check your watch against it, monsieur – this is a live picture. And the person in the white coat there is Dr Tan, whom you know...'

'She *is* dead.' Telonne looked frantic now. 'I saw Picot light the... It's a trick. You've rigged this up.'

Agnès raised her eyebrows. 'So you saw Picot lighting the rag, now?'

'Go to the heart monitor, Erica,' Ormans said. 'And then give the mike to Dr Tan.'

A steady trace. Telonne shook his head. 'It... it... it's not connected up.'

Véronique threw up her hands. 'She's alive, you idiot!'

Dr Tan looked into the camera. 'The patient inhaled very little smoke, which was crucial. She will need extensive skin grafts to her buttocks, legs, feet and back. That process is well established and the prognosis is therefore good. A very tough young lady, she has already given a brief verbal statement. And named names. I have placed her in an induced coma…'

Darac continued over the doctor's voice. 'You see, your right-hand man Picot didn't kill her. He drugged her because he wanted her to experience what it is like to be burned to death. But first, he told her that was what he was going to do.'

'No… I don't believe… How can you know that?'

'Because she told us. He administered the drug in a dose he calculated would wear off in the furnace. He did that, obviously, so she would suffer to the maximum possible extent.'

'Shut up!'

'She came round just as we were dragging her out of the thing. I wish you'd heard her screams, Jacques. I'll hear them for the rest of my life. Loud, unbearable screams as all that flayed skin on her back—'

'Alright! Alright!' A weird sound came out of Telonne's mouth; a sort of half gasp, half cry. 'It's over.'

'Did you kill Walter Picot?' Agnès said.

'Yes!'

As Telonne lowered his head into his hands, a collective sigh went up in the room.

'Did you conspire with Picot to kill your daughter, Laure Telonne?'

'Yes!'

The door flew open. Frènes marched in. And was by his master's side in a flash.

'This is beyond anything I have ever—'

Agnès held up a hand. 'Before you say anything else, Frènes, be aware of the kind of man you're getting into bed with. Monsieur Telonne has just confessed to one murder, complicity in a second, and there's a lot more to come.'

'Get out of here, you miserable little crumb,' Telonne said to him. 'Get out!'

Utterly deflated, Frènes sat down, instead. The golden goose had finally laid its egg and it was rotten.

Frankie had said nothing until this moment.

'Monsieur Telonne, why did you seek to have Laure killed?'

'Because… she was evil. She wanted me finished.' The man's face clouded with incomprehension. 'I built this city. Why wasn't she proud of me?'

'Greed,' Agnès said. 'Greed was your undoing. Thanks to Monsieur Delmas's recording, we know that somewhere in the bowels of the city lie the mortal remains of unregistered workers. People who died because of your corner-cutting methods. Your ex-partner Stéphane Chayer knew about it. He told you about a safety deposit box that contained an incriminating photo. A photo that would become public knowledge on his death. You had to retrieve it. And commissioned So-Pro to accomplish that.'

'It was a joke! A lousy joke!'

'But you didn't know that until it was too late. Afterwards, you got on with building your empire but there were people who could wreck everything for you, weren't there? People who had cheated Delmas out of his share of the reward money. A share he'd given up to his daughter. A daughter to whom he wanted at last to show his love.'

'I didn't know they had cheated Delmas. That's the truth. Picot told me about it only a matter of days ago.'

'And he would never have told you but for the fact that against all the odds, Delmas survived prison. Carl Halevy tried to kill him and was killed himself in the process. It was then you realised you'd been given an ideal opportunity to rid yourself of everyone connected with So-Pro; people who were in a position to cause you all sorts of trouble down the line including sinking your political ambitions. You set up the scheme with Picot and the Rigauds. We were bound to think it was Delmas who was killing off the gang one by one, weren't we? All you needed to do at the end of it was kill the true killer, Picot, and there you were – free.'

Telonne smiled as if he had actually achieved his goal. 'Yes. Free. Free of them all.'

Frènes stood with almost ceremonial gravity. 'Monsieur, be assured that you will not remain free a moment longer. How could you have dared to even contemplate adding your name to the honour roll of great men who have held office in our city? And on a point of information, Nice is *not* the city *you* built, as you are so fond of saying. When looked at in its totality, the contribution of Telonne Construction to our urban environment' – he snapped his fingers dismissively – 'is infinitesimal.'

Unable to raise any sort of hurrah at the point, Darac shared a look with Frankie. And then Agnès gave him a nod.

'Jacques Bertrand Telonne,' he said. 'I am charging you with the murder of Walter Picot…'

* * *

Darac gave Frankie a ride back to the Caserne.

'I wanted Marco's killer *so* dead, I can't tell you. But what that girl went through.' He took in a deep, nourishing breath. 'At least she didn't come to until we were dragging her out of the thing. I've never seen anyone in so much pain.'

'Burns. There's nothing worse. And think of the mental scarring.'

'She was scarred from the beginning, wasn't she?'

'Having a megalomaniac psychopath for a father isn't the best start in life.'

Darac wouldn't be sending her roses, nevertheless.

'I meant to tell you that it's Marco's funeral the day after tomorrow. And then on Thursday we're holding a memorial concert at the club.'

'May I come? To the concert, I mean.'

'I'd love you to.'

She put her hand on his knee.

'Remember Rama?' he said.

'Sticks? Of course.'

'He's flying in especially.'

'That's lovely.'

'And the city is going to put something together, too. Featuring JAMCA and the various other youth bands Marco worked with over the years.'

Frankie went to speak, hesitated, but then seemed to feel the moment was right, after all. 'I'm going to tell you something I've kept from you. Last year, I was obliged to investigate Marco. A girl's father made an allegation against him.'

The complaint had obviously gone nowhere or Darac

would have heard about it. Nevertheless, the thought made his blood boil. 'Listen. Marco may have been—'

'Yes, yes – he was innocent. Completely. The father was "annoyed" the girl had been dropped from one of the ensembles and was just—'

'Being a complete fucking arsehole.'

'Exactly. No, no, I soon discovered that Marco was propriety itself with the kids.' She gave Darac another look. 'He did his best to seduce me, though. Royally.'

Darac gave her a look. 'Well, he had very good taste.'

They left that one there.

'What's the latest on Freddy?'

'Freddy... We're back with mental scarring, I'm afraid. Big time, the poor kid. Among other things, he's talking about never playing again.'

'He will.'

'I think he will, too. I've made him a present of one of my other guitars, actually. And I'm going to keep an eye on him, I've decided. Take him under my wing.'

Frankie was interested in the view to her right, suddenly. Whatever it was.

Nothing was said for some moments. And then Darac slowly shook his head. 'I don't know, Frankie... You're born. You die. If you're lucky, you have some good times in between. What the hell is this all about?'

'That's what you've always thought, isn't it? I mean, you've always been happy thinking about life and death like that.'

'I suppose I have. It's just... What do *you* think?'

'Ask me when I'm dead.'

Darac gave a little chuckle. He could have said so much

at that moment. Instead, he put his hand on hers and squeezed it.

It was a good two hours later that he arrived back in the Babazouk. There was a hand-written note on his doormat.

I was here earlier but had to go. Ring me, Paul. Whatever time you get home.

All love, Papa xx

63

They drove through radiant light and blue shadows to the cemetery.

'That must have been tough.' The Peugeot rolled to a gentle stop. 'Finding them in bed like that.'

Martin stared at the gates. 'I've got no moral high ground when it comes to sex. Julie can live any way she likes. It's just that in this… big romantic thing I had going on in my head, there was only room for two.'

'There's got to be trust in a partnership, Papa.' He hadn't forgotten his own feelings for Frankie. 'Or what's the point?'

'Trust…' Martin said, looking his son in the eye.

'Let's go in.'

'A moment.' The effort of composing himself showed in every line on his father's face. 'I'm sorry, Paul. I'm so sorry for not trusting you. For not trusting you to tell the truth when you have never lied about anything in your life.'

'I lie every day. And not just to suspects.'

'You've never lied to me. And I should have remembered that.'

He put a hand on his father's cheek. 'Come on.'

They paused at Sylvie's grave, its *stèle* removed for the addition of her father's name.

'Did he find out before he died?' Martin said. 'That it was Picot who convinced the others?'

'Yes. You can hear him saying the name aloud.'

'Good.'

They set down a spray of roses.

'All these life stories,' Martin said, as they moved on between the neat rows of tombs.

The new grave looked splendid and, at first, banalities on the performance of the mason were all that passed between them. And then they fell silent.

'Where is she, Paul?'

He didn't reply immediately. He was trying to make a connection with the experience, trying to feel some energy emanating through the cool, clean stonework.

'I only know where she isn't.'

He raised his eyes to the mountains. Memories of his mother lived in their every rise and fall, as they did in everything she'd loved. It was a commonplace thought but, somehow, it hit him as it never had before. He felt a surge of happiness, suddenly, a bubble carried on a wave that broke in him and rose deliciously through his whole being.

'Actually, Papa.' He put his arm around Martin. 'I've just realised I know exactly where Mama is.'

ACKNOWLEDGEMENTS

My wife Liz has been my rock during the writing of this third Darac mystery, *Box of Bones*. As always, our immediate family, Rob, Clare, Katey and Bryan, has been a great source of help and inspiration, too.

For her time and for her invaluable insights, my thanks go to Susan Woodall. For their many kindnesses, I'm indebted to Lisa Hitch, Richard Reynolds and David Gower. Special thanks go to Katherine Roddwell for her translation work both from texts and during in-situ interviews with the Police Judiciaire in Nice.

Finally, many thanks to my agent, Ian Drury at Sheil-Land; and my editor at Titan Books, Sam Matthews.

ABOUT THE AUTHOR

Peter Morfoot has written a number of plays and sketch shows for BBC radio and TV and is the author of the acclaimed satirical novel, *Burksey*. He has lectured in film, holds a PhD in Art History, and has spent thirty years exploring the life, art and restaurant tables of the French Riviera, the setting for his series of crime novels featuring Captain Paul Darac of Nice's Brigade Criminelle, the first of which, *Impure Blood*, was named as *Library Journal*'s Pick of the Month. He lives in Cambridge.

IMPURE BLOOD

A CAPTAIN DARAC NOVEL

PETER MORFOOT

In the heat of a French summer, Captain Paul Darac of
the Nice Brigade Criminelle is called to a highly sensitive
crime scene. A man has been found murdered in the
midst of a Muslim prayer group, but no one saw how
it was done. Then the organisers of the Nice leg of the
Tour de France receive an unlikely terrorist threat.

In what becomes a frantic race against time, Darac
must try and unpick a complex knot in which racial
hatred, sex and revenge are tightly intertwined.

'Engrossing… an auspicious debut for Darac.'
Publishers Weekly

'A vibrant, satisfying read.'
The Crime Review

'Glorious setting and taut writing – a real winner.'
Martin Walker, bestselling author of *Bruno, Chief of Police*